In *WINTER HARVEST* Norah Lofts
turns to a new theme—a story from the
American frontier, the details of which
are so incredible, so shocking, that few
books reveal them in full.

It is a novel about the Donner Party,
which set out across Utah and Nevada
for California. Around the terrifying
story of their journey, Norah Lofts has
written a magnificent novel.

Fawcett Crest Books
by Norah Lofts:

☐ THE DAY OF THE BUTTERFLY   24359 $2.95

☐ THE HAUNTING OF GAD'S HALL   24272 $2.25

☐ JASSY   24101 $1.95

☐ THE LOST QUEEN   22154 $2.75

☐ NETHERGATE   23095 $2.50

☐ SCENT OF CLOVES   22977 $2.50

☐ TO SEE A FINE LADY   22890 $2.25

☐ WINTER HARVEST   24466 $2.75

WINTER HARVEST

by
Norah Lofts

FAWCETT CREST • NEW YORK

WINTER HARVEST

THIS BOOK CONTAINS THE COMPLETE TEXT OF
THE ORIGINAL HARDCOVER EDITION.

Published by Fawcett Crest Books, a unit of CBS Publica-
tions, the Consumer Publishing Division of CBS Inc., by
arrangement with Doubleday & Company, Inc.

ISBN: 0-449-24466-0

Printed in the United States of America

First Fawcett Crest printing: December 1973

15 14 13 12 11 10 9 8 7 6

I WISH, without delay or reserve, to acknowledge my debt to George R. Stewart, author of *Ordeal By Hunger*. To that beautiful and incomparable study of human beings in the grip of circumstance I owe, not only the impulse to write this story, but the geographical and other detail which made the writing possible.

I began to write when London was suffering daily and nightly bombardments and when news had just reached us of a shipload of evacuee children being sunk in mid-Atlantic. In the face of these things it did seem, for a moment, extremely fatuous to retail the trials of people long since dead. But this is a story of courage and endurance, of lonely battle and of the extremes of nobility and bestiality of which human nature is capable. As such I trust it will not be altogether untimely.

NORAH LOFTS

September 1940—March 1941

WINTER HARVEST

INTRODUCTION

It might seem improbable to many Americans that a train of Covered Wagon pioneers should strike an English writer as a subject on which to base a novel. But it will not astonish Westerners to know it was the Donner Party that appealed to Norah Lofts, of Bury St. Edmund's, Suffolk, as something of a classic story of courage and endurance, a story unequaled, as she has said, "to show the extremes of nobility and bestiality of which human nature is capable."

The actual Donner Party gathered in April of 1846 on the edge of the frontier in Missouri. More than a year later forty survivors of the eighty-seven members of it reached Sutter's Fort in California. The others died most horribly on the trail. During that twelvemonth these men and women suffered all of the rigors and misfortunes that were almost conventional with covered wagon trains, then they passed on to such tragedies as to set them apart from all other immigrants, before or since.

They emerged from the grasslands into the vague and mysterious region which the very maps they carried in their wagons designated in so many sinister words as the Great American Desert, or worse, simply as Unknown. Here was the biggest sun and the biggest moon and the biggest sky they had ever seen. There was also something that played cruel tricks: Mirages danced ahead of the wagons or flickered in their wake; and the children cried with joy, then wept bitterly as a handsome blue lake suddenly appeared, shimmering cool and inviting, then sank out of sight. It came to seem, in their increasing agonies of travel, as though both the horizon and their goal were moving in unison, that the horizon was always ten miles away, moving steadily with the wagons, and that California itself moved with the horizon.

The wind never ceased. It blew for weeks straight from the corridors of Hell, then shifted to pile up dirty murk that split in thunderous crashes. Out of the murk came castiron hailstones to stun the imagination, and to stun man and beast. Or, the wind coated throats and lungs with dust, carrying corrosive alkali into the eyes to grind the lids raw. There was of course no water.

Some said the sun was worse than the wind. There was no hiding place, nothing to break the relentless blazing of that immense and hated thing. Its everlasting glare played hob with eyesight and sanity. In its confusing brightness a gopher was seen plainly to be a coyote, a clump of sagebrush became a mounted Indian, a discarded wagon grew and grew until it loomed up as a monstrous barn topped by grotesque weather vanes that waved and glinted and mocked, then dissolved into nothingness.

This road through the desert and the threatening mountains beat all manner of things out of human beings. Men and women displayed prodigies of courage and self-sacrifice one day, on the next showed meanness, and worse. A man might live fifty years back in the States yet reveal fewer points of character than he would reveal here within a week. It was much the same with the women. She who quietly got into a wagon at Independence might emerge at Fort Laramie a virago.

Desperation was never far. It came dreadfully close when a thin sheet of ice covered a water hole in the foothills. Time did not stand still here in the great void of America. From the hour when the trains passed the one-hundredth meridian of west longitude, men began to think uneasily of snow. They knew you could not winter in the mountains. But that is where winter caught the Donners, and held them. It is why even their name brings a shiver.

Such was the Donner Party. Norah Lofts does not attempt to tell *their* story, though their story inspired her to write this sensitive and powerful novel. It matters not at all whether or not you ever heard of the Donners. In *Winter Harvest* you will meet a group of men and women you are not likely to forget soon, if ever. To watch how they variously met the melancholy tragedy that overtook them in the high pass by the small lake in the Sierra Nevada is a moving experience.

STEWART H. HOLBROOK

Portland, Oregon

CONTENTS

PART ONE

The Road

By the end of July the mornings and evenings found a faint premonitory chill in the air and the lupines were losing their towering blue. Grey-podded and stark, they revealed now the utilitarian purpose that had lurked behind the petalled loveliness. Midday was still hot and golden; on the far-away plains it was sweltering harvest weather; but at this last outpost of the emigrant road there was a secret sense of summer's passing, of a season grown old, of threatening change.

Two days ago, Jim Mason, the trapper who kept the store in summer, had seen a long train pull out in the early morning towards Fort Hall, and he had thought then that the season was ended. He was not sorry. The bartering, the chaffering, the sale of goods at extortionate prices enriched his pocket but grated upon his mind. He was happiest when alone; he resented being asked questions, being asked to bate his prices, being told the reason why this man was setting out on the journey, or tacitly asked to share the enthusiasm of another.

Yet, when a neat sturdy wagon, drawn by a sleek team, pulled into the camping place a few hours after it had been emptied, the mercenary element in his mind rejoiced. There were still saleable articles in the store, and here was a customer. He went out to greet him with a tolerably good grace.

There were no women in the wagon. That was a pity. It was the women who listened to his talk and bought the things he so warmly commended—the Indian buffalo robes against the cold of the desert nights, the dried bear meat with which to eke out the salted pork, the hard ships' biscuits which needed no cooking in the stretches where fuel was scarce. Women, Jim reckoned, were tormented by an itch to possess things. Some of the things which they carried in the wagons made him smile his crooked, mirthless smile. How many of them—china tea-sets, rocking-chairs, copper cooking pans—ever

16

reached California, and how many were jettisoned on the slopes where the wagons lurched and swayed, on the desert where the oxen failed and fell, at river crossings where the wheels were under water and the wagon beds a-wash?

There were no women in that neat wagon. There was a hired man, groom or teamster, with a sharp brown face and a mouth twisted from chewing a tobacco quid; and behind the wagon was a queer little creature, almost a dwarf, who drove a few loose cattle, four of which, three heifers and a bull, were beautifully marked, white heads and rear quarters with broad black bands around their barrels. And there was a man on horse-back.

At the sight of him Jim's regret over the women increased, for the man was obviously a person of substance. His manner, as much as his clothes and the quality of the mare he rode, betrayed that fact. Jim wondered a little that he should arrive at the outpost alone. Travellers who were well-to-do generally had satellites.

But a short conversation with the traveller enlightened the storekeeper and at the same time undermined his hopes of selling much of his surplus stock. For Kevin Furmage had made the crossing before and had prudently furnished himself with everything which experience suggested as necessary at stores where goods were plentiful and cheap. As though to soften the blow of his refusal, however, he invited Jim to drink with him, and over the pewter measures of good brandy, oblivious as to whether his listener were interested or not, explained something of his business.

He told about his journey to California two years previously with his invalid wife and household. The country, he said, was all that it was said to be, a land of fertile soil, congenial climate and boundless opportunity. He had intended to settle and spend the rest of his days there. But one day he had fallen into conversation with a Frenchman named de Brielle, who had crossed the mountains a year before by a new route. It was shorter and easier than the old one, and involved only forty-eight hours of desert travel. De Brielle had crossed alone with a couple of pack mules, but he swore that the road was suitable for wagons. Except to make a rough map with distances and directions carefully noted, the Frenchman had done nothing to make the new road known, and at the end of the conversation he had tossed the sheet of paper to Furmage and told him to make what use he liked of it. This journey was the result. Kevin had returned East, collected the beginnings of the Frisian herd which he hoped to introduce into the new country, and was now here, ready to leave the old road and try his luck on the new.

A more sympathetic listener than Jim Mason might have noted the almost fanatical light in the pale blue eyes as Kevin spoke of the new road, the tenderness in his touch as he drew the map from his pocket and spread it out; a more human onlooker might have wondered why this man, obviously well-to-do, should, having made the crossing successfully and settled satisfactorily, have undertaken the task of making the journey again for the sake of trying a new route and transporting a few special cattle. Jim was neither sympathetic nor curious. And had he been, his questions would have remained unanswered, for Kevin Furmage's reason for his action was buried so deeply that he seldom acknowledged its existence, even to himself.

There was, at the moment when he talked, trundling towards Fort Mason in a shabby wagon, a woman, learned in her Bible, who could have told him the story of Absalom; a man engaged upon a desperate venture, a man without an heir, who reared a pillar that should bear his name, lest, should he die, it might be blotted out from man's remembrance. And Kevin was like Absalom. Married to the woman of his choice, mated to an invalid, he was forever, almost unwittingly, searching for some means to perpetuate his name. And at the moment when the drunken Frenchman had thrown him the dirty chart of the new road he had been visited by a vision. The Furmage Road. That was what they would call it. Thousands of men, some of them still unborn, would set their feet upon that road and bless him for that discovery. And the three young black-and-white heifers and the young black-and-white bull were part of the dream. The Furmage Herd. It would be famous. It would, somehow, be linked to the road, as well. The old name—he cherished its history— might not be borne by any living person, might end with him, but it would go on in these two vital things, the Road over the mountains, the herds in the meadows to which the road led. Furmage.

Of all this, of course, he said nothing. His sanguine, lively mind, indeed, was hardly aware that it was there to be said. He was obsessed with this new idea as he had been with old discarded ones in the past. That they had dwindled or failed or palled meant nothing. To-morrow, as soon as Joe Sterry had fitted Persephone with a new set of shoes, he would be off, making, as he travelled it yard by yard, the new road. Jim Mason had a little forge. The charge for using it for an hour was a dollar. Kevin handed over the coin and stood up as a sign of dismissal. He meant to turn in early.

Jim went off to the rough log building which served him as store and dwelling-house, threw sticks on his dying fire, heated the kettle and took down his gallon jar of rum. Brandy was all very well in its way and he never refused a free drink, but the evening for him was not completed without his tankard of hot rum with sugar and a sprinkling of nutmeg.

Kevin, finishing his cigar before going to his bed, was the only one to see the other wagon arrive. In the dusk its colours were barely discernible, though the glow of the fire which the teamster and the cowherd had made lit up the gilt scrolls which decorated it. It came to a standstill not far from Kevin's own and almost immediately a hoarse female voice began to utter orders. Scanty and Janna, Floribel and Klara each had a task assigned and for some minutes everything around the newly-arrived wagon buzzed with activity. Kevin, who, unlike the storekeeper, liked and was interested in his own kind, leaned back in the dusk, drew on his cigar, and watched.

The oxen were unyoked and watered and fed, a table was brought out and a fire lighted by forms that seemed to have no faces. Two others, with faces and hands that caught the light, flitted to and fro. But the voice that gave the orders, the voice that complained and admonished, the voice that urged speed at one moment and care at the next, came from within the wagon. Kevin saw at last, as the fire kindled and the scent of cooking rose on the air, a stout heavy figure descend carefully and walk with little tottering steps towards a table which was set near the fire. He heard the hoarse voice say querulously,

"The eggs are hard again, Janna. You'll get no breakfast in the morning. Cook me two soft ones at once, damn you."

Janna, faceless in the darkness, threatened with short rations on a journey that it was difficult to make free servants embark upon, is black, and in all probability a slave, thought Kevin, and mused upon the destiny of the country that he had chosen as his own. Already in 1840 there was the question whether California would veer to the South or the North in the question of slavery. Without a single thought of the new-comers as possible sharers in his venture, he threw away his cigar-butt and went to his bed.

The morning had that premature autumn chill and Kevin rubbed his hands briskly as he went to the breakfast which little Hendriks had prepared. He was so small, so apparently fragile, that, in a world where men wanted brawn for their dollars, little Hendriks had found employment difficult to obtain. His sound good sense, his deft skill in small matters and his courageous handling of large ones, his loyalty, were not immediately apparent, and the little Dutchman had been on the verge of starvation when Kevin, visited by one of his impulses, had offered him work. Never had master found a more faithful servitor. Kevin had no cause, like his unknown neighbour of last evening, to complain of the eggs, which, preserved by a layer of lard on their shells, travelled in a box amidst wisps of hay.

He looked to his right as he ate and saw the painted wagon. The body was blue, decorated with scrolls of gilt, and the wheels were scarlet. It was one and a half times the size of his own. A fire burned on its far side and as he watched, the black girl, Janna, bore into its interior a tray laden with silver jugs and covers. From beyond, where the fire burned, came the sound of a shrill girlish voice and a deeper one with a curious accent. A black man, huddled against the morning chill, was washing the dust of travel from the body and wheels of the wagon.

From the forge behind the log cabin of Jim Mason's store came the sounds of Joe Sterry's labour on Persephone's new shoes and Kevin looked at his watch. Eight o'clock. They would be on the road by nine. He fingered the map again and looked towards the South-West. The dusty rutted trail that ran from the camping place led off to the North, towards Fort Hall. Kevin thought, with a strange upwelling of excitement, that when Joe returned and yoked the teams and his own wagon rolled away to the South-West it would be breaking a new trail. The earth had existed for a thousand thousand years and never a wheel had been rolled across that soil. His would be the first. He pushed away his plate and shouted to Hendriks to pack. Lighting a cigar, he began to stroll towards the forge to ask how long Joe would be. But a voice hailed him. He turned and saw, waddling towards him, the owner of the querulous voice.

Early as was the hour, the woman was painted, powdered and curled. Her bulging figure was tightly incased in a dress of black silk, with ruffles of white at neck and wrist which emphasized unkindly the sagging discoloured chin and the mottled claw-like hands. Her frizzed hair, impossibly black, made an unsympathetic frame for her furrowed raddled face, but beneath the wrinkled lashless lids her eyes were black and alert. The short nose, surprisingly fleshless, was arrogant as the voice.

"Madam?" said Kevin, turning back questioningly.

"Madame Jurer," said the old woman. "I would like to speak to you for a moment."

"That's easily arranged," said Kevin amiably, waiting.

"For you maybe. For me to stand is agony. If you would be so kind . . ." She waved towards two elm elbow-chairs that stood by the now dying fire on the far side of her painted wagon. Kevin followed her, waited until she was seated and then said: "Well?"

She breathed hard for a moment.

"I went into the store last night. The fellow was asleep but there were things I needed, so I woke him. He talked a bit, after he had tried to sell me a lot of rubbish. He says you are trying a new road . . ."

She paused expectantly. Kevin said:

"Well, as a matter of fact I am. What of it?"

"Is it a good road?"

"I don't know. I only hope to find out." Columbus, Magellan, Cook might have spoken with such proud modesty.

"The shark in there," Madame Jurer nodded towards the cabin, "said that it was shorter." Her voice stated the fact, but her eye held a question, and there was something about it which was almost hypnotic. It defied him to prevaricate or hide anything.

"It is shorter, by some days, especially in the salt desert. But, as I say, I don't know it. I am only going to find out, to explore as you might say."

Nancy Jurer made no immediate reply. She looked at him. And there was probably no woman in the whole of the length and breadth of America more able to judge a man than she. She made her reckoning: optimistic, up to a point, sensible, reliable, choleric, but fair-minded, fond of living and the good things of life, no fool, certainly not the man to throw away either life or comfort in a mad venture. (The inner self, the fanatic, the gambler who was set on this exploit was not a visible part of Kevin Furmage and so not physical evidence to the experienced eye.)

"I ask because I would like to travel with you," she said.

"Well, of course, that is for you to say," said Kevin. But in his mind the dream formed of a party, not a single wagon, safely taken across by the new route. "Mind you, I can take no responsibility."

Madame Jurer laughed. "Responsibility! It is the breath of life to you. Don't pretend otherwise. Don't tell me you shrink from responsibility! Inconceivable. But if you mean that you fear we'll be a drag on you, say so. But let me say first that we have ample stores. Ten oxen, and little in the wagon save food. But time matters to me, and if there is a shorter way I choose it."

"The choice is yours, naturally. And naturally I shall not dislike company. But I must tell you that the trail I follow has only been laid by one man with pack mules. I cannot say what difficulties lie ahead. The Fort Hall road is known and tried. I crossed by it myself two years ago. You have, madam, the choice between the tried and the untried, the proved and the experimental. I would not have you think that I persuaded you."

He pushed back his chair and stood up. Nancy Jurer ignored the gesture.

"To me time is important," she repeated. "Besides, there seems to be the choice between travelling with you and travelling alone. The last party for Fort Hall left yesterday morning, the storekeeper says. But—and that was why I asked you, really—one of my wheels needs attention and my driver says it can't be roadworthy until to-morrow. Would you wait until then?"

"I intended to leave this morning. But if you are set upon trying the new road with me I would gladly wait until to-morrow. A day more or less cannot matter much."

"Then, if you please, Mr. Furmage, we will set out together to-morrow morning." The hooded, vulture's eye wore a look of cajolery.

"Very well," said Kevin, cautiously. "So long as you don't hold me responsible, or feel that I have persuaded you."

"On the contrary. *I* have persuaded *you*," said Madame Jurer with all the graciousness of one who has gained her point. "To-morrow morning, then. Early."

Kevin pursued his intention of going to the forge, not, as he had originally intended, to hurry Joe Sterry in his work, but to take Persephone, and since he had time in hand, to make a preliminary survey of the road over which the wagons would roll to-morrow morning. He was secretly pleased to have gained a recruit, as any explorer would be. The old woman was not, perhaps, the companion that he would have chosen, but she seemed sensible and pleasantly disposed; and her good wagon and team would not be likely to give trouble or impede the march.

By riding out to survey the land Kevin missed the arrival of two wagons which reached the camping place within an hour of one another.

The first, a rather shabby affair, drawn by inferior, ill-matched oxen, was drawing into position level with

Madame Jurer's big painted one, when a woman stuck out her head and said in a clear, carrying voice:

"Not there, Ben. Over to the right is a better position."

Ben Smith, who seldom queried or disobeyed any of Mahitabel's orders, performed the manœuvre necessary to avoid proximity with the Jurer wagon, halted his team, pushed back his hat and turned to the woman who had by that time alighted and joined him.

"Tha's a good sight, Mahitabel," he said, indicating the other wagons. "Reckon we ain't so late after all."

The relief in his voice told of the fear that had dogged him for many days. Back home in Weston, Missouri, he had been known as Bad Luck Ben, and even now, with the old life cut away entirely and his face turned to the new land in the West, he seemed still to qualify for the name. Countless trivial, unavoidable, infuriating little accidents had delayed the wagon: and Ben, who had counted upon company during the most difficult part of the march —the part which was now beginning—had been terrified of having to make the crossing alone. The sight of two well-found wagons at the jumping-off point for the westering road was as lovely as anything he had ever seen.

To a degree Mahitabel shared his relief, but as she looked again at the wagon which she had taken pains to avoid neighbouring, it occurred to her that there were worse things than lonely travel.

The big wagon had obviously been constructed for comfort on a long journey, not hastily converted from a farm vehicle, like the Smiths', and the glistening white cover of it had an opening at the side, like the door of a house. Just within this opening sat Madame Jurer with a hand of cards (the devil's own playthings, in Mahitabel's eyes) laid out before her. A bottle and a glass stood at her elbow, but her whole attention was not concentrated either upon the game or the liquor. Frequently her hooded eye looked downward to the space beside the wagon where two girls, with bright painted faces and bright flashy clothes, were laughing and talking to a brown-faced fellow and one who looked rather like an ape in men's clothes. And in full view of the men, and of anyone who entered the camping place, hung a line of linen, much of it of so

24

intimate a nature that Mahitabel would have shrunk from exposing it to the eye of her own husband. The garments were sufficient indication of their wearers' characters, flimsy, frilled—Mahitabel's mind shied away from the word seductive. No good housewife, whatever her need, would have strung that line of washing within the sight of men.

Swiftly Mahitabel set about her own duties, making her fire on the side of her wagon farthest from the painted one and most earnestly keeping Mary Ann, her daughter, occupied throughout the morning. There was plenty to do, for this would be the last stop of any length, please God, before Calfornia. It was a necessary one because the iron tyre of one of the wheels had worn thin and loose and as soon as the team was unyoked and watered Ben and his son had gone off in search of the forge.

Soon the good scent of new bread crept out from behind the Smith wagon and pervaded the camping place. Soon Mary Ann was sent with an armful of linen to be spread on the sunny side of some bushes quite a distance from the camp. Soon the regular routine of household tasks eased the tension of anxiety in Mahitabel's mind and she forgot the painted girls and the dreadful old woman and her own fears for her son and her daughter. She baked and washed and made a stew for dinner, while little Ellen, late and rather surprising fruit of marital duty, crawled about on a rug in the sunshine.

But for Mary Ann, eighteen years old, strictly reared, expected to behave like a woman and think like a child, the damage, as her mother would have called it, had already been done. So far the trip, which had promised freedom and excitement, had been dolefully disappointing to the girl. She was heartsick for home, for familiar places and people. The long days of riding in the wagon or walking beside it for exercise, the evenings so strictly supervised by her hawk-eyed mother, had palled intolerably. She had shared her father's pleasure at finding other wagons in the encampment; she had shared her mother's interest, though not her disapproval, in the young people talking and talking and laughing beside the big wagon. But her interest was sharpened when she was able to dissociate the young women from one another and saw in Floribel Toit a striking resemblance to a friend left back in Weston. There were the same prematurely opulent curves to this girl's figure, the same gloss on her curls, impudent tilt to her short nose, friendly glance in her dark eye: and every resemblance battered shrewdly at Many Ann's lonely homesick heart. The friendship at Weston had come to a sad ending, Mahitabel, always intolerant of it, having finally forbidden it altogether. And on the surface she seemed to have been justified. Mary Ann's dark-eyed laughing friend had been married only just in time. Still, she was married, and the baby was very nice indeed. And Mary Ann had had many delightful hours in the forbidden house and learnt a great deal of which her mother deemed her completely ignorant. Now, if the wagons travelled together and the glossy-curled girl were as friendly as that first glance had implied, Mary Ann would know again the thrill of surreptitious meetings and grown-up conversation.

The day passed without encounter, but Mary Ann kept busy, kept within eyeshot, nevertheless watched her chance and was not slow to seize it when it came.

Ben Smith, with the newly-shod wheel safely in place again and the main meal of the day eaten, lighted his pipe and ventured into the store. The mingled scents of leather and lamp oil, of candles, cheese and tobacco, brought to his mind the store in Weston main street where he had spent many an evening hour listening and contributing to the general opinion about the weather and the crops and the state of things. It gave him a sudden twinge of nostalgia and also a sense of home-coming, which vanished when Jim Mason looked up from the scrap of paper on which he was doing some rudimentary accounts and thrust a stub of pencil behind his ear, saying: "Well?"

Jim had seen Ben earlier in the day, had noted the shabby wagon, the ill-looking team, as now he noted the careworn face, lined by anxiety and weather, the ploughman's stoop, the slow heavy tread of the tiller of the soil. He had no great hope of making much of a sale here. Still, one could always try. He invited Ben to take the stool, to refill his pipe from the tobacco-jar on the counter and reached down for his rum.

"Will ye take a sup?" The question lost its hospitality on Jim's lips and somehow stood out, starkly betrayed for what it was, a softener before the business talk. But Ben, feeling low, feeling homesick, feeling bothered, saw no motive but friendliness in the offer.

"Tha's kindly," he said and dropped on the stool like one prepared to make a long stay. Soon he was telling the storekeeper one of those stories of which he was so very tired; trying to explain why he, a family man, past his prime, with all desire for adventure worked from his blood long ago, should be preparing to face a long and difficult journey and to begin life anew far from his home. He told about the little farm at Weston, carved by his grandfather out of the wilderness, and how for three years the drought had lasted, reducing the work of three generations to a heap of dust.

"Wheat, she came up 'bout so high," he said, measuring with his hand a careful two-inch space from the counter, "then she turn yeller and dry off. Man can't weather that sorta thing year after year."

Jim did not bother to conceal his boredom. He had heard exactly the same story from men so like Ben Smith that they might have been figures endlessly reflected by opposing mirrors. He could have told it himself. But he waited, grunting his assent now and then, until Ben had finished, and then, leaning over to pour another sup—a very small one this time—into the tin mug which his guest had emptied during the recital, he began his talking.

"Howa y'off f'ammunition? Plenny game in the mountains this tima year. An' they's allus Injuns.

"Got 'nuff happing agin the cold? Powerful cold in the deserts o' nights.

"How 'bout carrying a supply o' biscuit? Mighty handy when there ain't n'fuel."

To these and similar blandishments Ben listened patiently, even a little longingly, but at the end, after much deliberation he shook his head.

"No. Mahitabel bid me get a bread crock. 'Cepting that, we broke it back at Shibboleth, we reckon to carry all we need. To tell you the truth, mister, we spent all we could spare on the outfit. We gotta make do."

As though these words, actually deadly in their familiarity, had suddenly kindled a light in his brain, the storekeeper slapped his thigh hard and leant forward with a more eager expression than had shown on his face during the whole interview.

"If tha's so whyn't you take a passinger? One that'd pay?"

"And where in seven hells would I get a passenger?" Ben retorted.

"Right here," said Jim with the air of a conjurer, who, after a dreadful moment of doubt, produces the indisputable rabbit, alive and kicking. "Blast me, I fergot him, clean fergot. He's back there in my room. He's sick. He come here way back in June with a party that aimed t'make the crossing, but the woman took sick an' they went home. Mr. Cooper, tha's his name, bin waiting ever since. But all the wagons went through here they was so full o' children, looks to me as though Californy'll soon be overcrowded. Nobuddy'd take him. I meant to ask Mr. Furmage, but I fergot. Whyn't you step through and take a look at him, talk business, eh?"

Ben shied away from the suggestion like a nervous colt from a piece of blowing paper.

"Sick you say. How sick? Catching?"

"Lor no. He got the joint evil, pore young man. He c'n barely turn his head. Reckoned the climate'd do him good. Step in and see'm."

"No," said Ben firmly, unfolding his long legs from the stool, "sick folk is women's business I reckon. If you don't mind I'll call in my wife and hear her say."

"Right. And mind you tell her what you'll be needing, the same as I told you."

Ben stooped his head at the low doorway and made his way back to the wagon. Although Jim Mason could hardly have guessed it the suggestion pleased him very much. The trader's talk about the cold and the Injuns and the spaces where fuel was improcurable had impressed him against his will and he yearned to fill every space in his wagon with the vaunted remedies. And there were men, he knew, who would have gone through and struck the bargain and presented the passenger to their wives and let

28

them grumble as they might; but not Bad Luck Ben, whose sole piece of good fortune in fifty years had been the winning of Mahitabel to be his wife.

On his way back to the wagon he noted that two more had come in. Somewhere a baby was squalling furiously. Ben picked his way through the newly arrived obstacles and reached his own wagon, where Ellen slept peacefully in her wooden cradle and Mahitabel and Mary Ann, stooped forward to catch the light of the one lantern, plied their needles. To Mahitabel, in a few trenchant phrases, he explained the position, and she, dubious, but always ready to investigate anything for the family's good, swung her cloak about her shoulders, smoothed her front hair, and accompanied him back to the store.

Her last words had been an admonition to her daughter to stay by the baby and not strain her eyes by sewing too long. But as soon as her parents had gone Mary Ann stepped down from the wagon and walked to where she could see the fire by the side of the painted wagon. Her eyes fastened on it longingly, and as though some subtle telepathy were at work it was only a few seconds before the plump dark girl strolled over and said:

"Whyn't you come over and drink some cawfee with us?"

Her voice was strange, as though she were just getting rid of a heavy cold, but the low hoarse tones were music in the ears of the lonely girl. With hardly a thought of the wrath to come she stepped across into the enchanted circle and was welcomed by the queer fat old woman, who put a hand on her shoulder and said: "Pretty little thing, what a pretty little thing you are," in a curiously uncomplimentary, gloating voice.

A cup of hot sweet coffee was brought to her by the big red-headed girl, who spoke very oddly and whose name was Klara. Madame Jurer, the old woman, cut a cake which for richness and plumminess Mary Ann had never seen equalled, even at Christmas. She discovered that the brown-faced young man was Joe Sterry, and the little dwarfed creature was called Hendriks. The big dark man whom Klara had invited to the coffee-drinking was Dave Glenny and by some unknown means he frightened

Mary Ann for no reason that she could see. But even the panic which seized her every time she heard his voice—though he addressed no word to her—could not detract from Mary Ann's enjoyment of this, the first company she had found since she had said her reluctant farewells at Weston. Every now and then the new goddess, Floribel Marietta Toit, would address her in that husky confidential voice. She asked her name and when told, "Mary Ann Smith," laughed heartily.

"Why, that's the name we girls give to . . . nosey-parkering people! Fancy you being up to that dodge. Go on, what's your real name?"

"That is my real name."

"God love me! How funny! Was that your baby I saw you with this afternoon?"

"Heavens no. That was my sister. I'm not married." And then, as if to excuse this admission, "I'm only eighteen."

"How old would you say I was?" Almost instinctively Floribel threw out her bust and drew in her waist and composed her face in serious, adult lines.

"Twenty, at least," said Mary Ann. The errant friend at Weston had been twenty.

"You've got me beat by two years. I'm sixteen," said the girl complacently.

Sixteen! And what perfection. What confidence. What curves. What clothing. Earbobs too, dangling under the glossy curls.

Floribel, who had been missing the rough give-and-take, the friendships, the quarrels and the alliances of the house in New Orleans, and who had found the dumb Polish Klara Bolewska a poor substitute for her lost friends and enemies, noted the light of admiration and affection in Mary Ann's candid face. She preened. And then, quite suddenly, she said with great earnestness:

"Which way are you going, Mary Ann Smith? The new way or the old?"

"I don't know what you mean." Oh, what a small timid voice.

"The Fort Hall way or Mr.—Mr.——Furbish . . . say, Joe what's the name of the man you drive for?" Joe

Sterry, avidly waiting to engage Floribel's attention to himself, said: "Furmage," and then stayed, leaning forward, anxious not to be forgotten again.

"Furmage," said Floribel triumphantly. "Are you going his way or the old way?"

"I don't know," said Mary Ann again. "I didn't know there were two ways. I don't think Pa knows either."

"Well, we're going the new way. It's shorter and easier and you spend less time in the desert," said Floribel eagerly. "You persuade your Pa to come that way, too. We could have good times, eh? I'll show you how to do your hair and you can tell me what you use on your face. I never saw such a complexion."

The vivid cream and carnation of Mary Ann's cheeks was blotted out by a hot and painful wave of color. Partly it was caused by the knowledge that she would eventually be driven to confess that nothing ever touched her face except soap and water, and partly because when Floribel said: "Persuade your Pa," she remembered that it was not Pa who chose where the Smith family should sojourn, but Ma; and at that thought her conscience had stirred uneasily.

She set down her coffee cup and stood up.

"I would like it if we could travel with you," she said with remarkable earnestness. "But I really must go now. I was supposed to watch the baby."

"All right," said Floribel easily. "I'll see you in the morning. Mind you travel our way."

Mary Ann said her shy, punctilious good-nights all round, not omitting the frightening dark man who had attached himself to Klara, and scurried round the intervening wagons back to her own. Mahitabel had returned but, though displeased with her daughter, she was not so furious as the trembling girl had feared.

For Mahitabel had scored a notable triumph. Led in by the storekeeper to the room at the back of the shop, she had lost no time in seizing the reins of the situation. Her "Well, Mr. Cooper," had shown every one of the three men that she intended to do no business through a third person. Long experience in tending the sick, as is every Christian woman's bounden duty, lent her wisdom now. The poor young man was suffering from no contagious complaint, he was simply suffering from what Mahitabel called "set rheumatism," and her heart went out to him because never, in all her days, had she seen a case of it cured. The sufferer just stiffened and stiffened until he was a corpse to all intents and purposes, and then at last it reached the heart and he could be buried decently.

But if, in that little room, his sickness was evident, so was his worldly station. The good gold watch and chain that lay on the table beside the bed, the thick ring on his little finger, the fine linen of his underclothing, the good broadcloth and silver buttons of the coats that hung on the peg on the door, even the silver mountings of the stick that announced his infirmity, all told of worldly substance. Mahitabel sat down on the chair by the bedside and her manner was a nice blend of motherly concern for his sufferings, respect for his status, and downright uncompromising honesty.

Frank Cooper, who had enlivened many an hour of enforced inactivity by study of his fellow creatures, liked her on sight. A good honest creature, he thought, and he would consider himself lucky to travel to California under her care. Now and then as they talked—Ben and Jim standing by in watchful silence which neither dared to break—he smiled a bitter-sweet smile which lent his pain-worn countenance a strange beauty. Soon it was all fixed. He was to pay a hundred dollars for his passage and Mahitabel was to provide the shelter of her wagon, care and attention and the necessities of food.

"If you're fanciful, Mr. Cooper, you must provide for your fancies. Plain fare is the most you can hope for from us." And then, because this young man had never lived at Weston, and could not know that there the names of Dewer and of Smith were synonymous with honest dealing, she added: "You can pay half now and half when you're safe landed on the other side. Will that suit you?"

"Perfectly," he said, and fished under the pillow for his purse. He counted fifty dollars into Mahitabel's hand and she put it into her cloak.

"We'll see you in the morning," she said. "My son will come to help you into the wagon. Good night."

"Good night, and bless you. Good night, Smith," said Frank Cooper with another of those bitter-sweet smiles, and Mahitabel and Ben, closely followed by the trader, passed out into the store.

"Now," said Jim, his eyes boring into the hidden place where Mahitabel had stored the money. "You've fifty dollars to spend. Ammunition I think you said, mister, and an Indian robe and some ships' biscuit, wasn't it?"

Long years of married life and her own sensitiveness lent Mahitabel wisdom.

"Ben," she said in a voice of wifely affection. "I'm a little worried about Abe. Would you please see what he's doing?"

She knew and Ben knew that Abe had been asleep beneath the wagon these three hours, but she did not intend to shame her husband before the storekeeper. Ben shambled away and Mahitabel turned her shrewd bright eyes upon the resources of the outpost store.

"The bread crock my husband bought, and the wheel rim has been fixed. Now Mr. Mason, what else do we need? No, no, how should you know? Let me think. Oatmeal. I think I must give that poor young man porridge whenever possible. Half a bag of oatmeal then. And with another mouth to feed I may be short of beans. A bag of beans I think." She checked a few items on her fingers, murmuring "Coffee, sugar, flour," oblivious to the storekeeper's fury. "That will be all. Bear meat? Oh dear no. I don't care for the sound of it. And I have salt pork and dried beef aplenty, besides we have two steers that we aim to slaughter some time, for fresh meat, you know."

Sublimely unconscious that Jim felt himself cheated, she paid for her modest purchases and ducked her tall head at the low door.

Jim Mason followed her with his eyes. Skinflint, shrew, harridan! Didn't she bear out all he had ever said about masterful women? Hadn't he just got her a good passenger, one he had been saving for just such a simpleton as her husband, and then she must weigh in, skinflinting, cheeseparing. Curse her! Wasn't that clodhopping fool damn lucky to have such a woman to keep his purse? Seven hells, as the clodhopper himself had said.

He threw back the Indian robe and the bears' meat and the ship's biscuit and the ammunition which he had clawed down to tempt Ben and he cursed Mahitabel with every curse within his range. But even he was not to guess how bitterly, how desperately, his bad customer was to regret that rejected bear meat, that despised ship's biscuit. Even as he cursed her, had he foreseen, he would have regretted. For he was not an evil man, merely disillusioned and avaricious.

Ben was waiting, in his faithful fashion, just outside the store and he chuckled happily as Mahitabel showed her purchases. Then he grew suddenly serious and said in his most earnest voice:

"Mahitabel, yon fellow did say something that made me think. That man on horseback, him you said was a gentleman, is trying to follow a new path across the mountains, he says. It's shorter than the other, and easier. I bin wondering as you talked . . . I mean I thought . . . what would *you* think about travelling with him?"

Ben's voice was diffident, his mild blue eyes anxious; his big brown hands clenched and unclenched themselves nervously. Decision of any kind had been made agony for him by the many occasions when he had been proven wrong. Fifty years of sustained ill-fortune takes confidence from a man. It was a tribute to the resilient sweetness of his nature that he looked now towards Mahitabel without resentment.

She deliberated for a moment, drawing her thin straight brows into a line above her nose. Then she said slowly:

"I'm for sticking to the known road, Ben. It's not for people like us to go experimenting and exploring. There's no family in that other wagon."

"No," agreed Ben. A little sigh escaped him as he thought of his own family responsibilities. Those hard-won, long-loved acres at Weston should now have been coming more and more under Abe's care, they were his heritage. And there should have been a little money put by

34

so that Mary Ann did not go penniless to the man who married her. Even the belated baby, Ellen, should have been rapturously welcomed, not rather sadly accepted as an additional responsibility. But the years of ill-luck and the final disaster of the prolonged drought had altered everything that a man could expect from life. He was fortunate to have so reliable and sensible a wife.

"You're right," he agreed. "We can't afford to take chances."

There was one sincere hope in his heart. When the wagons rolled out of the Fort Mason camping ground, he trusted to God that at least one of the other parties would hold to the Fort Hall road. There was safety in numbers, and confidence in company.

The matter might have ended there, settled, as most things were, by the dominant member of the family. But for once, for almost the first time in her life, Mahitabel found her will opposed, not only by Ben's unspoken preference, but by Mary Ann and Abe as well.

While his parents had been in the store Abe Smith had wakened from his bed under the wagon, lain for a little while with increasing restlessness, staring at the sky, and then gone wandering about the camp. It had increased in size. Two more wagons stood, with their poles lolling, upon the space of beaten earth.

One had brought in a big dark handsome man with a sullen brooding face, an undersized anxious boy of about twelve years old, and a woman who, for some reason not connected with physical beauty, made an appeal to the watching Abe such as he had never experienced in his life before. And Abe, at twenty, was far from being the innocent boy that Mahitabel supposed him.

Drawing away a little into the shadows, Abe watched the newcomers and came to several lightning decisions. Brought up with animals and of a kindly disposition, he noticed that even the stolid and insensitive draught oxen shrank from their master as he unyoked them. The rangy young riding horse in the same ownership had a wild and uneasy eye. The boy seemed timid and nervous, a little over-alert to perform the orders which the dark man issued. Once, when he stumbled over a carelessly thrown-down yoke, the man aimed a blow at him. The boy dodged with the agility of long practice, but his face seemed to contract into a narrower, less youthful mask of anxiety.

The woman, small and neat-moving, with a pale triangular face framed in a cloud of black hair, busied herself in starting a fire. Before it was burning the man was impatiently demanding his supper, declaring that the scent of coffee from the vicinity of the neighbouring red-wheeled wagon made him ravenous. Thereupon the red-haired, queerly-spoken girl who travelled with Madame Jurer invited him, with an effrontery that Abe had never seen equalled, to come over and drink a cup with them. The dark man accepted the offer with alacrity.

When he had gone the woman and the boy seemed to straighten themselves, as though a burden had been removed from their shoulders. She spoke for the first time.

"Which way is the water, Evan?" She lifted an empty bucket as she spoke.

"I'll get it for you."

"Indeed you will not. You've carried enough for one evening. You don't have to work for *me*."

Although the sentence was emphatic it seemed to lack conviction; to be a mere statement of fact.

"Aw, I'm all right. Gimme the bucket," said the boy and laid a hand beside hers on the handle.

Then Abe, who was shy of strangers and seldom impulsive, moved forward and said in a voice stiff with nervousness:

"Allow me, ma'am; I'll fetch it for you."

Boy and woman looked up, startled, almost apprehensive. Then she said in a low quick voice: "Oh, thank you. Thank you very much," and gave the bucket into his hand. She smiled a little and Abe felt his face grow hot. His knees were stiff with self-consciousness as he walked away. When he brought back the bucket, brimming silver, he waited until she was stooped over the fire, then set it down unobtrusively and hurried away.

It was getting dark. Around Madame Jurer's fire the gathered faces shown redly. He recognized Mary Ann with a start of surprise. She was sitting close to the dark plump girl, who, as he passed the group, looked up, whispered to his sister and then looked at him again, gaily, invitingly. But Abe was in no mood to join them. He shook his head, not at Floribel, but at Mary Ann, and moved away.

Another newly-arrived wagon, crookedly halted, stood by the edge of the camping ground, and beside it, by the light of a lantern recently kindled and not ·burning well, a little man was working with a clasp-knife upon an ox-bow. Abe heard him swear softly as the knife slipped on the hard wood; then he sighed and paused to toss back a heavy lock of grizzled hair which fell forward again as soon as he bent his head.

Abe, who had paused, in the immemorial way of men who see a fellow engaged upon a task, however familiar, was for the second time within an hour startled by the sight of a strange face. As Cordy Warren tossed back his hair the lantern, with gathering power, threw its light on his features and Abe thought that he had never seen a human face so worn and scoured. The wide, noble brow, so placid in outline, was marred, ploughed and furrowed; the eyes—shortsighted to judge by the way he bent over his work—held a look of settled anxiety; the mouth had the lines that suggested firm closing upon insult and reproach. And yet the whole face was incongruously complete and calm and trustworthy, and as he looked upon it Abe was conscious that he too had been lonely upon the long march from Weston, that he too had been dumbly in search of congenial companionship, and that for some strange reason it was offered here in the person of the little man making such a poor job with the knife.

Once again Abe abandoned his habitual reserve and moved forward into the circle of light, which grew brighter as night encroached upon the camping ground. Cordy Warren looked up and said: "Good evening," with a smile that was at once friendly and detached, as though he were prepared for Abe to move away again immediately. But Abe squatted down beside him, and asked with rather more than his natural diffidence:

"You trying to bore a hole in that?"

"That was, roughly, my aim," said Cordy, his smile

and his voice edged with irony, "but like many others it seems to be doomed to failure."

"Whyn't you burn it through? You'll never do it that way. Hot iron's the only tool for that job."

"'Oh wise young man'," said Cordy, sitting back on his heels and dabbing his brow. "I hadn't thought of that. I suppose a poker would do—if I can find one, which I doubt. Camp fires seem not to need poking."

"Reckon I can lay my hand on the very thing, straight away," said Abe, rising. He went over to the Smith wagon and returned immediately, carrying a short thick length of iron, pointed at one end, and a pair of bellows. With the deftness of long practice in practical things he knelt by the fire and blew it to a fierce core of heat around the iron. When the iron itself glowed he slipped off his coat, wraped his hand in its sleeve and withdrew the tool. Neatly he burned the hole at the spot scored by Cordy's hacking, turning his head away from the cloud of acrid smoke that rose as the iron ate home. He held out the completed job.

"I'm infinitely obliged to you," said Cordy warmly. "You're very handy. I'm afraid I'm not; and I've been finding out lately just how necessary handiness can be."

"You come far?"

"Umm." There was a sound of hesitation, an almost imperceptible pause and then: "Yes. From Pennsylvania. Where're you from?"

"Weston, Missouri. We're both a long way from home, aren't we?" A long way from the places and people that we knew; a long way from the friends we had; cut off; lonely. Cordy could hear all that in the boy's voice.

"A long way, indeed. But I've made a longer journey in my time. I'm from England originally."

"I thought you spoke different." Abe watched as Cordy, with an air of relief, closed and replaced the clasp-knife. The thought went through his mind that only a Limey would have set about such a job with such a tool. Yet the thought did not make him like Cordy less.

There was a five-minute silence. Try as he might Abe could think of no way of breaking it, except by taking leave. Reluctantly at last he unfolded his long legs.

"Oh, don't go," said Cordy, as though suddenly reminded of his existence. "Have some coffee. It's just here." He set a battered metal coffee-pot amidst the red embers and from somewhere about the wagon's tail produced two cups.

Gladly Abe sank back again, accepted his share of the strong black liquid and renewed his struggle to produce some remark acceptable to his companion, something that would mark him as a fit associate for an older, more educated man.

Cordy produced a pipe and pouch and proffered the latter.

"I never have smoked," Abe was obliged to admit.

"Listen," said Cordy, leaning forward, once the pipe was alight. "I went into the store directly I arrived and the fellow there said something about a man called Furmage who intends to try out a new road. D'you know anything about it?"

"No," said Abe. "And I reckon if anything like that was said it'd be said to Pa, not me. But he ain't mentioned the matter. The Fort Hall's the on'y road I ever heard of."

"Or me, until this evening. But this new way is supposed to be shorter and easier, and God knows that would suit me. I've got a wife and three young children in there," he jerked his head towards the wagon, "and they present a problem on a trip like this . . . milk and such things. I shouldn't be sorry to shorten the journey."

"I don't think anyone would. I don't mean that I don't enjoy it, sometimes. But, well, I've alwust lived in the one place and I've a fancy for getting up mornings and seeing th'old things round me. I'll be glad when we find a little place again."

"You aim to farm there?"

"Nothing else we *could* do. You ain't a farmer?" No, a farmer would know more about tools.

"No." Again that trivial hesitation, and again the confidence hard on its heels. "I'm a newspaper man, printer, editor, reporter, jack-of-all-trades in that line. I've got a little press in the wagon, and I should like . . . it's a bit ambitious maybe . . . but I should like to find a grow-
39

ing place where there wasn't a paper, and start one. I'm too old to make much of a new trade now."

"I don't think changes are much good," Abe agreed, pontifically. "We wouldn'ta changed, but we was forced. Three years with hardly a drop of rain, summer or winter. We was drove to change. You can't fight the weather, as Pa says."

"Change was forced on me, too," said Cordy, "but not by the weather."

Either the fireglow died suddenly or a shadow came from within his darkened face. Against his will he remembered the uproar in that peaceful Pennsylvanian township, which in certain circumstances he would have been happy to have made his home for the rest of his days. He recalled the cackle of spiteful tongues, the pointing fingers and the averted faces of erstwhile friends, Ruth's cold determination, his own acceptance of the inevitable. Forgetful of Abe's presence, he groaned aloud as he often did when alone; then, as the boy stirred, he tried to cover the harsh sound of misery by a cough.

"I hope you'll find the place you're looking for. P'raps after all change ain't a bad thing. Us Smith's never did much good stopping in one spot, that I do know. P'raps we'll all make our fortunes in the West."

It occurred to Cordy to retort that making a fortune was not the sole aim of life. But he remembered in time that the boy was young, with health and vigour in him, with life and love and many years ahead of him. For such, given fair opportunity, any land, east or west, offered chances of happiness. But for himself there was nothing to hope for, save patience and fortitude of mind, and health of body so that he might continue to support Ruth and the children. He would not even think of the forgetfulness that passing time would bring, he scorned its dull medicine. Oh, my dear lost love, torn from me by circumstances so brutal, your memory must live in my mind, so that we are not separated utterly, so that life does not seem completely wasted since I can remember the happiness we once had. . . .

Abe's voice, dreadfully uncertain, broke in upon his musing.

"About this new road . . . if there is one. Say, will you travel by it, or stick to the old?" It mattered, it mattered somehow more than anything had mattered since the boy had left Weston.

"I shall go by the new one if it sounds at all feasible. I must try to find out more about it. In fact I think I shall go now."

The words dismissed Abe, who, in shyness, rose over-hastily and with a muttered word of thanks for the coffee, shambled away into the darkness.

But later on, when mention was made of the choice of roads within the family circle, the knowledge that his new acquaintance was minded to try the new one made Abe side with his father, who was activated by his desire for company, and with his sister who was infatuated by Flori-bel Toit, rather than with his mother, whose native readi-ness to meet adventure had been worn down by the certainty that the woman who was married to Bad Luck Ben could afford to take very few chances.

That the black-haired woman's direction of travel was unknown hardly occurred to Abe; even if he had known it, it would not have influenced his vote. She had roused in him an emotion that he did not understand and was not anxious to experience again. Pain was in it, and pity, as well as bewilderment and excitement. But she was married to the sullen dark fellow whose beasts feared him, and that fact set her so far away, in Abe's simple sight, that to him it seemed natural that they should go their separate ways in the world without further contact.

Mahitabel, like all benevolent tyrants, was quick to sense opposition, however veiled and dumb. Of her three opponents only Ben gave a reason for his preference, which had become stronger when he learned that both Madame Jurer and Cordy Warren intended to follow Mr. Furmage in his experiment. Possibly the dour-faced man who had been last to arrive, and whose name, it was learned, was Dave Glenny, might favour the old road, but even so, with the Smiths he would make but a weak party, nor was Ben much taken by his looks. Ben preferred, like all timid souls, to be a member of the majority; and for once in his life he openly expressed his opinion and was surprised and delighted to find that his son and daughter, in less obvious fashion but quite certainly, favoured the new road.

Mahitabel did not capitulate easily. She repeated her words about not taking risks and about the tried ways being best. She was not obviously disconcerted when Abe, nervously fidgetting, muttered:

"But Ma, if everybody always thought that, nothing would ever have been discovered at all. We shouldn't even know that Californy was there, jist over the mountains."

Unwillingly, however, she at last said that Ben might try to speak with the man who wanted to travel the new road and hear for himself what the advantages were.

Upon this non-committal statement the family retired, nursing their separate hopes and fears.

The camp was astir early in the morning. Abe was dispatched to fetch Frank Cooper from the store, and Ben picked his way through the bundles and the people and the teams, towards Kevin's wagon. Hendriks and Joe Sterry were bustling about but there was no sign of their master, and when Ben, rather diffidently, asked the cowherd his whereabouts the little man said gutturally:

"He's in his bath. I just poured'n. Round odder side," and he pointed to the far side of the wagon.

The idea of a bath during the morning hours of a working day wrung a grunt from Ben, to whom the process was confined to a Saturday night ritual, back home in Weston, when the weary, sweat-damped, earth-caked, chaff-irritated body was made fit to wear its Sunday clothing. Nor could his inelastic mind entertain the notion of either seeing or being seen by a perfect stranger in a bath. So he hesitated until a hearty resonant voice came from behind the wagon: "Somebody wanting me? Come along round."

Reluctantly Ben rounded the wagon, and there, with his hands vigorously rubbing his head with a towel whose ends draped his shoulders and left the rest of him naked, was the man whom he sought. He stood in a shallow crock, like those used for standing milk for cream, but it was wider and deeper and it was full of soapy water

42

which still gave off lazy spirals of steam. Ben, caught in a similar position, would have been speechless with confusion; as an onlooker he suffered considerably; but Kevin Furmage, lowering the towel to his neck and seesawing it to and fro merely regarded his visitor with interest and said:

"Good morning. You wanted to see me? Let's see, I don't know you, do I?"

"I should say not. The name is Smith. I kinda wanted to ask you summat, but I can wait till it's more convenient for you."

He turned away, gladly, for Kevin had begun towelling the more private parts of his body and Ben was growing hot with embarrassment.

"No, no, don't go. Be finished in a minute. What did you want to know?"

He stepped out of the water, flicked the towel rapidly over his feet and legs and reached for the pile of clothing that lay on the bleached grass beside him. He dressed himself with swift deft movements and in two minutes Ben was able to look at him squarely, and then he saw a man of about forty years old who bore his years lightly, with a ruddy complexion, bright choleric blue eyes that protruded a little, and a thinning crop of crisp pale ginger-coloured hair. His shoulders were broad and flat, his flanks thin and his legs the well-muscled, slightly bowed limbs of an habitual horseman. He made Ben, for the first time in many years, conscious of being heavy and thick and slow.

"Now?" said Kevin with a grain of impatience in his voice.

"I wanted to ask you about this here journey. Round about they're saying that you've been over the old road once and now you're looking for a new one. Is that right?"

"Quite right."

"I wanted to know which you'd advise a man with a family, and with a sick man aboard, to try."

The earnestness in his voice as he put the question and hinted at his liabilities touched Kevin.

"Now, you know, that's hardly a fair question. I'm not here to give advice. I came here prepared to start out by myself to follow a map and to travel a road of which I know nothing save that I have heard it favourably described. I don't mind saying that *I think* the new way has inestimable advantages, the chief one being that the desert drive is shorter by at least a couple of days, but I'm not taking any responsibility for folks who think they'd like to travel with me. Three lots have chosen to do so, but I want to make it quite clear that I didn't advise, or persuade or even much wish them to do so."

"You mean the three other wagons 'sides mine are going your way?" Ben breathed harshly. "So if I set out this morning on th'old road I go by myself?" Just what he had feared all along, the very shape of fear!

"That's about the size of it. There's the old lady with the Negroes, a little man with a wagonful of youngsters, and the other fellow who came to see me late last night, big dark man with a Welsh sound to him. I told them just what I've told you, but the choice was theirs, as it is yours."

"Nobody could say fairer than that," Ben admitted. But in truth the fairness of it disappointed him; he would have liked more definite assertions, more persuasions, strong reasons that he could have carried back to Mahitabel. He stirred the dust of the camping ground with the toe of his heavy boot and tried to draw out the assurance that he needed.

"But leastways," he said slowly, "you being a man of experience, like, you'd say that it was better to travel in company, would'n'you?"

"For myself I usually prefer it. I don't know that I would make it the deciding factor."

"I'd rather travel with others," said Ben, and for once his tone had no hesitation in it. "And specially I would like to go with folks as had been before. This ain't my sort of country; nor I don't care for mountains and such. . . ." Gropingly he tried to express his countryman's distrust of the unfamiliar. "I think, mister, if it's all the same to you we'll just hang along of you."

"I'm glad to hear it." Once the decision had been made without influence from him and he could therefore detach all responsibility from himself, Kevin was able to speak freely. The old fanatic glint shone in his eyes as he detailed to his new follower the advantages of the new route. He spent five minutes in praising it, and at the end of that time Ben had a sheaf of arguments with which to tackle Mahitabel.

When he had hurried away Kevin sat down to his breakfast. He was usually a hearty feeder, and the food this morning was as well cooked and served as ever, but for once his appetite failed him and after the first few mouthfuls he pushed aside his plate and called to Hendriks that he might do the final packing. As the last bundles went into his own wagon and into those of the other travellers, Kevin walked to the place where Persephone was picketed and with one hand on her neck, surveyed the busy scene.

He was conscious of mounting excitement; yet below this pleasurable sensation there ran, dark and cold, like an underground stream, a little creeping thread of uneasiness that was almost fear. For the first time he realized the magnitude of his undertaking. It was all very well to say that he had not encouraged or persuaded these people to follow him; it was all very well to announce his repudiation of all responsibility; the fact remained that what had begun as a lonely adventure had developed into a matter of leadership and for a moment he doubted his ability to undertake it. The raddled old woman had been wrong when she had said that responsibility was the breath of life to him; she was either mistaken, or—more likely—speaking with intent to flatter. It was one thing that he had never sought, nor willingly accepted. Now, in this moment of mental clarity, he saw that there lay the reason for his frequent failures. The spectacular thing, easily accomplished, had always been his aim.

This journey for example . . . He had meant to follow de Brielle's map, mark the new road, make a record for speed and then announce his triumph. In a sense, of course, he would have been responsible for Joe Sterry and Hendriks, but they had understood what they had committed themselves to, and were only servants anyway. But these people who had so trustingly confided their lives to his guidance were different, so different that he was visited by a momentary longing to shout to them all, that he would not have them follow him, that they must pull out to the north on the Fort Hall road and forget that any other route had ever been mentioned.

The longing vanished almost instantly. The old optimism welled up, displacing his self-mistrust. He knew that the road was good, he trusted de Brielle, he trusted, despite his past failures, to his ruling star. This was the biggest thing he had yet attempted and, by God, he would see it to a successful conclusion. And these people, they would yet be proud of this day's work. The first party to enter California by the Furmage Road. It was the only vestige of distinction that any of them would ever know.

Kevin threw back his shoulders. Leadership had been thrust on him, but he would bear it worthily. He would govern his temper, check his impatience, provide enough courage and cheerfulness for a party twice the size.

Lightly he swung himself into Persephone's saddle; confidently he watched his followers assemble their teams.

Across the camp Mahitabel Smith wedged in the last pillow that was to keep poor Mr. Cooper firm and comfortable on this, the first stage of the journey. Her hands were as deft and busy and her manner as alert as ever, but eyes wandered now and then to the well-worn track that led to the Fort Hall road, and then a little frown drew her straight brows together. Ben had come back with irrefutable arguments in favour of the new route and she had given way, but a certain uneasiness remained at the bottom of her mind. She had climbed into the wagon while the family ate their breakfast and there, alone, she she had fallen on her knees and requested of God one definite sign, one tiny clue of guidance. But nothing had been vouchsafed her, and Mahitabel, in these days, was versed enough in the ways of God to feel neither distress nor disappointment. If a sign had been needed He would have given it before; obviously it was immaterial to His purpose which way the Smiths headed. And yet . . . that faint uneasiness remained.

She wedged the cushion and returned Frank Cooper's smile of gratitude with another as candid and sincere if less sweet, settled the baby, looked around to see that

46

nothing had been forgotten, and went to the head of the team where Ben stood patiently waiting.

"Everything is ready," she said. And she meant, not only that bundles were in place, casks firmly secured, passenger and baby made comfortable, but that she herself was ready to walk, and heave and push and pull, to cook and scheme and contrive so that at last all the people who had been entrusted to her care should emerge upon the other side of the mountains if that should be God's will.

"Keep clear of that painted wagon if you can," she added, glancing at it from the corner of her eye. "I'm sorry it's coming this way. That little wench is the spitting image of Dulcie Jepson, back home. You remember the trouble I had with Mary Ann over *her*. And that one was grinning and making signs to her all the time we were packing. Where's Abe?"

"Lending a hand."

"Who to?" Mahitabel's voice was sharp.

"Fellow called Warren," answered Ben calmly. "He didn' seem able to yoke up so good. Ain't very handy, Abe says. You gotta be neighborly on a trip like this, Mahitabel."

"I don't mind neighboring the Warrens," said Mahitabel, who had watched Ruth's motherly ministrations. "They seem a decent little family." One kept one's standards, even when one was a nomad, far removed from the environment that had given such standards birth.

The chill was still in the air, though the cloudless blue of the sky gave promise of another hot and perfect day as the wagons followed one after another off the beaten earth of the camping ground and lurched down the decline which divided the store from the first steep upward slope. Jim Mason emerged, bleary-eyed and tousled-haired, to watch them go. Hitching the belt of his trousers he threw back his head, sniffing the air like an animal. Like an animal he knew in his bones that it would be an early winter this year. Good for trapping, though bad for emigrants.

He watched the train draw out. Damned ornery spenders, he thought. Them that could have spent, Furmage and the old trollop and the Smiths after they'd taken their passenger, wouldn't; and them that would have liked to, that dark whisky-craving fellow, Glenny, and the Mrs. Warren who wanted things for her babies all the time, couldn't. And most likely they'd be the last he'd see this year. Still, it hadn't been a bad season, on the whole. This craze for going west seemed to grow stronger every year. He might as well close the store now and have a rest before going back to his real work.

The haze of dust of its passing was already obscuring the wagon train as Jim turned away. He didn't think of the travellers again. Why should he? They were only a party of ordinary people who were seeking in the West what they had missed or lost in their old home places.

He was not to know—could anyone have known?— that at the moment when the wagons followed one another down the slope, the good and bad angels were already mustering for the battle in which these few "ornery spenders" were to be both warriors and field. How should he know that these unremarkable men and women, in their very blood and bones, were to be the agents through which was to be asked again, and partly answered, the immemorial question, *What is man?* Is he an animal that has somehow acquired the gift of speech, an upright posture and a trick of co-operation, props which adversity may knock away and leave the brute beast to gibber and wallow and betray his fellows? Or is he a God-remembering being, who, exiled from Heaven, yet bears with him the memory of decency and beauty to guide him through the world and to set him standards that he must observe?

These people, on their earthly journey, with their faces turned to the earthly West, were going, though they did not guess it, to pile up evidence for argument upon either side. And four of them, Mahitabel Smith, Nancy Jurer, Dave Glenny and Cory Warren, were going to put to the test the allegiances of a lifetime.

The wheels rolled over the faded lupines. The sun defeated the chill in the air. The wagons reached the bottom of the valley and the oxen leaned forward for the upward slope, stiffer than any behind them, foretaste of those to come.

The journey, and the story, had begun.

PART TWO

The People

MAHITABEL SMITH—WHO LOVED GOD

Mahitabel Dewer was the third and only surviving child of her parents. Theodosius, her father, was a leather-worker in Weston, Missouri. He made not only footwear but harness, windproof jerkins and leather-thonged chairs. He was industrious and God-fearing; and was wont, when asked how he did, to reply, not with a report of his physical health, but with the words: "God gives me strength and health to work hard." His wife, Maly, was a little round woman, very placid, except when roused to anger, when she could be very violent.

There was nothing in either parent to account for Mahitabel, the tall strange girl who flashed through the quiet, leather-scented house, like a darting ray of light. She was not the child they would have chosen. They had done their best to rear her properly, and Theodosius' leather strap had had no small part in her upbringing. Until she was fourteen, after which age corporal punishment was no longer seemly, she had been beaten with remarkable regularity. Maly, who was lethargic and rather idle, was inclined to favour her because she was so remarkably energetic, and was sometimes heard to say that no harm could come to a girl who was such a good worker. If Mahitabel could have behaved rather better in service time her mother would have supported her with more fervour and assurance. But almost as regularly as the Sabbath dawned, Mahitabel was in disgrace. Either she appeared unsuitably dressed; or she made some un-Sabbatical sign to a fellow rebel in the congregation; or she criticized the sermon. And until she was fourteen Theodosius beat her almost every Monday.

When she was seventeen she was very attractive, not from any regularity of feature, or delicacy of proportion, but because she was so obviously healthy and happy and pleased with herself. She had a sense of style that was certainly not inherited from Maly; she could tie a mere bow of ribbon so that it caught the eye, and pin a brooch of ordinary silver so that it looked like a decoration. The girls of her acquaintance were not slow to recognize this gift and cultivated its owner, at first, perhaps, from ulterior motives, and then because, at this stage, Mahitabel was irresistible. She was careless, and witty; and wherever she was the boys were bound to be.

It was odd, at that time, for a girl so tall, so outspoken and so daring, to be popular; but Mahitabel was outside all rules. The boys of the neighbourhood laughed at her sayings, encouraged her in her unfeminine physical feats —like running across the field where the Averys' bull lived, or mounting Mr. Kruger's new and surprisingly vicious horse—and then, suddenly and without warning, they would make sheep's eyes at her and attempt hot but unskilful kisses.

It was a period of early marriages. Life was not so secure and certain in Missouri in the early years of the century that you could wait until you were thirty before stamping your mark upon the next generation. But though several of her friends were married at seventeen and eighteen, the popular and much-sought-after Mahitabel reached the age of nineteen and was still unmarried. Theodosius, more puzzled than ever as his daughter grew beyond his control, grumbled so continually at her behaviour that Maly, although she knew that she would miss her daughter's presence and energetic help, was heard to say more than once that she did wish Mahitabel would marry and settle down.

But Mahitabel went happily on, out to tea, out to supper, dancing in this barn, taking charge of this table at a tea-meeting, rushing away, unknown to Theodosius, to visit a circus in Sandwater, trying the latest style of hair-dressing, making her severe, Maly-chosen clothes look like models.

To Mahitabel life was very good indeed; and she accepted its goodness as a gift from God, just as Theodosius accepted his increasing tendency to rheumatism, and Maly her distressing flatulence. The grim and terrible God of the meeting-house, with His regrettable jealousy and strict ideas on human behaviour, was not real to her at all. Hers was the God who had made the sunshine, the flowers, the madly vocal spring birds, the capering young lambs. She had a vague, but very pleasant idea that He liked to see you enjoying yourself.

Amongst her many friends were the Kenyon girls; and this was a tribute to her personality, for as the doctor's daughters they ranked amongst the aristocracy of the little town, and they had attended a Ladies' Academy at Sandwater. But, being pallid and languid and slothful they revolved gratefully within the radiance of Mahitabel's orbit.

Early during the summer after Mahitabel's nineteenth birthday the Kenyon girls greeted their friend with the news that their cousin Barny was coming from New York to spend the summer with them. He had been ill, and his sister, Dr. Kenyon's well-married sister, had decided that a long stay in the country, under his medical relative's eye, was the one thing that was needed to restore him to full health.

She had not added that his physical frailty had been outgrown for several years, and that her real reason for wanting to secure Barny's absence from New York was that he had been conducting a regrettable intrigue with the wife of his father's very junior partner.

The Kenyon girls, who were motherless and entirely inefficient housekeepers, solicited Mahitabel's aid in entertaining their sophisticated relative.

Barny arrived, furious with his exile and in a mood to despise everything and everybody in Weston. The sulky look that had been almost permanently upon his face for the last few months, lent his thin, highly-coloured face a strange childish charm. His manners, his voice, his very clothes marked him as something apart from the fustian youth of the small mid-Western township.

Within an hour of his arrival, Mahitabel, the heart and soul of the party that she had organised to welcome him, was conscious of a new element in her life. She fell in love with him as quickly and as thoroughly as she did everything. Towards her Barny's feelings were very mixed. Superior as he was disposed to be towards everything in Weston, he did not find it possible to ignore her, she was too vital for that; it was obvious on that first evening that though the company met in Doc Kenyon's house and ate his food, it was Mahitabel's party. Mahitabel remembered the forgotten dish languishing in the kitchen; Mahitabel mopped up when something was spilled; it was Mahitabel who cried: "Now we'll play so-and-so." So at first Barny disliked her, thought that she was noisy and domineering and outlandishly dressed. Then, gradually he came to realise that of all the girls in his cousins' circle Mahitabel was the only one who would show to advantage at Rattier's or the Green Parlour, and he rather wished that he could appear in one of these places with her, and meet Agnes Fulmer there and wring her heart with jealousy as she had so often wrung his.

But although he was beginning reluctantly to admire the tall dashing girl, the dregs of his original dislike remained. He liked women like Agnes Fulmer, small, frail, fair and secretive, the very antithesis of Mahitabel Dewer. Nevertheless, one warm summer evening, when he was accompanying her home after a picnic, he kissed her, idly and experimentally. The result surprised him.

Hot-bloodedly but cold-mindedly he used her, partly to amuse himself through a summer's stagnation, partly to assuage his longing for Agnes. Mahitabel gave herself whole-heartedly, glad that she had resisted so many young men with hot mouths and heavy hands, glad that she was still unmarried and so mistress of her own affairs.

Despite her religious upbringing and strict training she was not once conscious of sin. Even when sometimes on Sundays the dreadful word "fornication" occurred in one of the Lessons, she never associated herself with it. The God of the meeting-house, of Theodosius and Maly, had no concern with this affair; this was a matter for the God of the sunshine and laughter who had always been her friend.

Barny was astonished at the ease and completeness of

his conquest, and before long he did admire Mahitabel ardently; for her talent for deception, for her vigorous response, and most of all for her lack of feminine wiles and claim-staking. In public not the most acute observer could have guessed that there was more than good comradeship between them; in private she never mentioned marriage or the future, or appeared to regret her lost virginity. She just enjoyed herself.

Her love for Barny flavoured all her life. Even the long Sunday services were endurable now, for from her place she could watch his black head between the fair curls and flowered bonnets of his cousins; and now and then, in a psalm, mostly, an odd sentence would strike home to her heart. "My flesh shall rest in hope," "So shall the king greatly desire thy beauty: for he is thy Lord." For many years the barbaric beauty of the Old Testament had washed unnoticed over her head, but now her ears were open and many a stray, inapt phrase sent her into such a trance of mingled memory and anticipation that Maly, with a secret glance sideways, was led to hope that Mahitabel was entering the company of the elect at last.

And then Barny tired suddenly, and with boredom came the thought of the future. He wrote urgently to his mother and she, secure in the knowledge that Agnes Fulmer had gone to the sea for the hot weather, wrote, permitting his return. In the interval between his satiation and the arrival of his mother's letter, his own good manners and Mahitabel's peculiar faculty for seeing her own vigour and vitality reflected in other people, kept the affair going and she was at least spared the gradual disintegration of their relationship.

In the second week in August she went, reluctant, but ungrudging, to nurse an aunt at Sandwater through a trifling illness. Barny had promised to come over and lighten her exile, but he did not come and Mahitabel light-heartedly assumed that something else had arisen to occupy him on the appointed day. But she was eager to see him, when, at the end of ten days, she returned to Weston and stopped at the Kenyon house before going home.

Bella Kenyon was in the kitchen, inexpertly sealing

down some currant jam, and Mahitabel, after the first greeting, took the paper and the white-of-egg and the brush and finished the job with despatch and skill. "Now," she said, pushing the finished jars into line, "tell me what you've been doing while I've been pulling Aunt Kitty out of the jaws of death."

"Nothing much," said Bella disconsolately. "Barny went two days after you left; and with him gone and you away it's dreadfully dull."

For many a summer Mahitabel could not smell the scent of hot currant jam without a sickening of the heart. On this morning the red, white-capped pots, the egg basin, the brush and the scissors and cut paper swung in a whirling arc before her eyes. She laid her palms on the table and leaned forward on them, steadying herself. And she said, in a voice that even to her own ears sounded unreal and hollow, "Well, I bet you haven't had such a dull time as I have."

Bella Kenyon noticed nothing; she took up the argument, as Mahitabel had intended, upon the respective merits of Weston and Sandwater and it lasted until Mahitabel said she must go.

It was about half a mile from the Kenyon's to her own home, and since she wanted to see no one she walked across the field and through the corner of the wood. The way led her past the place where Barny had first kissed her; and she stood there, fighting the hardest battle of her life. She did not remind herself that this was what might be expected to happen to a girl who fell in love with a summer visitor; nor ask herself what she had hoped. She stood there with her hands clenched together and let the knowledge that he had gone, without even a farewell, and that she would never see him again, sink into her soul. She would have liked to throw herself on the ground and grovel and cry; but in a few moments she had to face Maly; and she could not excuse a ravaged face by saying that she had a headache, she had never had one in her life; and above all things she knew that she must behave entirely normally.

She stood there, with the sun dappling through the leaves upon her shoulders, until she had set her feet upon one spot of unquaking ground—she could bear it so long as no one knew or guessed. She loved Barny; she would never love anyone else, but she could bear the pain of her loving so long as she could bear it alone, free from anyone's scorn or pity.

She went home and regaled her mother with the details of Aunt Kitty's illness and the latest news of Sandwater. She was unmoved when Maly said, "I've been waiting till you came to make the currant jam." Nor did she flinch when, over supper, her mother said, "Bella and Meg will miss their cousin, I should say. We'd better ask them to tea on Sunday."

The remaining days of August passed and September came. The new month brought with it the shattering knowledge that something had overtaken her that could not be hidden. The fresh blow, coming so hard upon the heels of the old, and following three weeks in which every word and action must be watched and controlled, almost unhinged her mind. What should she do? The shame, the disgrace, the misery that she would bring upon Maly and Theodosius: the pointing finger, the whispered word, the watching eye—she endured them all in the first few days after that discovery.

Her tortured mind went round and round, entertaining and rejecting one possibility after another. They were limited by her innocence. She might go away, find work, and bear the child in a place where at least no one need share her shame. But she could only do housework, had never been farther afield than Sandwater and had never in her life slept under a roof that did not belong to a relative or a friend. Or she might marry one of the young men who favoured her; the wedding could be hurried through on the plea that just after harvest was the most favourable time for country marriages. But that plan involved great deception and considerable risk of a discovery that would ruin life forever afterwards. Or she might confide in her parents and, backed by them, compel Barny to marry her. She dismissed this most rapidly of all. First there was the awful moment of confession to face—and she was not at all sure that she could even put the case into words with Maly or Theodosius looking at her: and after that there would be Barny's disgust and his unwillingness to endure. If he had ever thought of marrying her he would not have gone away like that. Also New York was as far away as another country, to her mind, and she had talked to her lover enough to have learned that his life was too far removed from hers for her to even visualise it clearly. She could not possibly intrude upon it, unwanted and shamed. In the last resource she might kill herself. Avid and eager as she was for life, deeply rooted as her joy in it had been, this was the plan which appealed to her most.

And then, sudden as the light which blinded Saul of Tarsus on the road to Damascus, the thought of God struck upon her shrinking mind. Not the gay God who had been present in the musty, corn-scented barns or the grassy places where she and Barny had lain, but the stern God of her parents and the meeting-house, the jealous God who had said, "The wages of sin is death." It may have been a trick of her exhausted mind, or it may have been a genuine revelation, but, quite certainly, as she sought for some solution to her problem, she was suddenly conscious that other possibilities than those of mortal action were open to her.

She had been in bed at the time, enduring the nightly torment when she must face herself and the future without even a pretence that all was well to veil the full horror of her plight. She slipped from the bed and went over to the open window. She knelt there with her elbows on the sill and her eyes on the star-sown sky.

The disregarded Sunday preaching had at least taught her that God must be circumspectly approached; and that the first condition of forgiveness is that one should be sensible of sin and sorry for it. So, kneeling there, she remembered every word spoken, every touch, every excitement of that happy summer, and by an alchemy of will she converted it into an orgy of vice. The secrecy that had been half the fun of it was vile deception; she had been carnal and lustful, she had mated without God's blessing; in short she had sinned grievously. She had used a gift which was intended for the procreation of children and the glory of God without thought of either children or God, merely for her wilful pleasure. She delved further

59

and saw that in this last summer of her life she had only put the crowning touches upon nineteen years of unsanctified living. She had always been vain, proud, headstrong, worldly and thoughtless. The trouble in which she now found herself was merely the logical outcome of a youth spent as hers had been.

She pondered this thought for a long time, and then, lowering her elbows, she clasped her hands upon the window-sill, lowered her head upon them and began to pray. The prayer was an intricate mixture of Old Testament phrases, remembered scraps from prayers in the meeting-house and sheer outspoken girlish supplication. When it was ended by her inability to make new sentences or repeat old ones any more, she crept back into bed and the relaxation of her body was accompanied by an ease of mind. She knew, for the first time, the joy of having cast her burden upon the Lord, and she slept more soundly than she had done for weeks.

But morning brought no miracle.

God was teaching her patience, she thought; and with strange new meekness she admitted the need for the lesson. Sometimes, during the ensuing string of disappointing days and prayerful nights, she found her mind reverting to her original plans for helping herself; but she forced her mind away. To engage in speculations as to what she would do if God did not help her was a flagrant breach of faith. She must trust Him, implicitly, and prayerfully. And every night, while the house slumbered, she knelt by her window and poured out her eager supplication. It was less scriptural now, less flavoured by memories of the meeting-house: gradually it became Mahitabel Dewer asking an enormous favour from the one source that had power to help her. At last, gripping the window-sill in her strong hands as though to wrest a response from the wood she merely prayed, over and over again, "Oh God, don't let me have a baby, for Christ's sake!"

A whole month passed; and as though, in her case, a month was far longer than a month minus one day, she noticed the date and fell into a veritable paroxysm of terror. It was no good; God had not heard her, or if He had, had chosen not to answer. She knew that her will would not support her through that day under Maly's eye, so she dispatched her household tasks in an hour of frenzied activity, and went—she said—to spend the day with the Kenyons.

She went no farther than the wood behind the house. There was a yellow touch on some of the leaves now and the bramble sprays along its edge shone ruby and wine-coloured. The year was turning. She had always loved the autumn—as in its turn she had loved every season of all her years. But all that was ended. She would not see the misty mornings or help with the apple gathering, or make bramble jelly, or attend the Christmas dance in the Kenyon's barn; the wages of sin was death, and she had sinned and must take her wages.

She carried with her into the wood her most intimate possession, a thick book of lined paper which she had once cajoled Theodosius into binding with leather for her. She had had it since she was twelve, and there, written in a small crabbed hand—for she intended it to last her days and hoped to live to be eighty—was a detailed record of her simple life. Every punishment, every joy, every disappointment and every excitement that she had known for seven years was recorded there in straightforward language and indifferent spelling. The entries stopped abruptly with the remark that she had helped the Kenyon girls to prepare a bedroom for their cousin and had promised to go over next day to help them with the welcoming party.

She had come home after that party and from long habit taken the diary from her drawer where it reposed under a heap of neatly mended underclothes. But when she came to write about Barny words failed her and she knew that she had never before had anything of importance to record; that was why keeping a diary had hitherto seemed so easy. She had put it away and she had not added to it since.

Now, perhaps from a desire to clarify her thoughts, or from her natural inability to leave a job uncompleted, she took the pencil from the slot on the cover (one of Theodosius' more cunning devices) and wrote the whole story, sparing herself nothing. She wrote how she still longed for Barny, though he had treated her ill, how, in different circumstances she would ask nothing better than to bear his child, and how, prayer having failed she was determined to make away with herself.

"Some people think that to kill yourself is a crime, but I think that to live and bring disgrace to your parents is worse. I shall only hurt myself, and they need not even guess that I did it. The bridge by Goosegreen has needed a new rail for a long time and anyone might step off it in the dark. I don't think that what doesn't hurt anyone else can be so very bad. And anyway God has turned His face away from me already so perhaps it doesn't matter much."

There was a good deal more in the same strain.

When it was finished she read it through and then turned the pages idly, reading bits here and there. Events and people came vividly before her as she read; and she realised with a new spiritual insight that to-night, when she was drowned and the book, well weighted with a stone, would lie on the bottom of the river, this life that was here recorded would have been wiped out as though it had never existed. Mahitabel Dewer, who had a light hand for pastry, who could mend lace so that the tear was invisible, who could dance straight through the Master Maze without putting a foot wrong—she would have vanished from the earth. It was a heavy thought.

Nevertheless she set about her preparations with her usual thoroughness. She had said that she was visiting the Kenyons, so to their house she went. She cut out Meg's new winter dress, with whose paper pattern she found her tearfully struggling, and basted the longest seams together. She helped Bella make a rabbit pie and managed to eat her share at the midday meal. In the afternoon they went nutting in the shrubbery at the bottom of the garden, and then, at Mahitabel's suggestion, made some nut crackle candy. She turned it into the buttered tin to set, and thought, "By the time it's fit to eat, I shall be dead."

She washed her hands and picked up her little fringed cape. "I must be going," she said. "I promised ages ago that I would look in at Francie Pett's and see the new baby. I've never been and it'll be the old baby by the time I see it."

Frances Pett had been one of their friends and had had three babies before she had been married two and a half years, so some laughter greeted this sally. Meg Kenyon remarked that it would be dark before Mahitabel reached home and wished audibly that she had her courage. Bella walked a little way with her and then turned back.

It was still daylight along the road to Francie's home and Mahitabel reckoned as she walked how long she must stay admiring the baby before it would be dark enough for a person familiar with the bridge to miss it. Suppose too that the rail had been mended. But no, as she crossed it, trying not to look at the water, the bridge on one side was still unprotected. It would be mended to-morrow, or next day, she thought.

Beyond the bridge the road to Francie's lonely house ran between a field on one side and a little belt of firs on the other. Mahitabel had no sooner set a foot on it and begun to walk slowly along it than she was conscious of hurrying hoof-beats coming towards her. She did not feel that she could face anyone else; the chatter of the Kenyons and presently the feeble complaining of Francie was as much as she could stand. So she looked ahead, determined that if the rider were known to her she would shelter in the coppice until he had passed.

She recognised him. It was Mr. Kruger, Francie's Dutch neighbour, riding his vicious horse. He had bought it cheap, not knowing its vices, and when more knowledge-able neighbours had commiserated him upon his bad bar-gain he had been too proud to admit that he had been deceived; so he persisted in keeping it and in riding it, though he was terrified of it and it had played him some pretty pranks. (Mahitabel had once climbed upon it for a "dare" and the thing had stood like a lamb.)

To-night it came along, swiftly but steadily, and recog-nising horse and rider Mahitabel gathered her skirts pre-paratory to darting into the coppice. But it chanced at that moment that a partridge chose to run from the field across the road to the shelter of the trees on the other side. The horse, as though it had been waiting for some excuse for foolery, promptly reared, and danced madly like a circus horse. Mr. Kruger, whose thoughts had been so far away that he had not even seen the partridge, fell first backwards and then sideways, and, but that one foot slipped through the stirrup, would have fallen to the ground. As it was, he dangled, and when the horse, now somewhat surprised in its turn, came down on all fours again, his head hit the ground. Thoroughly startled, the horse bolted, straight towards the place where Mahitabel, with her eyes wide and her hands pressed to her bosom, stood on the edge of the coppice.

An emergency never found her paralysed, at the mercy of nerves unstrung. She did not even think that she was going to die to-night in any case. She stood until the exact second came and then, leaping out, caught the bridle and swung on it with all her weight. The horse plunged to a standstill and she dragged the rider clear. His face and head were covered with blood and gravel and his body was as limp as a sack. She pulled him to the side of the road and began to run towards Francie's house.

And before Francie's husband and the hired man had lifted the yard gate from its hinges and gone to bring in the injured man, the miracle for which Mahitabel had prayed had happened, very suddenly and completely and painfully.

It was a very different Mahitabel whom Sammy Pett dropped at the door of the saddler's shop on his way to fetch the doctor later in the evening. Her grey pallor and her shaking hands and lips, however, were amply explained by the experience that she had been through. Maly put her to bed with a hot brick at her feet and a pint of scorching ginger wine inside her, a sovereign remedy against shock. But as soon as she had fussed away Mahitabel pushed back the clothes and tumbled out on to the rag rug beside the bed. Her legs shook so that she had to help herself towards the window by clutching at the furniture between, and there, falling on her knees, she burst into tears and offered up, almost wordlessly, the most heartfelt prayer of thankfulness and praise that had ever been breathed by mortal lips. Not only had the miracle happened, it had happened in such circumstances that her physical state might go unquestioned. No one but God could have arranged it so. She thanked Him with her whole heart; and she vowed that throughout the rest of the life that He had bestowed upon her she would have no thought but His will. She would spend the rest of her days in His service.

She "rested" for a whole day after her shock, and Maly was busy all day answering the door to enquirers who had heard the story and were eager to congratulate the heroine of it. Next day she appeared, as usual, for breakfast. She was very pale and the prominence of her nose and cheekbones forecast what she would be like at her mother's age. Her black hair was brushed smoothly from her forehead and tucked into a little knot at the back. She wore her plainest dress, unadorned by fichu or brooch; and her nose, lacking its morning application of rose-water, caught the morning light. Her manner was quiet and subdued. Maly, fussing round her, came to the conclusion that her daughter was not so iron-nerved after all; and as day followed day she found herself perversely looking forward to the moment when Mahitabel would re-act from the shock and indulge in some wild prank.

But the day never came, and gradually the new, quiet demeanor became accepted as normal. At Christmas time Mahitabel presented to Bella Kenyon the much embroidered, many frilled petticoat upon which she had been working when disaster overtook her. It had been intended to crackle with starch and peep provocatively from the uplifted skirt as Mahitabel tore her riotous way through the Christmas festivities. It was quite all right for Bella to own and wear it; Bella was balanced, vanity would not lead her into mortal sin.

The many invitations which came to the Dewer house that winter were almost all refused. Questioned, Mahitabel said that she was too old to dance mazes or pull candy or skate any more.

But there were things far harder to forego than parties or provocative petticoats. God must have, not only her outer life, but her heart and her mind; and that meant dethroning Barny. She had to beat down the longing which even now would occasionally beset her, for Barny's lips and the touch of his hands. She must learn to hear his name casually spoken without a quickening of her pulses.

Above all she must pass those places where savage, sweet memories were inclined to disturb the contrite mind with which one should pass the scene of one's sin.

It was a hard task; but she accomplished it, always reminding herself that where Barny had abandoned her, God had upheld her. She became one of the few people who really love God without either fearing Him or seeking further favours. She prayed often, but for years her prayers were only for strength and guidance.

When she was twenty-four years old, and a settled old maid, both in manner and appearance and in the eyes of those about her as well as her own, Benjamin Smith, who had regarded her with admiration and hopeless longing during the old bright days, summoned his courage and asked her to marry him. Only pity for him—he was known as the unluckiest man within a radius of twenty miles—kept her from refusing straight away. She looked into his shy, humble eyes and knew that they could never hold a glance that would stir her; but because they were shy and humble she murmured some uncompromising sentences about needing time to think. Ben, who had dreaded a downright refusal and steeled himself to bear it, was immensely cheered by this delay in the delivery of his sentence and perked visibly.

Like everything else that had puzzled or troubled her within the last five years, the sudden proposal was laid out for the Almighty's inspection, with a request for guidance. She imagined that it might come in a change of attitude towards her suitor. If God wished her to marry him, she would feel more kindly; if not, some active repulsion would take the place of her indifference. But at the end of a fortnight (which period, for some unknown reason, was regarded as "time to think" amongst the young women of Weston) her feelings were just as neutral as ever, so on the Sunday morning Mahitabel, judging that this was a matter beneath God's notice and therefore left to her to decide, set out for meeting with the intention of refusing Ben, kindly but firmly, when he approached her at the end of the service.

The reading of the Old Testament that morning fell

upon the forty-fourth chapter of Genesis, and Mahitabel, less attentive than usual because she was trying to frame a kind and unhurtful sentence in which to convey her decision, was startled by the words, "And the cup was found in Benjamin's sack." A hot flush washed over her face and her heart began to race. Was this indeed the voice of God, speaking, not even in parables, but in clear ordinary language, naming actual names? She dared hardly hope for so much divine attention. But she straightened herself and listened with avid attention. The name had shown God's awareness of her problem; a definite solution might be on its way.

The New Testament reading for the day fell upon the seventh chapter of Corinthians—a mass of contradiction to the detached mind and an interesting sidelight upon the psychology of St. Paul. But all that Mahitabel, sitting bolt upright with her hands folded in her lap, carried away from the reading was the sentence, "For it is better to marry than to burn." It was clear enough.

And outside, under the shade of the ancient elm tree she beckoned to the diffidently hovering Ben. She said, having drawn him out of hearing, "I will marry you—but I have something to tell you first."

At the hour and the place which she appointed she told him her pitiable little story, withholding only Barny's name. Ben had loved her since her giddy days and he remembered—being a lover—what the rest of Weston was forgetting, the merry dashing girl who was always the centre of attraction, dancing through life on sprightly feet, shedding laughter and brightness around her. The fact that she was here, meeting him by appointment, almost prepared to marry, dazed him so completely that he listened to her story without really gathering its implication at all. Some other man—but of course, a dozen had hung on her lightest word, he had seen them—why make a coil about one of them now?

And to Mahitabel in that moment, as she told the story that no one else had heard, or would ever hear, a comforting revelation was vouchsafed. She could now speak of that cataclysmic summer without feeling anything at all, except the overwhelming gratitude which had reoriented her life. Memory, rigorously beaten down, or left to take its course, must die of itself, else we should all weep for our dead every day. Barny, of the dark sulky beauty, the demanding passion and the faithless heart, could now be dismissed in a sentence beginning, "There was a man . . ."

She married Ben after harvest and Theodosius, surprisingly delighted by the match, dug into his savings and gave her a thousand dollars for a wedding present. Neighbours who had commiserated with Ben when his swine died of fever and not another case was known in the district, when his cows slipped their calves, and his horses broke their legs in a plain pasture, watched to see whether, under Mahitabel's able hand, his luck would change.

So far as human wit and forethought, care, intelligence and prudence could control it, it did. Mahitabel was as good a wife as any in the country. She managed everything, worked day and night, advised, admonished and rebuked. But Ben's stars were cast in an unfortunate order and even she could not guard against every ill. It was, however, his evil fortune that endeared him to her; the woman was hardly born who could live with a man so humble, so industrious, so kindly and so unquestionably cursed as Ben, and not love him. And when he said, "Ah well, Brewster's crop, seeded outa the same bag and set the same week, is a bumper, and mine's rotted; but a man can't have everything and I've got a good wife," or "If it wasn't for you, Mahitabel, I think I'd own I was beat," her heart was warm and tender towards him indeed.

And presently there was Abe, and then Mary Ann, for her to admonish and defend. They too, following Ben's example, regarded their mother as the prop and stay, the infallible judge, the unbeatable manager. Her pride, which, unknown to herself, had received a shattering blow at Barny's defection, revived under this domestic adulation. She carried her little world on her shoulders; and when the burden became too heavy she had always her own secret source of strength and refreshment. Above, around and within her, closer than breathing, was the presence and the power of Jehovah; terrible, jealous, easily provoked, but also just and merciful and blessedly personal. He knew you by name; He understood even the trivial problems of everyday domestic rural life, and if He chastened you it was because He loved you. With that assurance you could face any affliction, look life straight in the face and know that, unless you released your hold upon your belief, nothing could beat you.

She needed every scrap of faith and support during the twenty-one years on that farm at Weston. Materially they prospered not at all. And when Abe was seventeen a disaster struck the whole neighbourhood, one which people with money saved and farms well-stocked might weather, but which dealt hardly with people like the Smiths who were never more than a season away from beggary. For three years a great drought lay on the land. Except for the wells, and the river where Mahitabel had once thought to end her struggle, there was no water for miles around, and the dripping, creaking water-carts went to and fro all day. But no man could water the field crops.

For all her prayers Mahitabel saw the farm reduced to an unprofitable dust-heap. A slow but steady exodus began to take place and amongst the remaining people the question, "What keeps us here?" was beginning to be asked. Ben, toiling to save his livestock, patient, suffering and uncomplaining as the beasts he tended, was incapable of making plans. It was for Mahitabel to take stock of the position.

With her dowry—untouched, or at worse borrowed from and replaced almost immediately—and what they could make in a sale, they mustered between two and three thousand dollars, and with this pittance they could not afford to gamble. They must make a bid for a possible certainty while they still had health and strength to convert into an actual one.

From somewhere the notion of California crept into their consciousness. There the soil was rich, the climate reliable, and land was to be had for the asking. It became, to Mahitabel, at least, firmly associated with the land of Canaan, and to her mind it was comfortably possible that the drought had been sent and prolonged in order that they might be driven to seek the Promised Land. She never mentioned this aspect of the matter, it was too secret and intimate even for Ben's understanding, but it was there, sustaining her through the upheaval, the demands that such a venture made upon mind and sinew, the sorrow that lay in leaving the familiar place where she had been born.

But all was arranged at last; and when, in the fullness of time the wagon train pulled out of Fort Mason there went with one woman, at least, as surely as the casks of salted pork and the sides of bacon, as real as the sack of potatoes and the barrel of flour, sound as the wagon and active as the oxen, the consciousness that God went with her. The age-old problem, was she made in His image, or He in hers, only events could prove. The answer lay ahead.

She had clung, through all the years and all the intersecting, overlapping claims on her attention, to the leather-covered diary. Busy and long as the day might be and tired as she was at the end of it, she never retired without entering, however briefly, a record of the day's doings. The book was filling up now and the long scribbled entry which she had once thought would be the final one, was far away in the early quarter. Being of methodical mind, she had divided it into sections, marking the end of each with a thick wavy free-hand line. Such a line came beneath the entry, "I shall marry Ben Smith to-morrow"; another came above the words, "My son was born early this morning"; and beside these there were the natural divisions between the last day of December and the first of each new year.

On the night before leaving Fort Mason Mahitabel drew another line. She did not know it but that thick crooked scrawl marked off a mere domestic journal from a record of historic value and importance. The book had originally cost two dollars, including the leather which Theodosius had used for the cover, and at that moment it was worth nothing. It had been "spoilt" by the scribble, which, though of interest to the curious as an account of small-town life in America at the beginning of the century, and to the student of human nature as a searchlight upon one woman's soul, was of no interest at all to the wider world.

But that which was written after the last line was drawn was to be read, printed and reprinted, pored over, wept over and regarded with pity, amazement and horror whenever human eye should convey its substance to human understanding. And the book itself, greasy from handling, with tear-blisters on some pages, and upon the corners of one section a brown, more sinister mark, was to take its place amongst pioneer bibliographia, shielded by glass from the questing hand and curious eye. For upon those last pages is set down, very briefly and in rapidly deteriorating writing, the history, not so much of the Furmage party, though that is included, as of the travails of Mahitabel's soul during those days of ordeal when she begged of God the final miracle that was not forthcoming.

But not by a word, in that lucid and invariably candid document, did the writer convey the slightest doubt that her God had forsaken her. And herein may lie the truth of the matter. It may well be that in her unshaken faith is proof that sustaining and supporting her was the hand which had already wrought a miracle more wonderful than the bestowal of bread, the hand which, from a handful of clay and a cluster of animal appetites, had carved out, clear and shining, the indomitable soul of man.

Sister Barbara closed the book from which she had been reading the Life of Saint Ursula, and began to walk around the class with silent, flat-footed gait. Each girl, as her turn came, rose to her feet and laid in the Sister's hand the piece of fine needlework upon which she had been working during the reading. Sister Barbara inspected the stitches and returned the work to its owner.

Praise was practically unknown at the Convent of the Annunciation, so the silent glance and the absence of rebuke denoted satisfaction. Here and there a crooked stitch, or one over-large, or the mark of a hot young hand upon the fine linen, provoked comment which was received humbly, or sulkily or with indifference, according to the needlewoman's nature. The rebukes were mild enough until Sister Barbara, reaching at last the place where Nancy Jurer sat beneath the window, received a piece of crumpled white stuff into her thin dry hands and stared at it for a moment with incredulous eyes.

"You have made no progress," she said coldly. She stole a glance at the pale impish face beneath its cluster of frizzy dark hair and an old dislike lent acidity to her voice as she added, "You are a very idle girl. In an hour you have done nothing except soil and crumple your work. You will not leave with the others, but will stay and sew— thus far." She drew a pin from the recesses of her voluminous clothing and stuck it firmly in a spot some six inches along the seam. "The rest may fold their work and go."

A rustle of activity pervaded the quiet room as the young hands, slim and plump, reddish, white or coffee-coloured, folded the work neatly and wrapped it in the thin white paper before laying it in the drawer where it would remain until next sewing time. Twenty pairs of eager feet bore their owners to the door. Twenty young voices began the chatter which rose in scale and increased in volume as the classroom was left behind.

Nancy Jurer ran her needle in and out of the emery strawberry that was provided for the polishing of needles, shifted into a more comfortable position on the hard upright chair and settled to her work with a sigh of resignation. The punishment was deserved, and she was not anxious to go home for a little while. She might as well sew.

But after five minutes of earnest stitching her needle moved more and more slowly until it stopped. Her eyes strayed to the window and rested there upon the motionless green tops of the trees in the Convent garden. She was thinking again of Mama and Philippe, running through her puzzled young mind the things that she had overheard last night from her bed, wondering how much of that deliberate bitterness had been really meant, and whether Philippe had repented this morning, as Mama had obviously done, and whether the quarrel had been made up by now. If not she wondered what effect it would have upon her own future. Would Mama move from New Orleans now? She had come there four years ago for no other reason than to be near her lover, that Nancy knew. She hoped that if the affair were truly ended last night, she and Mama would resume their queer nomadic life in which it was impossible for her to be sent to school. To have Mama to herself again—for none of the earlier affairs had encroached like this upon their life together— and to be free of the Convent sounded like a forecast of Heaven; and with childlike optimism she brooded over the pleasant prospect and forgot for a moment what Mama had said that she would do if Philippe really left her.

Sister Barbara's cold voice broke in upon her dreams:

"Kindly remember that I am waiting for you to finish."

Stitching quickly Nancy tried to control her mind's wanderings by concentrating upon ordinary things. From the door immediately below the window by which she sat she could hear the sound of the other girls' leaving.

There was Maxine's carriage being driven off with a flourish; there were the bells of Claire's white pony; now came the perpetually chiding voice of Thalia's black maid, "Miss Thalia, you done come out in yore house shoes again."

Every one of them was being met by someone; every one of them was returning to an ordinary, orderly family life; every one of them was sheltered and carefree, with nothing to worry about except the preservation of their complexions, the cultivation of their slim little waists and the not too-exiguous demands of Sister Barbara and the other nuns.

Stitching away, the young girl did not reflect upon their lot with envy, nor positively compare it with her own. At the age of thirteen she had out-grown self-pity. Too many demands had been made upon it, especially since her surprising admission to the Convent school. Wrong clothes to wear, wrong words to use, wrong part of the town in which to live, these were her lot. There was no one to meet her and escort her safely through the swarming, colourful, fascinating streets; no one to pay a formal visit to the Reverend Mother and discuss Nancy's progress in sweet, lilting, complimentary tones, and to drop, upon leaving, an ostentatiously unostentatious contribution into the alms box from fingers discreetly covered with pale tight gloves. Even her fees were wrong, always a little overdue, made up of odd coins, obviously scraped together and handed over by herself.

For four years, ever since her arrival in New Orleans and her admission to the carefully guarded circle of young ladies, these small bitternesses had been her daily fare. Most of them had mercifully lost their power to hurt her.

Mama had meant well. She had hardly settled into the house on Tighle Street before she had said that now Nancy could go to school, learn many things that would be useful and make many pleasant friends. Nancy had instinctively shrunk from the prospect and hoped that it would be forgotten, sink away to join many a dozen other of Mama's schemes. But the day had come when she was roused early from her bed to find Mama dressed at that fantastic hour in her street clothes; she had been washed and combed with more than usual thoroughness, dressed in her best clothes (so highly unsuitable) and led to the gate in the wall of the Convent garden. There Mama had behaved in a most unusually nervous fashion, telling Nancy to ring the bell and go straight ahead, everything had been arranged and would be all right. She had seemed anxious not to be seen and had hurried away before the pealing bell had been answered. The nine-year-old child was puzzled by this behaviour from Mama who was always bold and pushing, not in the least averse to meeting people: but now she understood. She had aged a great deal in the four intervening years; and learnt much besides the stilted lessons of Sister Barbara and the rest of them.

She had made no friends. All the other girls had friends, generally one special one and a little circle of companions. They visited one another's houses, knew one another's relatives, enjoyed many mild pleasures together. Maxine D'Obrée, it is true, dwelt in splendid isolation, arriving each day in her shiny carriage and each day departing in it to her rightful sphere in some charmed and indescribably exclusive sphere. But her isolation was a matter of choice; there was not a girl who would not gladly have been her friend. Nancy's loneliness was thrust upon her; it was impossible for her to pretend that she despised everyone, as Maxine did; there was nothing to back up such a pretence, no carriage with coachman and footman, no titled relatives, no richness at all. Besides, in the early days she had been so like a stray puppy, eagerly responsive to a chance careless kind word, easily and often snubbed.

All that was now lived down; the attempts at friendliness forgotten, the earlier wounds scarred over and immune from further hurt. She came and went unnoticed. Occasionally Sister Magdalena, who was old and ugly and taught reckoning, would praise her lines of neat and accurate figures; but in her heart Nancy despised the praise because the sums were all of a kind that didn't really need setting down at all; she could do them in her head and knew the answers before she had finished copying down the items. "If two gardeners can dig a plot in three days, in how long can five dig it?" Too easy to bother about.

More often, indeed, she was being rebuked for idleness, lack of attention, or, more unfairly, lack of some item of equipment. And to that, too, she was almost impervious now. She had noticed that the bouts of rebuke had often coincided with lateness of fees. She had even, though not until this year, become resigned to the fact that had hit her hardest—that in the Nativity Play which the Convent pupils acted each Christmas, she would be cast for the role of sweeper, who, in sacking apron, wielding a birch broom, swept the yard of the Inn at Bethlehem, and with deplorable lack of perception, failed to move respectfully out of the way of the ass which bore the Blessed Virgin. The coveted part of Mary fell inevitably to tall fair Maxine, who could no more act than a block of wood, but who could, on these occasions, fill the entire front row of the auditorium with tall swaggering or tall swaying relatives.

Apart from the time spent in school, Nancy was happy enough. At home, if her mother was alone, they laughed and talked together, cooked highly flavoured and indigestible dishes, furbished up old dresses, or discussed new ones, went shopping amongst the shops and stalls of the cheap quarter, sometimes patronised the theatres. When Madame Jurer had callers, Nancy either went to bed or ran across the little paved court-yard to the house of Madame Schwartz, the good-natured dark-faced woman who was their neighbour and landlady. She was able to treat the fat dull daughters of the Schwartz family with some of the scorn with which she herself was treated at the Convent, and so lay balm to her own hurt feelings; and although she was uncomfortably aware that Madame Schwartz pitied her, she was willing to forgive a pity which evinced itself in a kind welcome and little tit-bits to eat.

"I am still waiting for you to finish," said Sister Barbara. Nancy had reached the pin; but now, from pure perversity she took it out and drove it in again, farther along the seam. Let her wait, cold-voiced, impatient old thing. This staying on after the others had left had been her idea, not Nancy's. And she herself did not want to go home yet.

Mama had been a pitiable sight this morning, so pale and heavy-eyed, so oddly uncommunicative; she hoped that Philippe would have called in during the day, or sent a message, and she did not want to arrive home before the quarrel was made up. She hated to see her mother extinguished and distressed. She promised herself that next time Philippe, in his patronising way, brought her candies or fruit or little cakes, she would throw them at him. Mama was far too easily reconciled, that was largely her trouble. Still, if the reconciliation had been effected home would be happy this afternoon, and Mama would try to make up for her manner this morning. Nancy had seen this kind of thing happen before. Though never had such things been said as were said last night. . . .

"Have you not finished yet, child?"

Nancy recognised in the "child" a note of defeat; Sister Barbara was appealing to her to hurry. Stubbornly she shook her head.

"Bring it here." The cold voice was uncommonly soft.

In the line of tiny stitches the original pin holes showed plainly.

"You moved the pin. . . ."

Never deny the obvious, that was one of the things she had learned. She stood silent. Sister Barbara leaned her cheek on her hand and studied Nancy.

"Now why?" she asked.

"It fell out. I suppose I put it in farther along."

"Well, you have performed your imposition. You may put away your work."

The nun's eyes followed the child as she returned to her place, drove home her needle and with neat, unhurried movements shrouded the stuff with paper and tucked in the ends. It occurred to her that any other little girl, kept after hours, would have hurried when given the word of dismissal. When the drawer had been opened, the work laid inside and the child straightened herself after closing it again, Sister Barbara said, in the same soft voice, "Come here, Nancy."

She stood by the table, detached and impassive.

"Are you sulking about being detained? We have to make up for wasted time, always, you know."

"Yes, Sister."

"Then tell me—why did you deliberately sew on past the pin marks? They were plain enough. And why have you taken so long in putting away your work? Is it perhaps that you are not anxious to return home?"

As she asked this question Sister Barbara's thin cheek coloured a little. Gossip was a worldly vice and one to be eschewed; but there was a mystery about this pupil. She came from a part of the town that was redolent of discreet disreputableness; and the Mother Superior had once, in an unguarded moment, admitted that she had only accepted her because some hidden influence from a high place had been brought to bear. Might the child's answer reveal some detail of a way of life shrouded in mystery?

But the change in the nun's manner had rung a warning bell in Nancy's shrewd young mind. The question was friendly enough, and there had been a day when it might have brought forth an answer, when she would have been glad to pour into some sympathetic ear the story of this day's worries and anxieties. But that time had gone. She had learned that she had no friend within the Convent walls. The behaviour of everyone over the belated fees had proved that. The nuns might talk about charity and the wrongs of malicious thinking, but they were just as inconsistent as everyone else. Not one had ever tried to shield her from the knowledge that she was unwelcome because she was poor, wore the wrong clothes, lived on Tighle Street and had no established family. So now, in answer to the question she returned a stony silence, thinking to herself, "Wouldn't you like to know?"

"Is something troubling you, child?" persisted Sister Barbara, who could see, now that she looked at Nancy closely, with individual attention, that the thirteen years had carved marks of maturity on the little ivory-skinned face. A wariness of eye, a firmness of chin and a line of concentration between the silky black eyebrows made her look older than sixteen-year-old Maxine. "If so, you know that we are your friends, able and willing to help you." She paused expectantly.

Oh yes! And what would happen to your flat squab's

78

face, I wonder, if I told you what was bothering me and why I am not in a hurry to go home. Let's see—— Dear Sister Barbara, I am concerned about my mother. You see, she isn't quite like other people's mothers; for one thing, she isn't married. But she has a lover; he is so rich and important and well-known that I daren't even mention his name. I am not supposed to know it; but I have a way of finding out things. He pays for the house on Tighle Street, and he gives my mother money. He is generous and we should be very comfortable if it weren't for Philippe. He is the one whom my mother really loves. She gives him money. And when my shoes are too small and my stockings are what Sister Magdalena calls a disgrace, and my fees are late, it is because she has given the money to him, and yet still has to seem to have plenty, lest the rich man should suspect something. Also, dear Sister Barbara, it costs a good deal to be a mistress; you have to have clothes, such clothes as you never dreamed of, paints and powders and lotions and scents. And if a man makes you a handsome allowance you are expected always to have wine in the house when he calls.

But I am not concerned about the money, though not having any makes me unpopular and ensures that I can never be anything but a sweeper in the Nativity Play, not even the Innkeeper's wife. I am worried because Philippe has a chance to marry a very respectable young woman with a snug dowry; and so he is going to leave my mother. He told her so last night, and then they said terrible things to one another. She made a threat which I think might bring him to his senses, but I want it to be all right again by the time I get home. Because, although you would despise her, I am fond of my mother and I cannot bear to see her as she was this morning, pale and limp and hating life. I am quite happy to stay here here and sew, or stand silent under your questions until I can be sure that Philippe has had time to make up the quarrel. . . .

"Sister, I have finished the task that you set me. Have I your permission to go now?"

"You may go." Defeat, laced with relief, was in the nun's voice.

Her house shoes had been outgrown for several months and when, driven by the asperity with which the nuns had remarked that her outdoor shoes were not suitable wear on parquet floors, she had applied to her mother for new ones, there had been no money. Since then she had gone through an elaborate pretense of changing her shoes and had stoutly maintained, when questioned, that these *were* her house shoes. Today, alone in the cloakroom, there was no need to pretend; but she must not leave the door without her hat on her head and her thin mittens on her hands. She tied the faded ribbon strings of the wide straw hat in a careless drooping knot, put on the mittens, and thus protected from criticism, emerged from the gate in the wall. The wide street with its shady trees was quiet and dull and she hurried through it until she reached the central market-place.

Here there was plenty to look at; stalls of clothing and of foodstuffs that made her mouth water; beggars soliciting the charitable coin; business men going home from their offices; ladies of the town taking the air demurely and yet somehow managing to flaunt their charms and advertise their trade; proper ladies just emerging to drive for a while in the cooler air of the afternoon. Nancy watched them, quartering the market-place with leisurely tread. Philippe often made an afternoon call; she would stay out until the reconciliation was over.

Tiring of the market she climbed the steps of the church and spent some time in its shady, incense-scented interior. Occasionally she had been taken to Mass and if asked her religion would have replied unhesitatingly that she was a Catholic. But even now, at a moment when dawning adolescence so often turns the child's minds towards Mysticism, Nancy was not conscious of any presence or reality behind the elaborate ritual of the Church. She enjoyed going to Mass because it offered a spectacle, colour and movement and scent; but it meant nothing. She much preferred the theatre, which, offering the same ingredients, provided the mind with problems as well. Why did such and such a person behave in such a manner, why did the victim never suspect the swindler or the murderer, how could any woman, not obviously blind or stupid, trust the villain for one moment?

Now, with a perfunctory bob towards the altar, she made her way around the church, studying the Fourteen Stations and noting for the hundredth time Saint Veronica's remarkable likeness to Sister Elisabeth who taught drawing and was always satisfied with Nancy's work except on those occasions when fees were overdue. She observed that Saint Christopher had been regilded, that one of the arrows that transfixed Saint Edmund had been broken off, and that someone had offered Saint Anthony a little wreath of paper flowers.

When she reached the table where the votive candles stood it occurred to her that it might help things if she lighted one for her mother. She had no money to slip into the heavy iron box with the hungry slotted mouth, but lack of money was no novelty to her; it was a condition that must be ignored. She chose a small candle, lighted a taper and kindled a flame. When it burned strong and steady she knelt for a moment and prayed, without much feeling but with intent seriousness, that Philippe might renounce the well-dowered lady and continue his association with her mother.

She left the church by the north door, emerged upon the side of the market and discovered, as she stepped into the dusty sunshine, that she was very hungry. The Convent provided the pupils with a midday meal but it was never appetising, seldom satisfying and on several days in a month definitely inedible. To-day had been such a day, and normally she would long ago have satisfied her hunger, either at home or in Madame Schwartz's warm, garlic-scented kitchen. She crossed the corner of the market and entered the little shop where cakes and coffee and sweet syrups might be obtained.

She explained her lack of money and demanded credit,

which the proprietress, who had had demands of the kind before and had never failed to be paid, readily gave, and Nancy ate four sticky cakes of varying flavours and drank two glasses of syrup, varied of name but indistinguishable in flavour. Then, replete, she set off by the steps of the steep street, home.

As she reached the arch which gave upon the more shady quarter of the town a clock somewhere chimed the half-hour. Half-past five. She could go home now.

For some distance small dirty shops, lodging-houses, drinking dens and brothels lined the road. Then, turning sharply to the left she entered the peculiar precincts of Tighle Street. It had an air of hushed quietness only attained by most streets in the early part of a Sunday afternoon. Most of its length was composed of high walls, pierced here and there by a door or grilled gateway on the ground level and by a window above. Such houses as showed themselves upon the street were primly curtained, well painted and often decorated by little shrubs or flowering bushes in green tubs. Outwardly it was a model of decorum. Yet Tighle Street was more infamous than the street of drinking dens and brothels that flanked it. It had somehow become the home, not of the exponents of momentary and fleeting pleasure, but of the intrigue which had, for a time, the permanency of marriage. To set up a woman in Tighle Street implied that she was necessary to your happiness and that you were prepared to pay for your pleasure. Many of the women who lived in the street had been installed there when they were young, and upon their protectors' death or satiation had received enough money to continue to rent the expensive, demure little houses that long custom had made into homes.

Nancy knew the street so well that she passed along it with unseeing eyes. She entered one of the iron gates set in the wall and stood in the little court-yard, oblong in shape, full of flowers and draped upon all its sides by heavy blossoming creepers. To the right was Madame Schwartz's house door, to the left her own, and feeling that she had wasted enough time, and anxious now to share with her mother the rejoicing of hope restored, she pushed open the green door and ran across the tiled hall.

She had never been in the home of any of her class-mates so she had no standards of comparison, but at least half of them would have thought that Madame Jurer's house was luxurious in the extreme. The stairs were laid with thick red carpet, heavy velvet curtains hung within the gossamer muslin ones that draped the windows, there were ornaments and knick-knacks and glittering chande-liers in every room. But Nancy knew that almost every-thing in the house belonged to canny Madame Schwartz, who had long ago inherited the whole house from her protector, had married, upon his death, a common fellow who worked in an abattoir and, in order to supplement the family income, had removed herself to the servants' quarters, where her brood was hard pressed for room, and left off the real house to people like Madame Jurer.

Mama's rooms were on the first floor and Nancy sped up the stairs on feet made soundless by the red carpet. When she reached the landing there was a sound of many voices and her heart rose. Mama had recovered and was entertaining her friends. Tugging off her mittens and throwing aside her hat she opened the doors of the sitting-room.

All the subdued chatter ceased as she appeared in the doorway, and all the faces—set into expression of horror and pity and avid interest—turned her way. Then, out of the crowd struggled Madame Schwartz, the brown creases under her eyes shiny with tears, her plump hands outstretched, her comfortable bosom offered for Nancy's comfort.

Before her head was forcibly dragged down to this shelter the child's eyes ranged over the assembly, search-ing in vain for that one face. There was the apothecary and his wife, the eldest of the Schwartz girls, three or four neighbours and Father Julian. But Mama was not there. The bedroom door stood slightly ajar and through the opening she could see a corner of the tumbled bed and the faint suggestion of someone lying upon it. She struggled towards it; but Madame Schwartz held her firmly. Little murmurs arose from the women: "The child . . . poor thing! She did not think of the child. Ah, the poor mother-less creature. What will become of her?"

It was borne in upon her shrinking mind that when, last night, Mama had cried in torment that without Philippe she would not, could not live, she had spoken no more than the truth.

It was over at last, the excitement, the speculation, the gossip and the secrecy. Madame Schwartz was fanatically anxious that the affair should be kept quiet. A tragedy of this kind aimed a shrewd blow at the very heart of the Tighle Street tradition; and, more to Madame's concern, at the prospect of quickly re-letting the little house. No other pretty lady would be anxious to be installed in a house where her predecessor, in time and trade, had died by her own hand because she was threatened by a loveless future. In addition there was Madame Jurer's protector to consider. He, poor man, always so punctual with the rent, so generous, so discreet and, within clearly defined limits, so faithful, must be spared from knowing the truth. So Madame Schwartz invented a clever and circumstantial story of sudden illness, collapse and death. In the midst of her sorrow Nancy was appalled to discover that what she had regarded as her mother's secret, unwittingly shared by herself, was in reality common knowledge in the Schwartz family.

The question asked on the afternoon of the tragedy as to what would become of the child, remained after the scent of death had gone from the house and Madame Schwartz had stripped down the curtains, taken up the carpets and thoroughly cleaned each room, as though by material scouring she might rid the place of its im-material taint. The bed with its ill-associations stood for two days in the sunny court-yard and then came back, stripped to the mattress, but piled with clean sheets, blankets and pillows. Madame Jurer's wardrobe was emptied and an old-clothes dealer, with dirty predatory fingers and the eyes of a vulture, made a bid for the lot. Nancy's own clothes were taken out of the wardrobe too, in order that it might be freshly papered within, and they did not go back, but were laid in the little valise as though ready for immediate removal.

But despite this suggestion of transitoriness, despite the cleaning and upheaval, despite the pointed hints and open invitation to cross the court-yard and stay for a while with the Schwartz family, Nancy clung to the house with the perverse fidelity of an abandoned cat. On one occasion, when she had ignored a hint from the landlady and that good-natured woman had veered a little from the course of kind tolerance to the bereaved which she had set herself, Nancy had fixed her sloe-dark eyes upon her and said flatly, "I shall stay here until the end of the month. The rent is paid till then."

"But it is not right that you should be alone to brood. Come, bring your things and let me lock the house. My Gerta will be delighted to share her bed with you. It will be good for you to be in the cheerful company of the young."

"I would rather stay here, Madame Schwartz, thank you," said Nancy, and sat down in the bare window-seat from which the cushions had been taken for beating in the court-yard. There was no mistaking the determination of the gesture and Madame Schwartz retired.

But the end of the month drew steadily nearer and would not be ignored. Nor could she ignore the efforts which Madame Schwartz was making for her final disposal at the end of that period.

"I could take her, yes!" Madame explained one evening to a crony in the court-yard just below Nancy's window. "And there are those who say that with so many one more is not noticed. But that is not true. A child does not need food only, there are clothes and shoes. And after there is the matter of employment, and the question of behaviour. Am I to make myself responsible for one whose father is unknown and whose mother was . . . ?" The hearty voice dropped to a sibilant hissing. The crony muttered something and Madame Schwartz began again:

"To place her will not be easy. She has no gifts. She cannot cook or mind babies. And although she can sew, sempstresses earn so little. I do not know what I am to do."

A window slammed above their heads and both women looked up guiltily.

"I am sorry for that. It is hard to learn that you are unwanted," said kindly Madame Schwartz.

"We are not to blame for that," said the crony with a significant note in her voice. "And why do the nuns not do something for her? Have you thought of the Orphanage?"

Having closed the window Nancy did not hear the suggestion. But Madame Schwartz heard and wondered that she had not thought of this obvious solution herself.

In collaboration with Father Julian who was partial to her because she was a faithful supporter of his church, Madame made complete arrangements for Nancy's reception into that home of the lost, abandoned and unfortunate, the Convent Orphanage.

Two days before the end of the month she conveyed to Nancy the double information that the house was let and two days were needed for its refurbishment; and that she was to enter the Convent Orphanage on the first of the new month.

"So bring your things and come with me now. Gerta and Johann are coming in to lay the carpets here and hang the curtains. You would be in the way. You can come over and help Elsa and me to make a spiced cake. We will have all the things you like to eat until you go."

"Gerta is calling you now," said Nancy.

"My ears must be failing, I do not hear her," said Madame Schwartz, smiling. "You gather your things and come along." She bustled away.

When Gerta, strenuously denying having called her mother, went, with Johann, to the green door across the courtyard, she found it locked. From the window above Nancy announced her intention of staying in the house until the time came for her to leave. The Schwartzes, fundamentally kind, forbore to press the point. They even laid food on the step of the locked door and were sorry to find it untouched next day.

The news of what was to become of her jerked Nancy out of her stunned misery.

The Orphans were housed in another wing of the rambling Convent and made no contact with the school. But every day they could be seen from the classroom windows, taking their set exercise in a piece of ground at the bottom of the garden. They did not gambol, or laugh, or play together. They walked round in twos, evenly spaced, silent, prematurely old beneath the eye of the supervising nun. Their dresses were of grey print, their shoes wooden, their hair cut short beneath little basin-shaped caps. They were an affront to the eye; an insult to the name of charity. To pity them had been Nancy's privilege, almost her only one within those walls. Out of shape as her own life was, she had at least a home and a mother. They had nothing.

And now, through the action of that mother whom she had dumbly and undemonstratively loved very dearly, she was to be sent to join those drearily marching figures. And from the windows above Maxine, and Claire and Thalia, would see and recognise her, and probably deem that she had found her rightful place at last. Then, in a year or so, she would be sent out, with a certificate for industry, honesty and piety, to become the virtual slave of any seemingly good Catholic woman who wanted someone to wash floors and dishes, haul wood, clean shoes, do all the menial tasks of a house.

She faced the prospect with the realism of an adult, shot through by the feverish imagination of an unhappy child. She reckoned the social stigma, the loss of personal freedom, at the same time as, on her feet, she felt the unyielding embrace of the wooden shoes, and about her neck, the rasp of the high print collar. She looked into a future lightless as a long tunnel and shrank from the prospect.

For the first time she realised, a little too early for her own good, the stubborn and exiguous demands of the flesh. It was this body that raised the problem; this lump of flesh which must be fed and clothed, housed and bedded. When people wondered about her future and tried to make arrangements for it, it was of the stocky thirteen-year-old body that they were thinking. Of the mind, the inner person, the thing that made her Nancy Jurer, they took no heed at all. How that might suffer mattered not a bit so long as the mouth was provided with food and the limbs covered decently. When they thought of Nancy Jurer they thought of some eight stones of bones and flesh that was hungry and obtrusive and impossible either to ignore or escape. Even when it was dead and finished its disposal would be a matter of concern—she had seen that, recently.

Her mind slipped a cog and she thought, detachedly and for the first time without sorrow, of her mother. She had been loved by two people, by her daughter, and by the stout, grave, dignified elderly man, who had wept, Madame Schwartz reported, when she had personally and discreetly conveyed the news to him. But their love had meant nothing. Because one had inhabited the body of a young girl, and the other of an ageing man, they had not been worth living for. It was Philippe, who lived in the body of a strong young man with black hair and brown hands, who had mattered. He had been unloving, greedy and finally faithless, but these things had not counted against his physical charm. The body was all-important.

The child crouched on the floor, with a dusty ray of sunshine finding its way through the sun-warped shutter and falling warm upon her hands. For the first and last time in her practical life she indulged in abstract thought. With a mind that was at once immature and precocious, ignorant and shrewd, she surveyed the whole problem of living.

It was a fateful moment. She might so easily, from childishness, or fear, or weariness, have taken the path mapped out for her by Madame Schwartz. She might have lived and died without ever owning anything except a sleeping mat in someone else's house and a few working clothes. She might have lived and died without ever being in a position to do anyone much harm. But destiny had already claimed her.

For as she sat on the floor in the slowly shifting ray of sunlight and thought her new thoughts about the claims of the body and the burden that its needs imposed upon the freedom of the spirit, a door swung slowly open in her mind. The troublesome body had a value. Mama's slim elegance and bright gold hair had been marketable commodities. There was a purpose for which the body could be used which did not involve the discomfort, nor—to her ill-trained mind—the shame that must attach to the entry to the Convent Orphanage. And what mind, thirteen-years-old, and exposed since its earliest days to the corrosive influence of easy-virtued Mama, could rightly draw the comparison between the print, the wooden shoes and the sacking apron, and the silks, furs, feathers and jewels which the body, in the right market, could earn for itself?

For the first time since that tragic home-coming she began to move about with energy and purpose. She heated water and washed herself thoroughly; she brushed the tangles from her neglected hair. From the clothes crammed into the valise she selected her brightest, most unchildish dress, a flounced pink muslin with ribbons of a deeper shade. Between the blackness of her hair and the brightness of the dress her small square face shone with the creamy pallor of privet bloom; her dark eyes were large and shadowy from sorrow, moping and semi-starvation. Her reflection, studied critically for the first time, displeased her; and from the drawer of the dressing-table which Madame Schwartz's fingers were itching to clear out and re-line, she took the paints and powders that had been part of her mother's armoury. Much watching had made her skilful in their application.

She descended the stairs, a quaint little figure, rouged and curled and powdered but moving with a childish freedom of limb. She unlocked the door, opened it a crack, and peered out warily. The afternoon somnolence lay over the court-yard and the house on its other side. There was food on the step and the sight of it reminded her that she had eaten nothing for nearly two days. Not daring to stop, she snatched up a piece of crusty loaf, and with it in her hand, darted towards the gate in the wall. She munched as she walked along the deserted street.

The food revived her; exercise and resolution dispelled her melancholy; she sniffed the air, felt the sun warm on her body, drew in the heat and colour of this outer world, so nearly lost to her for ever. It was like the Resurrection of which the nuns had spoken.

Near the head of the steps in the steep street there was a house with grilled windows and a narrow door. Within, amidst its plush and velvet, its gilt and marble, its tasselled cushions and nymph-laden ceilings, the brothel drowsed through the empty afternoon. Only the drab slattern who had left her mopping of the tiles in the hall to answer the pealing of the bell, was moving, and she was only half awake. Madame, she told Nancy with an envying yawn, was resting. Nobody called at this hour.

But Nancy, destiny-ridden and short of time, was not to be deterred. The slattern yielded at last and slipslopped away to report the importunate visitor. Presently she returned and led the child up through the sleeping house.

Nancy stood on the threshold of the dimly lighted, thickly-carpeted, stuffy, scented apartment and looked her future in the face. For there, with thin dyed hair painfully pinched into curlers, shrewd hard eyes peering from a lined face, innocent at the moment of cosmetics, was the image of what she was herself to be when the years had run their course. Even the husky, spirit-hoarsened voice might have been an echo from the future.

"Who are you? What do you want? I hope it is important. I do not like my siesta disturbed."

And for some strange reason Nancy was instantly at home and at ease. She, who had never found it easy to be articulate, felt no difficulty in setting her case before this old woman, who, once she understood the point of the ill-timed visit, raised herself on her pillows and listened attentively. Even the few, searchingly intimate questions that the old woman asked were answered without hesitation or embarrassment. It was as though the world had suddenly begun to speak a language that she could understand.

She explained her position and made her offer concisely. She would wait and serve, fetch and carry, attend the wants and run the errands of the young ladies until such time as she could take her place amongst them.

"And why did you choose to come to me?"

"Because," said Nancy gravely, "I have heard that yours is a very high-class house."

The old woman laughed, and raising herself higher said, "Draw back the curtains and then come nearer to me. I must look at you."

The shrewd old eyes, infinitely experienced, indescribably evil, studied Nancy steadily for several moments. They noted the stocky, vigorous little body, the bright wary eyes that squarely returned her stare, the crop of shiny hair that denoted physical vitality and endurance. She said at last, speaking slowly,

"Very well. You may stay. I do not think that you will have to serve long."

In a way it was a true prophecy. The period of menial duties, running errands, dressing hair, laundering clothes and cleaning floors was soon over. The novitiate lasted barely a year, and then the young recruit was allowed to enter the ranks that she had chosen. But in another sense the old woman spoke falsely, for on that sunny afternoon Nancy Jurer had entered upon a servitude that was to last her lifetime, servitude to herself. From that moment everything, every person above the earth and under the sun, became subservient to the well-being of this body, which, because of its needs, had once threatened her peace of mind and by virtue of that threat made itself master. Because, in this world, the body must be housed and clothed and fed, there had been that afternoon when the dark tunnel stretched before her and only immediate action had saved her. Very well, then. Since it was so important, let it be paramount. Tend it, groom it, see that it eats well and lies soft. Sell its pleasures, but see that you get the price and make sure that its real security is never for an instant in danger. For, the moment of the sale passes and leaves no mark; but the price remains, and the body remains, renewing itself from day to day, immutable, a solid and visible asset that has been made out of a liability.

This self-servitude demanded constant vigilance, especially in those earlier years. There were unsuspected weaknesses to be overcome. There were times when she understood why her mother had forgiven Philippe his sins, and preferred him, penniless, greedy, faithless, to lovers both rich and generous and kind. There was a young man with silvery-fair hair and innocent blue eyes who wandered into the house in the steep street in a search for experience, and who, without greatly enlarging his own, infinitely increased that of the black-haired, sloe-eyed creature who shared with him an unexpected moment of rapture. But Nancy had seen the end of the path down which love, gently cajoling, enticed you; she rallied her defences and scored another victory over the weakness of the mind. For these things were not of the body; to that grim Moloch one man's flesh was no more than another. It was wiser than the mind which went about inviting slavery. The body forgot; the mind remembered. The mind was vulnerable; the body could be made impregnable.

There were other weaknesses, too, that must be combated. A tendency to hasty temper was one of them. The cause of Nancy Jurer's well-being demanded that men should be pandered to, women placated, friends deceived and enemies forestalled. For these ends a steady, cool, even temper was essential, for a time at least. And although her natural temper was violent and easily roused she battened it down, telling herself that she might do as she wished when she was firmly established; but when that time came habit was strongly ingrained and even the people who hated her most often had cause to admire her self-control.

But, as the years went by, and experience followed experience, she learnt that the most deadly enemy of self-interest was pity. It could ruin the soundest plan, defeat the best-laid scheme. It was most dangerous because it was more often called into action than either love or bad temper. You could, if you liked to permit such colossal folly, even pity the customers of the house who were, after all, merely men, weak and human, in search of they hardly knew what. You could pity them, on their endless quest; and you could pity the women within the house, who sold what should be given. And such pity disturbed the whole equilibrium of life. It must be uprooted and thrown on the lumber heap where so much, freedom of choice, fastidious-ness, respectability and the world's esteem, had already been cast. Never for one moment must you admit that any person could be other than a potential enemy or a possible tool, never for an instant must you believe that any inter-est mattered save your own. So you would survive and prosper.

And Nancy Jurer prospered. For the body is an easier taskmaster than the mind, and, served wholeheartedly, not niggardly with its rewards. As soon as she knew that she was recognised as an individual, an attraction to the house who was asked for by name, she struck a shrewd bargain with the madame; and after that, coin by slow coin her hidden savings grew.

Just before she was thirty, with her own savings and the backing of a man who recognised her rare qualities, she opened a house of her own, became "Madame" herself and hereafter plied her trade through the bodies of other women. For nearly twenty years she occupied a distinct, unshakeable position in the social structure of the town. Her name was synonymous with shrewd but honest deal-ing. Her prices were high, but her measure just. Her house, too, was orderly, so that respectable citizens could fre-quent it without fear of any disturbance that might incur publicity.

Her own brief premature attractiveness waned early, and as soon as she was installed in her own house self-indulgence made her very fat. She waddled about on dis-proportionately tiny feet, richly clad, intensely observant and heartily feared. She had an eye for female form that many an Eastern worthy would have coveted for his harem master; a pretty face could not deceive her, nor a graceful form, nor a sprightly manner. That eye probed beyond such superficial charms. She knew the trade down to its most trivial detail, and in New Orleans in the first two decades of the century it was held, with some justification, that you had not whored until you had visited Madame Nancy's.

Before she was fifty she retired, bought a small elegant house in a shady suburb and devoted herself entirely to pandering to her own tastes. It was so engrossing a pastime that she did not notice her loneliness. All her life she had been surrounded by people who must be controlled or placated; now she was free. She hardly realised that she had no friends, or that now that her natural function was abandoned she was merely a gross, lonely, déclassé old woman who ate and drank far too much. Riding in her comfortable carriage behind her perfectly matched, satiny plump horses, or seated at table, grossly devouring her favourite foods, or sinking at night into her billowy bed, she was perfectly happy, at once the priestess delighting in serving her goddess and the goddess gloating over her votary's service.

This happy state of affairs lasted for twelve years; and, since her money was shrewdly invested, seemed likely to last her lifetime; but some obscure and unfathomable juggling upon the part of politicians and financiers whose very names were unknown to her, brought the halcyon days to a sudden end. Shortly after her sixtieth birthday she awoke one morning to find herself ruined.

She was not alone in her misfortune; dozens of people shared it with her. In New Orleans alone there were several shrewd men who had believed themselves secure and their families comfortably provided. Most of the money lost in this venture had been new money, worked for and saved by men as capable and businesslike as Nancy herself.

She told herself savagely that there was no shame in losing money, no stigma in a bad investment. But within herself she was bitterly ashamed. She had been misled and fooled in some untraceable fashion, and must now begin to earn her bread again. In itself this did not disturb her unduly; some secret current in her blood moved more swiftly at the prospect of battling again with the world, stealing marches on her rivals, bullying her subordinates. But, as she faced the situation squarely, she could not deny that the thought of re-opening a business in New Orleans was indescribably distasteful to her. It meant announcing her failure and admitting that she was either an optimist who had retired on too little, or a fool who had invested her money unwisely.

Her body was now unwieldly and slow, the blackness of her hair due to art rather than nature, but the brain behind that furrowed brow was as clear and vigorous as in her prime. Within a few days she had decided her course. There was a new country in the West, a rich country, full of men, most of whom had no women with them. If her trade were established there at all it would be crudely and rustically established; there would be room for her. Women were always scarce in a new country and the essence of salesmanship is to offer goods in a market where they are rare.

Speed of action was essential; she was over sixty and used to her comforts; this new penury must not be unduly prolonged. Quietly and quickly, without mentioning a word of her losses, she sold her house, her furniture, her carriage and horses and a little strip of building land which she had bought as a chance investment. For an old woman of sixty, content to live frugally, the proceeds of the sales would have sufficed for life. But frugal living was not in Nancy's creed.

Without a word about her losses or her intentions, without a farewell to anyone, she left the town which had been her home, and sometimes her milch cow, since she was nine years old. Three people went with her, Scanty, who had driven the coach horses, Janna, his sister and Floribel Toit. Scanty and Janna belonged to Nancy, she had owned them for about five years; her claim to Floribel was less valid.

Four years before her retirement one of her girls had borne a baby, and because she was a good valuable girl (no other reason would have sufficed) Nancy had allowed her to stay in the house and keep her baby there. Floribel's early life had much resembled Nancy's own, and at sixteen the girl was accomplished in her own line, besides being very pretty. Madame Nancy had never accepted any responsibility for her, and had not given her a thought until she considered setting up business in California. Then she remembered. On the night before she left New Orleans she paid what she called a friendly visit to the house, looked the girl over with her expert eye and proceeded to dazzle her with promises of fun to be had, money to be made and an ultimate rich marriage. As soon as Floribel had consented to go with her, Nancy easily overawed the owner of the house with talk of legal guardianship; they left the house together.

Klara Bolewska was picked up at an inn, somewhere on the journey. Some attraction, not immediately apparent, arrested Nancy's professional attention, and to the big, red-headed, raw-handed, discontented Polish girl she repeated the promises that won Floribel Toit. It was a very easy victory; and when the big red-wheeled wagon moved on again the inn was without hired help and Klara sat on a padded seat, removing, with some lotion lent her by Floribel, the traces of menial toil from her strong, square-tipped hands.

The wagon rolled on over prairie and meadow land, over plain and hill, through forest and river. It ended its lonely journey at Fort Mason, and when it rolled on again it was in the ill-fated company of those who were going to carve out a new road to the West. And just as Mahitabel's God had accompanied her on the journey, Nancy Jurer's god rode with her in the shape of an ageing woman, gross, greedy and cynical, stripped of illusion and incapable of pity. There was no question here of which was the maker and which the image. Long ago, so long that she had forgotten the fatal day, the woman had glimpsed her god and remained unswervingly faithful ever since. Moreover the god had grown with the years, as is the manner of dieties that must either grow or diminish. It now weighed fourteen stones, a mass of pampered flesh, caring for nothing but its own well-being, knowing little but its appetites. Comfortably provided, painted, powdered, dyed and bejewelled, Nancy Jurer went out to put to the test a life's philosophy.

That she remained completely faithful to her creeds throughout the experience that awaited her is not to be wondered at. Changes of heart are rare at sixty-two. Her share in the drama that was to be enacted has been often condemned, not solely by those who witnessed it. And

96

even the most charitable human judge could hardly know that she had once been a child, alone and bewildered with sorrow, who had had to choose her path while she was still too young to understand.

When Cordy was nearly twelve the oldest of four children and tough and well-grown for his years, the Warrens moved into Milchester, seeking amongst the new mills that had ruined them, a new source of livelihood.

Simon Warren, the father, was a weaver, an industrious and competent craftsman, and for the first ten years or so of married life he had supported his family comfortably enough upon his earnings, eked out by the produce of the acre or so of land that surrounded the cottage. There had been a cow, some pigs and a few chickens; there were trees that bore fruit in their season; a patch of well-tended garden had yielded enough vegetables to last the winter. The children had flourished in the good air; and though Simon was growing bent and hollow-chested from the long hours at his loom, well, most weavers grew that way and thought nothing of it.

But the time came when the hand-loomers could no longer compete with the swift and tireless machines. The farms around were amply supplied with labour. The acre or so would not provide, unaided, for the family's needs. After careful consideration and a good deal of discussion with Mary, his wife, Simon decided to move into Milchester and carry on his trade in the new fashion. So they left the cottage where the pigs had run beneath the apple trees and chickens clucked about the door and the gilly-flowers had opened their velvet petals beside the path, and moved into the raw new town, where they were fortunate enough (though they did not realize it immediately) to rent a two-roomed house in a row of identical ones. Mary mourned the lack of a "backhouse" in which to wash and bake. There was no inch of ground in which to keep a hen, or dry a line of linen in the sun. There was no oven in which to bake the good bread, the oatcakes, the substantial rabbit pies. There was only a rusty little stove in one of the rooms and a little low cupboard beside it for the housing of coal. Instead of the well in the garden there was water in a pump at the extreme end of the row.

Mary's regret at the lack of convenience soon gave way to more anxious feeling. Lack of oven, lack of cupboard space could no longer disturb the housewife who found little to cook in the one or store in the other. Only one thing in Milchester was plentiful and that was work. But the mere rumour of the plentiful work had drawn men and their families by hundreds into the vicinity of the mills and the sheer weight of competitive labour had driven wages to the point where, by working twelve, fourteen, sixteen hours a day, a man could barely support himself, leave alone his dependents. Perversely enough, however, since trade was booming and labour piteously cheap and plentiful, the mills expanded and kept up their demand for new hands. There was work for Mary too. Driven by the inexorable need of bread for herself and her children she abandoned everything that had made her life, the cleaning, the cooking, the making and the mending, the careful upbringing of her children. She joined the ranks of the toilers.

To this pair, as to thousands of others, used to hard but undriven work in their own homes, the hurrying, clacking, inhuman mill was Hell made evident, and for a full six months after the beginning of their sorry experiment, they combined in their determination to keep their children out of it if it was in any way possible to do so. The sight of the children, so young, so overworked, so pitilessly used, so wastefully exploited, shocked everything that was decent and paternal in them. Of course Cordy had worked in the country. He had made long journeys collecting the yarn from the spinners, he had carried home the finished cloth. He had scared rooks from new-sown fields and led a horse at harvest time. But he had not crawled under the machines, picking out with his hands the accumulated dust and woollen fluff that no broom could reach, while above him the unceasing machine, unguarded, was alert to snap

99

off a finger, an arm, or a scalp unwarily exposed. He had not worked for fourteen hours a day in a stuffy, dust-laden air, or been beaten, as these children were when they were drowsy or slow or stupid with exhaustion. Contemplation of the pit into which they had fallen themselves and seemed likely to plunge their children also, filled Simon and Mary with horror and despair.

Still, it was obvious that something must be done. Wages continued to fall; in the first winter of their mill work they dropped to four and sixpence, unprecedented little. And bread was dear. Moreover there was the iniquitous custom of the "truck shop". The mill owners, ever avid for profit, had established shops of their own close to the factory gates, so that women, who, however weary they were at the end of the long day, must not return home empty-handed, could make their purchases without going along to the competitive market. At first Mary, after an inspection of the prices and the values in the truck shop, had tried to deal elsewhere, refusing the advice of more experienced women who tried to point out her error. This passive resistance lasted only a fortnight, at the end of which, on pay day, she was informed, in no very kindly manner, that she was expected to patronize the shop that was attached to the mill.

Prices there were high and the accounts by no means strictly kept. No debts were allowed, the amount of the purchases being deducted from the worker's pay. Often enough there was no money to draw. Cordy, rising eleven, must enter regular employment.

Mary's last struggle in the cause of individualism was made in the dark days of that winter. On Sundays, her only free days, she tramped about trying to find some respectable trader or craftsman who would either receive her son as an apprentice or employ him for a modest sum which would enable him to live at home without being a burden upon the family exchequer. But she soon learned that her ideas were outdated. The old system of apprenticeship was dying out. These few workers who still had their own freedom, cobblers, bakers and blacksmiths mostly, either demanded a premium or were already supplied with pauper slaves to whom the old honourable word "apprentice" was wrongly and debasedly applied. Mary received only one offer, and that was not for Cordy at all. A chimney sweep, passing and overhearing her argument with a shoemaker, crossed the road and inquired the age and size of the child. Mary told him eleven and well grown.

"Too big," said the sweep. "Ain't you one smaller?"

Mary thought of William, five years old. And then, looking across the road she saw the pitiable infant who was awaiting his master. Scraped raw in places, starved to the bone, dejection and timidity in every line of him, he leaned against the sack of soot which he had removed from some twisting chimney-stack. Bursting into tears Mary hastened away without replying. Even the mill was preferable to that.

So Cordy joined the ranks of those child workers who, with their mothers and fathers, toiled and often died in order that the exports of cotton cloth to India might be kept up, that the flag might follow trade to distant Africa, and that men might grow ever richer and richer and build great houses from which to issue now and then and vote against any measure that might bring amelioration to the lot of those upon whom they battened.

Cordy himself was relieved when his mother made up her mind, even though she cried when she communicated the news to him. He had acquired in that terrible six months a sharp and precocious knowledge of ways and means. He thought, not of the labour that he would have to perform, but of the two, perhaps even three shillings which he would bring home at the end of the week. With his "piece"—a thick slice of stale dark bread, thinly smeared with fat—which was to be eaten at midday, in his hand, he strode out manfully in the dark hours of the winter morning, feeling that he was taking his place in the world at last.

Only once, and that many years after and in a distant place of which the child Cordy had never heard the name, did he mention to anyone the experiences and torments of the days that followed. And upon that occasion he spoke (he who was always calm and concise and levelheaded) with such burning passion, such deadly gravity, such trenchant eloquence, that those who heard him were amazed and convinced against their will. It was as though he had carried that bitter burden for years, as an oyster may bear the pain and irritation of the invading grain of grit, and working upon it with the virtue of his patient and kindly endurance, had at last produced it as a thing of worth.

The room was stuffy, but it was an offence to open the window, for the air might dry the atmosphere and cause the taut threads to break. Water lay—in the interest of this same dampness—three or four inches on the floor. The whole building rocked and vibrated with the clangour of the machines. And here the children, "piecers" as they were called, often covered twenty miles a day, joining broken threads at this machine and that, keeping an eye upon the dancing bobbins, marking and replacing the empty ones. At midday they were granted half an hour's respite, but it was often a matter of eating while attending to some duty that had been left undone and must be caught up before the afternoon spell started.

The children themselves were pale, dwarfed and misshapen. A few were idiots, especially amongst the pauper children who had been sent to the mills from workhouses of the South. A number of the free children were the offspring of parents, either brutal or brutalized, who were content for their children to toil in their interests. But here and there a carefully washed face, a smooth head of hair, a neat patch upon some poor garment, testified to a motherly instinct, dumb and outraged by economic necessity.

Into this heterogeneous collection of young martyrs Cordy Warren was tossed, a sturdy, well-built little boy with the faint remains of country rosiness and tan left over from last summer and a curly crop of sun-bleached hair. His first sight of the room in which he was to work appalled him, the noise made him feel stupid and the task to which he was set was puzzling because he could not see its end or its reason. Twice in the first hour men, harried and bullied themselves, spoke sharply, bade him make haste and speeded him on his way with a push. A child to whom he once appealed for help turned on him the blank senseless look of the idiot, and mouthing something indistinct and useless, went back to the task which it had, by repeated punishment, just mastered, though not understood.

The six hours until midday seemed endless, longer than any whole day he had known in his life. His head and his legs ached and his fingers were already sore, as they would continue to be until the merciful callouses formed. Hunger gnawed at his stomach and he thought of the "piece" tucked away on the ledge of the loom.

At last the hour came. The smack and knock of the machines ceased. The older workers who had, by right, the first turn at the privy and drinking water in the yard, made their way out of the room. The children, with deep unconscious sighs of relief, drew, from pocket and hiding-place, their pieces. Most of them consisted, like Cordy's, of bread, scantily smeared with fat, or the red anonymous jam of the truck shop; in a few cases a boiled potato in its jacket was eaten jacket and all; a very small minority were privileged possessors of a particle of cheese. Not one meal was adequate to the appetite of its owner, not one was capable of doing more than keep life extant and hunger within bounds.

There was one child who had nothing. Cordy's attention was drawn by the fixed stare, wistful, anxious and yet not really hopeful which the other boy fixed upon his slice. Uncomfortably, yet not knowing the reason for his discomfort, he let his gaze travel to the boy's hands. They were empty. He was making no move towards pocket or hiding-place. He just stared, and a tiny dribble of saliva gleamed at the corner of his white-lipped mouth.

Looking away deliberately Cordy bit into his slice. Hunger can savour the dullest provender and the stale crumby bread with its meager greasiness set all his gastric juices working strongly. He bit into it roughly, chewed hard and swallowed zestfully. He was almost finished, far, far too soon, when he became aware once more of those wistful eyes.

"Gimme just a bite." It was no more than a whisper. But a little girl, with the face of a wizened old woman, overheard and said, with a belch as her own hastily gobbled potato hit her stomach:

"He's allust beggin' Timmy is."

Whether it was a hint to generosity or a warning, Cordy did not know. She made the statement flatly, giving Timmy an indifferent glance as she did so. Cordy hesitated a moment and in that moment the last bite had found its way into his mouth and was being crushed between his teeth. The resigned patient look of the dinnerless child smote him with a sudden pain where he had never felt a pain before.

"H'an't you had any?" he asked, knowing very well what the answer would be, knowing too why he had averted his eyes while he ate his own.

Timmy made neither answer nor answering gesture. It was not necessary.

"Why not?"

"There warn't none."

The wizened child had been looking through the window and now she said: "Water's free." There was a general rush for the door. They lined up in what was obviously an established order of precedence to take their turns at the tin cup that hung by a chain above the water pail.

And then the dinner spell was over and the afternoon's work began. Half-way through it Cordy, who had not yet received his first painful lesson in attention to work no matter what happened, became conscious of a commotion near-by and craned his neck to see the cause. Timmy lay huddled in the aisle between two of the machines. The man who had worked one of them stepped out, looked at the supine body and stepped back again. Along the aisle came the room overseer, taking off his belt as he came. The leather thong rose in the air and came down with resounding thwacks upon Timmy's back and shoulders, but he did not stir or cry out. It was Cordy who flinched and gave a little whimper. Without making any apparent effort the overseer stopped and lifted Timmy by taking a handful of his garments, like a woman lifting a pudding by its cloth.

The man at whose machine Cordy had been piecing bent over and took his ear between a savage finger and thumb.

"Tend your work, good-for-nothing, or you'll get something as'll give you reason to yell," he said.

The overseer, returning, flicked his belt across Cordy's hindquarters before rebuckling it about his waist.

"Don't stare at what don't concern you," he said, almost amiably.

"You got off light," said the weaver threateningly.

But Cordy was suffering from something far worse than a twisted ear or a welted bottom. The pain that had assailed him as that last mouthful passed out of reach in his gullet, was growing worse and worse. He could not locate it. It was in his head and in his chest and in his stomach, everywhere, and it was like being hungry and like being bruised and like having a scraped knee all at once. Later on when he understood about conscience he could look back and remember the very moment when his own first made itself felt.

Once, as he squatted down to clear a joint that had clogged, he caught sight of his own legs, bare because the wet floor made it advisable to roll the trousers to the knee. He saw, for the first time, the sturdiness of his own body. Mum had certainly talked a lot, since their arrival at Milchester, about starving; and there had been days when he too had gone dinnerless. But not for many days together; and it hadn't hurt him, look at his legs! He remembered Timmy's sticklike limbs, dangling from the overseer's grasp. And he had refused him one bite. For he was sure now that Timmy was dead. No living body could hang limp like that, or be unresponsive to such welting.

The afternoon, though it, like the morning, lasted for six hours, seemed much shorter; for unconsciously and uncomfortably he stumbled, so soon, upon the secret for defeating monotony—mental activity, agonising as it might be. When the machines shuddered to a standstill again he put on his boots, turned down his trouser legs and went to wait, as he had been told to do, at the gate, where his mother soon joined him. A little light from an unscreened window fell on the cobbles, and Mary, edging him into the glow of it, looked at him anxiously, her hand beneath his chin.

"Well son, how did you manage?"

"All right."

"Did you eat your piece? I oughter told you. If you leave it about sometimes it gets took."

"I ate it."

"That's right. I expect you're tired."

"I am a bit."

"Still, step out and maybe we'll be back afore your father."

She put her hand behind his shoulders, and, weary herself, tried to help him along. She was conscious, despite his sturdiness, of the vulnerability of his young body. How long before he too had the out-sticking shoulder-blades, the crooked spine, the spindle-shanks of the children on whom her wincing sight fell so often? She sighed. The sound reached Cordy and stopped, almost on his lips, the story that he was about to pour out about Timmy. Mum was worried enough about food for her own family, worried, now at this moment, about his having to go into the mill. He stepped sideways, avoiding the hand.

"I can manage, Mum. I ain't so tired now." And then, after a stumble that shook him into the realization that he was almost asleep as he walked:

"I like it there, Mum. It ain't so bad at all."

Well, perhaps he had been lucky and struck a kindly soul who would shield and spare him, as she, God knew, tried to spare the young ones whose circle touched hers.

"That's my man," she said fondly.

The words struck something in the depths of Cordy's mind. Of course, being so big and strong he was almost a man. And he had refused that poor skinny child one bite of his piece. He could never forgive himself.

Next day, however, he learned that Timmy was not dead. Even to those who are deserted by God and man alike death does not come so easily. Grey-faced, sunken-eyed, Timmy was in his place next morning. Cordy was delighted almost to choking-point when he saw him. Surreptitiously he fingered the piece, which to-day, warned by his mother, he retained in his pocket. Between his sore finger and thumb he pressed and broke it unevenly. He longed for the time to come when he could take it out and

106

proffer, in dumb amendment, the precious morsel that was the larger share.

But when the long weary morning had run its course and he was able with a joyful heart to offer the fragment of food, Timmy had already dragged out and bitten into a small cold potato.

"Me gran' pieced me terday," he mumbled through the first mouthful. But Cordy's conscience was not to be outdone.

"Here y'are," he said firmly. "I brought it for yer. Get it down."

Timmy needed no second bidding. He almost snatched. And Cordy turned away to eat his diminutive portion so that his lie should not be exposed. All through the afternoon he soothed his physical pangs (so much easier to bear after all than the undefined ones of yesterday) by comparing his size and fatness with those of the starvelings about him.

It was strange that he should have started life with the idea of his physical superiority, for all his life after he was undersized. That first twelve years' growth was never matched again and yet all his life Cordy was to remain one of those to whom everyone else was one of those "little ones" on our attitude to whom our spiritual stature must ever depend.

The year dragged on in toil and misery. Cordy's own lot was slightly easier than that of some of the other children because, being mentally alert and physically active, he could manage his work better. But after that day when pity made its first and fatal assault upon his peace of mind it was all too easy for him to suffer vicariously. Especially did he hate and dread the last few hours of the long day, when every ten minutes' passage was marked by the wailing of some child, suffering from unavoidable punishment; not the noisy crying of a child who is anxious to draw attention and so sympathy to itself, but the low sobbing misery that must find expression. Nobody heeded it; the mill clacked on, but when the belt, or the even more dreaded iron stick called the "billy-roller", fell upon the defenceless flesh the white line would appear around

Cordy's lips and the sickness would stir in his stomach. It became an obsession, so that he must look at the sights which shocked him, so that his own sufferings, the blows, the cracked chilblains, the skinned knuckles and heavy colds in the head that came his way, were almost welcome because he could reflect that now he was knowing pain, sharing it, bearing his part of the burden.

Insanity lay that way, and as he exhausted the reserve of strength that he had carried into the mill as a legacy of a happy and healthy childhood, he might have become a useless neurotic. But a whole series of misfortunes saved him.

First Simon with his weak chest developed "weavers' cough", the dreaded consumption that claimed so many whom ill-feeding, unremitting toil and the sudden change from the hot and stuffy atmosphere of the mill to the chill streets outside laid open to its ravages. Without complaint the man continued to work until the morning came when he could not leave his bed.

"A day's lay-in will set me straight," he told Mary, and she, not daring to absent herself, gave many instructions to Alice, now nearly ten years old, and went heavyhearted to her work. In ten days Simon had coughed away what remained of his lungs and was dead.

Mary, looking wildly about for some compensation for the loss of the chief wage-earner, let off half the two-roomed house to an Irish family, a man, his wife and two children. They were rough and noisy and Mary feared them, even as she welcomed their promise to pay half the rent. But the promise was never kept. A week's payment would be made, then for a fortnight they would miss. Mary's pleas and protests were brushed aside or countered with: "Sure and we paid you. You've forgot." Argument, however logical, was unavailing; nor could the harassed woman think of any action short of physical eviction, which she was not qualified to undertake.

Three months of semi-starvation for the whole family produced a situation that had only one cure: Alice and William must go to the mill and little Lisbet be left in the insecure keeping of the Irish children. The decision caused Mary less pain than she had felt before allowing Cordy to go into the mill. There was no more rebellion in her; the inevitability of things was bringing numbness in its train.

During the following summer an epidemic of scarlet fever swept through the mills, decimating the ranks. Alice fell sick first, then Lisbet, then William and then Mary herself. When the mother struggled out of her four days' delirium it was to find that of her family only Cordy lived.

The bereavement—or possibly the enforced rest—ended her apathy. At all costs Cordy must be saved, and now that there was no family to consider, revolutionary action was at last possible.

"We're going back to the country," she told Cordy. "Perhaps to Groton. I'm known there as a respectable woman and a good housekeeper. Parson'll speak for me. A woman with four children is tied down, but a woman with one is freer. Soon's as I get about agin, Cordy, we'll be shut of this place."

So, on one of those mornings when the mist lies pearly over the gleaned fields and the trees gleam golden in the sun that bathes their uppermost boughs, Mary and Cordy set out on foot with all their worldly goods in a bundle. The Irish family were left with the house for which they were now responsible and a junk dealer had given Mary five shillings for the bits of furniture that remained. It was all they had in the world.

They slept under the hedges or under the newly made stacks in the edges of the fields, and when, days later, they reached their own village nobody recognised in the dishevelled haggard woman and the pale bony child the remains of the tidy little family who had left it only two years before. The housekeeper at the Rectory was not at all pleased when she found them on the doorstep. Another pair of beggars, she thought, who had been told that the Rector never sent anyone away without a meal, upsetting her careful housekeeping. But when Mary said: "You don't remember me, Mrs. Potter? I'm Mary Warren, as used to live at Hunter's Cottage," the woman threw up her hands and cried: "Lor, how you have altered, you pore dear. Come along in." And she pulled a chair forward and a stool beside it, emptied the larder on to the kitchen table and reached down the tea-caddy. Presently she said: "And this'd be your youngest, wouldn't it?"

Mary's expression was a comment upon all that had happened. She said simply: "Nay. Children don't grow that fashion where we bin. This is Cordy, my eldest, and all that is left to me."

Mrs. Potter reached out and refilled the cups; her unspoken sympathy was in the gesture.

The Reverend Mr. Forsdyke said, and Mary did not contradict him, that the hand of God was in the situation. It so happened that a friend of his, the Rector of Sibley Strawless, was wanting a woman to keep his house. To-morrow, if it were fine, he would ride over and call upon him, and if the post were still vacant he would commend Mary so warmly that her engagement was certain. Only Cordy wondered, when the matter was successfully arranged and he and his mother installed at Sibley Strawless, whether the deaths of his father, his sisters and brother which had brought about this desirable state of affairs could be rightly called the hand of God. But of this, as of the other matters working in his mind, he gave no sign at all.

The Reverend Mr. Hawthorn, of Sibley Strawless, was seventy-four years old and had outlived his housekeeper and seemed likely to outlive her husband who tended the garden and looked after the horse which the old man had not bestridden for years. He was not sorry to find that his new housekeeper had a son, a likely boy enough who could help in garden and stable, sing in the choir on Sundays, and, after feeding and training a little make some runs for the Sibley Strawless cricket team. At the moment the boy was too thin and pasty-faced, and over-quiet for his age, but good air and good feeding would soon alter that. A very faint and well-censored picture of life in Milchester had reached him from his friend Forsdyke who had it limned for him by Mary. The good old man's limited mind looked forward to seeing Cordy burst forth into bucolic louthood.

But the boy remained thin and undersized and quiet.

And one winter's afternoon the old man, entering his study, found him, with the log-basket on his arm, poring over a book that lay open on the desk before the replenished fire. The book, the recently published *Waverley,* was hardly calculated to interest the immature mind and the old man said mildly: "Hardly your kind of reading, is it, my boy?" Cordy started and a sudden painful colour stained his cheeks.

"I was only wondering," he said defensively.

"Wondering what?"

"How you do it. How do you know what the marks mean? I can see that the same things come over and over again. But how do you know what they mean?

"You cannot read?"

"No." And then suddenly shaken from his reserve by the strength of his longing: "And I do so wish I could."

From being an old man, no longer able to follow hounds, liable to indigestion after drinking port, doddering from study to garden, from Rectory to church, there to preach a sermon composed twenty years ago, an old man with life behind him and one foot in the grave already, Septimus Hawthorn suddenly became a man who had a great gift to bestow. Benevolence and generosity, interest and enthusiasm beamed upon his face as he said:

"Put down that basket and draw up that chair, Cordy. We'll soon put that right."

He was probably, from all academic standards, the worst teacher in the world. It did not occur to him for one moment that Cordy, faced with written words of the English language, was as helpless as he himself would have been confronted by a page of Chinese. He had no notion even of starting his pupil with simple words. He plunged straight in. He meandered, he digressed, he forgot. He explained the meaning of a simple word by using lengthy and erudite synonyms. But in a month he had Cordy reading fluently from the beginning of a page to its end. And if the meanings of the various words were obscure, well, there was Dr. Johnson's Lexicon on the side table. Partly the success of the teaching was due to the teacher's enthusiasm and dogged patience, partly to the pupil's eager application and Milchester-born habit of endeavouring to give satisfaction in order to avoid punishment.

New worlds opened before Cordy's wondering eyes. All the stories and all the wisdom of the world lay open before him. It was like being given another pair of eyes, another body altogether. Nor was he the sole beneficiary of the transaction. To the Reverend Septimus for whom life had been spinning upon an ever narrowing orbit this new interest proved vital and restorative. He searched his memory for books that he had enjoyed as a young man, tottered into the attic, and fumbling among the debris of years, recovered the volumes themselves. He talked endlessly as this allusion or that recalled some experience or some memory of his days at Charterhouse or Cambridge. He dealt with Cordy's almost virgin intelligence as a child deals with a clean slate. He scribbled all over it, gladly, without design, but with infinite gusto.

The old groom-gardener, who had first resented Cordy's intrusion and then leaned heavily upon his strength, muttered and complained. He could no longer manage all his work. Then find another boy, any boy. This one was sacrosanct. This one was what his reverence had been needing ever since hunting had failed him as a pastime. Here was a new and fascinating chase. Down through the centuries, over the fields of paper, the hedges of grammar, through the coverts of philosophy, the ditches of doubt, his mind hunted Cordy's. Away and away! Such sport had never been his before.

This entry into the world of letters, like his entry into the life of the mill, might well have turned Cordy's brain, ill-adjusted as it was to the sudden onslaught. But all the while Mary was there, unlettered, but instinctively wise: piling the plate with food, inventing the errand that involved some walking, taking away the candle and so making night reading impossible. She preserved his contract with the familiar and the tangible.

In her heart she was proud of him; and, ashamedly, grateful that out of her family he should have been spared. Vaguely she knew it was something of this sort that she had intended when she had set out to walk from

Milchester to Groton on that autumn day. But to her flesh he remained her little boy, to be watched and cared for and, when necessary, chided. The hand that could wield pen on paper must deal faithfully with the porridge spoon; and the eye could be drawn from the printed page to the crisp brown crust of the apple pie.

She lasted long enough to see him through the chase. And then, on a bright spring morning she died, very quietly, of heart failure, the knife with which she had been peeling potatoes still in her hand.

Cordy, eighteen years old, small and spare, as he was to remain, followed her to the grave beneath the trees that darkened the study windows. Returning, he shut himself into the small room that had been his for six years and gave himself over to the processes of thought. When he emerged he went to the study and announced his intention of returning to Milchester.

The old Rector argued, ingeniously and persuasively; renouncing his dignity as never before, he pleaded. But Cordy was in the grip of an idea, deaf to argument and immune to cajolery. He must go back to Milchester because he was haunted, because, through all these six peaceful years, he had remembered that which had disturbed his peace. He could explain now; he turned the weapon that the old man had forged, against him, and finally he conquered.

"Get along with you then. And when you're sick of reforming and realise that you are a very ignorant fellow, come back and I will teach you Greek."

Working men were downtrodden because they did not understand their strength. They were abused because they were dumb. They were like animals, patient, accepting, exploited. They had only to unite, to state firmly that they would not tolerate conditions as they were and things would improve. He, Cordy would go back to them, working with them he would gain their confidence. Lucid of mind he would lighten their darkness; he would speak for the dumb; fight for those that were oppressed.

He worked and spoke and fought for fourteen years.

Macclesfield, Leeds and Manchester, Northampton, Coventry, York. Nottingham, Middleton and Bradford. Working, speaking, writing. Hounded about. Called fire-brand, agitator, disturber of the peace. Followed from place to place and sometimes forestalled by messages that went through the new towns like tom-tom messages through the jungle: "Fellow called Warren. Agitator. Chuck him out." He worked for a fortnight and starved for a month; he lay sick in Norwich workhouse; he lay chained in Leicester gaol. He talked, in those fourteen years to thousands of people and accumulated such a weight of evidence regarding injustice and abuse as would, one would have thought, have sent revolution flaming the countryside. By his fervour he wore himself out; no other visible alteration was accomplished.

For the people themselves were against him. They might listen to him, agree with him, corroborate all he said at those furtive meetings in cellar, attic or field; but that was all. They feared to be seen in his company, would deny, when questioned, that they had ever heard his name. A considerable number of them would join with the owners in breaking up his meetings and hounding him from place to place.

Largely this was due to fear, apathy, ignorance and helplessness on the part of those whom he sought to rouse; but in an appreciable degree it was due to Cordy himself. He was not, despite his inspiration and his burning fervour, a leader of men. He was himself too vulnerable, too susceptible, too lacking in detachment. He could make, few men better, a sharp and sudden appeal to the emotions, but because of that very fact the emotions that he raised, courage, fury, enthusiasm, would, when they cooled, leave the emotional sphere open to the oldest and strongest feeling of all—fear. When he talked of bad conditions, the inequity of the truck system, the greediness of the owners, the injustice of the law, men's hearts burned within them to alter these things. But when the moments had passed they were left with the sour taste of the information he had given them. Aye, things were bad for sure. So bad . . . better not draw any

114

more misfortune upon yourself by getting mixed up with agitators.

Or the reason may have gone deeper still and concerned itself obscurely with the fact that Cordy himself was not an inspiring figure, that he was small and starved-looking, with a voice which, starting off with firm resonance, quickly grew hoarse and weak; that he was a workman who had suffered and would surely suffer again. It is a notable fact that the men who lead reforms and revolutions come seldom from the class whose wrongs they work to redress.

In any case, and for whichever reason, Cordy laboured for fourteen years in a stony and unresponsive field. But it was not until one summer evening in Milchester that he realised the extent of his failure.

He had been drawn back to the town which he knew so well by rumours of trouble. A threatened cut in wages had followed a lengthening of hours. Like the petrel bird that heralds the storm, Cordy hurried to Milchester to organise a standing-out against the double imposition.

It seemed that it was easier than usual to arrange for an outdoor meeting. The field was chosen, the cart from which he was to speak dragged into position. The secret had been well kept, but pickets were posted to keep watch for the dreaded yeomanry. For one never knew when a coward or a favour-currier would act as Judas.

It was a warm evening, the scents of hay and beanfields mingled sweetly on the air. Cordy's heart rose as he mounted his improvised rostrum. Perhaps here, this evening, in the place where he himself had received initiation, the movement would begin. At this meeting might be lighted the taper that should start the cleansing conflagration sweeping through all the pestilent places of the kingdom. Here, at this moment the first snapping of chains might be heard. Man might rise in his strength and defy his oppressor. Cordy's heart was full and his eyes moist as he began to speak.

The audience was smaller than he had hoped or expected. And it was unsympathetic. Close-to, the pale faces were raised attentively, he recognised converts and disciples of years' standing. But outside this little circle unrest and muttering began before his first few sentences were completed.

"They strook at Maanchester, dennen they? and what happened theer?"

"How many was killed at Preston when they tried that game?"

"What happened to Joe Sherwin at Stockport?"

The gibing questions, the recountal of the failures of men like themselves, poured out with a dreadful and surprising relish. It was as though they delighted in the realisation of their own helplessness. A sudden intolerable depression laid hold of Cordy, as crippling as a physical sickness. He clutched the rail of the cart with one hand and raised the other in the air. He said, almost inaudibly: "My friends, listen ..." and knew that thus early in the evening, with his speech unmade, his voice had failed him. He swallowed convulsively and the sweat broke out on his forehead. Old Tom Maxton, a veteran weaver and his friend, climbed stiffly into the cart beside him, prepared to hold the fort until Cordy's unreliable voice recovered. But before the old man could speak a shrill voice cut sharply through the undertones of muttering dissension.

"Go away," it said. "You only make things worse."

Cordy's mind noted, without immediately recording it, the real despair and unhappiness in that shrill indictment. He gulped and felt the muscles of his throat taut and strong again.

"If you let them do this to you; if you go back and work for those longer hours for that lessened pay, then it will be you who have made things worse. . . ."

A short stick, thrown vigorously, twirled through the air and struck him on the head, midway between ear and eye. He fell back into the cart like a log.

It was probably thrown by a professional troublemaker, one of those who, for a shilling or so, would attempt to break up any meeting, or, failing that, make a disturbance which would bring discredit upon the gathering and justify the calling in of the soldiers. But Cordy, seeing it coming, had not troubled to duck his head, for the thought had flashed through his mind: "So that's how they feel," and despair held him immobile.

Despair dogged him into the depths of the breakdown that followed. His unconscious moments were restless and noisy with repeated pleas and exhortations; his conscious ones spent in gloomy recountals of his failures. In vain did old Tom, sheltering his body at considerable risk to himself, attempt to solace his soul.

"You'm not alone, lad," he said often. "There's men working through the length and breadth o' the land, aye and in the high places, too, for the cause that you have to heart. It takes time. Evil be strong and the Devil be wily. You'm beat now, but you'll gather yourself and go on fighting."

But in his heart Cordy knew that he was defeated. He no longer believed that men could save themselves. They struggled, some of them, against their own apathy and their own fear as well as against the conditions of their world. But with what result? That the laws were tightened against them, the gyves more firmly riveted upon their wrists. The sharp voice that had said: "Go away. You only make things worse," had spoken the dangerous half-truth which in his desperate state Cordy had accepted as the final word. He thought of the blows that had been dealt upon the defenceless by the mailed fist of power and privilege; he remembered the meetings broken up, the skulls split, the hungry men carted off to gaol, because they had disturbed the peace in which they were expected to labour and to starve. He said:

"I've tried, Tom; but it's too early. To go on is like forcing a birth, you only ruin the thing that is to be born. Those fellows who shouted about the Manchester riots and Joe Sherwin at Stockport and the woman who screamed that we made things worse—they were right. I've done harm instead of good. I'm harming you now. If I were found here you know what would happen. I'll go away."

Consideration for Tom enabled him to beat down his weakness, to rise from the makeshift bed which seemed like a haven in a world gone awry, and to leave Milchester. He decided to go to America, the Mecca, at that period, of the misfits, the dreamers and the disappointed who were determined to try again.

Fate led him, without much preliminary buffeting, to Craddock, a Pennsylvanian village that was growing into a township overnight following the discovery of coal beneath its green fields. And there James Digby, printer and owner of the *Craddock Times,* took him into his business, his home and his heart.

Digby, bald, wrinkled, dried out, an old man at sixty, was a reformer, too. But he did not believe in meetings or speeches.

"The power of the press, my boy," he would say, "that's what will do it. People listen and know what they hear is right, but they go away and forget and begin to doubt. When they can all read they won't have a chance of forgetting. Moreover we'll build up, out of paper and printers' ink, a new thing called public opinion. It will be a roll of honour and a pillory, all in one. This is what will do it, my boy, this!" And he would lay his skinny hand, with the indelible rim of printers' ink in the nails, upon his old-fashioned press. Caressingly; prophetically.

He was a widower. His daughter, Ruth, a stout, quiet mouselike creature, ran his house, mended his shabby clothes, made one dollar do the work of two, kept the meals hot when the press broke down and must be nursed without regard for domestic arrangements. She was thirty-two, a settled old maid in her own eyes and those of her acquaintances, when Digby brought Cordy into his home. Within a month she was shyly and painfully in love with him.

Cordy, being without interest in her, and lacking in male vanity, was quite blind to the fact and oblivious to the significance of the neat piles of carefully mended underclothes, the frequent appearance of the dishes that he had enjoyed, the steady knitting of hose, mufflers and mittens that began with the cold weather.

For him the drama of life in Elm Street, Craddock, Pennsylvania, was centred, not in the neat, always rather chilly, old-maidish house, but in the "shop" as Digby called it, where the stuffy warmth of the atmosphere was sliced through by treacherous draughts, and every available space was deeply covered with papers, gritty with dust and turning yellow at the edges; where the press thudded out its messages and Digby, dimly sighted above the rampart of paper, wrote his acrid, critical, intelligent editorials beneath the yellow halo of the hanging oil lamp.

Here he learned to set up type, work the press, frame advertisements, sort out notices of births and deaths and marriages and, once a week, just before going to press, write a column which summed up, succinctly and honestly, all the events, social, political and civil, that had occurred since the last printing of the paper. "IT HAPPENED LAST WEEK" was its title and its contents varied from the information that Mr. Oatflanger's bull, advertised as lost in the previous issue, had been safely restored to its owner, to the dramatic announcement of the murder of Mr. Clay and the arrest of his wife and her lover who had become weary of waiting for the course of nature.

During the middle of the week the press, half casually, tossed off bills of sale, church notices, obituary cards and similar unnoticed trifles. When it stood idle Cordy and Digby were either out in search of material, advertisements, gossip, or working in the big overgrown garden at the side of the house.

Season followed season. Four happy years went by in a flash.

Now and again a slight uncomfortable pang shot through Cordy's mind at some new and special evidence of Ruth's devotion; and it seemed at times that he had to say "Thank you" rather often; but since her service was akin to Mary's motherly care, which he had missed during his wandering years, he accepted it without much curiosity as to its implications. Digby, to whom it was quite clear, said nothing. He was not the interfering kind except where the paper's policy was concerned.

In the fourth winter the old man fell ill. Sharp arthritic pains racked his limbs. He moved slowly about the office until at last, when he could not leave his chair without aid and his handwriting was an illegible waver, Cordy and Ruth persuaded him to go to bed. Even then he refused the services of a doctor, ministering to himself with hot rum and a homemade compound of blackcurrant, and allowing Cordy to rub his knees, elbows, ankles and wrists with some horse oil that flayed even the masseur's hard palms and fingers.

He stayed in bed for a week and the pain eased. It had been a week of threatened trouble at Black Dive, a mine in a neighbouring village; as soon as Digby had the use of his legs again he insisted upon being driven to the place, where he spent the whole of a bitter day collecting information which, as he confided to Cordy on the return drive, would provide material for the most inflamatory editorial ever written.

He never saw it in print. The dreaded pneumonia crackle made itself heard in his chest next day, and that week's issue of the *Craddock Times* bore a black border. Within, side by side with the scathing editorial denouncement of the Black Dive's conditions and policy, was the obituary of the writer.

In one of his brief lucid intervals before the end Digby had whispered to Cordy that he had left him the paper and the shop and trusted him to "look after Ruth." That was all. He did not mention what he knew—that Ruth had loved Cordy since his arrival; or what he hoped— that Cordy's care for her would take the form of matrimony. Such things were better left to themselves. He said "look after Ruth," and died.

And there was the business, just capable of supporting the pair of them if they stayed together under the one roof. And there was Ruth, piteous in her bereavement and her black clothes, turning confidingly to Cordy for everything, from comfort to the assurance that the paper should be run as before. There was not enough money for her to take and go away; and if, on the other hand, Cordy himself should leave, who would edit and print the paper? Bert Wader, a printer, sacked for drunkenness from the *Courier,* the *Times'* troublesome rival, came in to help Cordy on press days, but he was not reliable and only capable of working under orders.

And anyway, Cordy reflected, neither he nor Ruth was very young any more. He was thirty-six and he suspected that she had reached if not passed that age herself. So he settled down, and amidst the confusion of muddle and debts that Digby's death had revealed, thought no more of the matter until one evening, entering the house, he found Ruth puffy-faced from crying. His gentle enquiries elucidated that people were talking about them, saying that it wasn't decent for them to be living alone like that. Coyness sat oddly upon her tear-swollen face as she repeated the gossip.

"Oh well," said Cordy at last, when the final word had been repeated, "I must get a lodging. I'd have done it before if I'd thought of it. But your father, Ruth, didn't have much business sense. He didn't even keep receipts and lots of bills have come in that I'm nearly sure would have been paid before now. So there is not much money and I shall be able to draw only very little in the way of wages. Still, don't you worry any more. I'll manage."

To his surprise and discomfort fresh tears welled into her eyes. Ruth, too, had lately given her age some consideration, and now she saw what she considered her last chance of a husband and some children slipping away from her. A rebellious streak in her nature cried out that he was a blind, stupid fool, but outwardly she said that lodgings were expensive and uncomfortable, and that she would be very lonely, very lonely indeed without him.

"Then we must find someone to live with you," said Cordy, conscious of irritation beginning to shoot through his pity. "It's obvious that in this place we couldn't go on living like this unless we were married."

He said the last words as he moved to the mantelpiece for his pipe, and Ruth's sudden onslaught almost bore him into the fire. She had, in a literal sense, thrown herself at him as he spoke the magic word, and was now laughing and crying and babbling about how much she loved him, and how glad she was that he had asked her, all at once.

The Reverend Mr. Hawthorne had thought Cordy a clever little boy. Mill crowds had thought him a clever speaker. James Digby had rapidly developed a good opinion of him both as a paper and business man. But

121

he was not clever enough for the situation in which he now found himself. Nor, of course, nearly hard enough. It was impossible to dash that radiant happiness from Ruth's ravaged face by an explanation that would hurt her and free him.

He said: "Why Ruth . . ." and then, feeling that something more was expected, kissed her clumsily on the brow. She kissed him in return with a violence that surprised him, and then said:

"You'll put a notice in the paper, won't you, Cordy? So that it's in this week?"

They were married three weeks later, Cordy still with the mourning band on his hat and sleeve, Ruth in a new gown, black, but more gaily cut and ruffled than her usual ones.

Her behaviour during their brief betrothal, and for a few weeks after the wedding, often caused Cordy an uneasy pang. She seemed so happy that his own inward unmovedness shocked him; and she was so obviously delighted with the turn of affairs that he felt brutal for having made her wait so long. He was reminded of Timmy, whom he had also kept waiting for the thing he wanted.

That his wife was temperamentally cold and physically unresponsive he only dimly suspected, putting down their failure to achieve felicity to his own secret lack of passion. So he brushed away his feeling that something was wrong, turned a deaf ear to the inner instinctive voice that said: "It shouldn't be like this, you know," and threw his energies into settling the business straight.

Late in the following autumn Ruth bore a son, Digby, who had, immediately after the wedding, become the subject of her prayers and hopes. Promptly her true nature was revealed. With almost disconcerting suddenness she diverted the full stream of her devotion and almost all her attention to the child. Cordy realised that although she had wanted him and married him, he personally had meant little to her. Any man, tidy in the house, regular in his habits, of kind disposition and capable of fathering children, would have done as well. He drew a little comfort from the thought that Ruth had not been cheated as much as he had at first feared.

One night during the following winter, Cordy, after carrying up the cradle and bidding Ruth not to wait for him as he would be working late, went back into the office and sitting in Digby's chair, gave himself up to the paper's accounts. Digby had never troubled with such things, and the muddle and the debts that had to be sorted out and settled after his death had inspired Cordy to evolve a more satisfactory system.

It was a wild night, with a north-east wind that howled like a banshee around the building and flung spurts of sleet at the window. Now and then a particularly violent blast cut the back of Cordy's head with an icy knife and made the oil lamp that hung from the ceiling swing backwards and forwards. He worked on, oblivious to draughts and shifting light, until a low but imperative knocking sounded upon the side door. He weighted down the papers against the draught that would result from opening the door, and with his pen still in his hand, went and shot back the bolt. A woman, battling to hold her cloak against the wild fingers of the wind, stood on the step. Her rather breathless "Good evening" was snatched from her lips and swallowed up on a long banshee wail. The gust blew her sideways and she fell into the office where all the loose papers were fluttering madly, and she steadied herself for a moment by clutching at Cordy's arm. He pushed the door closed with some difficulty and drove home the bolt to steady it.

"What a night," said the woman in deep clear voice, "and what a grand fire."

She went straight to the glowing iron stove that stood in the centre of the office and stretched her hands over its top. Cordy, coming closer, could see the firelight through the thin, semi-transparent palms. After a moment a drop of rain fell from the front of the cloak's hood and trickled down her cheek. She put up one hand and pushed the hood back on to her shoulders, revealing a worn young face with faint hollows below the cheek-bones and a mass of reddish hair, curling in the dampness.

She said: "I did find it then? You run a paper?"

Cordy nodded, still looking at her. Under the cloak she

wore a thin sprigged dress, mired at the hem, and as she thrust one foot towards the warmth he could see that her unsuitable shoes were soaked and muddy.

Four years with Digby had taught him that the old man's acrid kind-heartedness had many calls made upon it. He imagined that the worn young woman had come to ask for help in some difficulty. Therefore as he dragged forward a chair and asked her to sit down his voice and manner were very gentle. She sat down and straightened the thin shoulders upon which the damp cloak had hung too heavily.

"I want to put an advertisement in your paper," she said. "And they told me at the shop that all advertisements must be in by Wednesday night. You go to press on Thursday? I want this to have a prominent place. I don't mind paying extra for that."

From somewhere within the cloak she drew out a sheet of paper and handed it to Cordy. Turning towards the lamp he read, in neat shaded copperplate:

"Mrs. Susan Brede wishes to announce that her school for young ladies and gentlemen (the latter to the age of ten years) will open at Number Eight, Jackson Street, Craddock, on November the fourteenth. Inquiries are invited. Mrs. Susan Brede, who has had experience with some of the best families in New York and Boston, is well-qualified to teach music, dancing, embroidery and deportment as well as the usual academic subjects. Board can be provided if desired. Terms will be moderate."

"It's not like some of our advertisements," said Cordy. "I often have to rewrite them to make sense. Then if the answers are unsatisfactory the advertisers are inclined to think it's because I messed the originals about." He smiled as he spoke, but Susie remained grimly serious.

"Do you think it's any use? The school I mean. I chose this place, after a lot of consideration, because there wasn't a school here already. You see, I've got to make a living somehow, for three of us. I'd hire out, but scrubbing breaks me in bits and it's so difficult with Anna, and my little boy. They need a home. So I thought of a school. I can teach him with the others, and Anna can look after the house. What do you think?"

124

She looked at him as though the whole future of the school depended upon his answer. He was acutely aware of her pathos.

"I think there's an opening," he said cautiously. "As you say there isn't a school. I'll put this at the top of the advertsement column, with a border, I think. And I'll make a mention of it in my column of weekly happenings. I'll say what a good thing it is that the torch of learning is being re-kindled in Craddock ... something like that. They like flowery terms."

"Thank you. And how much will that be?"

"Half a dollar for the advertisement."

"And the mention?"

"Oh, no charge for that."

She drew out a manly leather purse and searched amongst the coins in it for the one she required. She laid it on the desk and remained standing, pulling up the cloak's hood and drawing it about her.

"I envy your stove," she said. "I wish I could take it with me. You see, we only arrived to-day, and I don't think anyone has lived in that old house for ages. None of the stoves would draw a bit. We couldn't even have coffee."

A vision of the blackened tin coffee-pot which Ruth invariably left at the side of the kitchen stove came before Cordy's eyes.

"If you could spare a moment ..." he said diffidently. "I have some coffee waiting for me."

Susie sat down promptly. "More tuneable," she said, "than lark to shepherd's ear."

It was with a strange sense of uprushing excitement that he collected the coffee and the extra cup and found Ruth's rich fruit cake in the pantry. And when the pot was empty and the thick plummy slices no more than crumbs on the plates, friendship between the two was firmly established. Susie had told him two things which he was appalled to think she might have told to anyone who was momentarily kind to her. One was that she was not a widow, as in Craddock she intended to pretend. Her husband had left her. "He was no loss," she said. "And it serves me right. Everybody begged me not to marry him, and I would. But I can't go back like the Prodigal and *grovel* about it, can I? Not till I've tried everything." The other was that she had never taught in her life. "Notice, I didn't say that I had taught in the best families. I said 'had experience with.' And that is true. Parties and things." Either fact would have doomed the school from the start should it leak out. Cordy told her so.

"Oh, but I've only told *you*," she said looking at him wide-eyed, so that he was stabbed anew at the thought of her defencelessness, "and you wouldn't tell anyone."

"Of course I wouldn't. But I don't see how you could know that."

"I don't either. But I just did. I knew I'd found a friend the moment I looked at you."

She made no protest when he fetched his hat and coat and announced his intention of accompanying her back to Jackson Street. Once there it was a simple matter to enter and take a look at the recalcitrant stove. The big old house felt damp and unfriendly. The recently unpacked furniture stood around looking ill at ease.

"It'll soon be nice," said Susie, leading the way with a dripping candle. "I thought this for the schoolroom, near the garden—God, what a wilderness that is too— and no stairs for the little ones to tumble on. And this for the cloakroom. Then I shall live in here, it seemed the friendliest room. Will you come and see me when I get all straight?"

"Of course. If I may."

It was midnight when he left, smirched from his wrestling with the stove, but happily conscious that he had left it burning, a warm core at the heart of the unfriendly house. That a similar source of warmth had been kindled in his own being, when she put her thin hand in his and thanked him for all his kindness, was not so immediately apparent, although afterwards he knew that he had fallen in love with her on that first evening.

Hitherto he had only served causes. Now he was to bend brain and sinew to the service of a person as resolutely as ever Ruth had done. Subtly—for by no means completely unworldly—he canvassed pupils for the school.

126

And when they were found he screwed pegs into the walls of the cloakroom for their clothes and nailed shelves in the schoolroom for their books. He mounted maps on rollers; he mended torn pages and worked out sums which Susie must learn before she could teach. He found out from Ruth the best places for groceries and butcher's meat and the most reliable sources of fresh milk and vegetables and retailed these scraps of domestic wisdom to Anna, the dour old woman who had been Susie's nurse and who had followed her into the exile of her mésalliance and stuck to her, grumblingly, ever since. Anna was of the opinion that Miss Susie should have gone straight home to her family when her husband decamped. There she could have lived in comfort and reared her son properly. She bitterly resented the school and despised the loud-voiced children whom Susie— through her own stupidity—was compelled to teach. Meeting one of them in passage or doorway she would fix it with a cold stare and say: "Make way for your elders," in a voice that none of the pupils dreamed of disobeying. Susie, they thought, was "soft", but Anna reminded them of their own mothers and grandmothers, and was mightily respected.

After a few weeks of criticism and narrow watching Anna accepted Cordy, and the whole situation, much as elderly female attendants upon attractive young women have traditionally accepted unorthodox relationships. He was certainly not as dashing and handsome as Miss Susie's men should be, but Anna had seen her mistress come to grief over one handsome, dashing young man. She was glad now there was someone to keep Miss Susie happy, to give her advice and to remind her that she was still young and attractive. Anna often closed the door of the sitting-room behind Cordy in the gentle, knowing manner of one who understood and sympathised with an intrigue.

Cordy never entered the house without a rare sense of homecoming. He had at last found the woman whom he would have liked to marry.

That she had entered his life years too late and that they were neither of them free people any more, were facts which, since they ruined the pleasure of the moment, must be thought about as little as possible. One further fact—that their friendship, if ever exposed to public view, would be the ruin of them, was not so easily ignored, and Cordy, aware of this, developed a new sense of caution and secrecy, timing his visits with care and covering his evening absences with ingenious excuses which Ruth, wrapped in the care of the child and in her own happy complacency, never even thought of questioning.

With every visit to Jackson Street Cordy fell more deeply into the habit of regarding it as his life's centre. Within that house he seemed to become a different person, more free, more gay, more positively alive. He found that he could talk to Susie as he had never been able to do to Ruth: Susie found his dry remarks amusing and delighted to his descriptions of the people with whom his work brought him in contact; Susie thought him very clever because he could cast up a column of figures with swift accuracy; Susie appreciated him as a person. All these things flattered his vanity which had, almost without his knowing it, suffered at Ruth's hands.

But that was only one of the charms which she held for him. She was utterly different, he discovered, from anyone he had ever known before. Even while he deplored her extravagances he delighted in them because of their novelty. It was easy to see that her poverty was of comparatively recent origin, imposed upon the surface of her mind, not part of the very stuff of life as it was to Cordy and most of the people he knew. She resented the petty economies that gladdened the heart of good housewives. She liked rooms warm enough to allow her to wear thin dresses, even in winter; she scorned the wooden-soled, leather-thonged pattens in which other women clumped through the winter streets. When she secured six pupils as boarders she housed and fed them so well that their keep absorbed their fees and, as Cordy pointed out, she was teaching them for nothing. But although Cordy, helping her with her muddled accounts, would urge and actually suggest economies to her, he was bound to admit that extravagance, like her flippancy, her bright dresses, her frank hedonism and easy laughter, became her.

The days between his visits were now flat and grey, though they followed the pattern that he had hitherto regarded contentedly enough. Across them the night of their next meeting shone like a beacon seen across a strait of dull water. Sometimes he was a little frightened of his dependence upon her. Suppose the school failed and she moved away; suppose she realised that life would be easier in the home of her parents; suppose the errant husband returned to claim his own; suppose—worst of all—that she tired of him and withdrew her friendship. In many ways she betrayed traces of a fickle nature. She liked altering the furniture of her house, she liked trying new ways of dressing her hair, she admitted that the faithful Anna, though useful, was maddeningly boring since her every word and action could be foretold. And once she confessed that she had been tired of her husband long before he left.

"He was another," she said, "who always said or did the thing that you expected. He couldn't even leave me without going through all the normal preliminaries. I knew a fortnight before he went that he was contemplating a move."

"But you let him go?"

"I let him go. I never was one for keeping things in cages."

Cordy hated himself for thinking suddenly of his own home, where Ruth, now well-advanced in her second pregnancy, was an unconscious but inescapable gaoler. He looked at the woman beside him and the turn of her head showed him the nape of a thin white neck, like a child's, with little tendrils of russet hair curling against it. As often before desire moved in him so overwhelmingly that his hands trembled and his voice was uncertain as he said: "I must go."

But the night came, when, as he struggled with the dear temptation and prepared to flee before it, she turned to him and he saw the answering desire naked in her eyes. Her "Don't go," was no more than a breath, but he heard it.

Before that they had often, in the course of their talking, said that life was short and people fools who did not catch at what happiness it offered; said that the only evil in behaviour lay in hurting other people; hinted that in a civilised world one mistake should not be allowed to ruin a lifetime. All these things they had said with a sharp and mutual knowledge of the implication of the words. None the less, when the moment came to test the theories, each met it with a little shock of surprise, and a wonder whether, by seeking more, they had spoilt a precious thing.

But doubt was quickly swallowed by delight. For this union, hidden from men and unblessed by any god save those old pagan deities who knew the value of the flesh, was complete and perfect. Cordy found that there was no room, even for thought, in the dark narrow space where two people who had travelled down the years to meet at last in this moment, came together with joy. Even when dubious and self-condemnatory thoughts were forced upon him he never swerved from the belief that this was his true marriage and his legal one a pale and forced adultery.

When the second child, James, was born and weaned and Ruth's mind turned again towards the daughter whom, since Digby's birth, she had desired, Cordy found it difficult to offer the crust of charity with deceptive conviction. For one moment something stirred uneasily deep in the depths of Ruth's comfortable complacency; but by summer she was pregnant again and disquietude slept. She was sure that it would be a girl this time, a girl with Cordy's slender build and big grey eyes. She would be beautiful as her mother had never been; through her the woman would savour the things that she herself had missed ... the sweethearts, the yearning young men, the white wedding and the flowers.

Ruth dreamed on and left Cordy free to lead his double life.

The paper, under his energetic control, enjoyed a period of prosperity. He canvassed subscriptions for it, sought advertisements, thought out ingenious schemes for making it attractive. He was prepared to work for twenty hours a day, if the work could be found, in order that Ruth might have a hired girl to help with the house and the children, might have the new brass bedstead that she coveted, might have rich clothes to deck her portly body. He owed her these things and was eager to meet his obligations. But the inner allegiance, the heart of care, the yearning hand of love, these were for the woman who would not accept so much as a load of logs from him.

"But why not, Susie? There's no danger. Half the town knew I was going to Abbott's mill. I carried twelve orders for people. And surely I wear out your fires enough, sitting by them."

"I don't care," said Susie, searching for her manly leather purse. "I don't want you to give me anything that money can buy. It's very easy, you know, to drift into being a kept woman."

He knew then that Susie had her soul-searching moments. He felt an agonising tenderness towards her.

Ruth's daughter, named Zillah for her mother, was born and proved a wailing puny child. Since disturbed nights were bad for Cordy, who had to work hard during the day, Ruth and her daughter moved into another room, sharing the new brass bedstead. Cordy was free to come home later and later, enter the office door and make his way in the furtive darkness to his lonely bed.

So it was almost twelve o'clock one night when he and Susie leaped from the couch before the dying fire in the "friendly" room at the sound of a fall and frenzied screaming overhead. Other shrieks followed the first and Susie, dragging her thin blue dressing gown about her, made for the door, hard followed by Cordy, feeling rather ridiculous as he struggled into his coat.

They reached the foot of the broad shallow stairs as a flame-enveloped figure came to the top, and throwing up its arms, stepped out blindly, stumbled, and with a final shriek, fell, still blazing, to the bottom.

Cordy ran to the pegs in the hall and snatched his

topcoat, a stout garment of frieze. He wrapped it about the little body and extinguished the flames.

The six boarders, ranging from little Erik Rosenbaum to big fifteen-year-old Madeline Dixon, were crowding down the stairs, and as Susie bent to examine the face beneath the coat one of the girls said: "It's your Richard, Mrs. Brede." And another added, as if by afterthought, "And the passage is on fire."

Richard had left his bed which he shared with another little boy to go to Susie's room for a drink of water from the carafe that stood by her bedside. Returning he had knocked over the small lamp that stood on a table at the turn of the passage. The window curtains and his nightgown had been caught by the licking flames.

It was a matter of a moment to tear down the curtains and crush out the fire while Susie carried Richard to the sofa of the sitting-room and covered the burnt limbs with a sheet. As soon as he had dealt with the fire Cordy ran out to the house of Dr. Miller, fortunately not far away. The doctor, informed through the window of the accident, hastened to dress and ran back with Cordy.

Susie devoted herself to the nursing of Richard who lingered for four painful days before he died: the school was dismissed. The six boarders returned to their six homes with six varying and highly-coloured stories with which to enliven the dullness of their family dinner tables. Three of them volunteered that it was Mr. Warren who put out the flames; two of them merely said "a man" did it; the sixth, a romantic little boy, claimed the honour as his own, but that story did no harm since his family had had previous experience of his inventive power.

Two of the mothers met on the following Sunday morning after service at the door of the church. They conferred together. The mother who knew the name of the man passed it on. Moreover she called her daughter away from her mild flirtation with a young farmer and said: "Madeline, what time was it that the accident happened to that poor little boy?"

"Nearly midnight," returned her daughter carelessly. "The clock struck before the doctor came." She went

132

back to her flirtation without knowing what a coil she had started.

Respectable widows who taught school shouldn't be sitting up at night with newspaper men while their children burn in their beds. The morals of a woman who sat up alone at that hour were open to suspicion. Oh me, oh my, Mrs. Satterthwaite, Mrs. Rosenbaum, Mrs. Dixon, will you be letting your young one go back to Jackson Street after this? Your Elsie, Mrs. Rutherford, is a noticing sort of child, has she ever said *anything*? Now I come to think of it it was Mr. Warren that first spoke of the school to my husband. And do you know, last autumn when Mr. Warren came to our place to get particulars about the church social I gave him some cuttings of my gipsy geraniums that he admired and I'll swear they were in the Jackson Street garden this year. I'd know them anywhere, they're the only plum-centered ones in the county. I didn't want to *start* anything, but since it's being said . . .

Throughout the week that followed Richard's funeral the gossip spread with the rapidity of a prairie fire. It withered good sense, consumed charity and made short crackling work of incredulity. It leaped, in the person of two good friends of Ruth's, into her parlour, and there, over the teacups, found fresh fuel. Cordy returned to supper to find his home ablaze.

He denied nothing, made no excuses. He said that he was sorry, in a flat and beaten voice that fanned Ruth's anger to greater heat. And once, when strange obsolete words, largely Biblical in origin, were hurled at Susie in denunciation, he said: "It wasn't quite like that, Ruth. The fault was entirely mine."

He let her talk herself into silence and then asked:

"What would you like me to do? You realise, don't you, that you have ample evidence for a divorce. I'll try to arrange about the paper so that you have enough to live on."

"Oh yes," said Ruth bitterly, "very fine. Very fine indeed. Then you can go to *her,* I suppose. Well, let me tell you that will never be. You're my husband and the father of my children. You haven't acted right by us, but

133

that don't alter the facts. Mind, I'm not saying that I shall take you back as a husband again," the flush on her round cheeks deepened duskily, "but a father my children shall have."

Cordy accepted the verdict quietly. And at least, he reflected, his immediate problem had been solved. He must get together some money for Susie and send her away; and he must work hard for the rest of his life to try and repay Ruth for the suffering he had caused her. The extreme bleakness of the prospect, the hollow dimness of life without Susie was terrible to contemplate, but it was, he told himself sternly, no more than he deserved.

He went as soon as possible to see Susie. He made no furtive visit on this occasion, but called at four o'clock in the afternoon. Susie was seated in the sitting-room, dispensing a rich and highly indigestible tea to a gawky twelve-year-old girl, Constance Summers, and a little swarthy boy, Johnny Baune. She rose, very thin and frailer than ever in her black dress, and saying: "Help yourselves, children. You pour out, Constance," led Cordy into the schoolroom. It was bitterly cold there, the fire had not been lighted and she shuddered as she poised herself on the edge of the ink-splashed table.

"I don't know what to do with that pair," she said. "None of the others came back, I can't really tell why. Old Summers drove up in his gig yesterday and deposited Constance and when I went out and shouted that nobody else was here he didn't take any notice. He's deaf as a beetle, of course. And then Mrs. Baune—or at least she calls herself Mrs. Baune—arrived with Johnny in the afternoon and said that he was such a different boy since he had been living with me that she thought she would send him back despite everything. More than that she would not say."

"I can tell you the rest," said Cordy. "Come here."

He took off his coat and spread it across the most comfortable chair in the room, saw her seated in it, wrapped the coat about her, and sitting on the table beside her, put his arm about her shoulders. He explained everything.

Except that her pallor deepened a shade and her eyes

134

grew dark with the widening of her pupils, Susie gave no sign of distress. When he had done she said:

"I suppose it was only to be expected, one day. But I'm so sorry for you, my dear. Your home and everything . . ." She reached up and touched his cheek with her hand. "Poor Cordy."

"I'm all right," he said. "Your school is finished, I'm afraid."

She straightened her shoulders with the little gesture that was all her own.

"Don't worry about that," she said. "I can start one in some other place. It would be best for me to go away, wouldn't it? Then I can start afresh and begin with all the cunning little economies that you have commended to me. And at night I shall lock the boarders in. Oh dear, thinking of that night has reminded me of Richard. I'll be all right in a moment." She walked to the window and stood there crying for a little while. Then she turned back and said:

"Listen, Cordy. Do you want this to be the end of everything between us? Be honest. Don't try to spare my feelings."

A desolate misery for which there were no words swept over him. He put his hand to his head and groaned.

"Ending it will be like ending life," he said at last. "But I can't think what else to do. Ruth is my wife; she wants me to stay, and there are the children to consider. If only there were more money, Susie; if I could leave her knowing that she would always have enough for her needs—and theirs—I shouldn't hesitate for a moment. We'd go clean away somewhere."

"That would be Heaven."

"But darling, my hands are tied. I've got to stay with the paper."

"I know, Cordy, I know. And I must go away. You needn't worry about me. I haven't . . . Richard any more; and I think I'll send Anna north to her people. She's longing to go, really. I'll easily get work of some sort. I don't think I'll try another school."

"I hate to think of you, drifting about the world, alone,

working. Oh, why haven't I been successful and made some money, so that I could look after you!"

"Because you're not that kind, darling. I shouldn't love you if you were."

"I've spoilt your school," he said irrelevantly.

"And I've wrecked your home. But I wouldn't do otherwise, if I had the chance again."

"I would. I would be far more careful."

She eyed him sharply. "Careful? What do you mean by that?"

"Not to be seen here; not to be caught as we were."

"Oh," there was a note of relief in her voice. "That. Yes, we should have been more careful. But I'm afraid this was bound to come, my dear. It's the normal ending of affairs like ours."

It was as though the last farewells had been already spoken; and although he stayed for some time after that neither of them found anything new to say. The ending was as inevitable as the beginning had been. They could only recognise the dire necessity, and endeavour so to act that the parting might not be made more painful.

With the utmost dispatch Susie disposed of the house and sold her furniture. Suddenly she was gone, and Cordy, aged both in mind and body, turned his face towards a future utterly devoid of hope or cheer. Even his thoughts of her were soured by the nagging sense of anxiety for her well-being; she was so little fitted for dealing with life alone.

But, after a short interval, her letters began to reach him. She gave the address of a farm at Saraset, and said that she had been very fortunate in finding a job as housekeeper to an old farmer who was extremely kind to her. It was a most comfortable place, and if only there were a chance of seeing Cordy sometimes she would have been perfectly happy.

The letters were gay, inconsequent and loving, just like Susie herself, and they cheered Cordy mightily.

He needed support at the moment; for the little scandal had borne two troublesome results. One was a sharp drop in the circulation of the paper. The community was still largely Puritan in feeling, with a leavening of Catholics, and Cordy's behaviour had shocked almost everybody. It was not that scandals were unknown in the district, but people had liked and trusted Cordy, respected his opinions and been influenced by his views. To discover that he was a common adulterer was far more painful than to learn that a neighboring farmer had made free with his hired girl. There was an unspoken, but very strong feeling, amongst the paper's readers that a man who could not manage his own life properly was unfit to retail reliable news, and positively unfitted to offer any comment upon it. Reader after reader cancelled his subscription: and their wives, who were more inclined to blame Susie and turn a lenient eye upon Cordy, were deprived of the pleasure of reading the newly instituted corner which Cordy had devoted to feminine topics. Advertisements and casual printing also fell off proportionately. Cordy had stayed by the paper, but the paper had deserted him.

The other result was Ruth's growing unhappiness. She never went out without returning with some report of having been slighted in a shop, or looked at pityingly by some woman or another in church or at a social gathering. One day she returned from an outing with a dark flush upon her round cheeks.

She flung off her outdoor clothes and flounced about the house, saying nothing definite yet obviously trying to draw attention to her mood. At last Cordy asked mildly what was the matter.

"Matter enough," she said, snatching at the opportunity of complaint. "I've lived in Craddock all my life and always been respected and well thought of. Now any jumped-up, dragtailed hussy thinks she can insult me."

Familiar sickness gripped Cordy's stomach, but he had no choice but to hear the story. Ruth had been to the Ladies' Sewing Meeting, and there, over the cups of tea at the end of the afternoon, that common ignorant foreigner, Mrs. Baune, had lamented loudly and deliberately, within the wronged wife's hearing, that Johnny, who had been such a good boy with Mrs. Brede, had reverted to all his old naughty ways since the school was closed. Susie

137

was the only person whom he minded at all, and Mrs. Baune openly deplored her leaving.

"I should be heartily glad if we could leave this town," Ruth finished. "I've lived here all my life and never thought to leave it; but there are some things that can never be lived down."

Unable, without hypocrisy, to offer sympathy, Cordy could only ask:

"Where would you like to go?"

"Anywhere, so long as Mrs. Brede had never been heard of there," said Ruth sharply; and was delighted to see, by the white line around her husband's lips, that she had wounded him.

Cordy did not take Ruth's suggestion of leaving Craddock very seriously. She was too deeply entrenched into the town's structure. The slights, he thought, were mostly in her imagination and when her first anger died away would cease to occur. So he threw himself into the work of resuscitating the paper, a difficult task, entailing great energy, a good deal of insult-swallowing and no little hypocrisy. And the results were not encouraging. Men who had taken the rival paper, the *Courier,* were quite satisfied with it, they said. They gave foolish reasons, the print was easier to read, it didn't use such hard words, it had advertised a corn-plaster that had worked wonders. Cordy found conviction oozing out of him as rebuff followed rebuff. Perhaps after all the *Times* had been a bad paper and people had just taken it out of sympathy or habit. Maybe the *Courier* gave folks just what they wanted and was the paper of to-morrow as the *Times* was of yesterday. Possibly it would not be a matter of leaving Craddock, but of being driven out of it in search of bread.

Within doors life was nearly as wretched. The hired girl, Bessie, who had been with them since just after Digby's birth, and whom it had given Cordy great pleasure to be able to provide for the lightening of Ruth's labour, gave notice suddenly. Ruth pressed for a reason and the girl said that, although she had no grudge, it was a good place and she had been happy in it, her mother insisted upon her leaving. It wasn't the right atmosphere for a young girl; so she would go at the end of the month, if Mrs. Warren pleased.

There were tears that night at supper to which Cordy returned after a dismally disappointing day of canvassing. And there were tears and worse shortly afterwards when Mrs. Rutherford gave her annual children's Christmas party. She had decided, for this year, to ask no children under seven, because on the previous occasion several of the youngest guests had been sick or tearful or otherwise destructive to the festive spirit. Ruth, not knowing this and too proud to ask, only knew that Digby was not invited, and she saw in his exclusion the beginning of a lifetime of social ostracism for her children. Even Bessie's leaving had not hurt her so much.

"When I was a child I went to all the parties," she said thickly through her tears. "I can see what it is, they're going to visit the sins of the father upon the children. They'll never have a chance at all. Cordy Warren, we *must* go away. We must find some place where this dreadful cloud won't follow us. And we must do it before the children begin to notice and wonder what is wrong with being a Warren."

She looked at the three infantile faces and burst into fresh floods of tears. Tortured Cordy could not point out that she was exaggerating and imagining things. It was his fault that this suspicion had come to poison her normally happy domestic and social life. He could only wince at each fresh implication and repeat that he was quite willing to leave Craddock. But even that sentence had to be bitten off short, for he dared not add: "If I can sell the paper." For the paper was unmarketable for the same reason that Craddock was uninhabitable. Oh God, what had he done!

When he approached O'Casey, owner and editor of the *Courier*, his last hope was shattered.

"Buy it!" exclaimed O'Casey, mouthing his cigar. "I don't need to buy it. Sure, it's walking across to me on its own two feet."

"That's only a temporary business," said Cordy. "It'll die down, and the *Times* will be as flourishing as ever."

"Don't you believe it. It's done." He pushed back his

hat and eyed Cordy narrowly. "I'm sorry for you, Warren, 'pon my soul I am. As a token of which I'll take the press if you like. Looks as if I'll need another at this rate. And I'll take any paper you have in hand. I might even print that corner of yours for the ladies, if you care to write it up. Three dollars a week, so long as you don't tell anybody you're doing it."

"Your generosity is going to lead you into trouble one of these days," said Cordy and went out of the office with a jaunty step that belied the leaden heaviness of his heart.

Well, he thought bitterly, as he made his way back to his own office, so much for pity. The weak did a great deal more harm than the strong, the kindly than the ruthless. He had needed only to push away that evening and say, politely but firmly, "That wasn't a proposal, Ruth. It was a statement of fact. I don't want to marry you!" Then he could have gone into lodgings and when Susie appeared they could have come to some sort of terms. But no, that moment's weakness had been the first step in an endless coil, and by it he had spoiled Ruth's life, ruined her home town for her and irrevocably wasted her patrimony.

He sat down in his office and took up a pencil, chipping away shreds of the cedar wood with his thumb as he thought. He had to get Ruth out of Craddock, she was obsessed with that idea now; and he had to get the money wherewith to do it. He sat there evolving wild schemes, all more or less dishonest, he who had never cheated anyone (save Ruth) of a penny in his life. But none of the schemes was capable of becoming action, he knew that even as he schemed. One thing however stuck out— O'Casey had gained virtual possession of the *Times;* it was O'Casey who must loosen his purse.

At last, moving like an automaton, he changed pencil for pen, threw back the lid of the heavy brass ink-pot, reached for paper. Adding word to word, slowly and experimentally as though to see how they looked when written down, he penned a request to Susie.

When, some days later, the answering letter came he fell upon it with more than usual eagerness. Yes, bless her, she had managed it. Dear, inconsequent Susie who couldn't work a simple sum, or effect an economy, or punish a naughty child, she had done exactly what he had asked.

He laid the enclosure aside and read Susie's own letter. It was just as usual, a spirited outpouring, a testimony of affection, laced with a nostalgic longing.

Presently he put on his hat and set out for O'Casey's office. He had decided upon a line of conduct and adhered to it like an actor who had been given a part upon which his whole future depended. In O'Casey's office he appeared to hesitate in stating his business, refused a chair and fidgeted round, picking up movable objects from O'Casey's desk, studying them and returning them while he made uneasy remarks about the weather, the latest news and local gossip. Finally O'Casey, exasperated, said:

"For God's sake, man, sit down and say what you've come for. Decided to sell me the press?"

"Well, no, O'Casey," said Cordy coming to a standstill midway between desk and window and looking uncomfortable. "The fact is ... Now look here, O'Casey. We've been rivals, but we've always been on good terms personally and I did have a feeling that I shouldn't do anything definite without mentioning it to you."

"Mentioning what?" demanded O'Casey impatiently.

"The offer I just had. You see, if I take it there's no doubt it'll knock you about a bit and I can't forget that you were very decent to me that time I ran out of paper. ..."

The simple softie, thought O'Casey, studying Cordy's mild, troubled face.

"What sort of offer is it?"

"Pretty good." He took the crisp folded paper that had been enclosed in Susie's letter and laid it under O'Casey's eyes. There, on the good headed paper of the *Saraset Sentinel,* beautifully written in shaded sloping script, O'Casey read that Mr. Jacob Brennan, hearing that the *Craddock Times* might be for sale, was interested in the purchase of the paper with a view to running it in collaboration with the *Sentinel* and converting it into a similar tri-weekly publication. A mass of figures, some of which showed that the well-informed Mr. Brennan, though conversant with Craddock's growing population, had not seen the latest returns of the *Times'* sale, followed, and he stated clearly what he thought the paper was worth to him.

O'Casey looked as stunned and startled as though Cordy had hit him heavily on the head with his own pewter inkstand.

"You see he says, 'Confidential' at the top. You wouldn't mention the matter to anyone, would you, O'Casey?" asked Cordy plaintively.

O'Casey brushed aside the request.

"What you going to do about this," he demanded.

"Well, I guess I couldn't leave the paper in better hands."

"Sure and you couldn't. But look here, old man ... what am I going to do? Why the Hell did he have to choose Craddock. How'd he hear about it?"

"They have people always on the look-out for a paper in temporary difficulties."

O'Casey stared down again at the letter, reading it from beginning to end as though in search of some flaw. But there was none. It was a very good letter, it showed what Cordy could do if he tried. The letter's author, tiring of his role, felt a strong impulse to cry out, "For God's sake make up your mind and put me out of my misery," but he sat still, looking at O'Casey with a gentle commiseration in his regard. O'Casey, glancing up, saw the look and was deceived by it. One of the best, Warren, straight as a gun-barrel, never been known to tell a lie or do a shady bit of business in his life.

"Look here," he said finally, "he musn't have it. A triweekly affair like the *Sentinel* would run the *Courier* off the road in six months. Suppose, Warren, I equalled his offer, would you take it? I'd better it if I could, but the simple truth is it's more than I would pay if it wasn't forced on me. How about it?"

Cordy, who had exactly matched the fictitious offer with the value of the *Times* before the fatal day of Richard's death, hesitated a moment, and then said, "Well, I suppose it's no business of mine who has it. Your money is as good as his. But are you sure that you want it? Do you think you can afford it? I'm afraid I want the money down, right away."

"You can have it. You can have it by ... Saturday. Will that do? And I must say, Warren, I'm obliged to you. After what I said the other day ... well ... lots of people wouldn't ever have mentioned the *Times* to me again."

"I suppose not. Well, that's settled then?" He rose to go, was half across the room and then whirled round.

"I've thought of something, O'Casey. We've got to be careful, or at least you have. If it ever gets out that you bought the *Times* over his head, old Brennan is capable of starting a new paper right here, under your nose and running you out of business, for pure spite. You know what he did to Bellamy. We don't want a repetition of that. I shall write and simply say that the paper is already disposed of. And you'd better never mention that you knew Brennan was interested, or that you only bought it to keep him out. See?"

O'Casey saw. It dawned upon him that his erstwhile rival was a damned clever fellow. How clever he could not rightly gauge.

Ruth's delight at the news broke down for a moment or two the frigid reserve with which she had treated Cordy since the trouble began. They were therefore able to discuss their destination with something approaching unity. Ruth was anxious (though at the moment she did not repeat this reason) to go somewhere so far away that no one in the new place could possibly have heard of Susie Brede. Cordy was also eager to disappear completely from Craddock. O'Casey would keep quiet for a time through fear of reprisals, but one day he would talk and it was within the bounds of possibility that he might learn that Jacob Brennan had nothing to do with that letter except to provide the paper upon which it was written. Susie, obedient to the last detail, had slipped it into her muff when she called at the *Sentinel's* office to place an order.

Ruth now remembered that a cousin of her father had once spent some years in California. Upon his return he had visited Craddock and drawn comparisons much in favour of the new country. The incomparable richness of the soil, the lovely climate, the opportunities that awaited men there, had all come in for their meed of praise. James Digby, indeed, had meditated going there, saying that there would be an opening for a paper. But he lacked incentive, his affairs were too muddled even then to allow him to leave Craddock and the cousin had eventually returned alone, saying that he would lay his bones there. California had sunk into Ruth's mind, a fabulous country of fruit and sunshine, and been forgotten. But it rose now, the stronger for its incarceration. And Cordy, to whom all places on earth, except forbidden Saraset, were the same, and who was anxious not to disturb this newly-made truce, was not hard to persuade. It meant cutting adrift from Susie entirely; even the frail link of their letters would be broken then, but he must not consider that; it was part of the price.

But it was not demanded. Two days before they left Craddock for ever, the south-going mail brought Cordy a dirty letter addressed in a completely unfamiliar hand. Almost, in his innocence, he opened it before Ruth; but at the last moment something warned him and he carried it to a place apart. There was a sealed packet inside, and a half-sheet of paper torn from a common exercise book.

Dear Mus Warren, he read, *Ms breed bin with me som time, she arsked me to sent this you see i done it i am soory about her she was a reale nice lady i done my best with her but it was no yuse. Yuor respektable servant alice Foster midwif.*

His trembling hands ripped the inner covering and his eyes, scanning the page as though every word were a lash laid on them by a whip, devoured its contents.

My own darling, I am writing this to-night, but I hope that in a few days time I shall be tearing it up and sending you quite a different letter. But I wanted to say goodbye to you in case anything happened. Mrs. Foster has promised most faithfully that she will post it for me.
You didn't know, did you, that when I left Craddock

I was in what they call an interesting condition. In this case I suppose it would have been a true description, lots of people would have been interested to know it. So you see, even if that fatal evening had never happened I should have had to go away sooner or later.

I am not sorry about it, and I should hate it if you were. If it gets born I shall love it dearly for your sake; even more than I loved Richard, because, apart from its own sake I shall love it for yours. But, having had Richard, I am rather afraid that things are not quite right with me, and that is why I am writing to you, Cordy darling.

Our love was the loveliest thing in our life, and I can say quite sincerely that I am content to have lived and to face death, having loved, and having been loved by, you. You have not only restored my faith in human nature, but, a little, in the chances of something going on after we are dead. I even made a poem about it the other day, imagine me! Here it is—

> *Once in the tale of Eastertide*
> *I only saw the Young Man dead*
> *Who saw the trees he loved so well*
> *Blossoming round Him as He bled.*

> *Now love, though coming bitterly*
> *Lights one bright candle in the gloom,*
> *I cannot think your lovely soul*
> *Could find an end in any tomb.*

I'm afraid it isn't very good and the punctuation is bad, as mine mostly is; but it shows you how I feel and I mean every word.

I deceived you about the farm, I'm afraid. It was shocking. The man was very mean and knew the whole Bible by heart; he could quote most furious passages in the most inapt circumstances. He even reminded me once when I was lighting the fire that Elijah's widow was gathering "two sticks" for her fire and if that was enough for her it should be for me! Imagine it. I said that I didn't know that Elijah was ever married so his widow was news to me. He nearly had a fit. When I had to leave I had a lot of interesting things about the whore of Babylon, whoever she was, said to me. Cups full of fornication and so on. I did manage to say that a cup full of anything would have been a treat.

Darling Cordy, I didn't mean to run on like this. I meant to write you a very loving dear letter that you could keep in memory of me if anything happened. I do love you darling and if I get to Heaven nothing will please me there until you come; if, as is more likely, I go to the other place I shall wait for what is known as my fellow sinner.

But perhaps, after all this bother, there is just a great peace.

Good night my dearest, darling Cordy. Thank you for all your sweetness to me. It made the whole of life worth while. I hope it hasn't upset yours too much. I do beg of you not to be sad about me. I wasn't any good really. It would have been better, perhaps, if I'd never come to Craddock. But I am glad I did, because indeed your love blessed me above all women.

Good night, and good night. I shower your dear face with kisses. I love you beyond all hope of expressing.

Susie

He crawled to the door of the denuded office and locked it. Then with Susie's letter held in one hand he put his arms across the desk and laid his head on them. Groaning sobs that seemed to tear his chest wrenched their way out of him, but his eyes were dry. This was a grief beyond the consolation of tears.

Ruth tried the door presently and called his name, but he gave no sign that he had heard her and she went away thinking that he had left the house.

When, later on, he emerged unobtrusively and began to concern himself with the last preparations of their leaving she was surprised to notice how white and drawn he looked. Evidently he minded leaving Craddock more than she had imagined. But although she fussed, almost in her old manner, about his physical welfare, she could not really pity him. After all, this thing had happened through his own fault. And the lurking thought that perhaps some of his depression might be due to a longing for Mrs. Brede prevented Ruth from offering sympathy by word or gesture. Cordy did not notice the omission. He knew that his heart had broken and that there was nothing that could comfort or interest or inspire him again. He felt that he had killed Susie as certainly as though he had knifed her and he would most willingly have died himself. But there was Ruth, and there were the three children—four strangers who looked to him for support: broken heart, bereaved body and tortured mind must be bent to their continued service. Somehow the weaknesses and failures of the past must be redeemed.

So he came to Fort Mason where opportunity came alongside him and, unseen, measured pace with him along the road.

Dave was eleven when the letter came; the first letter that had ever been known in the little house in the wilds of Pant Glas. His father took it in and broke the seal with a businesslike air and then hesitated.

"Now it iss then," he said in the sing-song Welsh speech that he had brought with him from over the border, "that the lad can show what it iss that he learnt in the school, yess!" He laid the sheet over Dave's clean-scraped plate and waited expectantly.

The thin sloping script, much flourished, did not greatly resemble the thick black letters of the horn-book from which Dave had learned to read in his two years of schooling, but tenacious perusal and a little guesswork at last yielded results and to his admiring family Dave read the letter. It was from his mother's uncle, Tom Lloyd, the apothecary. After inquiries about the family's health and well-being, it offered a home and good training in business to the apothecary's eldest great nephew. The London boys, he wrote, were idle and careless. He was tired of wasting training upon them; but to a country boy, of his own blood, who would, moreover, remind him of his well-beloved niece, Megan, the old man was willing to open his home and heart. His business flourished and he was no longer young, so the lad's future would be assured.

When the young voice had struggled through the rather pompous phrases Megan Glenny said, "That wass very goot, Dave. Go out now and feet the pigs."

"Oh, Mum, can't I know?" She shook her head, and Dave, well-trained in obedience, reluctantly left the kitchen.

148

- "I do not like it," said Megan, as soon as the door was closed. She reminded her husband of the time when a doubly bad season had reduced them to borrowing, and they had paid Dame Price—latter Dave's teacher—a whole chicken to write them a letter to Uncle Tom, begging his aid.

"Dit we get any answer? No," she exclaimed, voicing a ten years' rancour that it had been Evan's poor family, not her comparatively wealthy one, which had come to the rescue in those dark days.

"It iss but that he wants a cheap boy," she announced. "And why should it be our boy?"

But Evan Glenny, weary, at thirty-six, of toiling incessantly on his unproductive acres, saw in the offer the promise of an easier life for his first-born. It seemed to his simple mind that the ambitions which he had entertained when he sent Dave to the dame school and which had wilted in the chill blast of penury, might now be realised after all. No one with sense would hesitate if asked to choose between life as a poor farmer in Pant Glas, and life as an apothecary in the rich city of London. The boy would probably inherit the shop.

"When we are young," he pointed out, "we like strangers better than our own; but when we grow old the blood calls. Your uncle Tom has heard the call and answered to it. I think the boy should go."

Megan's protest that Dave was already very useful about the farm was countered by his remark that young Evan, only eleven months his brother's junior, was shaping well and would work harder when he was unable to leave everything to Dave.

The truth was that Evan Glenny, in marrying Megan Lloyd, had hoped great things from her family, well-known to be "warm". The hopes had not been realised, but Tom Lloyd's offer cancelled out all disappointments. And at last, seeing her husband so set upon Dave's going, Megan gave an unwilling consent. It was not for a mother to divulge her inmost heart or admit to favouritism, and never once during the discussions did she reveal that her most honest reason for opposing the plan was that Dave was more dear to her than all the rest of her brood put together.

So at last a letter, written by Dave himself and taken into Shrewsbury to post, accepted the offer; and a week later the boy followed it.

His own feelings were rather divided. His father's talk of the joys of the apothecary's life (of which he knew nothing) and of the splendours of London (which he had never seen) had fired the boy's imagination. On the other hand, in order to experience these joys and splendours he must leave his mother, whom he both loved and respected. She had in her a streak of hardness, of practical good sense which answered to something already within him; provided he was not the cause of it, he enjoyed seeing her in a temper. She was altogether more vital and fascinating than his dispirited father.

Once she was resigned to his going she became very anxious that he should make a good impression upon her relative, busied herself far into the night in setting his scanty wardrobe in order, and warned him that in London he would probably be required to eat with a fork. His father merely told him to remember his prayers and to be a good boy.

The young creature who eventually set out on the long journey to the metropolis was a wide-eyed, innocent thing with unlimited capacity for development. He was alert, rather above the average intelligence, well-grown for his years, and above all intensely malleable. Although he was eleven, no very formative influence had been at work upon him yet; he had learned to be active on the farm, to say his prayers—vague meaningless gabble for the most part— and to take a fairly thorough wash on Saturday night. Neither of his parents had had the time or the surplus energy to bother about Dave's soul or psychology; and had he stayed in their care he would probably have grown up to be a little less crushed than his father and a little less practical than his mother. As it was the trundling coach, making its laborious way from Shrewsbury to Worcester and from Worcester to Gloucester, and so eventually to London, carried him to quite another destiny.

Uncle Tom, lately so often discussed, met the coach, and Dave's first sight of him was disappointing. He was a tall old man, much bowed, with a suety yellow face upon which a network of purple veins had been woven. His brindled eyebrows met in a heavy bar across his eyes and the eyes themselves were like crumbs of coal, alert, observant and shifty. He was shabbily dressed in a heavy topcoat with many collars, the top one polished with grease, and his beaver hat was crumpled and worn bare in places.

In appearance he was far from being the wealthy relative who was to make Dave's fortune. But his greeting was exceedingly affable. He told Dave that he was a big boy for eleven and the very spitting image of his mother, and no compliments, however flowery or carefully chosen, could have pleased the boy more. They set out to walk to the New Lane where Uncle Tom's shop was situated, near the river at the back of the Strand.

The Lane was New in Elizabeth's day; name had outlived fact, and when Dave first set eyes upon it in 1812 he experienced his second disappointment within an hour. He had no pre-conceived notion of what an apothecary's shop should look like in London, but this was much inferior, to his eyes, to Mr. Bridger's shop in Shrewsbury, where he had once been taken by his father on a market day to have oil of cloves applied to a nagging tooth. It was a dark narrow building with an upper storey that oddly resembled Uncle Tom's eyebrows, and its windows, what with the tiny leaded panes and the accumulated dust of years, showed little of what lay within.

Mr. Bridger's had been sparkling bright and filled with glass globes in many brilliant colours, red and yellow, green and purple, so that Dave, seeing them for the first time had been reminded, for no reason that he could have expressed, of the lists of jewels in some parts of the Bible. The coloured globes were certainly there in Uncle Tom's shop, but one had to peer closely to see them; they, as well as the window panes, were obscured with dust.

The door was locked, and tied to the heavy handle was a dirty ticket, bearing in Uncle Tom's flourished script the

151

words, "BACK IN ½ HOUR". Uncle Tom slipped it into his pocket after turning the key, with the words, "That's what you are to save, my boy. In future when I go out you'll keep shop for me, eh?"

The words carried a pleasant suggestion of authority to the eleven-year-old mind, and Dave acknowledged it with the smile which was one of his chief charms. But Uncle Tom added:

"Not that I go out much. Well, come on in."

The interior of the shop was musty, as though there were not air enough to bear the burden of the many different scents that lay upon it. A big bell, swung on the door, jangled as they walked in, and another far away inside the house, answered it. Everywhere was very dusty and untidy.

Uncle Tom led the way to a narrow lobby behind the shop and hung his hat and coat on some pegs. Dave did the same with his.

Several doors opened off the lobby; Uncle Tom opened one of them and ushered Dave into a room unlike any he had ever seen or imagined. It was panelled throughout with wood, dark and polished with age. A good fire burned in a dirty ornamental grate. The carpet, also dirty, was of thick rich pile and there were several chairs with padded seats and headrests. Velvet curtains with silk fringes shut out what light the dirty windows at either end of the room admitted, and at least three of the little tables that stood around bore brass lamps and there were also several silver candelabra on the mantelpiece and the sideboard.

Near the fire, flanked on either side by a padded chair, stood a round table on which, spread on a filthy cloth, was a fine repast. Two cups, a silver teapot, a caddy and a milk jug stood on a big silver tray; there was a large ham, pink and succulent, a dish of sliced brawn, a jar of pickles and one of jam, a crusty new loaf and a slab of butter. Dave's eyes glinted. Not even at Christmas in Pant Glas did one find ham *and* brawn on the table. His heart, slightly depressed by the dingy appearance of the shop, rose again. Uncle Tom, apparently, was rich after all, and he spent his money on things that mattered. That was the explanation.

Tom Lloyd stooped and set a kettle over the fire.

"I expect you are hungry," he said kindly. "Help yourself to what you fancy and begin. I'll make the tea today, but in the future you can do it. So watch me as you eat."

Dave watched carefully. But he had leisure to note that his mother had been quite right. Both places at the table were laid with forks as well as knives.

"Well, now, my boy," said Uncle Tom, as the meal got under way, and Dave had twice scalded his mouth with the unfamiliar beverage, "what sort of a boy are you? Honest? Industrious? Teachable?"

To each adjective Dave, rather embarrassed, nodded his head slightly.

"Good," said Uncle Tom, "very good. But in business there's one thing more important than any of them. I wonder can you tell me what it is?"

Dave tried to remember his mother's maxims, and hesitated a moment between mentioning washing on Saturdays, and saying one's prayers regularly. Uncle Tom did not look as if he washed much at any time; his long ridged finger-nails were deeply margined in black; so Dave said:

"To say your prayers." He knew that he had chosen wrong immediately; for Uncle Tom's glinting eye opened wide for a moment and then disappeared amid mirthful creases.

"So you say your prayers, do you? Well, good enough. But it wasn't of them I was thinking. No, my boy. The best thing that anybody can have in business—especially a person like you, just beginning—is a still tongue in his head. You remember that, Dave, a still tongue! In business, more particularly my business, hardly a day passes that you don't hear or see something that somebody else would like to hear about. Fools talk and so they lose their business. Or they ask questions, which is nearly as dangerous." He bent forward and fixed Dave with a stare which was suddenly malignant. "I'm telling you right away, my lad, that if you start asking questions, or go tattling abroad anything you hear or see in *this* house, your name'll be Walker. Do you see?"

"I see everything except about my name," said Dave. "My name is Glenny, you know."

Uncle Tom gave a short bark of laughter. "What I meant was that you'll be walking back to Pant Glas. On the other hand, if you're a good boy and a help to me, and keep your eyes open and your mouth shut, your future is assured."

The very words that his mother had used in conveying to him the news that he was going to live with Uncle Tom. An assured future; such a change from the chances and uncertainties of life on a farm where too much rain or too little, an untimely frost or a vicious hailstorm, could place a whole family in jeopardy.

Full of food and good intentions Dave sprang up at the sound of the jangling bell.

"Can I go, please?"

"You can come with me, lad. But you can't go into the shop alone yet awhile. Why, you might poison somebody by mistake."

Perhaps in order to avoid just such a catastrophe, Dave's first duties in the shop were the sorting-out of the multitudinous bottles, flasks, boxes and packages, and the labelling of those which had temporarily lost their identities. Over the latter task he gained a wholesome respect for Uncle Tom's knowledge. The old man had only to apply his long purple nose to a paper package or a bottleneck, and sniff, in order to be able to say:

"Horehound, my boy," or "Balsam, Dave."

Occasionally a substance would have perished with age and even Tom could no longer name it; liquids would have evaporated, powders lost all their flavour. It was then Dave's duty to wash out the bottle and return it to the shelf which held clean ones, or to burn paper and contents in the living-room grate. When he had been a month in the shop, and had even, in an excess of youthful zeal, climbed upon a stool and shaken the dust out of the bunches of dried herbs that hung from the low ceiling, the place looked quite different. He was so anxious that Uncle

Tom should notice the improvement that he cleaned the window. But the expected praise was not forthcoming.

"When you know more about this trade, Dave," said his uncle, "you'll realise that people suffer at times from things that they don't like to mention. The dark helps them. I'm used to it; I can see them quite well. They can't see me properly, so they open their minds easier. No, no. I know you can't put the grime back, but when it gathers again, leave it."

It was interesting, at that stage, to speculate upon the diseases which needed the darkness as cover. In fact the whole of life with Uncle Tom was very interesting indeed. There were the different people who came into the shop, for example. Women leading coughing children, men with sore eyes, people who would thrust out a swollen thumb with the announcement that it was just a cut but it didn't seem to be doing too well, countless cases of toothache. These were all simple and straightforward. But there were others. Fashionably dressed men would swagger into the shop and ask, airily enough, for Mr. Lloyd. But when there was only the counter between them and Uncle Tom they would lower their voices and sometimes look askance at Dave, wondering whether he could hear them. They were mostly elderly gentlemen, Dave noticed, or, if they were young, pale and tired-looking. To them Uncle Tom's manner was a curious blend of the respectful and the jocular, and once the potion had been handed over there was frequently some laughter.

There were women too, of every sort, who came into the shop and would have none of Dave, and whispered. Then Uncle Tom's manner was fatherly and faintly reassuring. There was no laughter with such customers. And sometimes a woman would come in with more than usual secrecy and hold a lengthy confabulation with the old apothecary. Then, very often, Uncle Tom would have the fire built up quite late, and a kettle boiling; and he would tell Dave to hurry off to bed and not to mind if the bell rang. But there was never any sign of tea having been made, when Dave came down in the morning; and once, on sofa and floor there was a big wet patch. Dave asked about it; but Uncle Tom reminded him about not asking

155

questions. He was rather cross that morning and looked ill himself.

Exactly how and when all these secrets were made plain to him, Dave could not have told. His stock of sordid knowledge, too early acquired, grew gradually. Uncle Tom, tired of secrecy within his own household, betrayed a good deal, and some Dave merely guessed at and then confirmed his guesses by observation. But by the time that he was thirteen and had been in the New Lane for two years, he was familiar, not only with the ordinary facts of sex, but with the trials of lost potency and unwanted pregnancies.

· Uncle Tom seemed to have the measure of his knowledge; for shortly after the day when Dave had understood the reason for those late boiling kettles and midnight peals at the bell, his uncle, faced with unforeseen difficulty, called him down and let him assist at a particularly grisly operation.

A toe, relentlessly pressed by a shoe, develops a corn; a palm, regularly chafed, defends itself with a callus; and so this boy's mind, exposed while still young and malleable to the side of life with which most of his uncle's trade was concerned, grew tough and insensitive. The process was gradual. There was no moment when the innocence was stricken from his eyes; it faded gradually. His heart did not harden in a day; there would have been hope for it in that case; it hardened imperceptibly and from within, which meant that it hardened for ever.

For there was another side to all this sordid business. The old men handed over their guineas, gladly; the women brought out their hoarded or their borrowed coins. It was from them, not from the sore eyes, the cut thumbs and the toothaches, that Uncle Tom made his money. And no one, more particularly no one who had experienced the penury and the anxiety of the home in Pant Glas, could ever despise money. The regular, good meals, the great fires, the warm · bed, were all bought by money. As he grew older there were the outside pleasures that could only be bought with hard cash; new clothes, visits to the theatre, respect in shops, evenings in pleasure grounds; none of them yours unless you had money. He drew the obvious conclusion. Uncle Tom was right; anything was worth while if you had due recompense for it.

Without his knowing it, Tom Lloyd watched him closely. He had had apprentices before; some had been stupid, some garrulous, one or two possessed of undesirable scruples. But as the days progressed Uncle Tom congratulated himself over the inspiration that had made him send for Megan's son. Day by day he took him more completely into his confidence, matching each fragment of revealed knowledge with some material advantage.

His beautiful gold watch, for instance, was gained through a curious bit of business.

One morning the shop bell jangled, and as Dave looked up from the big flask of Lloyd's World Famous Cherry Cough Cure which he was preparing against the coming winter, a wave of subtle perfume met his nostrils. Just inside the doorway stood two female figures, one tall and buxom, one small and slight, both heavily veiled and plainly dressed. But the masterful way in which the taller of the two demanded to see the proprietor of the shop, and the tones of her voice, conveyed to Dave that here was a customer of no ordinary quality. He hastened to call his uncle.

To his surprise, after a few quiet words, Tom Lloyd led the pair to the inner room. As they passed the corner where he was working Dave stared at them covertly and saw that the smaller woman was crying quietly behind her veil and that the curls which showed at the back of her neck, between the bow of the veil and the collar of her cloak, were of a peculiar shade of reddish gold.

They were gone for some time; and when Uncle Tom ushered them through the shop again, his manner was unexpectedly servile. Later in the morning Dave saw him take out the bunch of keys that never left his pocket and pull from under his bed the heavy iron-bound box, which, Dave knew, held his savings. There had been a time when he had kept the box a secret from his nephew, but that, like other things, was now a secret no more. He was rubbing his thin veined hands together in a pleased manner when he emerged from the bedroom.

Nothing happened for two days; but on the evening of the third day, Uncle Tom, after supper was over, said:

"Dave, I want you to go out for me. You know Croome Square, don't you? You've delivered things there for Lady Fawcett. Well, those houses back on to Cotton Lane. There's a door in the wall, two doors down from the 'Shepherd and Dog.' I want you to wait by that door until a young woman comes out. She'll know you by this white scarf. Put it on and put it well up against your chin so that it shows in the dark. You needn't say anything. Just bring her here as quickly as possible. That's all."

The night was foggy and the few lights in the streets were hung about with golden haze. Cotton Lane, save for the lights in the windows of the "Shepherd and Dog" was as dark as a tunnel. The door at which Dave was to wait was quite a long way down the lane, and set in a high blank wall over which some bare tree-tops showed. It was cold standing still and he kept warm by beating his hands and stamping his feet and walking briskly to and fro, ten yards to one side of the gate and ten yards to the other. His back was towards the gate when he heard the scream of the rusty hinges. He flung round suddenly and the young woman whom he had come to meet gave a little gasp of terror or surprise. He said, "It's all right," and she came towards him, rather timidly, lifting her eyes towards the white scarf. Dave at sixteen had reached his full height and the girl's head hardly reached his shoulder.

She laid one small gloved hand on his arm, and Dave awkwardly bent his elbow, so that the little hand lay in the crook of it. She was still veiled but he could smell the same perfume and realised that it had haunted him for three days.

Unfamiliar and indescribable feelings coursed through his body, beginning at the spot where the little hand lay pressed between his arm and his side, and running to the remotest cell of his being. He began to feel his breath shorten, as though he were walking too fast, or carrying something too heavy. He was obliged to open his mouth in order to breathe without snorting.

He knew all the short cuts and they were at the door of the shop in a few minutes. Neither had spoken. But on the doorstep, the girl drew back and said in a tearful voice, "I'm frightened." Another curious feeling shot through hitherto unused channels in Dave's being and he could feel her fear in his own flesh; it was almost as though he were threatened too. He said awkwardly and without much assurance, "There's nothing to be frightened of," and set the key in the lock. Uncle Tom seldom stayed alone in the shop after darkness without locking the door.

He had heard their entry and was waiting at the door of the living-room, which was brightly lighted.

"Come in, my dear," he said in his most fatherly manner, and to Dave, "Thank you, my boy. You can lie on your bed, but don't undress. I want you to take the young lady home. We shan't be long."

The door closed and Dave went upstairs. He folded back the top cover of his bed, stretched himself and drew the cover back over him. He lay still, but his mind was wide awake. For the first time in his three years of knowledge he found himself wondering about what was going on downstairs. The facts were known to him now, he had shared in the business, but his mind had never been exercised on behalf of the patient before. It was now. He could see the tilt of her head as she looked for the reassuring evidence of the scarf; feel the little hand tucked into his arm; smell the perfume and hear the terror in the voice as it cried, "I'm frightened." A light sweat broke out on him, so that he pushed back the cover and was immediately gripped by the cold of the room.

Time passed very slowly. The house was so quiet that he could hear the ticking of the grandfather clock in the lobby below; but though he strained his ears he could hear nothing else. When the clock struck at last, shattering the silence, he counted the strokes. Eleven.

Then suddenly there was a patter of slippered feet on the stairs and a shrill voice, not immediately recognisable as Tom Lloyd's, calling, "Dave. Dave. Come here at once."

He tumbled from the bed and blundered out on to the stairs. Half-way up stood Uncle Tom, a candle guttering in his shaking hand, his face a sweat-drenched mask of dismay. He said in a whisper, as though they were not alone in the tall house, "She's dead, Dave."

They went into the brilliantly lighted room together.

Between the lamps and the candles and the great fire the room was overpoweringly warm. Everything was in disorder, except the body of the dead girl, which lay on a sofa near the fire, covered from chin to ankle by a coloured shawl. Her head, turned a little sideways, made a hollow in one of the silk cushions and against the pale smooth cheek those reddish curls clustered caressingly.

"Are you sure?" asked Dave.

"Quite sure," said Uncle Tom testily. "The thing is what are we going to *do?*"

"It wasn't your fault, was it?"

"Not in the least. But do you think her Ladyship will believe that? And even if she did, think of the scandal. Of course you don't know who that was. It's a trifle late for introductions, but you escorted here the Lady Eleanor Fitzmark, younger daughter of the Marquis of Inchwater. And there she lies, dead on my sofa. What the hell are we to do?" His voice rose hysterically.

Dave went to the ornate sideboard and took out the brandy bottle and a glass, and then, after a moment's hesitation, a second glass. Uncle Tom, always generous about food and drink, had always kept the brandy for his own consumption; but to-night was an abnormal occasion and Dave himself felt shaken and a little unreal. He splashed out a generous measure of the liquid and thrust the glass into the old man's shaking hand. He tasted his own smaller portion, but, not liking it much, set it aside.

Uncle Tom drank his as though it had been water. He shook a little less violently, but he did not seem much restored. He crouched in his chair by the fire, which was beginning to burn hollow at the middle, and every now and then his eyes rested upon the face of the dead girl and then suddenly turned away again. At last Dave was compelled to break the silence.

"What exactly are you afraid of? The law?"

"Oh no indeed. That doesn't bother me. It's that I don't know what to do. You see, this was a tricky matter. The young lady was to have been married next month to Lord Sheer. Less than a week ago her mother—it was the Marchioness herself who came that morning, not trusting anyone else—discovered her condition, and also that she

160

had been having an affair with the groom. They asked my help. It didn't seem dangerous. Why on earth she had to die I can't understand. Lots of drabs have been in a worse case than hers, and walked out of that door as right as rain . . ." He broke off and cast a malignant, resentful look at the unanswering dead as though he had been wronged out of spite. "Now see, Dave. If we leave the body here until it's sent for, or if we take it back, you and I, and put it over that wall into the garden, either way there's going to be talk and the whole story will get out. And the Marchioness will never forgive me. That's what I fear, my boy. These nobs can ruin you overnight if they take a grudge against you. Why, she'd say I bungled it and take out all her own shame and confusion on me. I'll have to leave the place. I'll have to be out of this before morning."

He got up, shaking again with a violence that rattled his few remaining teeth; but Dave pushed him back into the chair and filled his glass again.

"Listen, Uncle Tom. . . . What would happen if we said that we never saw her? That she never came here again, eh?"

"That might serve. But there's that, my boy, that." He indicated the sofa.

"That might go in the river, Uncle Tom."

The glint which had been extinct in the old eyes, flickered into life again. "Naked," he said, as if to himself, "with nothing to show who it was. It might work, Dave, it might work. And if the great lady's daughter is missing, well, that's her trouble. It's worth trying. We can't be in a worse fix than we are, can we?" He seemed to beg Dave for reassurance. And then, draining his glass, he sprang to his feet, active and strong again.

They set to work.

It was very late before the job was over, and later still before Dave's overstrained nerves permitted him to sleep. In the morning he was disturbed from the very depths of unconsciousness by the ringing of the bell, not the one attached to the shop door, but one controlled by a bell-pull outside. He started up, but seeing by the greyness of his window that it must still be extremely early, lay down again, thinking that he had been dreaming. He lay for a moment between sleeping and waking; and the bell sounded again, an urgent impatient peal. Dragging on his trousers and thrusting his bare feet into his boots he clattered downstairs. Uncle Tom was already in the lobby, wrapped in a thick dressing-robe. His thin grey hair was ruffled and the candle that he carried threw fantastic heavy shadows about his eyes and nostrils and hollow temples.

"It'll be about last night," he whispered. "Mind what you say," he added as Dave opened the shop door; as though it were his plan, not Dave's, which had been carried into action in those dark hours.

Against the faint grey light in the street was outlined the tall majestic figure which had accompanied the little shrinking one on that first visit. She crossed the threshold swiftly and walked into the shop without speaking to Dave.

"Good morning," he said, closing the door and following her. "My uncle and I are early too. We were anxious to know what had happened. The young lady never came."

"What?" exclaimed the lady, coming to a full stop and beginning to wring her hands. "What are you saying? Take me to your uncle at once."

In the unusually tidy room at the back Uncle Tom had set light to the dry faggot in the grate and the flames were already leaping and crackling.

He stood up stiffly and said, "Good morning, ma'am. What happened? Did the young lady's nerves fail?"

"Was he speaking the truth then? Did she not come here? Oh my God! What shall I do?" She put her hand to her mouth and made a desperate effort at self-control.

"Pray be seated," said Uncle Tom, pushing forward a chair; but Lady Inchwater ignored it. Whirling round to Dave she said, "Did you go? To the right gate? Did you wait?"

"He did," said Uncle Tom.

"Let the boy speak for himself."

"I waited until eleven o'clock at the second door from the 'Shepherd and Dog' in Cotton Lane," said Dave. "I wore the white scarf. But the young lady who came here on

Monday never came out at all." Perhaps it was because the lady was veiled that he was able to look her straight in the face with an air of utter candour.

"Did anyone come out?"

"Well, yes," said Dave. "But not that young lady."

"How could you tell?"

"Because the one who did come out was dressed like a servant. And she had a little bundle. And there was a man with her."

"Ahh." The lady's escaping breath sounded like the air rushing from one of those blown-up bladders that little boys kicked about the streets. She now condescended to sit upon the chair that Uncle Tom had pushed forward, and staring straight ahead of her, muttered, "This is terrible. This is the worst thing that ever happened." She sat stricken for some minutes and then, turning back to Dave, rapped out:

"What kind of man was he?"

"I didn't notice him much. You see, as soon as I saw them I knew that they weren't ... that the young lady wasn't the one I went to meet. So I wasn't very interested. And it was foggy as well as dark. But he was ordinary looking and he wore leggings."

"That's it," said her ladyship. "Wretched girl, she took advantage of having the key and the five minutes' freedom. Dear God, what will her father say?"

Tom and Dave stood silent. And after a moment the lady seemed to realise that she was exposing a private grief to indifferent eyes. She manipulated her handkerchief under her veil and dabbed at her mouth and her eyelids. Then, slowly and brokenly she got to her feet.

"I need hardly say—not a word of this. We shall keep the secret for our part; and if so much as a breath is heard we shall know how it originated. I do not wish to threaten. . . ." But the denial, spoken in that voice was threat enough.

"Ma'am," said Uncle Tom earnestly, "our lips are sealed. We have nothing but sympathy for you. And by the way, the fee, paid in advance and alas, never earned." He held towards the lady the little netted purse, heavy with gold. She brushed it aside as though it had no value.

"Keep it for your silence, and for meaning well," she said, her voice heavy and flat again.

Dave accompanied her to the shop door and saw her hurry away through the brightening dawn.

"And all the shiners left with us in the bargain," said Uncle Tom, weighing the little bag in his hand. "Dave my boy, you're a genius. I shan't forget this day."

Dave rather hoped that Uncle Tom might empty out a shiner or two at least as a sign of his appreciation. For his uncle, although generous enough over food and clothing, was inclined to ignore that the needs of a growing boy were different from those of a child. But the money went back into the iron box. Next day, however, Uncle Tom left Dave in the shop for an hour, and when he returned, laid in the boy's hand a fine new watch and chain.

In the winter following this episode Dave found himself growing restless. Life in the shop, hitherto so interesting, began to pall. Uncle Tom, as though aware of the fact, would often hand out some trivial sum and bid the boy get out and enjoy himself. And Dave did so, sampling in the course of time most of the pastimes and pleasures of the London nightlife at that period.

One evening he found himself in Bully Baynes' Academy of the Fancy, and Bully himself, greatly condescending, went over to him, asked his age and told him he had a fine pair of shoulders. Dave at that time was easily flattered, professed himself interested in the noble art of self-defence and was soon taking lessons at sixpence a time. Bully proclaimed him a "natural", nimble on his feet and with more weight above the equator than below. Actually he was a born fighter, courageous, unimaginative and cunning. Before summer he had ceased to pay for instruction, but was instead receiving trivial sums in return for acting as practice opponent to the professionals whom Bully trained.

The atmosphere of the Academy, and the company that he found there, hastened the deterioration which life in the shop had begun. It rendered both mind and body a little more insensitive. To Bully and his associates nothing was sacred, no trick contemptible provided it went undiscovered, no swindle deplorable if it remained unexposed.

And in this circle, too, everything was judged by its monetary value. Even Bully, who had a certain disinterested love of his profession and recognition of a good performance, would prefer a crooked fight that won him money to a clean one which lost it. So Uncle Tom, with his "anything for money" motto, was not an isolated figure; he could be seen in his multitudes wherever men were gathered together.

But greed and brutality, though often allied, are not indivisible. Greed may be curbed, in certain natures by the fear of either inflicting pain or of suffering it. This fear Dave now cast aside for ever. With every pain that he dealt or received his greed became more firmly established and his ruffianly tendency more deeply rooted. By the time that he was twenty he was known, even in the rough circles which he frequented, as "a hard nut".

One thing might possibly have saved him.

There came into the shop one afternoon, a girl in a garish crimson dress and a wide hat tied with ribbons of a colour which to a sensitive eye clashed badly with the crimson. But Dave, moving forward to serve her, was conscious only of the big bright brown eye which the tilted hat revealed upon one side and the wide mouth painted in yet another shade of red. As he leaned towards her she lifted the brim of the hat and revealed that her other eye was almost closed and lay in a great circle of many differing hues.

"Got anythink for a black eye?" she asked in a soft, wheedling tone. "I tried a bitta steak d'reckly it was done but it weren't no use."

She was very short and she looked up into his face with a tilt of the head which reminded him of the golden-haired girl whom the river had taken, and as he leaned forward to inspect the damaged eye the strange currents began to move in his blood again.

"There's witch-hazel and elderflower water. That's good for bruises," he said. And conscious of the effort required he turned to the shelf where the remedy—a popular one in that quarter—stood ready in small phials.

"But will it look awright by ternight?" asked the girl

165

with anxiety in her tone and in her one eye that was capable of expression.

"I couldn't promise that," said Dave, with unusual frankness.

"I don't care what it's like underneath," she persisted. "I want it to look awright."

"Then you'd better try grease-paint. What the actresses use, you know. Lucky we've got some in stock." Once more he turned back to the shelves.

"Cor!" said the girl, examining the stick that he offered, "I dunno what to do with this. My complecshun's natural." She preened a little as the painted lips uttered the lie, and Dave, wondering at himself, said:

"I can see it is."

"Can you reelly, dearie? You're a bright one. Tell you what. Lemme come round there under the lamp and you fix my old pudding and pie for me, eh? You'd make a better job of it."

Not exactly unwilling, but hoping that Uncle Tom would not enter and catch him so engaged, Dave lifted the flap of the counter and let her into the inner sanctum. There, perched on his stool with the hat in her hand, she lifted her face to the light with the calm assurance of one who realises that but for an unavoidable accident her appearance is beyond reproach. Under the rouge and powder her face was smooth and young and unblemished; the undamaged eye was bright and clear; even her teeth were intact and white between the reddened lips.

Rather timidly Dave applied the grease-paint, even asking whether it hurt as he rubbed it in.

"Nothing much. I can bear it," said the girl. "Anything rather than go out looking like a bad plum."

"You can't see the black now," said Dave at last. "But it looks a bit shiny. It needs powdering. I've got some. We generally sell both together."

"Oh don't bother," said the girl. She lifted the flounce of her skirt and from the top of her stocking dragged out a lump of dirty swansdown, folded over to preserve its powdery surface. She offered it to Dave, who did not notice its dirt, but only that it was warm from contact with her body. He powdered around the eye with meticulous care and brushed the surplus powder from brow and lashes. Then he gave back the swansdown and the girl replaced it, performing the action leisurely and giving a good display of a shapely leg encased in a coarse white cotton stocking.

"Got a glass?" she asked.

There was none in the shop, so Dave galloped upstairs and brought down the mirror before which he shaved each morning.

The girl, who had evidently expected a miracle, studied his handiwork critically.

"The colour's awright,'' she said rather grudgingly, "but it still looks sorta shut up."

"I didn't pretend that paint would open it, did I?" Dave asked. "The swelling may go down quite suddenly. Anyway I did my best."

"Aw! I know yer did," said the girl, flashing a smile at him and putting on her hat coquettishly before the mirror which he still held. "You're a angel outa Heaven, that's what you are," and leaving the scarlet strings dangling, she leaned forward over the mirror and kissed him full on the mouth. Leaning back again, she tied the bow under her round chin, eyeing him provocatively the while.

All his pulses were racing; for a moment he could not speak for breathlessness. Silently he put down the mirror, lifted the counter flap and stood aside for her to pass. Then, suddenly, he gasped out:

"What's your name?"

"Alice."

"When'll I see you again?"

"Next time somebody blacks my eye." She saw him stiffen with offence and added: "I'll look in. I live about 'ere. Goodbye, and thanks ever so much."

The door-bell jangled and she was gone.

It was some weeks before he saw her again; and the fever which had heated his blood was dying and needed deliberate evocation of memory to recall it. He had left Uncle Tom with his paper and his pipe and his glass, and was going out himself at about half-past nine in the evening. Before leaving the step he reached backwards to make sure that the key had turned—it had been rather tricky of late—and finding the door still unlocked, he swore and took out his key again to make good the omission. As he did so there was a patter of feet in the alley, followed by a heavier tread; a soft light body threw itself upon him, pressed against the still unlocked door and almost fell into the shop.

Thinking that it was some new trick of thieves, Dave followed the stranger within, pushed the door and locked it with the key that was still in his hand. It was dark in the shop and he put out his hand blindly. His hard grip closed on soft material with soft flesh beneath it, and the weight of his clasp brought forth a frightened whimper. A woman.

He said: "Stand still. The door is locked," and walked to the door that opened on to the lobby where a candle was burning. He called: "It's only me," in case his uncle had been disturbed, and returning with the light, closed the lobby door behind him.

The candle glow showed the face of Alice; not the perky assured Alice who had said: "Next time somebody blacks me eye," but a pale dishevelled Alice, breathless and wide-eyed from terror. She bent over and touched the toe of her shoe, sure remedy for a stitch in the side. Then, straightening herself, she gave him a rather watery smile.

"Thank God you was there," she said, with feeling. "He'll do for me yet. You was all I could think of."

"Sit down," said Dave, hooking forward the customers' stool with his foot. He went to the back of the counter and poured out a little measure of Lloyd's Raspberry Cordial, a restorative highly esteemed by ladies who thought brandy vulgar. Uncle Tom made gallons of it in the raspberry season, steeping the ripe fruit in cheap raw brandy for two months and then drawing it off into elegant flagons with fancy tops.

Alice, who knew and liked brandy, drank her portion at a gulp and gasped: "Cor! That was good. I feel better awready." Her smile grew more certain and her hands began to flutter over her hair, her hat and the torn flounces of her bodice. "I bet I look a guy," she announced. "But so would you, so would anybody that'd just got outa that grip. Lucky to be alive, that's what I am."

"Why? Who is he?"

Alice's expression tightened. Dave could see her thinking that it was wiser to name no names.

"Damned great bully," she said. "And I ain't working for 'im no longer. No, not if he kills me I ain't. Do yer think he's outside?" Terror reigned on her face again.

"It doesn't matter where he is," said Dave boldly. "You're with me now. And I put Bully Baynes' best man to sleep in the second round the night before last. You're all right with me."

"Then let's go out, eh?" said Alice, recovering fast. "Let's go to Balmer's. Fetch us that glass again, lovey."

"There'll be a glass there; if I go in again my uncle'll hear me. I'm supposed to be out now."

" 'Fraid for 'im to see you with a lady?" asked Alice.

"I'm not afraid of him at all. But he'd ask questions and stop us."

"Awright. Come on then."

Once outside the door, her manner changed again and she looked fearfully up and down the street, and clung to Dave's arm in such a fashion that he would have been severely handicapped if any attack had been forthcoming. But none was, and they reached Balmer's safely and there spent three happy hours, drinking and eating and being entertained by a young lady, "especially brought over from Paris," who after several gymnastic feats which included touching each ear with the toes of her opposite foot, threw off all her clothes in a simulated fit of temper and stood for one breathless moment mother-naked save for a pair of red shoes with studs of glass in their heels.

"She ain't much to look at reelly," said Alice when the thundering applause had died down.

"I bet you look much better," said Dave, and felt his blood roar again, partly at his own daring and partly at the vision the words evoked.

Under her lashes Alice regarded him. Green as green and raw as raw, she would bet. But young things were

169

generally generous; and he was old Lloyd's nephew and everyone knew that old Lloyd was made of money.

"Wouldn't you like to know?" she whispered.

The tumult could no longer be borne. He stumbled to his feet. "Come on," he said.

She took him up to her room, a narrow apartment under the eaves of a tall grimy house two streets away from the shop. A wide dingy bed took up most of the space, and in the remainder Alice washed and dressed and ate. She lighted two candles, held them sideways until they spilled little silver pools of grease and then anchored them in the pools, one on the mantelpiece and one on the table. She rummaged about and at last discovered the better part of a pint of porter in a brown milk jug. She gave Dave half of it in a sticky cup and drank her own from the jug.

Then, beginning with her hat and ending with her stocking, she tore off all her clothes, and to any eye but a prude's looked far more beautiful without them, for they were cheap and tawdry and soiled, while her body, not marked by its trade or the hand of time, was smooth and rounded and beautiful.

"There! I told yer," she said. And Dave, with hardly a glance, blew out both candles and closed his hands on that desirable flesh.

To both it was a night of revelation. Alice, who had feared clumsiness and shyness or the youthful ardour that overreaches itself, was pleasantly surprised. Dave was transported. The restlessness that had been at work in him for almost three years was assuaged now, the goal reached, the journey understood.

When he slipped into the shop in the early hours of the morning it was with the confirmed intention of asking Uncle Tom either to pay him a wage so that he might make a home for Alice somewhere, or to permit him to bring her into the house as his wife. Joy such as this night's must be bound down and made his for ever, for a future without it was inconceivable.

For just an hour or two, the time between his return to the shop and the moment when he made his proposition to Uncle Tom, he regained something of his former self. The callous young apothecary, the hard habitué of Bully's, were lost in something that faintly resembled the innocent boy who had come out of Pant Glas.

The resurrection was of very short endurance. Uncle Tom was as amiable and as understanding as ever. He offered no shred of opposition to the scheme. He was wily enough to know that to have done so would have hardened Dave's determination and taken all the value from the argument which he was about to produce.

"Certainly," he said, "certainly. You can do exactly what you like, Dave my boy. I'll give you thirty-five shillings a week, you're worth that to me; or you can bring the young lady here and make a home for you both and in that case I'll give you fifteen, because, you know, a married man has various expenses even when his roof and his food are assured. Maybe you'd be happier on your own. You must think it over and decide."

Dave had, for some obscure reason, been prepared for opposition from his uncle. They had lived together very amicably for almost nine years, and he knew quite well that he would have resented it if Uncle Tom had proposed either to break up the ménage, or introduce a third person into it. The attitude of friendly understanding surprised him and put him off his guard.

"Of course," mused Tom Lloyd, thoughtfully, "some men are cut out for matrimony, and some are not. If you are you can't be happy out of it—that is witnessed by the fact that men who have been most unhappily married will marry again if the woman who had made them unhappy happens to die. But if you aren't made for matrimony, born and reared for it one might almost say, then there's no more unhappy state on earth. Now for myself, I should hate it. Always to be responsible to someone else for your goings and comings; to give some woman the right to pry into your most intimate affairs, to spend your money and pledge your credit and even decide what you should eat for breakfast—why, I know a man whose wife can't abide the smell of onions or the sight of tripe. No ... I couldn't have borne it. So I kept out. Maybe you're different. After all your father is a great family man; and the Bible does say something about 'blessed is the man who hath his quiverful,' doesn't it? So I suppose your father is blessed far beyond your poor lonely old uncle, eh?"

In those few gentle sentences he had managed to call up a series of unpleasant pictures and the final one brought to mind the kitchen at Pant Glas, with the six young Glenny children round the table. The scanty food, the bickering, the admonishments. The Bible might say what it liked, Uncle Tom's state was far more enviable than his father's.

"I don't know which sort of person I am," he admitted with a rueful grin. "But I suppose I shall find out. All I know at the moment is that I want Alice."

"Which is rather a different thing, if you'll forgive my saying so, from wanting to marry her. And if you'll extend your forgiveness for a moment more I would perhaps take the liberty of adding that there *is* a little danger of the two things becoming confused. The good lover is not necessarily a good husband—or wife, as the case may be. Take me for example. I have have no more dispensed with the Alices of this world than I have with the other good things. I was reckoned a good lover in my day"—his smile had a veneer of infinite salacity—"but as a husband I should have been a calamity to some poor woman. I'm so selfish. I liked to have my fun, mark you, but I liked my glass and my pipe, and a quiet hearth." He managed to imply that these comforts were incompatible with the married state.

Throughout the days that followed, while professing an interest in Dave's intentions, asking him whether he had decided to live at the shop or elsewhere, asking him when he intended to marry, and where, he contrived to make the boy understand that only fools bothered with the ceremony; the clever ones were fly enough to get away with the bait while leaving the trap unsprung.

Dave's good intentions were not strong enough. Moreover he had already tasted the bait; and although it was good and he had enjoyed it he was in a position to reflect that the trap, so far, existed only in his mind. Alice had not seemed to expect or even hope for marriage.

The days went on, with the matter still unmentioned—save to Uncle Tom. And as Dave hesitated the moment when he might have bound Alice to him irrevocably, passed. They met often in that high cluttered room, and though each meeting fired Dave anew with a desire for sole possession, which only his doubts prevented him from making a fact, Alice's first pleasure and surprise were blunted. For a raw youth he gave a surprisingly good performance; as old Lloyd's nephew he would have been a desirable husband. But as a lover, possessive and jealous, he wearied her. She had her fun to find and her living to get; why should one behave like a wife while culling none of the advantages?

Dave, with his board and lodging found and his irregular sums from his uncle—amounting to about ten shillings a week, a considerable sum in those days—might have bribed her allegiance for a time, had he resigned himself to a temporary affair. But behind his own doubts and the regularly injected poison of Uncle Tom's philosophy there still lurked the ghost of his good intention. One day, not immediately, but when he felt a little more sure of himself, he might marry her; and they would live in the tall house where the old man's satirical eyes could watch his behaviour in the trap. So furtively, and hardly admitting the fact to himself, he began to hoard a portion of the money he made. He made Alice only trifling presents and took her only to the humbler places of entertainment.

The bully from whom she had fled screaming returned, promising amendment; half-fearful, half-fascinated, she took him back, and one evening Dave, appearing to keep a rendezvous with her, found the door locked, though from within there came sounds eloquent of the room's occupation. Alice's brittle cheerful voice and the deeper tones of a man reached the boy through the thin door.

He hammered upon it. And as his fist beat the panel he knew, beyond all doubt or cavil, the pangs of jealousy and (so strange are the ways of the human heart) the agonies of love betrayed. When the door opened roughly and showed the beetle-browed, heavy-jawed face of the man who had Alice's fickle nature in thrall, the vascillating victim of Tom Lloyd's insidious tongue was suddenly decided. To the brusque question: "What the hell are you doing here?" he returned a bold answer, "I've come for Alice."

The man laughed. "You're unlucky then," he said, and

173

would have closed the door without further parley, but Dave's foot was already in the opening and his hands were braced against the panels. One heave against the pressure of a figure unprepared for such action and he was within the room and the door clapped to behind him.

"Here, here, what is all this," protested the man, still unroused. "Don't you know your manners? What do you want?"

"Alice is coming with me to the Spring Gardens."

"Ho no, she ain't. She may have said so. But I'm back now. You be off, my young cockerel."

Turning to Alice, he said, still jocosely:

"Who *is* this young feller?" The mock pleasantry of the question was insulting.

"I'm going to marry Alice," said Dave loudly.

"That's the first I've heard of it," said the man, all the humour and patience wiped from his manner. "Now then, you young devil," he added, turning to Alice, "what's all this about?"

Three weeks ago Alice might have snatched at the promise of those defiant words, but Steve had been back for three hours and Dave had hesitated too long. She laughed now.

"Don't mind him, Steve. He's only fooling. I seen him a bit, that's all. You bin away a long time."

"Too long," said Steve sombrely. "Here, you, clear off afore you and me get wrong."

Dave had misunderstood Alice's attitude. Of course, this was the fellow of whom she was frightened, the bully who had lived on her earnings, from whom she had fled that night. That was why her answer was so placating. Poor little thing, she was terrified. A great warm wave of courage and chivalry, the last he was to experience in his life, welled up in him. He turned to the man and said truculently,

"Be off yourself. Alice don't want you here, nor do I. And if I catch you here again, frightening her, I'll give you something to remember."

The man looked at him with genuine astonishment.

"You silly young puppy," he said, almost gently, "you—young fool. Here, get out afore I lose my temper."

174

He tore open the door and put a compelling hand on Dave's shoulder. Dave hit him a swift and telling blow. Steve returned it heartily and in less than a moment they were staging there, in the tiny space between door and bedstead, a fight as eager and as desperate as any ever seen in Bully Baynes' Academy.

Steve was heavier and better versed in tricks; but Dave was younger and in better form. They swayed to and fro, grappling together, and then, breaking apart, met again with the heavy thud of well-directed blows. And Alice, huddled upon the tumbled bed, clutched her open bodice about her and followed the movements with her eyes. She did not doubt that Steve would win, and she wanted him to. She was a little tired of Dave.

But Dave was putting up a good fight. Her eyes brightened. It would do Steve no harm to take a knock or two and to learn that she knew how to choose her men. And, oh, how sweetly she would comfort him afterwards. Her eyes brightened; and she forgot to clutch the bodice, which fell backwards, disclosing the full white breast above the line of the soiled underclothes. Then suddenly her gaze sharpened with concern. Steve's blows were weakening, Dave's growing heavier and better placed as the other man's defence weakened. Cripes! There was Steve going over and Dave struggling on top of him, hands urgent at his throat, knees pressing him down. Christ! He was killing him!

Scrambling from the bed like a disturbed cat, she looked wildly round the room. On the corner of the table stood the basin at which she performed her scanty ablutions, and by its side was the half-filled ewer. Snatching it up, she rushed forward and brought it down with all her force on the back of Dave's head, just as he was turning to say: "There, Alice, that settles him." He saw the blow coming, but could do nothing to guard himself.

The impact of the blow shattered the ewer and knocked Dave senseless. When he came to he was outside on the bare boards of the landing at the top of the stairs; Alice's door was locked, and from behind it came sounds of the joyous reunion which he had interrupted. He got up, hauling himself by the rail of the stairs, and stood there for a

175

moment, reckoning his hurts. His ears sang and he felt giddy. The back of his head was cut and there was blood on his hair and on his coat collar. He had, besides, suffered quite enough from Steve's hands. But he was undaunted. He shook himself, tossing his head there on the deserted landing, with an action curiously like that of a bull about to charge, and then he fell upon the door. The unsubstantial structure shuddered, but it held at lock and hinge, and the blows that he rained upon it reverberated like thunder through the quiet house.

Doors opened on various landings and voices began to call out, demanding to know the reason for the disturbance. The unwanted attention was fuel to his fury. He asked nothing now but a chance to revenge himself upon Steve, and upon Alice. There was a splintering sound and a long crack appeared in the panel of the door. The sight gave him increased strength. Alice now began to scream, and continued to do so despite Steve's rough command to be silent; and within the house, other women, not knowing why but moved by the contagion of panic, added their cries to hers.

The mistress of the house, roused at last, crept like a slug from her bed of rags in the basement, and waked her son and her son-in-law who slept even farther from the scene of the disturbance. Neither was a man of valour and they were rebutting the old woman's suggestions of violence, when the watch, attracted by Alice's screams, appeared at the house door. He had heard the first of the yells but had prudently gone in search of help first. Supported by his fellow, he was now prepared to enter with all the authority of the law. The son and son-in-law, cheered by the prospect of being in the majority, and in the unusual position of being upon the side of the law, joined forces with the watchmen and set upon Dave from the rear. There was a wide crack in the door by that time and since, from within, Steve could be seen on guard with his knife in his hand while Alice was armed with a shoe, there is little doubt that Dave owed his life, or at least his immediate well-being, to the timely interference. None the less he resisted it all the way down the many stairs and into the street.

Once there, the two young men beat a hasty retreat within doors and shot home the bolts. The watchmen, left in charge of a young man whose clothes, though tumbled and torn, pronounced him a member of a privileged class in that vicinity, mumbled out a few admonitions, seasoned with apologies, and trundled away to preserve the king's peace elsewhere.

Dave, who had been roughly handled in the descent, and once hit in the stomach, staggered to some railings and, hanging upon them, was violently sick. And when at last he straightened himself and began to walk weakly towards the shop, he had purged himself of more than his supper. He was never to feel even half-sentimental about any woman again. Desire would know a rebirth, so would possessiveness, but his softer feelings had been laid low for ever by that treacherous blow from Alice's hand. She had established herself a memorial that was to last as long as Dave's memory served him. The delight which she had shared with him was forgotten, except as a spur which from that time forth forced him into women's company; the tenderness with which he had, when out of Uncle Tom's influence, occasionally thought of her was never to know even that momentary resurrection; but the expression on her face as she leaned over him with the ewer poised in her hand was to be remembered for ever, lurking like a skull behind the smiles and the inviting faces of the women that he chose. Dozens of times during his life he justified himself and wronged some harmless woman by the recollection of what he was pleased to call Alice's perfidy.

Uncle Tom was, of course, immensely tactful. He dressed the wound at the back of Dave's head and asked no questions. If he ever wondered why Dave never mentioned the regular wage or matrimony again he gave no sign. But he was more indulgent and more generous as the months passed; and Dave, busy with the work of the day, the pleasures of the evenings and the dissipations of the nights, never knew how narrowly he had missed the way that might have led him out of the toils of selfishness which life, and Uncle Tom, and his own nature, had woven about him.

When Dave was twenty-five Uncle Tom began suddenly to fail in health. He complained of no pain, mixed, as far as Dave could see, no medicine for himself; but every day he seemed to eat less, to notice less and to find greater difficulty in dragging himself away from his fireside and his arm-chair. He shrank, both physically and in personality, so that in a few weeks he had become just a shadowy little old man, doddering between arm-chair and bed, referring everything to Dave and seemingly piteously grateful for the casual kindnesses and attentions which the young man found time to bestow upon him.

One cold morning Dave, entering the bedroom with the basin of gruel which gave the old man strength to rise and struggle into his clothes, found him dead. His face was peaceful and his nightcap was in place. He had died in his sleep.

He had kept his promise with regard to assuring his nephew's future. The business and a thousand pounds were left to Dave by a will drawn up and signed only a year after the boy's arrival in London. Two thousand pounds were left to a Mrs. Letty Davids who lived at Brighton and whom Dave never saw, and fifteen hundred, together with certain articles from the house, a tallboy, the clock on the stairs and some of the silver, went to a Mrs. Agnes Pelham of the "Blue Boar," Bermondsey, who arrived to collect the goods and whom, when he saw her, Dave vaguely remembered as a woman who had occasionally visited his uncle during the first months of his apprenticeship. What dim and forgotten romances the handsome legacies remembered, Dave never troubled to wonder. He bore both women a grudge because their shares exceeded his and he was very uncivil to Mrs. Pelham on the occasion of her visit.

For a year or rather more after his uncle's death, Dave led a life after his own heart. He retired late and stayed in bed until almost midday, when he rose and spent about two hours in the shop. Apart from that time he left it in charge of a boy who knew little and whom he did not trouble to teach anything. With money in his pocket he was a welcome visitor to his old haunts and a flatteringly received newcomer at fresh ones. Never having had money in any quantity before, he had no idea of its elusive qualities; and he was far through his legacy before he realised that a thousand pounds is more easily spent than gained.

Most of Uncle Tom's money had been made by nefarious practices and in these Dave had neither the skill nor the subtlety to follow him. Nor was he thoroughly grounded in the regular apothecary's trade. The business in Lloyd's Cherry Cough Cure and in the famous Raspberry Cordial was lost during that first year when Dave failed to buy the ingredients in time, and often when it came to reordering stocks of ordinary drugs he found himself at a loss and his ignorance a prey to men who were more knowledgeable and as unscrupulous as he was himself. Finally, after a year and two months of unprofitable trading he disposed of the business and with this new capital and complete leisure, took a partnership in Bully Baynes' Academy.

But Bully, indulgent to his customers, demanded of his business confederates rather more than Dave was disposed to give of effort and sweat, and the ensuing months were marked by quarrels which grew bitterer as time progressed. Finally, when Dave had been absent for four consecutive days during a busy season when Bully was counting upon his presence, he returned to find his partner in a deadly sour temper.

" 'Ere, I wanta talk to you," he said, without preliminary, his fury reinforced by the sight of Dave's slack and debauched appearance, "come in 'ere." He threw open the door of his little office.

"I've got a lesson at eleven," said Dave, defensively.

"Oh no, you ain't. I put Peter on to it. 'Ow was I to know you was coming back terday? When I took you on, Dave, and give you a third share for a measly seven 'undred, I thought I was taking on a real live man, but what with your idling and drinking and your whoring you're no more good'n a bunged-up eye. The time 'as come for us to part, cully, no doubt about that. So see 'ere. You put in seven 'undred on the third of June. You've drawn out three in six months, one way and another, and you've earned next ter nothing. An 'undred went into the new gymnasium, with your permission, in fac' it was your ideer, the old place was good enough for me. So 'ere's your three 'undred balance and I'll be glad if you'll take it and not put me in no more muddles like I bin in this week on account of you."

"And what do I get for the hundred that went into the building?"

"You can go to law about that," said Bully succinctly, "but till then you get damn all. See? I'm sick of yer."

"I'll set up on the opposite side of the road," said Dave furiously, "and drive you out of business."

Bully laughed in a hearty, unaffected and wholly offensive way. "I'll risk that, boyo!" he said jovially. "You hafta get up in the morning and stay off the drink and the drabs in our trade—that's just what I'm telling you, Dave. No, you pop along and have a good time with that money and then marry a widow with a bit more than leg in her stocking. That's the best advice you'll ever get."

There was probably only one person in the world who could have spoken to Dave so frankly or treated him so contemptuously, and Bully was that person. He knew his power. Muttering and cursing Dave picked up the money that Bully had so carelessly thrown down on the table and left the Academy for the last time. He had forgotten that there had been a day when he had regarded the right of entry there as a source of pride and had been breathlessly flattered because Bully had shown interest in his muscles. He collected a few of his things that were scattered about the place and made for the outer swing-doors in a surly temper. He would have liked to have revenged himself on Bully's heavy body, but was bound to admit that the four days' dissipation just completed had left him with little heart for anything. He would have a good sleep and to-morrow meditate the project of setting up on his own. He must do something while the three hundred pounds lasted —goodness how the money went!

He was so deep in thought that he almost fell over the dapper little man who was negotiating the swing-doors just as he reached them. He went on, without a glance and without apology, and turned sharply, quarrelsomely, when a hand was laid on his arm.

"It's Dave Glenny, isn't it?" the voice, strange in accent but obviously pleasant in intent, forestalled Dave's contemplated brusqueness.

"What do you want with me?"

"I've been trying to catch you for a week now. I've a proposition to lay before you."

The hand on his arm was gently propelling him across the street to the "Cross Keys," and there, with the sanded floor gritting under his feet and the clean-scrubbed table before him, he found himself making the better acquaintance of Mr. Jonas Sandabur, United States citizen and Jack-of-all-trades.

The dapper little man was a genius in his way. Starting life as a pot-boy in a New York public-house, he had risen to flamboyant heights as a purveyor of entertainment in that city. But his star was uncertain and he was given to losing upon one venture all that he had made from its predecessor, and at the moment when Dave drew his attention he was humbly content to be scouting for minor talent in the prize-fighting line. The business which had brought him to England had been a disastrous failure and it had been in an attempt to escape his own despair that he had paid a visit to Bully's place. There he had been attracted to Dave. He thought him ill-trained, overconfident and idle, but he had seen, what Bully had glimpsed long ago and then lost sight of, the young man's natural talent, nimbleness and complete fearlessness. He now made him an offer, not a dazzling one, but very acceptable to Dave's mood. Without admitting it, without even realising it, Dave was sick of his present life. The long line of Alice's successors, taken without tenderness, enjoyed without ecstasy, had begun to pall, there was a limit to what a man could eat and drink, and his money was running low.

Before he left the "Cross Keys" he had agreed to accompany Jonas Sandabur to America.

For two years he fought his way through most of the Eastern states. In public halls, in large towns, in barns, in roped fields at fairs, he peddled his mediocre talent. The life suited him, though he was not calculated to attain any great heights in it. He lacked the even balance, the calm

181

temper, the disciplined attitude to his trade which are the requirements for success in the ring. He earned money, and spent it; he visited many places and met many men without learning either geography or humanity. When, at the end of two years Jonas Sandabur tired of him, as Bully had done, he had little to show for his labours, unless Lou could be counted an asset.

Lou was Jonas's daughter, and, like many men left without a wife and with a daughter, he had entertained great ambitions for her. Even at his lowest financial ebbs he had paid his sister-in-law to house her, paid her school fees promptly, made her incongruous and expensive presents. He had once, all unwittingly, allowed her to meet Dave and had spent a great deal of care and thought in keeping them apart ever afterwards.

But Lou had lost her head as completely as her heart: she was so obsessed by the handsome young man that the obvious flaws in his character—and to do him justice he made no effort to appear other than he was—were impotent to cure her. She knew that he was callous, faithless, unfitted to make any woman happy, yet, each time in that two-year interval, when by careful scheming she found herself in his company, she was overwhelmed anew by desire for him. When he and her father finally parted company she welcomed the break because now she could follow her lover without risk of interference. And she hoped greatly that he would marry her.

The hope died a slow death, but it was dead before Evan, child of the union, was born. By then it was too late, and for thirteen miserable years Lou followed Dave about, enduring poverty, humiliation and neglect, and frequently physical ill-usage. She had lost all power to make a life of her own and would have wilted away if deprived of the dubious protection that he gave her. Now and again she made an effort to leave him, but she always returned and was grateful, like a stray spaniel, that he took her in, even if abuse constituted the welcome.

Occasionally, as when Dave opened a shop, or at another period took an ale-house for a time, she was useful and so was tolerated. In the nomadic seasons which composed most of the thirteen years, she followed him about, contributing to the family funds by hiring out as cook or needlewoman, sometimes brought low enough to act as decoy for Dave's nefarious schemes. Her flashes of rebellion grew less and less frequent.

When Evan was twelve the opportunity came to her to escape. Jonas Sandabur died and left her everything of which he was possessed at the moment. It might have been nothing; it might have been a small fortune; actually it was about three thousand dollars. It would have started her in a modest line of business in a milliner's shop or an apartment house, but almost automatically she handed it over to Dave, who lost one-third of it in a week's heavy gambling.

The steady run of ill-luck, following hard upon the good which had given him the windfall, steadied him a little. Once more, as on that morning when Bully turned him out, he knew a desire to cut loose from his old associations. He indulged in an unprecedented review of his position and realised that he was forty years old, that many ways of picking up a livelihood were closed to him and that others would shortly close.

There was talk in the air of the new country in the West, a country where a man with his wits about him and a few dollars in his pocket, need suffer no lack.

So Dave bought a wagon, an ox-team and a riding horse, and since Evan, twelve years old, was now sensible and handy, and Lou, though her charms were fading, might be turned to account, he took them with him. And so he reached Fort Mason in time to join Kevin Furmage's party.

PART THREE

The Revelation

For days the journey was uneventful. Joe Sterry drove the Furmage team and Kevin rode his mare, Persephone, often scouting on ahead, trying out the trail and returning to warn those behind of troublesome inclines or river crossings. These at first gave little trouble, for at the end of a hot dry summer they were shrunken, low in their beds between the waterrounded boulders and the margins of sand.

The trail ascended steadily, but beyond each ridge gained there was the short sharp descent upon the farther side, more dangerous than the upward pulls, since here only care and skill prevented the heavy wagons from overturning or from over-running the slipping teams.

On the whole the life was pleasant enough, especially in the evenings when the fires were lighted and the smoke and scent of the cooking rose on the cool air. The lower slopes of the mountains abounded in mountain sheep (strangely long-legged and agile to the lowland eye) and in antelope. Often enough there was game for the pot.

Ruth Warren and Mahitabel Smith, though so diverse in nature that in ordinary circumstances they might not have found one another congenial, grew friendly, with the generous though cautious friendliness of the pioneer. Both were housewives, both mothers, both eminently respectable women. Ruth formed the habit of taking all her troubles to the older woman and they spent some portion of the evening hour together at every camping place. That neither of them approved of Madame Jurer and her lively companions was made obvious enough, but that did not worry the inhabitants of the painted wagon. It was forty years since any respectable woman had looked kindly upon Nancy Jurer and she wanted none of them. She wanted nobody. With plenty to eat and drink, a pack of cards to deal out in varying, complicated patterns, and a comfortable bed awaiting her, she could be happy anywhere. Klara Bolewska, on the other hand, was very glad that no one wanted to talk to her, for the evenings gave her opportunities to slip away and meet Dave Glenny, the dark, and to her eye, handsome man who was the only other person save their leader to possess a horse—obviously a man of status. The pair had come together with all the pleasure of two people of the same kind who meet in an alien land. And Floribel Toit, working towards Abe, through friendship with his sister, guileless Mary Ann, was quite happy too, waiting with the inexhaustible patience of the very young.

Abe had Cordy to visit and admonish, though now and then, when he could do so without being observed, he would direct some word or act of kindness towards Lou Glenny, who, but for him, would have been entirely alone. Both sets of women were kind to her, for it was easily seen in the first stages of the march that she was a pitiable creature, ill-used and neglected. But she was so nervous, so elusive, so curiously engrossed with something remote from common human experience, that whether she were talking recipes and motherlore with Ruth and Mahitabel, or skin-care and hairdressing with Floribel and Klara, there was an element of discomfort in her company that made people wish her away. A woman who sometimes screamed in the night; who wore two black eyes in a fortnight; who could not even stand up for her own child . . . no, no one could consider her seriously. No one, that is, except Abe, who was struggling with the last phases of his adolescence, and who had once seen, or heard, somewhere, the expression: "Our Lady of the Sorrows". That, to him, Lou Glenny was, and Dave Glenny was all the evil, past, present and to come. Dave was Pilate condemning Christ, Herod massacring the Innocents, Ahab betraying Naboth. Abe's learning was utterly Biblical.

The loneliest person in the company was Kevin Furmage. He could halt by any fire on any evening and be offered the best seat, the choicest tit-bit of the pot. Even Lou would defy her master to give him welcome, but spiritually he dwelt alone. No one in all the company could share his dream or his vision of the road that they were making, bearing thousands of feet wearing away to the West, to the land of promise. That was incommunicable. And although he often invited Cordy Warren to his fire and a glass of his brandy, and although the little man was the obvious choice of company, being literate, articulate and unabashed, those evenings were seldom wholly enjoyable. Cordy was unwordly, yet his wit, when it flashed, was acrid and dry; Cordy was kind, yet his tongue could be scathing; Cordy was friendly, yet at heart he was remote, squeezed empty, burnt out, no boon companion for Kevin, that simple, worldly, optimistic soul.

The brandy was wasted, because the hour for retirement came before it had done its work. If once Cordy had mentioned his dead lost love, or Kevin his abhorred sonlessness, they too, would have had common ground. But Cordy found Abe a better companion, and Kevin found himself, evening after evening, drinking his glass with raddled old Nancy Jurer. She understood men, and she understood liquor, she had dealt with both all her life. She could, in certain circumstances, cease to be a person, and become a symbol, the companionableness of woman when she was too old to stir desire, woman, when she was turning at last towards the level pastures of sexless living. Kevin enjoyed her anecdotes, her stories of New Orleans, which he had never visited, her racy descriptions of people, some of them well known.

So the journey went on, uneventful, laborious and in part enjoyable. Every evening Kevin traced on the map the trail that they had covered, and once announced with pleasure that they had already saved six days on the Fort Hall Route.

The first serious trouble came after they had crossed a ridge which they named, since it was nameless upon the map, The Saddle, on account of its shape.

The weather had grown colder as they ascended, and on this evening, Mahitabel, wrapped in her cloak, thought of the warm, dusty evenings of August, with the harvest in full swing, and the poppies and cornflowers speckling the sheaves, and the gleaners. But she took her diary, in which she had written on many such an evening at home, and turned to the next blank page. She recorded the crossing of The Saddle and the safe though laborious descent upon its western side, and that they had camped near a spring. She remarked that game was growing scarcer, but that Abe had shot an antelope, a forequarter of which she had roasted for supper, the rest being shared out amongst the company. She found space to add that Mr. Cooper seemed slightly better, though unable to move much. Then she paused. Halting her quill, she thought of Abe, as she had, at intervals, been thinking during the day's march. Last evening noises of strife, now familiar, had come from the Glenny wagon, and Abe had suddenly loped off in that direction, without either excuse or explanation. This morning when she saw him again he had a swollen jaw, a misshapen nose and no skin on the knuckles of his right hand. And there was an air, at once furtive and triumphant, about him. Mahitabel had refrained from comment, and had, by a sign, halted an inquiry upon Ben's lips; but she had found herself watching for Glenny's appearance and a shaft of quite unregenerate pleasure had reached her heart as she noted his discoloured, lop-sided mouth and bruised cheek.

She was glad, no mother could help but be glad, that her son had marked his man and apparently held his own; but beneath the pleasure sharp concern had stirred. Abe had always been so terribly susceptible to the woes of the ill-treated; most of the fights of his boyhood had been over some tormented dog or stray cat which the other boys regarded as a legitimate butt. Now it was a woman, with a pale face and clouds of dark hair, who was appealing to his indiscriminate chivalry, and the matter might not end with an exchange of blows and a blooded nose. It was a pity. Not that Mahitabel was not opposed herself to the treatment meted out to Lou; but the year was 1840, women had not given much consideration to their rights and the other woman's wrongs, and Abe's mother tended, like thousands of others, not to interfere. If a woman chose badly, or failed to stand up for herself, or to inspire respect in her partner, well, it must be hidden away, the suffering, and not dangled, however unconsciously, as a bait for hot-headed, chivalrous boys. Almost—even in her mind Mahitabel underlined the word—*almost* she had rather that he had been drawn towards the red-wheeled wagon. Those noisy girls who seemed to have such a fascination for foolish Mary Ann were bound to disgust him sooner or later, whereas Lou Glenny ... Mahitabel sighed as she closed the book, screwed down the inkholder, with its patent, non-spilling device, and wiped the quill on her skirt. She wondered where Abe was now, for instance.

Abe, at that moment, was sitting on a boulder which broke the soft grass around the spring. He could hear the hobbled oxen munching contentedly and the small ordinary sound brought momentary peace to his mind. His big knotted hands, clasped, fell between his parted knees and as he stared into the darkness he could see, limned upon it, a procession of small white faces with tragic eyes and patient mouths. The terror that had distorted the original of the face when he saw it last night disturbed the peace of the oxen's munching. Why had she ever married him? What could anyone see in a great coarse brute like that whose beasts abhorred his touch? What had she suffered? What had she still to bear?

He was conscious of physical pain as he thought of her. It struck him across the loins and along the inner surfaces of his thighs, so that he stirred in bewilderment, having known before only the superficial pains of a cut thumb, an aching tooth. He gripped his hands till the knuckles cracked.

Presently he sprang up restlessly and returned to the camp. Twilight was now threatened by the darkness and he heard, before he was near enough to see much, the noise of a number of men, talking at once, raising their voices to shout one another down.

Fearing, instinctively, for Lou, he looked towards the Glenny wagon, but there was only Evan, rubbing down the wild-eyed gelding which was sweating and blowing as though it had been ridden hard. Dave often rode out after camp was made; he seemed never to tire; and he seemed, too, to enjoy challenging Kevin's position as scout.

It was Dave who was shouting loudest in the group near Kevin's wagon, and as he drew closer Abe could hear him say:

"I tell you the map's wrong, or else you are. Nobody but a fool would attempt it."

"Only a bigger fool would suggest going back, now," said Kevin hotly, answering him. "We've been fifteen days

190

on the road. Going back would take longer, the climbing is steeper. It'd be the middle of September before you were back at Mason's place. Besides. I've seen the ridge. It looks tough, but the surface is good. Maybe you didn't stop to notice that."

"I noticed enough," retorted Dave. "I don't miss much. And I've noticed that though this was supposed to be such an easy road, it gets harder every day. You properly deceived us in my opinion."

"Did you expect to cross the Sierras in an arm-chair? And don't say that I deceived you. I won't have it. I didn't ask you to follow this road or to travel with me. What with one thing and another I should prefer your room to your company, Glenny. Go back. Go to Hell if you like, but don't come here bellowing at me."

Glenny spluttered. Cordy Warren's quiet voice broke in on the noise. "I doubt if one team will get you up The Saddle from this side, Glenny. It's almost perpendicular."

"My team'll go where I've a mind to drive 'em," said Glenny. "Besides, I haven't finished yet. Maybe Smith, or Madame, will realise before I've done that we're all being led by the nose by Mr. Bloody Kevin here who's got this bee in his bonnet about a new road that can't be travelled. Then they'll turn back and we shan't have to go up single-teamed."

"If you want to describe in greater detail the ridge that has frightened you, and try your persuasive powers, go and do it elsewhere. That is all I ask. I'm going to bed now and in the morning I'm going over that ridge. Those who care to follow can do so, and the others can go back and try again next year. Good night."

Kevin pushed his way out of the circle and walked away. The group re-formed. Glenny told again of the ridge, twice as high as The Saddle and twice as steep, which barred the path. A more popular person might have persuaded one of his listeners, at least, that to return was the only possible plan, but no one, not even Madame Nancy, liked him enough.

In the morning, very early, Glenny yoked his team, turned his wagon and pulled out on the backward trail. No one, save Klara Bolewska who had fallen in love with his dour good looks, and Abe who wondered what would now happen to Lou, regretted his departure.

Yet, when four days later, he appeared, he was welcomed with relief. When he strode, grey-faced with fatigue, his brow scored with fury, into the camp by the creek beyond the dreaded ridge, the assembled company saw, not a disagreeable travelling companion, a wife-beater and a trouble-maker, but an extra pair of strong hands, a sturdy pair of shoulders.

The ridge had been crossed with less difficulty than they had feared and the wagons had been taken cautiously, without accident, down the short steep drop on its western side. And soon, stretching ahead of them between the ramparts of the mountains, might be seen a wide green valley, rich in promise of easy going for the wagons and of good fodder for the oxen.

The hopes that it raised made doubly bitter the disappointment that was theirs when they drew nearer. This was no grassy bottom, but a dense, tangled thicket. Aspens and alders and willows, tough and stunted and bent over by the wind that blew along the tunnel of the valley from the north, grew there in hundreds. And between them, closely weaving willow to alder and alder to aspen, were brambles, thickly-fruited, sharply thorned, and wild-rose sprays with their hooked prickles and their fruit just reddening.

The ruddy colour faded from Kevin's face when, riding ahead, he saw for the first time the nature of the valley. He rode across it from one extremity to the other, seeking the opening that must be there. De Brielle was not a fool. Everything else that he had noted about the road had proved, in its travelling, to be true and well-observed. Three years ago the Frenchman had passed this way with his pack mules. How? Had he cut a path? Had the thicket grown since his passing? Had he been mistaken, or had Kevin read the map wrongly?

With a feeling of mortal sickness the leader turned away at last, satisfied that no opening was there and facing the unpleasant task of breaking the news to his followers. Furtively he checked his map, taking a reckoning by the stars as soon as darkness fell. There was no mistake. The trail
192

led to this valley and no other. And unless the party turned back to winter in Wyoming, they must cut a path through it by the edge of the axe. Besides, even those who were minded to return remembered the almost over-hanging descents of The Saddle and what had come to be known as Glenny's Ridge. Could they be climbed? They doubted it. So at last they were spared the agony of indecision. Before they slept that night men looked to their axes and tried their edges, laid picks and shovels ready to hand.

With the first light of morning they were attacking the thicket, hacking and hewing, throwing the loosened, living stuff aside. Now they learned how terribly weak in man-power they were. Only seven of them, and of those neither Kevin nor Cordy were hardened to constant manual labour, and Hendriks was handicapped by his smallness.

And this weak little company were facing a task that might have appalled a team of lumbermen. The tough little trees defied the axes; the brambles, even when severed, clung desperately to their supports and had to be dragged for feet before they could be flung clear. By the first breakfast-time even Ben, tough as hickory, and Abe, full of youthful vigour, and lively Joe Sterry, were panting and exhausted. Kevin and Cordy were regarding with dismay the puffy blisters on their palms. Only Scanty, Madame Nancy's Negro who considered that he was a driver, not a woodsman, and had spared himself as much as possible, was fresh and undistressed. But Madame missed very little with that hooded eye of hers and after breakfast she borrowed Kevin's riding-crop, and might, throughout the day, be often seen, tottering about the place of activity on her little feet, urging Scanty to greater effort. The sight, in other circumstances, might have been comic.

During the breakfast spell, while the men refreshed themselves with steaming coffee and plates of beans and bacon, Mahitabel took Ben's axe from the wheel against which he had leant it and stepped into the little clearing that the men had made. The action needed was different from that of splitting logs which she had done many and many a time and her first few blows were ineffective. But she caught the knack quickly and set about a little willow with force and accuracy.

Klara, with her mouth full of food, joined her. She had never, in twenty days, spoken to the terrifying Mrs. Smith, but she spoke now.

"I can do it," she said, speaking carefully. "I have chop down whole trees in Lupisu, little place where I live before." She was expert, and as strong as a man. Mahitabel thought better of her. And presently Janna, Scanty's sister, lumbered up, her black face a little sheepish.

"Sho muh," she begged. "Ah's better'n Scanty doing most things."

So they worked together, the respectable farmer's wife, the budding prostitute and the black slave. Behind Mary Ann and Floribel Toit cleared the debris as Hendriks had cleared behind the men. And Frank Cooper, looking out from his sheltered place in the wagon, knew to the full the bitterness of physical uselessness.

After that the three women took their turns with the work. Mahitabel grew thin. Klara's carefully tended hands hardened anew. Janna sweated and smiled.

Four days of gruelling labour, and just as they ceased work on the fourth day and dragged themselves out to the camp, Glenny, defeated by the western slope of The Saddle, returned, glowering. Lou had a fresh bruise on her face; Evan's ear was red and swollen; the oxen were patterned all over with whipwelts. But here were palms not blistered, a back not yet cricked. They were welcome.

Without saying a word to anyone, Dave, leaving the care of the oxen to Evan, drank a pint of coffee and lay down for an hour under the tail of his wagon. He lay flat on his back, his long loose arms stretched beside him, touching the ground. Cordy, aching in every limb, sent a glance at the supine form, and was reminded of the old story of the wrestler who, each time he was thrown, gained strength anew from the earth as he touched it. But whether Glenny were renewing his strength or merely abstracting himself from the company and its perilous situation none could tell for an hour.

At the end of it Glenny rose and stretched himself. The

grey look had gone from his face. He lighted two lanterns, got out his axe, and then, as Lou, obedient to a snarled order, set out to borrow more lanterns, he disappeared into the opening in the thicket, followed by his son. Lou, with two loaned lanterns, scurried after them. From the depths of the green tunnel the blows of his axe could be heard.

Suddenly Abe sprang up with a word that neither of his parents had ever heard upon his lips.

"——," he said. "What he can do, I can." He seized his axe and plunged into the thicket. For three hours more he toiled in a frenzy that was compounded of pride and fury, love and hatred.

After that they worked and rested in turns, day and night, so that at no hour of the twenty-four was the valley silent; and as they hacked and hewed there developed, unacknowledged and unspoken, a rivalry between Dave Glenny and Abe Smith. The work which they did in hatred, the competition in which they engaged, the defiant extra shift that each would work, waiting for the other to weaken, watching for the moment of collapse, did much to send the path forward.

Nevertheless it was the first of September before the narrow, uneven path was carried to the far end of the thicket. When the last bramble was thrown aside the men emerged into the open, scored and scratched, worn to the bone and utterly weary, but momentarily triumphant. Behind them stretched the path that they had made; and now they must turn and devote their depleted energies to the task of bringing the wagons through.

The brambles that swung beside the path, the branches overhead, clutched at the lurching tops as though in a last effort to hold back the defilers of their ancient solitude. But the oxen, at least, had rested for a fortnight and were of good heart. Creaking and jolting over the roughly hacked stumps that broke the path the wagons, one by one, emerged.

There had been no time for hunting while the road was being made, and the Herculean labours had inspired hunger. Now, as the casks and the sacks were sorted at the repacking, here and there a stab of anxiety went through the mind. God send that there would be no other unforeseen delay or the consumpton of food would have to be cut down.

From Mahitabel's diary, that exact and honest record, we may learn that it was on this day that she began to be concerned for the success of the venture. She was repacking alone, for Mary Ann, carrying Ellen, had gone with Floribel and Klara to the end of the path to watch the final barrier fall beneath the axes. And as she noted the inroads that had been made into her stores in a fortnight a premonition of disaster, which was a new guest in her busy mind, suddenly disturbed her peace. Suppose, after all, they should have stuck to the old road? Ought she to have been firmer, not pandered to Ben's desire for company? A sense of her responsibilities smote her heavily, three children, a sick man. . . . For a moment her hands were stilled and she looked ahead, across the valley, to the distant peaks which were just gilded by the sun. Fear and despair sat on her face, so that Frank Cooper, watching her, was troubled, though he feared to speak and to ask what was bothering her. But a line from a psalm slid into her mind as the light brightened on the mountain tops: "I will lift up mine eyes unto the hills, from whence cometh my help," and comfort flowed in upon her as though a dam had been loosened. It was all right. God knew all about their situation. He held them in the hollow of His hand. She must not insult His omnipotence by worrying because the food had gone a little sooner than she had expected it to. With a sigh of relief she turned back to her work, and as a faint cry came blowing back across the valley she turned to her passenger and said brighty:

"Did you hear that? They're cheering. We're through."

In the red-wheeled wagon Madame Jurer, her soft white hands idle, but her eye alert and watchful, also noted the depletion of her stores. She decided instantly that the Negroes and the girls should have less to eat in future. What would it matter if the girls were a little scrawny when they arrived? A few days of good feeding would soon restore their curves. As a preliminary, in order to frighten Janna into being economical whether she were under observance or not, she rated her for wastefulness and drew such a picture of possible starvation before the journey was ended that Janna turned grey and moaned dismally. Her own words frightened Nancy a little. Already she missed, sorely enough, the fruit and tender vegetables, the fish, the fresh butter and cream which for so many years had decked her table. Suppose the stores should really end before the journey and she found herself without the thickly sweetened coffee, the thinly sliced bacon, the pink ham and rich biscuits that she loved? She was compelled to reckon her stores again, just to reassure herself. And gradually her fears retreated. She had plenty really; and the frightened slave girl would aid and abet her retrenchment.

At almost the same moment, little Hendriks, housewife for the moment, happily discarded a keg of pork which he had opened overnight and thought inadequately salted, and he abandoned too, with equal light-heartedness, a bag of flour in which only two or three pounds remained. It was hardly worth packing a practically empty sack and he was too busy to remove the flour before jettisoning the canvas.

For six days they travelled without halt or incident and saw at last a gap in the mountains, which when gained was found to give upon a gentle slope that led to a wide plain. To their innocent Eastern eyes the sight was homely and reassuring. It was a pleasure to be free of the close narrow places where the sun never seemed to sink properly, but to drop behind some peak suddenly and plunge the travellers into immediate gloom. Across the plain on this evening they could see the colours of the sunset and millions of stars were sown after twilight upon the wide field of the sky.

But Kevin, drawing out his map and dotting in this latest camping place, warned them that this was the desert. They must carry water for fifty hours; they must cut grass and store it under the hoods of the wagons to preserve its succulence. To-morrow's sun would be scorching: to-morrow night icy cold.

Next morning, early, to take advantage of the hours of low sun, the wagons rolled easily down the slope and out on to the plain, scantily scattered with dry sage bushes.

The arid soil broke beneath the wheels and a cloud of dust gathered over and about the wagons, so that Mahitabel was reminded of the Children of Israel on their journey through the wilderness: they had the "cloud by day", but it went before, not after. The sun climbed high and shone with a fierceness not familiar in September—September with its turquoise sky, the mists at morning, the ricks rising in the fields and the glimmer of gold at the edges of the high elms.

No elms here, no inch of shade save where the stark rocks stood with their feet in narrow sharp shadows. At last even the sage fell away, defeated, and the dust took on a new quality. It hung on the lips, saltily. You licked them, but the taste remained and they dried again; presently a little crack appeared and the salt stung, woundingly. The rims of the eyes stung too, gritty and dry, and the nostrils were clogged with dust. Even the fingertips took on a rough woollen texture. And after the disappearance of the sage the surface of the plain became less solid. The oxen sank in at each step and the wheels moved more and more slowly. Fifty hours! And by the old route four or five days were the rule. No doubt Mr. Furmage was right when he said that this was the road of the future. Any road that shortened this misery would be the popular one.

With sunset the air became icily cold; so cold that it was difficult not to think that the white salt plain was an expanse of snow. There was something uncanny about it after the fierce heat of the day. It was as though the world had died suddenly.

Huddled together under rugs and blankets the people slept uneasily and the oxen moaned in the night.

The hills where the water was lay like a purple smudge on the skyline. By midday of the second day they should have loomed up out of that vague shadow; by late evening they should have been reached. But the fifty hours had run their course and still the white desert stretched ahead unbroken. And the surface grew worse. Beneath the salt crust was a bog into which wheels sank, and the ruts and the footmarks filled with water immediately. At first the sight of the welling liquid raised wild hopes, but the water was saltier and more bitter than brine. Again Mahitabel was reminded of the Children of Israel and the Waters of Mara which were sweetened by a miracle. Who was the worker of miracles here?

Not that one was needed yet. It was distressing to find the journey stretching out beyond the expected length, it was distressing not to be able to satisfy one's thirst fully, but there was no danger yet.

Kevin, with a sense of responsibility and uneasiness growing heavier with every hour, suggested moving through the night. It was moonlight and the extra labour would hurt the oxen less than prolonged shortage of water. No dissentient voice was heard, so after a brief rest and a doling-out of the remaining water the little train pressed on, with the wagons fanned out so that the teams need not tread in the churned wake of their predecessors.

The moon, although befriending them, bleached the last remnant of comfortable ordinariness from the strange world through which they moved. High in a cloudless sky she hung, pale, mad-eyed, remote; a dead moon staring at a dead world. The tiny human figures, trudging or riding by in their toy wagons, were inadequate assertions of life in an empty space where there was neither beast nor bird, neither flower nor tree nor the liveliness of water; only the tired, bewildered little people plodding onwards in an effort to save their lives.

It was a very quiet passage: the usual noises of the day were hushed; even the drivers' cries to their teams and the crack of their long whips (more frequently wielded as the hours stole by) were muted, lapped and laid away in the pervading silence. Joe Sterry started to sing once, but his merry voice was unbearably plaintive and the noise seemed to affront something that had laid a spell of silence upon the land; the song soon faltered and failed. It was as though the wagon train had been bidden: "Move softly through the desert and through the night, lest you disturb something better left asleep. Move softly that, unnoticed, you may pass unharmed." This was the part of the world where no life could flourish, its deadly feud against the living impressed even the least sensitive person in the train.

They travelled till moonset and then, in the dark before dawn, threw themselves down and rested their limbs though for many of them sleep was an impossibility. Anxiety nagged at them and in every mind was the question, would dawn show the watered hills within reach or not?

Kevin studied the stars and satisfied himself that his compass did not err. What mistake was his had been made when he listened to the Frenchman with his siren song about fifty hours of desert travel. He was going right by the map. But his confidence in the precious document was tottering; it had failed him at the Valley of Brambles and it was failing him here. And his failure meant more than it might have meant before the stay at Fort Mason. More lives were now at stake . . . women and children were in the train. Had he sacrificed them to his ambition? his fantastic need to assert himself?

Long before there was light enough to see by he was on his feet and studying the horizon. The hills, as the light rose, were visible, nearer, less smudgy, but they were more than a day's journey away.

The little water that remained was shared out; the grass was all gone and continuous travel was telling upon the draught beasts. The salt dust had caked whitely upon the stale sweat of their coats and the warming day brought little new sweat to dissolve the patterns of it; their bodies were too arid now to sweat easily. It was a day of misery for man and beast; a day of gathering fear and mounting panic.

In the afternoon, Kevin, tortured beyond bearing, saddled Persephone and rode round the scattered labouring wagons, separate atoms by this time. He collected empty water-flasks and bottles and announced his intention of riding on in search of water. He advised the others to press on until the oxen were past effort and then to unyoke and follow him on foot. He tried to cheer them by saying that distance in the desert was deceptive and that the hills might be nearer than they seemed. He pointed out to Ben and Abe, to Cordy and to Madame Jurer, the direction to follow, and then, looking about for Dave Glenny's wagon, he found that it was missing. In their misery and preoccupation the scattering company had not witnessed his going nor noticed his absence. He had probably fallen behind.

In the clear sunshine Kevin started off. The flatness of the plain was broken by low rolling eminences, almost as though a gentle summer sea had been frozen into immobility, and as he gained the top of one of these he could see, being mounted, the errant Glenny wagon moving steadily away to the north, away from the water. He checked the mare's gallop and bit his underlip, drumming his fingers impatiently on the pommel as he wrestled with his problem. If he rode straight ahead for water the wagon might be beyond recall by the time that he returned. Then Glenny and the woman and the boy would perish of thirst in the desert. And he would be responsible. On the other hand to circumvent the wagon meant a loss of time which might have almost equally evil results.

And he hated Glenny. Sitting there, pondering, he admitted the fact. His life had brought him into contact with many people and he was tolerant almost to a fault of many things that were popularly condemned; but Glenny was a brute and a bully and his manners were bad. He knew that if he liked the man he would have had no hesitation in riding after him; and almost as soon as he realised that his personal feelings were complicating the problem he saw that he had no choice at all. Dislike for the man must not lead him to condemn the woman and the boy. Swerving from his course he set Persephone's head towards the wagon.

The new direction brought the westering sun beating upon one side of his neck, and with heat and anxiety and a sense of time slipping past he felt a little sick. About the sun's rays he could do something; he took out his handkerchief and draped it from the inside of his hat brim, so that it hung like a screen.

As he rode he now and then glanced towards the hills on his left; how far? how near? It was, as he had told his struggling followers, difficult to estimate accurately in the desert. Glenny's wagon, for instance, was not so far away as he had first feared. He looked towards it again, and there, upon its farther side, he saw a horseman bearing down upon it.

Besides Persephone the only horse in the party was the wild-eyed gelding which Glenny was at this moment riding, and the sight of the other horseman sent a wild hope through Kevin's heart. Was some other party in the vicinity? Was his own not so miserably belated as, since the delay in the Valley of Brambles, he had feared? But with a sudden descent of spirits he realised the full folly of that thought. No other party could be travelling this road because no one else, except de Brielle, knew of its existence.

Kevin raised his right arm in the air. The strange horseman repeated the action faithfully. It was as if they greeted one another. Kevin leaned to one side in his saddle and the other mimicked him. Then he knew that this was the mirage, the pitiless mocker of the desert traveller, and was glad it was not reflected water that he saw in the hour of dire need. This vision hurt no one, it was even interesting. It vanished as suddenly as it had appeared, just before he came within hailing distance of the wagon.

At the sound of his voice Glenny turned his head, and then, with a deliberation that cut Kevin more than any verbal insolence could have done, turned back again, and flashing his whip over the backs of the draught beasts, urged them to faster pace. When eventually he drew alongside, Kevin allowed his fury to show itself in his voice.

"Where the hell do you imagine you're going? Oregon?" he demanded.

Without answering Glenny unleashed his whip again, and since the team struggled forward and the horse paced beside them, Kevin, who had reined in his mare, was forced to urge her forward too. And there are few things more irksome to the dignity than to address someone who will neither answer nor halt to listen.

"I suppose you know that you're going away from the water," he said, earnestness and anger blended in his voice.

"I'm going away from that bloody misleading map you've made such a coil about. And about that time too. Horiho there!"

"Will you stop and listen to me for a minute? Damn it, man, do you think I followed you for my health? You'll

202

lose yourself, you'll endanger the lives of your wife and your son if you persist in travelling this way."

As though his patience (*his* patience!) were now exhausted, Glenny shouted to his team and the animals halted willingly. Bearing on his rein he swung the gelding round and faced his pursuer. His demented bloodshot eyes met Kevin's with a flare of hatred in them.

"Listen," he said, "I left your party once, and though I had to come back on this blasted road, I left you then. I knew your map was wrong the night I told you so. And now—fifty hours in the desert! And we been three days wandering! Yonder's the water, look and see for yourself. I saw it a long time ago, but I knew if I mentioned it you'd blather about the map and your almighty experience. Get back now and collect the poor deluded fools that still believe in you and you'll find me with my beasts watered and my own belly full, hours ahead of you."

Following the line of the pointed whip butt Kevin looked and saw, distinct and clear and at no very great distance, a small lake, hemmed with green luscious grass and overhung by trees. Even the heavy-headed bulrushes could be seen, between grass and water. Knowing it for what it was Kevin could hardly check a sigh of admiration and desire. He said in a kinder tone:

"That lake is miles away, Glenny. It's a mirage. The sun and the clear air and the flatness are responsible for it. Why, just now I saw a horseman riding towards you, but as you see it was nobody but me. If you make for this you're done, man, done."

Glenny snorted with scorn.

"Rot," he said. "You mean it isn't on your map. Why, I can see it. And I ain't given to seeing things that ain't there as you seem to be." He ran the whiplash through his fingers and then added, "If you think I'm going to sun dry in the desert with water in sight you're wrong. Horiho there!"

Out flashed the whiplash and the team leaned forward.

The stubbornness, the dull cloddish ignorance, maddened Kevin. The hot blood rushed to his face.

"Don't think I care what happens to you, Glenny," he

said furiously. "I'm thinking of your wife and child. If you go on this way you'll all die of thirst."

A giant cry greeted these words and looking down Kevin saw that Lou Glenny had left the wagon and was now following, listening, her hand pressed to her mouth and her big deerlike eyes full of terror. The boy Evan, who had been trudging by the team all the time, and halting when it halted, now fell backward and joined his mother.

"Please," said Lou, approaching Kevin and looking up imploringly. "Please persuade him to turn back. I've done my utmost."

"Shut your mouth, you squalling bitch," said Glenny, "and get back in the wagon."

"I'm sorry, Mrs. Glenny. I seem to have no influence with your husband. But if you care to leave him we'll look after you. You can ride with me, and if the boy will begin to walk back I'll send someone to meet him. Believe me, that is the only way."

"Take her, if you like," said Glenny, wheeling back. "I've been trying to be rid of her for years. But the boy is useful. He stays with me. He's useful."

"I can't leave him," said Lou, still looking at Kevin and beginning to cry.

The trembling lips, the puckered chin and the tear-filled eyes were very moving; but the whole thing was an unwarrantable waste of precious time, and looking away Kevin said, quite shortly:

"You'll have to decide quickly, Mrs. Glenny."

She ran forward to Dave and gripped his booted leg.

"Come back, Dave—or if you won't do that, give me leave to take him. He's my boy, after all. Let me have him, for the sake of the old days, Dave, please."

Glenny, as impatient of delay as Kevin, pushed her away and then, as she still clung, brought the short butt of the ox-whip back and struck her in the face. She cried out and released her hold. Blood mingled with the tears on her face.

Without knowing that he spoke aloud Kevin cried, "All right, then!" and riding behind Dave seized him by the collar and dragged him backwards out of the saddle so that the big man's weight carried him over the horse's tail and onto the ground. The animal started forward in alarm, and Kevin, not taking his eyes from Glenny, yelled, "Catch him boy, catch him. Then get your mother up and yourself too."

Glenny was on his feet again in a moment. But instead of making for his mount and so frustrating the hopes of escape of Lou and Evan, he charged blindly at Kevin, who, with the co-operation of the nimble-footed Persephone, fended him off easily with his crop. Dave's whip, still in his hand, was too short in the butt and too long in the lash to be an effective weapon at short range, and while he stabbed and capered and bellowed Kevin saw Evan and Lou, insecurely mounted upon the nervous startled horse, go dashing away in the direction of the wagons. Once they were gone he pulled the mare round and was out of Glenny's reach in a moment.

Well, he thought, breathing hard, that was over and well over, and as he raised his hand to brush the sweat from his forehead he heard a crack, and a sharp pain, followed by sudden numbness, went through his left forearm midway between elbow and wrist. Persephone jumped sideways, and as he muttered a soothing word to her he looked at his arm and saw a hole in the cloth, its ragged edges darkening with blood.

"The bastard's shot me," he said aloud, incredulously. "It might have gone through my head!"

The thought stunned him. He had never been so near death before; never before roused murderous thoughts in another man's breast. He watched the dark patch widening around the hole, and more than the water shortage, more than anything that he had lately borne, that sight made him feel that everything was distorted, gone wrong, out of shape. Glenny had come up at Fort Mason and asked if he might try the new road—and now Glenny had shot him, not caring whether he killed him, and his bones might have whitened in the desert without anyone knowing, unless Lou and the boy heard the shot and guessed.

It was some minutes before he mastered his thoughts, took the handkerchief from his hat and tied it about his arm, pulling it tight with his teeth. God, he thought, as the knot was tied, suppose I had died . . . with the map on me, the map on me ... Glenny didn't think of that; but he should have. It's blind insensitive selfishness like his that does all the harm in the world. Because he is angry and must vent his spite nearly a score of people may die and he does not care. The world is well rid of him.

(But actually, almost as soon as the shot had been fired Dave had looked ahead and found the lake, with its grass and its trees and its bulrushes gone. Desperately and defiantly he had mounted the next ridge, and the next, peering out under his hand. But the angle of the sun had changed and the sky came down to the desert and the distance held no lake in its depths. Presently he turned his failing team.)

The numbness gave way to nagging pain, like magnified toothache. The tight folds of the handkerchief were speckled with blood. Thirst, which had been with him all day, now troubled Kevin acutely. He felt dizzy and there was a buzzing in his ears. But he must defeat Glenny. He must gain the hills and collect enough water to save the people.

Once he lost consciousness for a moment and his head fell forward, but his chin hit the pit of his cravat and he jerked upright, anxiously taking his bearings, seeing with relief that he was still riding in the same direction.

Persephone began to flag, her stride lost its rhythm, her breathing was audible. He chirruped to her and called through a throat that seemed lined with sand. And then, with a suddenness that justified his assertions about the distances in the desert, the hills were there, just ahead of him, and there was green again, the blessed green of watered land, and there were the willows dropping their leaves into the water. It was like an Eden poised on the very outskirts of Hell.

He flung himself from the saddle and drank with his face in the water, a bare foot from ripples caused by Persephone's plunging nose. Horse and rider, well-attuned as they usually were, were more one in that moment than they had ever been; both animals that must have water for their living, animals that had come out of the desert that did not tolerate their existence. They drank their fill, and then Persephone, plunging up with a shower of silvery drips from

206

her muzzle, fell to munching the good green grass, while Kevin lay, stretched on his back with his injured arm supported by the buttons of his coat.

But soon he must deny this pleasant languor, and with one hand, fill and stopper the flasks and bottles that he had collected. He dragged the mare away from her orgy and offered her a last drink. Then, wearily he climbed into the saddle; but his heart was light. He might tell his company that water was there, that only patience and effort were needed to bring them to it.

He started the return journey in the twilight, but the moon had risen before he met the first of his company, Klara Bolewska, the Warrens and the Negro brother and sister, driving their teams before them. Behind came the Smiths and Floribel Toit. The two members of the company who could not walk, Madame Jurer and Frank Cooper, had been left with the wagons when the oxen failed.

Throughout the late hot afternoon the travellers had had panic for company. The oxen had failed, the children were wailing, even the men and women had felt that they must drink or die. The decision to abandon the wagons temporarily came as a relief, for sound human instinct favours the untrammelled human foot as a means of escape.

Through the heat and panic and the haste and the thirst, good-fellowship and mutual responsibility survived and held; the men helped one another with the stumbling beasts, the women who had no burdens shared the weight of the children. And Mahitabel, by some means that she did not divulge, had found enough water to stay the children's thirst. She had remembered that Frank Cooper was her responsibility, and before leaving her wagon, by draining every cask and bottle, had collected a half-mugful of tepid water, and placed it beside him. Her baby was wailing all the time, but she restricted herself to moistening its lips. The baby was going to be carried towards the water; Frank Cooper must remain for an indefinite time without hope of relief, so his claim came first.

Just as she left her wagon she saw Nancy Jurer turn back into hers, having watched the departure of the main party. Always, if not happily, conscious of the old woman's personality, she was impressed now by her calm demeanour, and upon catching up with the others she inquired of Klara and Floribel whether there were any water in the painted wagon. The girls said they thought not, and Ruth Warren who had overheard the question, added that earlier in the day, when she had tried to borrow a little for her babies, Madame Jurer had replied that she had used her last drop overnight.

Mahitabel plumped Ellen into Mary Ann's arms and hurried, with her swooping, lapwing movement, back to the wagons. She poured, with apologies, half Frank Cooper's meagre supply into another mug and with it in her hand went to the other wagon. She disapproved of Nancy Jurer and resented the hold that she seemed to have gained over Mary Ann, but she knew courage when she saw it and was prepared to salute it in the only way within her power.

Her step was noiseless on the sand, and in the hot afternoon Madame sat with the flaps of the wagon hood open. Approaching, Mahitabel saw the old woman bend to her locker and take out the inevitable bottle of red wine and a big stone gallon jar. She poured out a little wine, and sat down comfortably on the built-in bunk that was one of the luxuries of the big wagon. She sipped, for pleasure, not for the quenching of thirst.

Something of the fury and hatred with which Mahitabel, halted in the sand, was regarding her, must have reached her mind, for she turned suddenly as though in answer to a call and her wary eyes hooded themselves for a second before returning Mahitabel's fixed stare.

"Well," she demanded—and there was a faint trace of uneasiness in the challenging voice—"and what are you staring at?"

"The beastliest sight I ever saw," said Mahitabel. "I've come back to bring you half the poor drop that remained to us, water I'd denied my own child, and I find you guzzling. You that wouldn't let Mrs. Warren have a cupful for her babies."

"And what," said Nancy Jurer calmly, "have Mrs. Warren or her babies done for me? If I had the foresight to store more water, or to use it more carefully, what is that

208

to anyone? I have myself to think of. And if everyone did that, you know, there would not be any cause for maudlin sentiment in this world."

"Maudlin sentiment," repeated Mahitabel, as though mouthing two words of an obscene foreign language. "I brought you what I had because I thought you were thirsty and suffering. If that is maudlin sentiment may you never be in need of it again, for believe me, you'd never get it."

With the faintest suggestion of a shrug of her fat shoulders Nancy Jurer lifted the glass and at the sight Mahitabel's control gave way. She pounced on the water jar and before the clumsy old woman could rise from her seat, had filled the pannikin that she carried.

"And may the rest choke you," she said setting the jar back on the table with a bang.

She replaced in her passenger's mug the water that she borrowed and with the rest held carefully, chased after the others. The water, shared amongst the four children, relieved their immediate pangs and they were quiet as one woman after another bore them along.

The sun set and the sudden chill, at first reviving, seemed to paralyse the weary struggling people; but soon after the moon had risen they met Kevin, with his words of cheer and his limited though refreshing draughts of water, put new heart into them. Towards morning they stumbled, one by one, out of the desert and felt the grass under their feet and fell on their faces by the water's edge, as ardent worshippers as ever went down the steps of Benares to receive the blessing of the sacred Ganges.

A day's rest, they reckoned, with plenty of water and grass, would give the oxen strength to bring the wagons out of the salt. So all day they lay on the grass beneath the trees, men and beasts together. Only Abe Smith went back on the good Persephone to carry water to the two remaining in the wagons. He was not to return, but to wait there until the other men brought back the oxen.

Mahitabel dressed Kevin's arm, using strips of linen torn from a petticoat flounce and making a sling of a hemstitched fichu. He said little about the accident, but that little, allied to Evan's few words and Lou's tearful apologies, laid bare the whole tale.

But to the travellers it was an interesting, not a depressing story, for they were suddenly in the holiday mood that follows an escape from pain or peril. They had, after all, beaten the desert, and save for Glenny they were all together and alive. The joy they found in this fact revealed the magnitude of their fears. Optimism rose in them. Nothing, they felt, that could now befall them could be as bad as the Valley of Brambles, or the discovery that the dry journey was almost twice as long as they had expected. They would make it yet.

(And all the time, hidden amongst the hills above the watering places, the little dark men were mustering. From their eyries they had been watching, for thirty-six hours, the slow approach of the wagon train. They had watched while Kevin watered his horse and lay in the shade; but they had given no sign, for to have done so would have warned the party with whom the oxen travelled. Waiting, they thought of warm ox-blood to drink and with which to be-daub themselves, succulent meat to eat, marrow bones to gnaw in the winter days that were coming, hides in which to wrap themselves and from which to cut strips for their bow-strings. Animals were scarce on the hills by the desert, and the little Diggers' bows were weak to bring against a flying quarry. But the slow stolid oxen were easy game. Hidden in the hills, screened by the bushes, the Diggers waited.)

Jim Mason had said, "And they's always Injuns": nor were the travellers utterly innocent of their menace. Tales —often true ones at first or second-hand—had been told by old people by many a comfortable hearth on winter evenings. But they had expected a screeching onslaught, openly conducted and easily routed by a little shooting. That had not come, and now they had forgotten the Indians. They ate the food which the women had prudently brought out from the wagons, drank their fill, and after their nights of labour and anxiety, sank into profound slumber. When all had been quiet for some hours the little dark men struck.

The noise of the stampede, of frantic lowing and bellows of pain, penetrated at last to the drugged brains of the sleepers. Men grabbed their guns with sleep-weighted hands, tried to kindle lanterns. But the damage was already done. A few dead oxen, and fatally wounded ones, lay about the watering place, horribly visible to the questing eye in the first light of morning; many had been driven off, others had run far afield in the terror of the moment, and even the living ones that were finally recovered, had the Diggers' arrows bristling from their hides.

After a first dismayed silence at the magnitude of their disaster the men broke into curses, at their evil luck, at their own carelessness, at the little dark men whom they had forgotten. And when they had expressed their futile rage, they rallied and began to tug out arrows and slap clay upon the punctures they had made. They worked together, but each man's eyes were furtively reckoning the marks that the beasts bore. Mine . . . thank God, only scratched! Another of mine dead, Hell! Dear Heaven, are all mine gone?

Scanty, with huge tears chasing one another over his quivering face, wailed that he dared not face his mistress with the news. Yet Madame Jurer had had what luck was going in the sorry affair; of her beasts five were there and on their feet, suffering only minor wounds. But Scanty mourned specially for the big lead ox, Chocolate.

"He just cudden be kilt by no liddle arrow like dat'n," he said at last, "great strong beast like he wuz. I done gotta find dat ox, Mr. Furmage, Mr. Smith, Mr. Warren. You all he'p me find Chocolate, den maybe I dast face it."

"But we've recovered all that were to be found," said Kevin impatiently.

"Maybe Chocolate done gone fudder dan dem udders. Mighty swift he wuz. Ah'm gonna look agin."

No one else would go on the hopeless quest, so Janna, tucking up her skirt all round, plunged into the undergrowth behind her brother, and as the company waited with what patience they could muster they could hear the musical voices of the Negroes calling:

"Choc'late! Choc'late! Come yo back here dis minnit."

While they waited the men gathered around Kevin and talked over what best to do. Kevin had four animals fit for service, Cordy three and Ben, true to his nickname, two only, least of all. They reckoned that these, with Madame Jurer's five, would make two teams for the two smaller wagons, Ben's and Cordy's; the red-wheeler monster and Kevin's must be abandoned. And things must be jettisoned from the two that went on, so that food for all might be transported. Here Ruth and Mahitabel broke in on the discussion, speaking up for this precious thing and that, precious enough to have been brought all the way from Pennsylvania and Missouri, doubly precious now when threatened with incarceration in the salt desert. But they were amenable enough after their first protests, weighed down by the seriousness of the situation, prepared to throw away anything if it helped to promote the success of the journey which was rapidly becoming nightmarish.

At last Scanty and Janna, both blubbering hard, returned without Chocolate, and then, driving their diminished teams, Ben, Cordy and Joe Sterry set off back into the desert. Kevin, who was in pain from his arm, was persuaded to stay with the women, "for protection" they said, and little Hendriks stayed too. The dwarf Dutchman seemed overwhelmed with misery. Of the four lovely beasts that he had tended for so long, given pet names to and trained to answer his call, like dogs, only one heifer remained. And his master, looking at it with eyes which saw, not only the one beast, but the end of his dreams of raising the Furmage Herd in the green fields of California, had said harshly, "Well, we can always eat her when meat gets short." Eat her, that precious, costly heifer, whose name was Tulip, and whose calves Hendriks had thought to see! When that day came, be he never so hungry and her flesh never so tender, Hendriks would not eat a bit.

As they had feared, Madame set about her slaves with shouts and blows, as though they had made the hills and the Indians and the bows and the arrows with the express intention of annoying her. But when Cordy, as spokesman in Kevin's absence, explained to her the plan for taking forward the two smaller wagons and leaving the heavier behind, she turned the full blast of her rage upon him. Fourteen animals remained, didn't they, and of those five were hers, didn't that give her the louder say in the matter? To her mind it did. And she had no intention of leaving her precious wagon with all its ingenious devices for comfort and place herself as a guest in someone else's rattletrap.

"But it's no question of whose beasts they are, or of who has the say in the matter," protested Cordy desperately—for all this was a further waste of valuable time. "It's a question of making the journey as safely and expeditiously as possible for everyone. I can see it's a good wagon and cost you money—but we've all to sacrifice something. In mine there's a hand-press that was to start me in business over there, but I shall have to leave it in order to carry food for everyone."

"Nor ma'am," said Ben, unexpectedly vocal, "it ain't no question of comfort, yours nor mine nor nobody's. Nobody'll be comfortable, it ain't to be expected. If Warren here leaves his wagon to take yourn you'll have to travel his children."

Joe Sterry tugged Cordy's arm and said quietly, "Leave the old bitch be, Mister Warren. Leave her with her wagon and her five beasts and see what she makes a *that*."

It might have worked—as a threat, but Cordy cancelled its value by admitting, "That's what I'd like to do—but that means our going on with only one wagon between us all."

They argued for a further five minutes and then both Ben and Cordy capitulated at the same moment. In the instant when they begin discussing which of *their* wagons should be abandoned Madame Nancy was certain of her victory. To mark it she said graciously, "If Mr. Warren, with his big family, takes *his* wagon, your passenger can ride with me, Mr. Smith."

Ben gasped at the audacity, "I should say so," he said. "Maybe you'd also be s'kind as to carry a few stores for us. Whose beasts is going to help out your five I'd like to ask you?"

"Well," said Cordy rather wearily, "which do we take, Ben, yours or mine?"

They walked over to inspect the vehicles. They had always been of a different order from Kevin's and Madame's, and now what paint they had was blistered by the desert sun and their timbers were dried out and gaping. There was little to choose between them. Ben said at last:

"You take yours, Cordy. That'll leave your missus boss

of it and it'll be better for the little 'uns. I'll go help poor Cooper across to the old harridan. I reckon she'll treat him better'n she would three babies."

There was no gainsaying the homely logic.

As swiftly as possible they gathered the food from the wagons that were to be abandoned and packed it into the two that were to proceed with the journey. Nancy protested, enough to support her sense of possession and not enough to madden the men into altering the scheme, as some of her goods were jettisoned. Then they set out; and the good stout wagon and the shabbier one, with their poles lolling, stood there, abandoned, strangely moving and desolate-looking upon the face of the desert.

When they reached the watering place it was to find that Dave Glenny had re-joined the party shortly after their leaving. He had abandoned his wagon, but had brought out three oxen with most of his foodstuff packed in unwieldy bundles on their backs.

This time there was no welcome for him, and as though feeling his ostracism, he remained, watering and resting his animals for twenty-four hours after the wagons moved away. But within a few days he had caught up with them again, since the free beasts moved more swiftly. And since he carried food and had animals that might be needed, nothing was said or done to prevent him joining the tail of the procession again. He did not wish to do so. He desired to push on with his light load; but the way was unknown to him and when he approached Kevin with a request for direction Kevin looked through him as though he were invisible and inaudible.

They went on climbing. Ascents beside which the almost-forgotten Saddle seemed like a gentle hillside were tackled and mastered; rivers were forded and crossed. The early optimism and good spirits of the company had gone, but in its place was something more durable, the stubborn purpose of people who have weathered disaster, and, in most quarters the clear unity of purpose of people who have shared in misadventure.

And then the cloud burst.

All day it had been clear and sunny, with an edge to the wind that chilled the sweat on neck and brow. Then, at three o'clock in the afternoon the wind dropped suddenly, and the tearing clouds settled low and still so that the afternoon took on the colour of evening.

The party was climbing a gully, steep and narrow, almost like the inside of a chimney-stack built of rock. The oxen, headed for the opening between two great boulders at the top of the path, gave the first sign of uneasiness, trying to swerve aside whenever the path widened and to take shelter behind the outjutting rocks.

There were men there who were wise in the ways of beasts, and Kevin had had a little experience of the mountains, but there was no one with both animal and mountain lore, and the oxen were relentlessly brought back to the path and forced onward and upward. And then the cloud overheard seemed to open and a solid sheet of water, powerful enough to knock a man down, hurtled through the air. It was not rain, no rain ever fell so solidly and smitingly. Clutching at one another, hanging on to an ox-yoke, snatching at a wagon wheel, the people tried to withstand the furious onslaught; but the supports themselves gave way. Mad with terror the oxen strove this way and that, smashing yokes and pole, hurting one another themselves. And to complete the chaos, from the head of the gully, which acted as a watershed, a great stream of earth-borne water came pouring, a tumbling brown cascade that filled the path and foamed around the rocks that hemmed it in. Cordy's wagon rocked and tilted as the ground beneath its far wheels was washed away by the flood, and it went over, slowly at first and then, carried by its own weight, with a tremendous thudding splash. From within it came, rising above the sounds of outer confusion, the shrill frantic screaming of Ruth's three babies and Mahitabel's Ellen.

As if that destruction had completed its purpose the downpour ceased abruptly; the flood water tore on down the gully and the drenched, bruised, broken people were left to pick themselves up and reckon their new losses. Surprisingly, the children had suffered least of all, having been flung against the rugs and blankets that composed the bedding. They were taken out unharmed. But there were broken limbs amongst the oxen; and Cordy's wagon had two smashed wheels. Ben Smith, who had been holding on to the wagon when it tilted, had a crushed foot, little Hendriks a long wound at the back of his head, and there were many bruises and cuts amongst the others. Madame Jurer and Frank Cooper, who had been riding in the second wagon, were, however, uninjured.

But the food which had been stored in the broken wagon was soaked and scattered about the path and some water had seeped into Madame Jurer's wagon, spoiling still other stores.

They bound up one another's wounds, shot the oxen that could not travel and cut off the fleshy portions. They moved the babies into the remaining wagon and heaved Ben—for whom there was no room—on to Persephone's back. By sunset they reached the head of the gully, and there, shattered and dispirited, camped early. Dave Glenny's oxen, free to take cover, had escaped injury. They were now pressed into service and his food thrown into the remaining wagon. But the wildeyed horse had broken away and gone tearing down the path, and though Glenny ran after it as soon as the deluge ceased, and went out again in the evening and in the morning, it was not seen again.

In the camp that night there was a curious stoic feeling that they had now suffered all that could be asked of them. The trail, the Indians, and now the elements, had all taken their toll. Wagons and beasts and foodstuff had been lost, but the people were still alive and together. The comfort that they took in the thought was significant—like Mahitabel's labour alongside Klara and Janna, it was a closing of ranks before the common enemy.

As though the cloudburst had ended their afflictions they were now cheered by four days of clear bright weather, rather cold, but sunny, and the trail was good. Cordy, who had proved their best marksman, shot some wild duck as they winged southward, and the suppertime at which they were eaten savoured a little of those old evenings when hopes were high and hearts unseared by anxiety. Perhaps the run of bad luck had ended. . . .

Even Kevin, looking at the range ahead of them, and pointing out that once they were across it they would have only downward slopes to negotiate, slopes that would end in the Sacramento meadows, even Kevin felt a little balm to his soul. With the map amended, and allowance made for the extra hours in the desert, it was a good road after all. The damage done by the Indians was due largely to the travellers' carelessness, and against a cloudburst no one could guard. If, despite these things, he could get the party across with its human complement intact, he need not consider the venture a failure.

So they pushed on through the shortening days and at last could see, outlined against the sky, the distant V-shaped nick between two heights which was the pass over which they would soon be travelling into California.

Kevin called their attention to it in a voice that was not quite steady. Some days before, when he had sighted the last barrier range and spoken of the Sacramento meadows, he had felt certain of entering them at the head of his party. But on this blustering afternoon when the actual Pass itself was visible, a new anxiety was taking possession of his mind.

He had, from the first, treated his wound with little ceremony. Mahitabel had dressed it for several days, bathing it with hot water and smearing it with some pungent homemade ointment which she found after a long search through her scattered possessions and which she swore would cure any wound not mortal. But after the cloudburst she had had Ben's crushed foot to tend as well as the long gash on the back of Hendriks' head. Kevin's wound seemed trivial by comparison and he had refused, after that, to allow her to devote any attention to it. But now he realised that it was not healing as it should. The clean hole was increasing in size and suppurating steadily. The dull nagging pain of it fretted his days and invariably woke him in the night as soon as the first sleep of exhaustion ended. He had been obliged to loosen Mahitabel's last bandage because his arm was swelling and on this day he was dismayed to find that his hand and fingers were puffy and discoloured. Nor did he feel well, as he put it, "in himself." And there was a half-memory of something that haunted him.

On the evening of the day when the Pass was sighted

he spoke of it to Mahitabel as he watched her dressing Ben's foot.

"I keep trying to remember something that I believe comes in the Bible, Mrs. Smith. Somebody who led some people somewhere and then didn't get there himself, quite. Is it Biblical?"

Mahitabel wrung out the cloth she had been using and looked at Kevin sharply.

"Maybe you're thinking of Moses. He saw the Promised Land from Mount Pisgah and then he died." Her tone was unusually curt and Kevin attributed it to a rebuke for him for not knowing his Bible better. But almost immediately she whisked round with a fresh pan of hot water in her hand and said:

"Take off that coat and let me look at your arm."

"It's all right," he protested, backing away from her. "It's better."

"Then what are you thinking about Moses for?" she demanded. "And anyway Moses was God's chosen servant and he was old and he hadn't been shot in the arm."

Kevin laughed, but even that sound was unlike his old hearty bellow, and Mahitabel, speaking in the voice that had quelled any incipient mutiny in her family, repeated her demand that he should take off his coat.

Kevin was stubborn; but he was no match for Mahitabel, and finally, with as much reluctance as though the wound were something to be ashamed of, he took off his coat, rolled back his shirt-sleeve and allowed Mahitabel to remove the bandage.

She bit back an exclamation of surprise and consternation at the sight of it, but her concern took the shape of abuse.

"You said it was better. Why, little Hendriks' is a king to it. But then he's got sense, he comes every evening, punctual as the clock. Really, Mr. Furmage, I credited you with more sense! Look at this bandage, stiff! And you that I've heard shouting all over the camp for a clean shirt on a Wednesday. Strain at a gnat and swallow a camel. You men are all alike."

Grumbling steadily she swabbed out the widening hole, smoothed on the ointment and replaced the bandage with

218

a clean strip of linen. She made a new sling.

"Now see that you keep it up," she admonished. "Else you may *be* like Moses, and nobody to thank but yourself. Ah ... and with all this I forgot to tell you that Mr. Cooper has been asking to see you. There's something on *his* mind, too."

Feeling a little as though he had been caught in a whirlwind, spun rapidly and suddenly released, Kevin walked to the wagon where Frank Cooper was propped on an improvised bunk. Throughout the whole journey the young man's condition had grown steadily worse, and since his removal to Madame Jurer's wagon the task of keeping him even reasonably clean had taxed Mahitabel's patience and ingenuity to the utmost. He was now so stiff that only his eyes and his hands seemed to have any life left in them. Even his voice was stiff and uneven, as though his affliction had reached his throat. But he greeted Kevin with his usual cheerfulness. Chained to the wagon, he had grown accustomed to Kevin's visits to Madame Jurer and knew that such visits generally entailed a sharing of some kind of liquid refreshment. Tonight his good leather valise was lying, half open, across his immobile legs, and as Kevin appeared he said, "Now Madame", and Nancy, as though at a cue, produced three cups. (The pewter measures had been jettisoned long ago.) She reached over and took from the valise a silver drinking flask.

"It's good brandy," said Frank, "calculated to save me *in extremis*. But we're going to drink it to-night because this is an occasion."

"Because we've sighted the Pass?" asked Kevin, in whose mind the journey was still uppermost.

"No, though we'll include that. Actually, Furmage, I've been making my will. And since it's the last bit of writing I'm ever likely to do, *I* call it an occasion."

Not for the first time Kevin received Frank's reference to his physical state with his embarrassment.

"Didn't you hear me say that we'd sighted the Pass," he said, "Why, man, before the ink is dry on your signature you'll be basking in the Californian sun and skipping about, limber as my mare."

"That, naturally, is what I hope for. But all the same

". . . to be on the safe side, will you see if this is legible and in order?"

He had borrowed Mahitabel's quill and the inkpot with the patent non-spilling device. Kevin took the sheet of paper—it had been torn from Mahitabel's diary—and glanced at the words upon it. The letters were cramped, uneven, difficult to read and he leaned towards the lantern in an effort to decipher it.

In simple phrases that yet contained a certain legal flavour the sick man had set down his wishes. His watch and chain, his gold ring and all other personal belongings were to go to Abe Smith; the five thousand dollars currency in his possession at his death were bequeathed to Benjamin and Mahitabel Smith, jointly, or in the case of one surviving, to that survivor. The rest of his property, his shares in the shipping concern of Cooper and Treeman, accrued interest and the Californian property bought in his name were left unconditionally to Mary Ann Smith as a token of his affection and esteem.

Kevin, who knew the shipping firm to be one of the biggest and most flourishing in the country though he had never connected Frank with it, found his first reaction to be one of amazement.

"It makes her a very rich young woman," he said.

"Comfortably provided for," said Frank. "But tell me . . . it seems to you legally valid and . . . not unduly compromising?"

"It's quite in order," said Kevin, rather at a loss. "As for being compromising, well, God, man we're not in Boston, you know."

"I know," said Frank, gravely. "Still, there is that to consider." He brooded for a moment and seemed to decide upon confidence. Lowering his voice he said, "You see, I'm very much attached to her. I don't think she knows and I'm glad. In my state it would seem silly, maudlin. Of course, *if* I get there and *if* I get better I shall endeavour to put things on a different footing, if she will let me. But as it is I wanted to be sure that she was provided for, at least. You think it'll be all right?"

"Perfectly. You haven't signed it, you know."

"No, I was waiting for you. I'll sign now and Madame and you can witness it, if you will be so kind."

With an effort that showed Kevin how painful the writing of the actual document must have been, he signed his name at the foot of the sheet. Madame Jurer wrote hers in slanting academic writing; Kevin affixed his scribbled signature and then hastily raised his cup.

"May it be long before it comes into operation," he said.

"Oh, it probably will," said Frank with a reversal to lightness in his manner. "Old Charles Freeman, my great-uncle, kept the whole family hanging on his slightest word on account of his money from the time he was sixty. When he died at eighty-four twenty different wills were found, but he'd married his nurse three days before and the last one left everything to his dear wife. It caused a lot of heart-burning I may tell you."

The lively glance shifted.

"I'm sorry to see that you've got your arm up again. Is it painful?"

"That's Mrs. Smith's doing. It's strange, isn't it, how these competent women can make you just about six years old again?"

"It doesn't need a competent woman to do that," chuckled Nancy. "The trouble is that you *are* all about six years old at heart, fickle and headstrong and very anxious to prove that you've really grown up."

For once Kevin did not reply to the old woman with his usual gay banter.

"I don't know about that," he said. "I only know that tonight I feel about a hundred, badly preserved at that. I think I'll turn in and see what a night's sleep can do for me. Good night, Cooper, remember the Pass is in sight. Good night, Madame."

"Good night, Mr. Furmage," said Nancy in her most graciously professional manner. "I hope you'll be restored in the morning."

When he had gone she said with considerable feeling, "That Glenny did a bad day's work when he fired that shot. Furmage has been a different man since, and he was the best of the lot of you." Then, with a sudden change in her manner she pushed aside the bales which had been so arranged that her disrobing was hidden from the sight of the man on the improvised bunk, and waddling forward she sat down near him.

"Listen," she said crisply, and Frank, turning his eyes to her face saw that it had set in a mask of determination from which the eyes, under their hooded lids, shone like crumbs of coal. "You bargained to travel with the Smiths, didn't you? What did you pay them?"

"If you must know, we agreed on a hundred dollars. I paid half and shall pay the rest at the end of the journey."

"So if you get to California they'll have fifty dollars, and if you don't they'll have, between them, all you own. Is that right?

"Yes. Why?"

"Why?" she repeated harshly. "Ask yourself why! Ask yourself whose wagon has carried you ever since the salt desert. Ask yourself where you'd be if I hadn't taken you in. And then, just to finish off with, ask yourself what I am getting in return for the inconvenience and unpleasantness of having a sick man lying in my wagon day and night. Well, what's the answer?"

A hot painful wave of colour swept over the pale wasted face. Dear God, was there no end to the humiliation which physical disability could inflict? How far better off was Joe Sterry, who owned nothing but his body and the clothes he wore, who could work his way and attend to himself and be obliged to no one.

"I must admit, Madame Jurer, that I had not asked myself those questions, nor had I any idea that they were troubling you. If I had thought at all I should have come to the conclusion that since the disaster at the watering place all notions of who owned this wagon or that had been abandoned. Some of Smith's cattle went into the team that drew us. . . . Still, I should much regret being under an obligation to you. It wouldn't please the Smiths either. Be so good to me as to hand me my bag again."

Kevin had put the will in it and replaced it under the bunk. Stooping with difficulty Nancy drew it out and watched greedily as Frank's hands fumbled with the clasps.

"The Smiths seemed not to find my presence either unpleasant or inconvenient, so we cannot reckon your remuneration by theirs, can we?" he asked coldly. "Will you be satisfied with two hundred dollars?" Many grasping people would have been deterred by his tone, would have prevaricated and protested; but it was many decades since Nancy Jurer had been handicapped by sensitiveness.

"Three would suit me better," she said calmly. "I'm afraid I can't afford to be either sentimental or generous. You need the transport and I need the money. And I don't suppose the Smiths will miss it whether you live or die."

Silently Frank counted out the money. Then he said:

"I'm sorry you had to ask, Madame Jurer. I should have thought of it myself."

"Oh, that's all right," said Nancy frankly. "I'm used to asking. And now here's the little Smith girl with your soup. I'll take my evening walk."

Mary Ann came in, her eyes fixedly downcast to the covered jug that she carried. Her mouth was set in as sulky a line as its natural sweet curves would accommodate.

In the period between the abandoning of the family wagon and the cloudburst she had enjoyed herself. Deprived of its focal point the Smith family had tasted a freedom hitherto unknown. Even Mahitabel could not forbid intercourse with the coloured wagon now that it carried part of her stores and her passenger. (What the necessary civility that she was obliged to show to Madame Jurer cost her, after the episode in the desert, no one but Mahitabel would ever know.) But after Ben's accident life for Mary Ann darkened and narrowed again; with two sick men to mind Mahitabel was obliged to leave a good many chores and much of the care of Ellen to her daughter. The giggling chats with Floribel were much curtailed.

Their intimacy had flowered apace and into Mary Ann's ear Floribel had poured a great deal that her friend had not known, besides much that she did not understand. Mary Ann had discovered that the round iron which Abe had used for boring the hole for Cordy was the very tool for heating and winding Floribel's glossy curls. Floribel had once returned the good office and Mary Ann's head had flowered like Medusa's; but with all her business Mahitabel

223

had had time to notice that and order the removal of the ringlets with a wet comb. It was on that evening that Mary Ann had carried in Frank's supper with marks of tears on her face and he had known, by the pang he felt, that he was in love with her. He had asked her the cause of her grief and she had innocently told him; and immediately afterwards she had hated both herself and him, herself for her confidence and him because of the tenderness in his voice and glance and because he put out one thin hand and patted her wrist.

Up to that time she had served him quite unthinkingly, had been sorry for him, anxious to relieve his tedium by little bits of gossip and to do what she could for his physical comfort. But afterwards the mere thought of him could fill her with a feeling that was part confusion and part nausea.

She had spoken about her change of attitude to Floribel —that followed naturally—and the other girl had listened greedily.

"He's in love with you," she announced rather groundlessly.

"Oh no!" said Mary Ann, horrified. "But that's a horrid thought! I hadn't noticed it before, but he's just like a corpse."

Madame says he soon will be one," said Floribel, "and she says he has plenty of money. Think if he married you and then died and left you rich!"

All Mary Ann's lovely colour faded. She stared at Floribel with unaffected horror. It was not the first time she had been shocked by this new friend's attitude; but it was the first time her own inner feelings had been concerned. Her mind—so newly informed, for poor erring Dulcie Jepson's disclosures had been innocent in the extreme compared with Floribel's—was passing through a very painful period of transition and enlightenment. Actually, though she was fascinated by it, sex, at the moment, was disgusting to her too, and the thought that poor crippled Mr. Cooper, for whom her mother had to do such unspeakable things, had any of *that* feeling for her made her hot and sick and angry.

So to-night, relentlessly called from a gossip, hardly begun, with the shocking but irresistible Floribel, she came to the end of Frank's bunk with silky mouth and downcast eyes. Unwillingly, trying not to touch his thin warm body, she propped the pillow behind his back and was careful to avoid touching his fingers as she handed him the soup. In vain he tried to talk and evoke some response. Mary Ann made monosyllabic replies, and kept her eyes averted. A little pulse beat rapid in her round white throat. He sensed something wrong and tried to probe the cause.

"Somebody been upsetting you again?" he asked.

"No."

He peered at her. "No? No curls? No rice powder?"

"No." And then, in a sudden burst: "I wish you could forget that. It was silly of me to tell you. It was childish. Besides, a girl shouldn't complain to people of her mother."

"You didn't complain. I merely asked you what was the matter, and you told me. But I'm sorry. I won't mention it again. You see, I'm afraid I've rather forgotten the proper way to talk to young ladies. You'll have to forgive me."

She almost hated him for the rather wistful kindness in his voice. She did not want to be pitied by someone who was himself pitiable in the extreme; she wanted to be properly dressed, prettily coiffured, and to have men at her feet, proper men like those in the stories that Floribel told, swearing they were true.

She said, "Oh, that's all right," in so grudging a manner that Frank was doubly sure of her unhappiness. She had been such a sunny little person. He himself admired Mahitabel, and no one in the world had better reason for gratitude to her, but he did think that she was needlessly strict in bringing up her daughter. And it was with the intent to comfort that he said:

"You know, Mary Ann, growing up is always rather difficult, but you've almost finished. As soon as you get into California you'll be married and able to please yourself about things. Your freedom will taste all the sweeter."

He viewed with alarm and consternation the effect of his well-meaning words. Mary Ann's face darkened unbelievably. Her eyes filled with furious tears. She said in a voice curiously like Mahitabel at her snappiest:

"I'll never be married. I won't marry anyone." And forgetting to take the soup jug, she flung herself out of the wagon and scampered away.

Frank might have gained some amusement if he could have overheard the whispered conversation between the girls later in the evening.

"I was right, then?" asked Floribel.

"Yes, you were right. He said something about getting married as soon as we were in California."

"And what did you say?"

"Oh, I refused him. I spoke kindly, but I made it quite clear that I couldn't marry him." Impossible for Floribel Marietta Toit to realise how the untruthful sentence was the fruit of seed she had sown.

"Well, Mary Ann Smith, you are the biggest fool I ever knew. Holy Mother, what wouldn't I have given for the chance. I told you, didn't I, that Madame says he's got lots of money."

"I don't care, I don't want it. I don't want it. I don't want ever to hear anything about it again." Her voice rose shrilly. "If you ever mention it again, Floribel Toit, you're no friend of mine."

Floribel shrugged her shoulders—a little less plump than they had been—but took no offence. She changed the subject without difficulty.

"Where's Abe?"

Strange, reflected Mary Ann, that Floribel who had, on her own showing, been attractive to almost every man she ever met, should have so little power to draw Abe. Once, very tactlessly, she had questioned her brother's feeling for her friend and Abe had expressed himself with unusual fluency.

"It's no good, Mary Ann. She's your friend and I reckon she's all right. But I just don't like her, that's all."

"But why not? Don't you think she's pretty?"

"No, I don't. I don't like the way she walks, for one thing. Nor I don't like all that colour on her face. Aw, Mary Ann, I'm sorry, but I just don't take to her. And she's wasting her time making eyes at me. Oh, yes, she is; think I'm blind?"

"It's because you've got Mrs. Glenny on your mind," said Mary Ann, stung by his scorn of the beloved Floribel. "And she married too. You ought to think shame to yourself."

With his sister Abe was neither shy nor easily embarrassed. Nor could he be teased by the mention of Lou's name as he had once been. It gave him a queer secret pleasure to hear it mentioned now. To Mary Ann's remark he replied with a smile, which in its serene assurance and suggestion of superior knowledge, showed how far behind he had left the old awkward boy that he had been.

For Abe all the disasters had worked together for good. The disintegration of the family units had given him freedom, the enforced communal living had offered him opportunity, and after Glenny's attack on Kevin there had been a tacit assumption amongst the travellers that Lou— who had remained faithful through personal ill-treatment— might now be permitted to ostracise Dave as the rest of them did. These were all circumstances favourable to the love-sick youth. But without Lou's consent they might have been useless. However, the gentle little woman, violently and finally liberated from an old and unhappy allegiance, was as ill at ease as a hermit crab whose old shell has been shed and the new one not yet discovered. She had a clinging nature, and there was no one to whom to cling, except Abe. She had a longing for kindness, and there was no one to offer it except Abe. Almost unconsciously at first she turned towards him; and Abe, shedding shyness and diffidence like an outworn garment, dropped his boyhood, too, and became of man's stature.

The most exciting moment of his life was the one when, during a stolen meeting after supper, she confided to him that Glenny had never married her. She proffered the information quite guilelessly and was surprised and considerably enlightened, by Abe's reaction. He seized both her hands from where they lay in her lap and wrung them in a grip that made her wince.

"Oh, Lou," he gasped. "That's the best news I ever

heard. Then you're free of him, really free. Oh, now I can look after you properly. You'll let me, won't you? You'll marry me as soon as we get there, won't you? I'll make up to you for everything." Sordid considerations broke in. "I shan't have much money, I know that. But Lord, how I'll work."

He made the promise on a note of ecstasy.

Lou drew away her hands and said in a small shaky voice:

"I shouldn't have told you that. You see, I couldn't marry you, Abe. For one thing I'm nearly thirty-four. And there's Evan, he's my son and I love him, but you couldn't take your wife's bastard into your home. And there're other reasons, Abe. I've told you a lot, too much indeed; but there are things I haven't told you, dreadful things. Nobody could believe what my life has been, the things I've had to do. Depths I've sunk to. I tell you either of those girls with the old woman is a clean decent creature compared with me. . . ." The speech trailed off miserably.

"I don't care," said Abe stoutly. "I want to make up to you for all those things. And I can't do that 'less you marry me. Aw, what do a few years matter? Happiest married couple ever I knew lived back home at Weston and there was twenty years between them; she'd taught him in Sunday School . . ."

"But Abe, you don't realise it, but I do now, and see what a wicked fool I've been. You only feel sorry for me— and pity isn't enough to get married on."

"It isn't that. I love you, Lou. I loved you the first moment I saw you. 'Member? The night I filled your bucket. I wasn't sorry for you then. You're just talking. And I reckon maybe I was a bit hasty, blurting out like that." His voice changed. "But you will, Lou, won't you? Marry me. I'd be the happiest man on earth."

"I'll . . . think about it," said Lou helplessly. "But . . ."

"There, we don't want no more buts," said Abe, and suddenly he leaned forward, put his hands on her shoulders and laid his mouth on hers.

His lips were soft. His chin, which needed the attention of a razor only once a week, was smooth as a girl's. And the kiss was as gentle and unpossessive as a kiss could

228

well be; but there was a wealth of tenderness and adoration in it. It moved Lou to tears. Abe shifted one big hand and brought her head to rest on his shoulder.

"There, there, my lovely, don't you cry," he said with indescribable gentleness. "Don't you cry, my little dear. Your crying days are done."

So now, on this evening when Mary Ann said: "And she married, too," Abe could afford to smile and be silent.

Only one person in the party shared his knowledge, and that was Cordy. It had been imperative to confide in someone and Abe had allowed himself a few cryptically revealing remarks to his friend. Cordy had very seriously warned him against encouraging an affection for someone whom he could not marry. His voice was so grave that Abe had felt compelled to tell him the truth. Confidence begat confidence and Abe chatted on, describing his plans and his hopes, too engrossed to notice that now and again a flicker of pain crossed Cordy's face.

It would have been easier to listen to, had it been the average boyish eulogy of the first-beloved's charms and beauty. But Abe, in one stride, seemed to have reached maturity and some of the things he said struck quivering chords in his listener's soul. "That is just how I felt about Susie . . . Thus might I have planned." Painful, unwarrantable affliction! He ended it for one night at least by saying:

"I hope it'll all come out as you plan it, Abe. And I hope, most sincerely, that you're one of those who are lucky in love. I know this kind of thing is mere meaningless words—but if you can avoid it, don't let this thing use up the whole of you. Because if you do and anything goes wrong you're left with nothing, finished, empty—like an old grapeskin. Yes, I know," he held up one hand. "It's your fault, you shouldn't try to confide in your grandfather!" He mustered a smile and Abe smiled too, but he had heard the underlying bitterness of that: "Finished, empty." Still, each lover's case was different; and in that case what could go wrong?

And so, weaving their little patterns as they went along,

they reached safely the mouth of the valley where the lake lay.

They were still concerned with trivial human things. Madame Nancy still thought of money and comfort, Kevin still dreamed of his road, Mahitabel wished that Ben's foot would heal and that Abe would come to his senses. A slight rash or a cold amongst her children still threw Ruth Warren into a frenzy; Cordy had his moments of mourning. Klara Bolewska and Dave Glenny worked their way through their sorry affair; Frank Cooper, Abe and Floribel nursed their loves; Mary Ann endured a few more growing pains. The little patterns shifted and changed like the colours in a kaleidoscope; but the big pattern remained constant. It was still a party of people engaged upon a journey. And the journey was drawing towards its close. One more stiff climb and they would be at the Pass. And high time, too. The year was sinking towards winter. Each day was colder and shorter than the one before it. The wild geese had gone southwards; there were only three days left in October.

It rained in the valley, sudden stinging squalls borne on the breath of an unkind, hurrying wind. The wagon bogged several times and had to be dug out by impatient hands. Their soaked clothes weighed heavily on them and it was difficult to make a fire to cook the beans and the coffee which their cold weary bodies craved. They spent two miserable days. But at least they had gained the lake and now, twelve hundred feet above them, ten miles travelling distance away, was the Pass.

And then, in mid-afternoon of a blustering day, the last of October, a strange weighted hush fell on the air. The lake lay, released from the ruffling of the wind, a mirror for the heavy low-hanging purplish sky.

Ben, propped on Persephone's back with his bad foot in a sling of Mahitabel's contriving, stared at the sky.

"If we was home I'd say 'twas threatening snow," he said.

The dreaded word fell like stone upon the heart of everyone who heard it.

"Too early for snow," said Kevin. "It may rain again." Raising his voice he called: "Bear away to the left, Joe. We don't want her bogged again." The team swerved towards the firmer ground and at that moment the first flakes fell. Casual desultory flakes at first that lingered almost carelessly on cheek and brow before melting; gentle unhurrying flakes that descended as though they knew what hopes they were laying to rest, and regretted it, yet must fall on.

Only a chance storm, people told one another. Remember, we are in the mountains now, the weather is different. It is too early, they repeated, for snow in any quantity. It is not November until to-morrow.

But the flakes continued to fall. The storm thickened. The ground whitened. Within an hour they were travelling through a snow-hushed world. The wagon moved more and more slowly. Winter, untimely but undeniable, had caught them in the mountains.

Now that thing which he had dreaded had come upon them, Kevin saw, without quibble or extenuation, the full extent of his responsibility. Three reasonably able-bodied persons would not have been trapped, even in this extremity. The Pass was within reach, and still open; one wild dash and the race with time would have been won. But this party, with its two sick men, its fat old woman and its four babies, was not capable of making a wild dash. Nevertheless they must be saved; and he must be the one to lay plans for their salvation.

He did so rapidly. He called Abe Smith and talked to him as the party struggled along.

"This may not be a chance eccentric storm, Abe. It may be the beginning of winter and in that case some, or even all of us, will be trapped this side of the Pass. We've very little food; almost worse, we've very few oxen left to kill and eat. I can only think of one thing. I want you to take Persephone and make a dash for it. You'll find that almost any one on the other side will help you to collect stores and men to bring them back, but I'll give you letters for various people. I'd go myself—but you'll do just as well on the other side, and if I went and anything happened it would look as though I'd ratted. Get your mother to pack you some food and wrap up well. I'll scribble some notes."

Dave Glenny, from his place at the rear of the party, had seen Abe taken aside. He watched while bundles, parcels and blankets were dragged from the wagon and Ben lifted into their place. He came up to Kevin, who was scribbling his letters of appeal, with his head, hands and paper just inside the cover of the wagon, and he tapped him on the back without ceremony. They had not spoken since their parting in the desert, but Kevin had forgotten his grudge in the stress of the moment.

"What is it?" he asked.

"You're sending someone ahead, over the Pass?"

"Yes."

"Who's going?"

"Abe Smith."

"I'll go," said Dave instantly. "I'm the person to send. I'm a horseman, he's not."

Abe, who had come up to take the letters, said hotly: "I'm a better horseman than you'll ever be."

Kevin held up his sound hand.

"I've no time to argue," he said, with a flash of his old spirit. "And it isn't a question of horsemanship, Glenny. I'm asking Abe to go because if we're snowbound and he gets through I think he'll use every effort in his power to come back and bring help. I haven't that much faith in you."

"That's a bloody offensive statement. And it's a lie."

"Is it? There was a man who saw a lake in the desert. He didn't care who died of thirst then, did he? That it wasn't water doesn't affect the question." He turned aside and spoke to Abe as though Glenny were not there. He watched the boy stow the letters in an inner pocket, gave him the date upon which to begin to act supposing the party had not by then gained a certain spot, offered him advice about what to do in storm, and then said: "Up you get, my boy. And God keep you. I needn't say that a lot depends on you." He thumped Abe on the back and then moved round to the mare's head. In the sight of the assembled company he took her velvet muzzle in his free hand and kissed her.

"Goodbye, old girl. Do your best."

Abe, with agility, if not with grace, swung himself into the saddle. His father had wrung his hand, Mahitabel had given him her rare brief peck, Mary Ann had embraced him and held up the baby's face to him. But Lou, regardless of who might see, had dragged down his head and kissed him as he had never been kissed before. It was a fitting beginning for a lonely and desperate venture.

The falling snow first blurred his outline and then hid him completely from sight. And as though his going had brought them to a sense of their desperate plight, the people now clustered about Kevin.

He had little of comfort to offer. He could only point out the facts of their position. It was still possible for the active members of the party to attempt to reach the Pass. But there were those who must stay behind on account of infirmity and they could not be left alone. It would be to their ultimate advantage if those who were able to make the attempt did so and thus eased the strain on the depleted stores. After all ten miles was nothing to people who had, in the last few weeks, covered hundreds.

There was a short period of disorganised activity which eventually resolved itself into order. Glenny, Cordy, Klara, Floribel and Mary Ann, Joe Sterry and Evan were to make the attempt. Madame Jurer, Mahitabel, Ben, Frank Cooper, the children and Hendriks were to remain behind. About Ruth Warren there was some doubt. If by going she increased the chances of her children, she was willing to do so, yet, as she pointed out, Mahitabel, with only Hendriks to help her, would be hard put to attend to four children as well as the two sick men. Hendriks stayed for choice. Since Mahitabel had dressed the wound on his head he had been her devoted slave. He now argued that she would need someone to chop firewood and, he added, until it froze, he could fish in the lake.

Frenziedly, in the darkening afternoon, those who were to leave bundled food and blankets together. Mahitabel, who had taken charge of the remaining group, urged the travellers to carry plenty of what stores were left. Those encamped by the lake were fewer in number, she said, and they could always eat the flesh of that last team.

233

It was, perhaps, this cheerless prospect which inspired Nancy Jurer to declare her intention of accompanying the travellers. No persuasion and no argument would serve to change her mind. Even Kevin's frank unwillingness to take her with him seemed only to strengthen her determination.

"I'm not asking you to pull or carry me," she said flatly. "Here I am, worse luck, and it's for me to say whether I go or stay. This pair of blackamoors are well able to help me along and I'm asking aid of no one else. Besides," she added, with the twinkle that often softened Kevin towards her, "all that ails me is my size. Exercise and short commons will soon remedy that."

Something very deep-rooted in Mahitabel rose and greeted that remark. For a brief and unregenerate moment she found herself preferring the old woman's tough decision of action to poor Ruth Warren's flabby changeableness. It seemed impossible for her to make up her mind. Stifling her own heartache at losing both Abe and Mary Ann in one afternoon, Mahitabel patiently reiterated her promise to tend Digby, James and Zillah as carefully as she did her own Ellen. Ruth finally set out with the party, but after the first hundred yards turned back, blinded with tears, and gathering her children to her bosom declared that they would all die together.

So Kevin, at the head of what was still the main party, set out for the Pass.

The faint remaining hope of gaining and crossing it was cherished by Kevin as a ruined miser might cherish his last remaining coin. Now and again as he stumbled along he recounted the times when he had been obliged to say: "All may yet be well." There was the Valley of Brambles; that dreadful moment in the desert, the hour when the Indians had attacked the oxen; the cloudburst, and now this. Never, he thought, had expedition been so ill-fated, never hope so constantly renewed and as often shattered again. And his arm hurt damnably. Strange how little Hendriks' head and Ben's foot had healed so successfully, while his arm had grown steadily worse. Probably, if he ever lived to show it to Doc Fletcher, he would whip it off; and for ever afterwards he would be "Kevin Furmage, you know, the fellow with one arm." Even in this extremity the thought appalled him.

It grew darker, and the wind rose again. The snow fell in eddies and whirls, blinding and confusing. But they were four or five miles from the wagon before it was evident that the Pass would not be gained that night. Then at last, beaten, not quite desperate yet, they huddled together in the snow, pressed close to preserve their bodies' warmth and wrapped in their rugs and blankets. They told one another that the change in the downfall boded well. It was a storm, no more. Morning would bring a thaw and clear weather.

The morning was cloudless; but the sun shone on a white expanse, broken only by tented shapes of the trunkless pines. In no place was the snow less than six feet deep; in places where it had drifted it reached ten or twelve.

Yet the Pass, so clearly visible in the bright morning light, tempted them irresistibly and some floundering attempts were made to travel in its direction. But the efforts, even of hope, even of desperation, are limited by the bounds of possibility and soon they knew that they were beaten. Almost without words they turned back and struggled towards the wagon and the lake.

At the lower level the snow lay less thickly. As the sun rose higher the pines sent great soft showers spilling to the ground. The lake lay greyly within its whitened banks.

Mahitabel had not wasted much time. The oxen, she had decided, could not find fodder because of the snow. They must be slaughtered. Already when the main party reached the wagon they found little Hendriks hacking the meat from a carcass. Ben, propped in the wagon's opening, was directing the operation, and he was the first to see the party's return. He called to Mahitabel, who was bowed over her log splitting, and she, axe in hand, stood for a moment watching their dragging progress. So, they had not escaped; the Pass was blocked; the last hope knocked away. Was one, so soon, demanded Mahitabel of herself, brought to regard the returning travellers merely as so many threatening mouths? She took note that famine might bring other disasters than starvation.

The next day and the two following remained clear and bright. A thaw seemed imminent; but the people had learned not to expect favours now, and they set to work as though it were a certainty that they would winter there.

For this one brief period Ben Smith came into his own. Drawing upon the experience of those long years at Weston when everything that was to be done had to be done by his own hands, he now directed the slaughtering of the remaining oxen, the hacking into joints and the stacking of the meat under mounds of snow. To him, too, was due the hastily but solidly contrived cabin of logs, reared as children rear houses with matches. It stood for years to mark their passing: to evoke the memory of their story. The roof was covered with pine boughs and with the stiffening hides of the oxen; the floor was cleared of snow, stamped hard and spread with pine needles. After the fourth day, when it snowed again, and the snow piled up against the walls, the cabin was a warm refuge; but it was desperately uncomfortable. Its own warmth brought melted snow seeping through the chinks of the walls; damp collected in pools on the floor; the air was always blue with smoke, and, for a time at least, rancid with the scent of cooking.

Ben and Frank were installed upon rough bunks just within the blanket-hung opening; the women and children slept as they could at the end nearest the fire. The other men occupied, for a while, the wagon which had been emptied of stores and stripped of its bunks, lanterns, stove and cunning built-in table.

They were scarcely installed before the snow began again and with brief intermissions it continued for fifteen days. Once a day the men struggled through the storm to share with those in the cabin the carefully rationed midday meal and to replenish the supply of firewood.

Closely housed, several of them ailing, all anxious and more than hungry, they endured the deadly monotony of their days with no more outbreaks of animosity and hysteria than might have overtaken any people in their circumstances. The most frequent cause of altercation was concerned with the food; for strange as it may seem, the idea of communal living was still accepted reluctantly. There was still talk of "my flour" and "your beans"; there were still bargains to be driven, favours to be extended, grievances to be aired. The cooking-pot was of necessity, a communal receptacle, but its contents were still personal and separate possessions.

Kevin, whose position and personality would ordinarily have given him the power to enforce a more economic system, seemed, in the eyes of Mâhitabel and a few other thoughtful observers, to fail in his duty. Mahitabel attributed his lethargy to his physical ill-health and she applied more and hotter fomentations to the stubborn arm; Cordy, who had come to know Kevin better during their enforced intimacy, knew that the cause lay deeper. The complete and utter failure of his scheme had struck at something more important and less resilient than his mere flesh. In good health he might have accepted his responsibility; in good heart he might have overcome the handicap of his sickness; but with neither advantage he fell an easy prey to despair and lethargy, enemies more dangerous at that moment than storm or shortage of meat.

During the third week of November there came a night when neither the pressure of bodies, the close-drawn blankets, nor the refuelled fire could provide warmth in the cabin. Ben, shivering in the cold, murmured: "It's freezing hard," and Frank, wakeful, replied: "It's what Warren and some of them have been hoping for."

In the wagon little Hendriks, also aware of the frost, worried lest the lake should be frozen. In the brief intervals between the storms he had sat, cold and patient, for hours on its banks, minding his pitiable tackle, dreaming of a great fish which he would present to Mahitabel. He had had no luck yet, but he had hoped on. The frost, if severe enough, would kill his dream.

It froze as no one had ever known it to freeze before. The surface of the snow was as hard as an oak floor; great branches snapped from the pines with a sound like pistol shots. No more water seeped into the cabin from the melting of the snow; within four feet of the fire the floor was frozen hard and icicles hung from the interstices of the walls.

For the last time hope raised its head amongst the ruins of Kevin's mind. If the frost lasted, some of the party might yet escape, and those behind, the sick, the frail and the children, might subsist on the stores that remained until help came.

It was a desperate venture. A sudden thaw—the thaw for which, before the great downfall, they had prayed—might send the travellers wallowing to their deaths in the softening drifts. To guard against such a chance, they made (frail defences indeed!) clumsy, improvised snowshoes. And Mahitabel, careless of whose the oxen were while they lived, sliced off strips of beef and dried them over the fire and used the last of the flour in order to make hard flat cakes; the traditional unleavened bread of privation and outpost and Passover.

The division between those who should travel and those who should remain behind remained constant, except that Janna, cowering and whimpering, pleaded to stay by the fire. Despite wearing every bit of clothing that she could muster or borrow she still suffered agonies from the cold. Her black face looked as though it had been dusted with mauvish-grey powder; her teeth chattered almost continuously. Her mistress, accurately gauging that each remaining mouth meant shorter commons in the cabin, where she herself, by general consensus of opinion. was compelled this time to remain, tried to force the black girl away. She assured her that walking would soon warm her. But Cordy, who had shouldered a considerable portion of Kevin's authority, and Glenny, who at least understood the jeopardy of their position, refused Janna's company as firmly as they had refused Madame Nancy's.

At the last moment Mahitabel, seized with concern for Kevin, drew Cordy aside.

"He's not fit to attempt it," she said.

"I have suggested that he should stay. But, of course, the argument about the food is unanswerable. I even wish I could persuade Ruth to leave the children. It would be to their ultimate good."

"She eats very little," said Mahitabel fairly. "And if she left them I doubt if she'd be in good enough heart for the

238

journey. No, Mr. Warren. It's me who should go. I'm in far better case than Mr. Furmage. Only ... you know who'd get the upper hand, left with two sick men, your wife and four babies. It's no use blinking the truth, is it? If Mr. Furmage stays and keeps order I'll go. I'd rather go."

"Shall I tell him so, or will you?"

Mahitabel looked into Cordy's face, thought that he looked like a worried monkey, and fell into the common error of underrating him.

"I will," she said.

She tackled Kevin a little too firmly. He had not yet reached the state in which he might be dictated to by a woman, however admirable and capable she might be.

"Nonsense, Mrs. Smith," he said with testy dignity. "I have no intention of allowing a trivial wound in my arm to relegate me to the company of sick men and little children."

"But you *are* a sick man," said Mahitabel in a frank, brutal voice. "We've all lost weight, but you've wasted. And don't be deceived by that colour in your face—that's fever or I never saw it."

"Tending your husband and poor Cooper has warped your view," said Kevin, recognising the truth of her statement but choosing to ignore it.

"You stay here," said Mahitabel, with as much cajolery as she could muster. "I'll go. You stay behind where at least there's fire, and see that things are kept fair and in order."

"I wonder that you deem me capable of such an onerous task. Delirium is seldom orderly."

"Oh, don't bandy words with me!" Mahitabel's patience gave out. "You'd be useful here. Ruth Warren would help you and the old woman would mind what you said. Out there you'll be nothing but a drag and a drawback. I wonder the others even *consider* taking you."

"It was hardly for them to consider, was it?" No one had ever addressed Mahitabel in such a tone. "On my singularly ill-starred journey I accepted some company, certainly, but I do not remember giving any of them the right to give me orders."

To his astonishment he saw Mahitabel's big clear eyes suddenly glassed with tears.

"You're a very foolish, stubborn man," she said. "And you've chosen to take wrongly everything I've said for your good. I reckon people in our predicament should think what's best for us all, not stand on our dignity and such foolishness. But if you will go, you will, I suppose. Let me do up your arm for the last time. I'll wrap it warm. The frost'll get it, slung up like that."

Kevin was silent as she went through the familiar ritual. Mahitabel was silent too. She was wondering what would have happened had she married a self-willed, stubborn man. Probably they'd have fought over everything that cropped up and ended by hating one another. Yet sometimes it might have been pleasant to have shrugged free from responsibility and been able to say: "All right then, have your own way."

As she arranged the shawl that was to act both as wrapping and sling for the injured arm, Kevin suddenly looked at her and smiled. "You'll do better here than I should, you know. I shall leave with an easy mind, knowing that you will look after them all."

Once again the party divided. Mary Ann kissed her father and mother and clutched Ellen to her in a last hard embrace. It was not a parting to be taken lightly; dangers known and unknown threatened those who left and those who stayed behind. Cordy lifted his children, one by one, grieved, even in that moment, that his feelings were muted and unpaternal. Poor innocent little things, born of error and spiritual dishonesty. He would have kissed Ruth, partly for appearance' sake, partly in kindliness, but over Zillah's head Ruth's dark eyes held a look of reproach that was more forbidding than dislike or anger. For the thousandth time that look implied that it was all his fault. The family should have been warmly and safely ensconced in the comfortable old house at Craddock and Ruth should have been happily occupied in secret preparations for another Christmas. As it was, Cordy knew only too well that the far-reaching result of his brief happiness had been to bring them all, not only to discomfort but to actual danger. He sighed as he turned away.

The travellers realised, within the first hour, the full and deadly power of the cold; and the women, with Kevin who had not taken a share in the expeditions for firewood, had their first experience of the weakening effect of a fortnight's incarceration on short rations. Nevertheless, it was with a sense of relief and escape that they tackled the first slope, a slippery and treacherous business. It was something to be moving again, to be going towards something, to be hopeful and active. They made seven miles and camped within three miles of the Pass.

A solitary cluster of ragged, wind-wrenched pines stood in a little hollow. Their trunks were invisible, and the boughs, sweeping downwards, sheeted with frozen cases of snow, looked like small white tents. They camped beside them. Joe Sterry, his natural handiness quickly asserting itself, began to make a fire. The wood burned willingly, and the frozen faces, the stiff hands and feet, yearned towards it; but soon an ominous sizzling sound mingled with the cheerful crackle of pine wood and one by one the logs tilted, hissed and were quenched in the puddle of melted snow. Quick to scent new trouble the people looked at one another with dismal faces. Without a fire the night would be intolerable. Yet how could they have hoped for a fire, since no snow, however frozen, could long withstand such a burden, and since no effort, however valiant, could hollow through such a depth of snow to the ground?

In the morning, despite their stiffness, they rose briskly, anxious to snatch at the first moment of daylight. Only Lou, with a disconsolate face, complained that her feet hurt her. Floribel and Mary Ann inspected one foot under the shelter of a shawl and found it swollen and mauvish in colour. They appealed to Kevin.

"It's frost-bite. You'll have to go back, Mrs. Glenny."

Lou began to cry and Evan moved over to the group with the dumb and puzzled wish to comfort that sometimes activates a dog.

"I'm sorry," said Kevin, "but there's nothing else for it. You can't walk with feet like that. I don't think you should even attempt to go back alone."

There was a moment's silence.

"Perhaps your husband . . ." said Kevin tentatively. "It's

only a day's march; less, going that way. And he seems in good fettle, he'd soon catch up with us again."

The words, addressed to Lou, since Kevin and Glenny were not on speaking terms, were overheard by the person they concerned. Dave's face was impassive as he turned it more fully towards the little group.

"I'm not going back," he said firmly. "I finished with her in the desert and she knows it."

"I'll go by myself," said Lou, with a flicker of pride quite new to her. But Evan, who had been biting his lips and turning red and white as first his father and then his mother spoke, said blurtingly: "I'll go back with her."

"But you wouldn't catch up again," said Kevin gently. The one day's march had shown already that the boy, though stout-hearted and uncomplaining, was handicapped by the shortness of his legs.

"I know that," said Evan, on a rather higher note. He was within a breathing space of tears himself. The journey had meant so much to him, had become a kind of symbol. With his first step he had determined to keep up with the men, especially with the loathed Dave, even if he died in the attempt; to have done so would have finished the process of emancipation that had begun on that day in the desert. Now his bid for equality was to be withdrawn, so soon.

There were hot tears in his eyes as he said good-bye to the others and helped Lou to muffle the foot which, once liberated, refused to be forced back into the shoe.

Mary Ann and Floribel walked together exchanging brief, breathless remarks. Floribel was rejoicing that she was out of Madame's clutches at last.

"You can come and stay with us," said Mary Ann boldly. Anything seemed possible now, if only they could get to California, even Mahitabel's hospitality to Floribel.

Floribel glanced with gratitude at Mary Ann and noticed that her nipped pallor had taken on a dirty green tinge.

"Whatever . . ." she had begun, when Mary Ann, turning aside, was violently sick.

There was nothing squeamish about Floribel. She held her friend by her heaving shoulders and when the last spasm died away helped her to clean her face and offered her fresh snow to melt in her mouth.

"God love me," she said at last. "I shouldn't have thought we could have been that much sick between us. Would you?"

Mary Ann shook her head, smiled wanly, and resumed walking.

But between that time and midday, when the party halted for stragglers to catch up and to eat a mouthful of food, Mary Ann had been sick four times and could hardly totter with the support of Floribel's arm.

"It's the cold," said Joe Sterry. "Chill on the stomach, I should say. You'd be better for some warm drink. But eat a couple of good mouthfuls and chew well."

Mary Ann obeyed instructions and was immediately sick again. She sat up at last and Floribel drew her head to rest against her knee. The others gathered round, helpless, until Kevin remembered a little hoarded brandy in his flask. He craned round and dived towards his pocket. Cordy helped him to drag the flask out.

"Take a good pull," said Kevin. "And if that doesn't settle you, you must go back too."

The threat was lost upon Mary Ann, who, having endured the bite of the unfamiliar spirit, was enjoying a brief sensation of warmth and comfort in her vitals. But Floribel heard it and shuddered. If Mary Ann were banished, ten to one she would have to go with her . . . and that meant good-bye to her hopes for a speedy arrival in California and a reunion with Abe.

More solicitously than ever she inquired how Mary Ann felt now; more tenderly she hoisted her to her feet; more firmly she helped her along. But just before the Pass was reached Mary Ann fell face forward and lay retching.

"It's no good; it's the cold," she gasped.

Kevin and Cordy, who had been bringing up the rear, joined them and both regarded Mary Ann with grave concern.

"All right," said Mary Ann, to whom discipline was not new. "I'll go back." She got to her knees again and pressed her head with hands that felt as heavy and numb as lead. Oh dear, sighed Floribel. And with Abe in California and that Glenny woman left behind, I might have made some headway. She looked at Mary Ann with some disgust. She might have known, she thought, those pink and white, golden-haired girls never did have any guts. She could remember one or two in the house at New Orleans; they were highly thought of and much in demand, but they never lasted. They went lungy or melancholy. Suffering Christ! thought the girl furiously, and she's been fool enough to hitch up with one! With the result that now she stood here, torn in two, while Cordy and Kevin talked about the ten-mile journey and how long it would take, and mumbled about a night to be spent in the open.

"I can go by myself," said Mary Ann, very much as Lou had done.

"I don't think you should," said Kevin; but a great sigh ripped itself out of him as he spoke. Oh, if only he had resisted that temptation to make a party out of it. Just he and Joe and Hendriks . . .

Then something that had been coming to fruition in the soul of Floribel Marietta Toit, something that had been growing secretly, confusedly in the dark, burst forth and flowered in the upper air of conscious thought. She had talked so much to Mary Ann about her brother that she now knew a great deal about him; and at this moment she realised that he was, not merely an attractive, aloof, shy boy with a long brown face, blue eyes and a kind mouth, but the living symbol of a whole range of ideas and standards which up to a month or so ago had been as far removed from her ken as a knowledge of Greek. He stood for something that made the old life seem dark and terrible, something that threw a harsh light upon Madame Jurer, something that had shaken her own plans for her future. And all muddled and dim in the little prostitute's limited mind, lay the notion that if she now pressed on towards Abe's physical presence, she would be separating herself from him by more than measurable miles; while by turning back she would in reality be moving towards him.

It was only an idea—and never in her life had Floribel been called upon to deal with ideas. She distrusted this one even as she acted upon it. I'm a fool, she thought, and embroidered the epithet with several choice adjectives. Yet her actual voice was saying, with every sign of confidence and energy:

244

"I'll go back with her, Mr. Furmage. Don't you think that's the best way?"

"If you can keep her moving," said Kevin, and his voice betrayed his relief. "There'll be a moon and you can't miss the way. Keep moving at all costs, because without a fire you wouldn't be able to keep one another warm."

"I don't want that you . . ." began Mary Ann weakly.

"Oh, come on. You're wasting time," said Floribel. "Here, have this shawl, and," she lowered her voice out of consideration for Mary Ann's scruples, "as soon as they've gone you shall have my flannel drawers. I've got two pairs on."

An unromantic, cataclysmic speech.

So the first thirty-six hours had sorted out the weaklings and the reduced party mended its pace. There was no need to consider Klara Bolewska, she strode along as freely as a man and at the end of the day and was able and willing to take her share in making the fire.

Joe Sterry had solved the problem of building a fire on the surface of snow. A platform of thick green logs, pressed closely together, was laid first and the fire laid on top of it. It was a good idea, for with the onset of darkness and the cessation of exercise the danger of freezing was always imminent.

Now they could sit by the fire and have light and warmth while they ate the dried strips of beef and the hard-baked cakes of flour and water which they carried in their packs. They had enough for the journey provided it went well and lasted only for the calculated time. So low were supplies in the cabin that they had been able to allow little margin for delay or accident.

But on the western side of the Pass they stumbled into bad weather, storms violent and prolonged, during which travel was impossible. Then, carefully hoarding their dwindling supplies they must watch and hunger through the long hours, piteously grateful for the fire's comfort and company. Complete warmth was impossible to attain— hands and faces bent towards the fire scorched, while the frost seized upon shivering back and shoulders, but each night's fire made a focus of comfort and proved that these

245

men, travelling in the wilderness, carried with them the heritage of racial knowledge.

On clear mornings they gladly abandoned the black wet hole where the fire had glowed and pressed on. They were cold, and unsatisfied hunger gnawed at their vitals, but they had more reason to hope than the people left in the cabin; they were active, busy with physical movement and so less beset by harrowing thought. But the mornings dawned when they could not move forward, mornings when even to seek fresh wood for the fire was a dangerous adventure, mornings when all they could do was to press closer together, sharing their bodies' heat, creating an intimacy that was superficial rather than real. Even Klara, pressing close to Glenny's big hard body, learned suddenly that there is no magic in mere propinquity. She would have undertaken, without regret, never to have set eyes on him again, in return for a good meal, a warm bed and release from anxiety. This frame, whose nearness had thrilled her in the warm nights that followed their exodus from Fort Mason, had become, in this frozen wilderness, merely a prop by day and a source of warmth by night. The warmth was given willingly enough, but as the days followed one another Dave showed an increasing tendency to walk apart from Klara and the others, to walk ahead, with occasional impatient backward glances, to endeavor to force the pace. He no longer tolerated Klara clinging to his arm, and the Polish girl learned reluctantly that a man who ill-treats one woman is hardly likely to use another with enduring chivalry.

Hunger struck the travellers long before those in the cabin were suffering more than mild privation. Made ravenous by the cold and their physical exertions, they ate more than they should have done in the first few days; then they were held immobile by a storm that lasted for two days and nights, moved through another day and were storm-bound again. The new storm lasted for four days, and when they could move again their packs were perilously light. Scanty, indeed, had consumed all his provisions, though he concealed the fact for forty-eight hours, knowing that he would be called "greedy nigger." Eventually hunger pains turned to cramp in his stomach and he was forced to complain. No word of reproach was forthcoming. Kevin broke his last bread cake in halves and Cordy gave him a strip of beef.

After that they noticed that when the descent of twilight told that within fifteen minutes they must camp, Dave Glenny, who had led the party all day, dropped behind, to appear again when the fire was made. Kevin, bitterly resenting his own one-handedness, and no doubt remembering its cause, said savagely that Glenny lingered behind in order to avoid his share of the labour. But one evening Klara Bolewska dawdled as well and then came rushing into camp to tell them that Glenny still had a good store of beef in his pack and stayed behind to eat of it unobserved.

"Good hearing," said Cordy, "provided he doesn't eat too much. By the look of things we shall all be depending upon his extra bit this time to-morrow."

When, on the next evening, Glenny fell out of line, Kevin, who for the last hour had walked leaning on Joe Sterry's shoulder, halted, and for the first time addressed his enemy voluntarily.

"No need to halt now," he said, "we'll camp by the next clump of trees."

Glenny stated in bald language his reason for halting.

"You were not so damned modest in the middle of the day," said Joe bluntly.

"You shut your gob!"

"The truth is, Glenny, that though we have no objection to cutting the wood and building the fire without your aid, we find ourselves this evening unable to break our fast until you join us."

Glenny looked stupid for a second, then, as Kevin's meaning dawned upon him, sly.

"I dunno what you mean."

"We haven't a crumb left. You, being wiser than we, carried an extra supply, didn't you? We're asking you to share it with us." The appeal was made with complete lack of graciousness, but the mere looking at Glenny could now raise Kevin's ire.

"I've nothing," said Dave. "You might have known that yourself. Ma Smith handed out the stuff, didn't she?

equal shares all round. Why should mine last longer'n yours?"

"A difficult question to answer, especially as you have eaten bite for bite with us. But compare the state of your pack with ours."

"I carry an extra pair of socks and a shirt."

"You lie terrible," screamed Klara. "I see the pack last night. It is full of meat. Nor is it the meat which Mrs. Smith did prepare. The strips she cut all the same."

"It's a bloody lie," said Dave. "I'm the same as you are. It's socks and a shirt in the pack."

His voice was so assured and his eyes met theirs so straightly that Cordy's heart fell. If that were the truth, then they were lost. But Klara was not so easily foiled.

"Show us, then, show us," she cried, dancing with rage and excitement.

Dave made no move to open the pack and Cordy's heart beat again.

"Come on, man," he said in a friendly voice. "You've teased us long enough. You were cleverer than we were and judged the thing better. Put us out of our misery and admit that we're all to share your bounty this evening."

For just a second Dave's eyes wavered. He opened his mouth as though to speak and one hand moved towards the pack. But he closed his mouth in its rat-trap line and let his hand drop.

"Come on, Glenny," said Cordy again, "you're torturing us."

"That's right," broke out Dave furiously. "Coax me now, wheedle round me like a pack of spaniels. You fools! You —— —— fools!" Nobody but Cordy heard the incipient hysteria in the rising voice of abuse. " 'Oh, Mrs. Smith, don't rob the others!' 'Oh no, Mrs. Smith, we shan't need that much!' 'Ten days should see us within reach of the settlements!' Ten days my foot! I knew, I tell you, I knew. It was a good road, wasn't it, full of ridges steeper than ten Hampton Courts piled on top of one another, full of brambles, thicker'n hell's smoke. It was a good road with only forty-eight hours in the desert, and all us fools taking it and believing you. Ten days to the settlements! So now you've been ten days and your grub's finished.

And serve you right. Not a morsel of mine shall you have. Yes, it's meat. It's beef off my own oxen, I had two, you may remember. It's mine all right. And I'm going to eat it."

He choked with fury and breathlessness. Kevin turned away with a gesture of distaste.

"Then there is no more to be said." Mentally he registered a resolve to die rather than touch the disputed meat. But Cordy and Joe, more reasonable, and Klara who had been hungry for longer than she could remember, stared at Glenny with wide eyes in which hatred warred with desire.

They moved on to the clump of pines. Joe, Scanty, Cordy and Klara took turns at hacking down a small pine and shared the labour of building the fire. Glenny stayed apart for awhile and then drew near. There was no Mahitabel in this company and he was allowed to stay. He lay down with his pack under his head.

Next day dawned clear and bright, but they were too weak to take full advantage of the good weather. Towards mid-day Glenny approached Kevin and said:

"Suppose I share the meat with you, will you give me the map?"

There was only one possible answer and after a pause Kevin made it. "I'll give you a copy."

"That's good enough for me."

But for Cordy's observation it might have passed unnoticed that Kevin, after fumbling one-handedly for map, pocket-book and pencil, paused, frowned, shuddered and then began copying the map upside down.

"Here," said Cordy, "let me do it."

Roughly, but accurately he marked the trail to be followed until the Yuba River was reached.

"After that you follow the river," he said. "Now, what about the meat?"

Very slowly Glenny unslung his pack and with furtive fingers dug out about a third of its contents.

"Half, at least," said Cordy, wondering at himself. Reluctantly Glenny added a few more slices. Cordy handed over the sheet of the notebook. Glenny glanced at it and tucked it away.

Klara flung herself forward.

"Take me with you," she said. "I will walk, I will not drag on you. You are the clever one, Dave. You and me we will arrive first and we will have the good times."

With a silent gesture of contempt he pushed her aside. He plunged forward into the snow.

"Let's keep up with the bastard," said Joe, linking his arm with Kevin's. For a few hundred yards they followed Glenny and then Kevin, gasping, said: "It's no use, Joe. Any of you that can go that pace, take your meat and go with him. It'd be the best thing. I can't do it any more."

"Muh neither," said Scanty, unaccustomedly breaking in, "ma empty belly kinda drag at muh."

"I took on to go to California with you," added Joe Sterry bluntly, "and God helping me I'm going to."

"Might as well admit," said Kevin, speaking as though with effort, "that I don't seem to see like I did. Everything seems blurred." He screwed his eyes fiercely.

"It may be the snow. I've heard of snow blindness," said Cordy.

"That's painful," said Kevin testily. "This isn't. It's to do with my arm. Every time it throbs it knocks against my eyes and makes things blur. I'm poisoned. I never could eat oysters." He seemed to realise that there was a certain irrelevance in that last statement. Scowling with concentration he added: "You musn't take any notice of me. Glenny said the right thing when he said—fool. You take the map, Warren, and press on. I know it well enough by this time, or I ought to. It's in the top drawer of my bureau if Miriam hasn't tidied it. She's a devil to put things away."

Klara giggled. Joe Sterry silenced her with a look of hatred.

"Lay hold of my arm, sir," he said, addressing Kevin with unusual respect. "We shall stick together, and if we don't land in California before that damned sharp-shooter, I'm a Dutchman."

"There *was* a Dutchman," said Kevin, with an air of suddenly remembering something. "Decent little fellow, wonderful with cows. Heifer called Tulip used to follow him like a dog. Follow along like dogs and build the Furmage Road. God damn you all, you should be proud.

250

Don't you know what it'll mean to you all to say that you were the first to cross by the Furmage Road? Even if it is all speckled. I don't suppose you realise how speckled it is. All pocked because Glenny would shoot at it. But it's a good road for all that."

"I think we'd better eat a little," said Cordy.

The food which Glenny had given them lasted three days under Cordy's careful handling. It meant that at each halting place they had about four mouthfuls each. They grew steadily weaker. Kevin, supported now on either side—they took turns in helping him—babbled almost incessantly, mixing sense with nonsense in a manner that made it necessary to pay him some attention. Once he turned gravely to Cordy, whose turn it was to help him along and said, gravely: "You have two sons, you know. In your place I should not let anything worry me. Money's no use, and an estate is only a bother, without a son to follow you. I've told you, Miriam, a thousand times, I don't blame you. You can't help it; but you must just allow me to have regrets." Yet when the Yuba valley showed, broad and clear ahead of them, he recognised it with a glad cry and added: "I wonder if that swine Glenny held to the right road?"

On the fourth and fifth days after Glenny's leaving they starved. Semi-starvation was now an old experience, but two days with nothing but a little scooped snow to quench their thirst was the worst that had yet befallen them. Klara and Cordy admitted to pain and walked bent double when the pangs seized them; Kevin, Joe and Scanty complained of hollow feelings and dizziness, but no pain. The pains seemed the lesser evil; on both evenings of those hungry days it was Klara and Cordy who showed most energy and determination in making a fire.

On the next day, the sixth of his absence, they overtook Glenny. He was squatting in the centre of a woven ring of tracks, his pack half-open between his knees and his scarf drawn over his eyes. Snow-blindness had stricken him down. There was still a small portion of meat in the pack and at the sight of it old feuds and resentments were forgotten. Cordy, since Kevin held back, shared the meat amongst the slavering company, tucked the tiny remainder back into the pack and then, unwinding his scarf, tied its end around Glenny's wrist. The other end he fastened to his belt and for the rest of the day he dragged Glenny along, much as a horse draws a cart. Strengthened by the meat, and somewhat encouraged at having caught up with the errant Glenny, the weakening party covered six miles that day, a record performance. They were cheered, too, to find that the snow was definately decreasing; it was not more than six feet deep at the spot where they camped by a dead tree, easy source of fuel.

Before breaking camp next morning they ate the last shreds of meat. Glenny cursed and swore over his portion.

"Keeping the five of you for four days," he explained, "has done me out of my three weeks' supply."

"Three weeks that you might have spent sitting in the snow or wandering round till you perished," said Cordy mildly.

"I don't grudge it to *you*," said Glenny, with a sudden tinge of feeling in his voice.

More than any other experience this day's march began to sort out their grades of endurance. Strangely enough Joe Sterry, whose lean tough build and brown face had indicated health and fitness, was the first to fail. He began to stumble and then to fall down, just as Mary Ann had done at an earlier stage of the journey. Set on his feet again and prodded into activity he moaned and begged to be allowed to stay where he was. If he could just rest a little, he muttered, he would feel better and soon catch up with them again. But Cordy, who felt that separation would be an admission of defeat, made Klara and Scanty support him on either side. He also untied the scarf from about his waist.

"You can't see, Glenny," he said, "but if you take Mr. Furmage's arm, you can help him along and be guided at the same time. Come on now, Klara, don't let your lot fall behind."

With fear warring against their weakness they pressed on.

Soon after midday a flaying wind from the north attacked them. After an hour it brought flurries of snow which grew thicker as the wind increased in fury and hardened into a genuine blizzard.

They were too weak to battle against it and too numbed by cold to rear a fire under such difficulties. Kevin, worn down by pain, made no attempt to deal with the situation and it was Cordy who selected a spot to the lee of a clump of pines, hounded the dispirited company together and spread the rugs and blankets completely over them. Even in their starved and frozen state their packed bodies exuded a little warmth, which gradually accumulated, so that inside the mound of flesh and blankets the air became humid. To lie still, to struggle no more and to feel the warmth creeping through frozen limbs induced slumber. Even when Joe Sterry began to move about restlessly and to describe, in stomach-rending detail, good meals he had enjoyed in the past and great feasts he meant to enjoy in the future, his movements and his words barely penetrated the consciousness of his companions. Snow thickened upon their covers and helped to preserve their bodies' heat. They slept on long after dawn had broken upon the storm-swept world.

When they stirred at last it was to find that Joe's tossings had exposed his head and shoulders. He was unconscious, but still breathing, and they dragged him under cover again and tried to restore him. His breathing became more and more shallow, however, and before midday he was dead.

They laid his body outside the covers, tucked in the edges again and crouched close. The thought that they might stay here until, one by one, they followed the groom on his new path, held all their minds for a time; but another thought came hard after. That would be their fate unless. . . .

They faced the unimaginable problem. Could Kevin, who had engaged the lively young fellow ("Thirty dollars and your keep"), or Cordy who had envied him his skill with the teams in hard places, or Klara who had regarded him as a possible second string, or Glenny who had resented the groom's vocal support of his master, could they ever have imagined the day when they would sit in the snow with their stomachs full of rumbling gnawings and their heads swimming from weakness and think of that smiling, active, brown-faced fellow merely in terms of meat?

He had died from a cause over which they had no control; and they would die themselves unless they abandoned the laws that govern the civilised. Yet for some hours, all through that afternoon, they sat while the blizzard howled about them, and respected the taboos of their kind. Perhaps each dreaded to be the first to move or speak.

But by sunset the one idea was so much in possession of all their minds that in the enclosed space it was almost palpable. Afterwards no one could remember what words, if any, were spoken, or by whom. But it was Cordy who crept out, knife in hand. Stimulated by hope they found strength to make a fire in a hole scooped out in the snow to shelter it from the wind.

After two days the storm died away and they rose up, stiff but strengthened, laid Joe's bones in the hole where the fire had been and passed on. The period of darkness had almost cured Glenny's sight and he was able to see his way, peering from beneath a handkerchief folded low on his brows.

Toiling up slopes, sliding and slipping down the declines, they covered the slow miles. And with every mile it became more evident that they would move faster without Kevin, in whom mind and body had failed simultaneously, so that, save for brief, transient flashes, he was now no better than an idiot child. Klara and Scanty were past rendering any aid; linked together they could still struggle forward slowly and support one another when one or the other stumbled. But upon Cordy and Glenny lay the burden of Kevin.

It became more and more difficult to get him to his feet in the mornings, or after the brief rests which their weakness necessitated. Like Joe Sterry, he would beg pitiably to be allowed to rest. The morning came when, Klara and Scanty having started off, Cordy bent over Kevin, urging him to make the effort to rise. Glenny stood fuming a little way off. Suddenly he strode forward.

"To hell with it, Warren. Leave him. He'll die anyhow. We can't make any pace with him in tow, and the meat's
254

nearly done and no sign of a settlement yet, nor of the Sacramento that he keeps babbling about. Damn it, he deserves to be left, he got us into this. Surely you can see that, Warren. But for his bleating about a new road we'd of stuck to the old way and none of this'd of happened. Leave him. Us that can walk can't afford to wait for them that can't."

"And why can't he? You know the answer to that, Glenny. You ought to be willing to carry him if he needs it."

"Well, I'm not. I'm not even going to heave him along any more, see? We've got to get along as fast as we can. We can't play about any more." His voice rang out harshly, then suddenly dropped to a confidential note. "But I tell you what, Warren; I ain't unmindful of what you did for me, back there. If you'll leave him, and join with me we'll give the others the slip too, and I *swear* I'll stick to you whatever happens. You're bearing up well at the moment, but you might need help, and not one of these is capable of lending a hand, you know that. Don't back the wrong horse too long, now, and be sorry when I've gone."

"But you're not going, Glenny. You're going to take hold of his sound arm and help me with him," said Cordy in a dangerous quiet voice.

"Oh no, I'm not."

"Then I'll shoot you," said Cordy calmly. And Glenny, looking back in alarm, saw that the little man had stooped over the prostrate Kevin and risen upright with a six-shooter, which he had drawn from the holster, in his hand. More threatening even than the shining barrel was the deadly quietness of his manner and the cold steady light in his grey eyes.

"My —— God!" said Glenny, voicing his most obscene oath. But he came back and attempted roughly to jerk Kevin to his feet. The sick man, who had sat, apparently witless during the argument, now moistened his cracked lips and said clearly:

"Everything that Glenny says is true. Go with him, Warren. It's a waste of time bothering with me."

"One after another, one after another," yelled Cordy so sharply that both the other men started. "You'll drive me mad between you. But you shall do what I say!" He pushed Kevin upwards and towards Glenny, saw their arms linked, and then, twisting his own arm beneath Kevin's out-stuck elbow, seized his belt at the back. The first hundred yards of the trail sloped downwards and with the strength of frenzy Cordy forced them along it almost at a run. They soon caught up with the other pair, whose first burst of energy was already flagging. Cordy forced them to keep ahead, his usually gentle manner charged with abuse. For it had dawned upon him, with sudden and dread completeness, that if these people were to be kept alive, kept moving and brought all together out of the mountains, it was he who must do the job.

During that day they noticed a further decrease in the depth of snow; it bore out one of Kevin's lucid statements, that during a normal year the snow-belt would hardly extend so far. There were more trees, too, and once, in a sheltered spot, they saw four leafless trees lifting their black branches amongst the sullen green of the pines. Oaks. They were getting on; they were moving into the levels where trees dropped their leaves in the autumn, where the snow was a natural element, not a deadly enemy, where they might hope for help from their own kind. It was an exciting moment.

But that day saw the last of the food they carried consumed, and when they camped Famine drew his gaunt frame into the circle around the fire. Not Glenny's eye alone noted the glaze in Kevin's, or the fever-patch burning on each livid, hollow cheek. If Kevin died, soon, there was hope for the other four. If not . . .

They ate, that night, what starving people in famines and sieges have eaten since leather was first tanned, the straps of Kevin's holster case, the case itself, pieces cut from their own shoes. It took the edge from their pangs, but it was not food. Cordy and Klara, whose stomachic reactions seemed to be akin, were violently sick.

In the morning they rose from food-haunted sleep and found Kevin still alive. In fact, he seemed better, said that his arm no longer pained him, and raised no objections to starting. While they were rolling their blankets and tightening scarves and belts Glenny approached Cordy and spoke with secrecy and caution.

"You can do one thing," he said, "to save four of us, your precious Mr. Furmage included."

"And what is that?" asked Cordy, though he knew the answer.

"Shoot the nigger. You can make it look like an accident."

"I couldn't do it."

"Then let me. I could."

"I can't connive at murder, Glenny. If we've got to die we've got to."

"It wouldn't be murder. He's only a black."

"He's walked with us and starved with us," said Cordy wearily. "He helped to guide you along when I got tired." He saw with a further fall of spirits that Glenny was looking meditatively at his big, square-tipped hands. "If you set about him, Glenny, I shall shoot you." And then he laughed very weakly, but with genuine amusement, and added: "Oh dear, every morning I have to say that to you. It's getting monotonous."

"You're mad," said Glenny staring at him. "Laughing with your belly as empty as a gutted pig. You're mad."

"Maybe," said Cordy, "and who could wonder? Come on, lend a hand."

"Blast me if I do," said Glenny, backing away. "Go on, shoot me. It's a better death than starving."

Pity, which had extended to Kevin and Klara and Scanty, but had missed the big black-browed man, stirred in a new channel of Cordy's mind. The poor brute was suffering.

"Come on," he said. "At this level we'll probably find something to shoot. Let's stick together for one day more."

"Three feet of snow—and you talk of finding something to shoot," sneered Glenny. Nevertheless he lent Kevin his arm again and the sorry procession moved away. There was only one idea in Glenny's head now. It was not Kevin, nor Scanty who must die, it was Cordy; since, with the six-shooter which he had craftily taken into his possession, the crazy little man stood between Glenny and his schemes. Once get the weapon, shoot Cordy, take his share of his flesh, and abandon the others. That was Glenny's plan, and he walked revolving it in his mind.

They covered three miles only. Then Klara, who up to that moment, had borne her troubles with fortitude, sat down and wept. Scanty sat by her and no effort of Cordy's could prevail upon them to take another step. At the same moment Glenny dropped Kevin's arm and stood still. The time for patience and sentiment has gone past; the time for action had come.

"You sit there," he said, with a thoughtfulness whose unusualness might have warned them, and indicated a fallen tree-trunk upon which the sun lay golden. The snow was soft in the grooves of the wood. Save for the depth of snow it was like a spring day in the east. "Warren and me'll go see if we can't find something to shoot."

Get Warren away from the others, fall behind him, set those big hands on his neck and squeeze. It would be easy. A fired shot would make it sound like an accident. And who would be interested anyway? They must all be as hungry as he was himself.

The most careful, hopeful watch throughout these last few days had brought no rewarding sight of furred or feathered life. Cordy remembered that, as he turned away, thinking that it did not matter which way they directed their steps. But Glenny led off towards some trees with an air of purpose. Cordy put his hand into his pocket and closed his fingers around the weapon. He had only the barest notion how to use the thing. Back in Craddock an angry father had avenged his daughter's honour with one, and Cordy, going to report for the paper, had been allowed to see it, as well as the mess it had made of the seducer. That incident, with Glenny's shooting at Kevin, composed Cordy's experience of firearms. He was glad that Glenny had apparently jettisoned his own weapon.

Deep in their own thoughts the two men passed between the trees and were out of sight. Glenny following his plan, ceased to lead, stopped to fiddle with his boot, fell to the rear. Quietly he stepped sideways behind Cordy's back.

From above the limp folds of a dirty ragged scarf the little man's neck rose, very thin and corded, the creases in the skin full of dirt which marked out squares and parallelograms on its surface. His ears, red and almost transparent against the light, stuck out from under the pressed-down brim of his old hat. His shoulders were bent, his head poked forward with short-sighted concentration.

Glenny raised his hands, big, chipped hands with blunt-tipped fingers and a growth of thick black hair from wrist to finger-joint. They were hands which, with the curves of youth still in their outline, had been put to ill-service long ago in Uncle Tom's business, and there were few things that they would have hesitated to do. Had Kevin or Scanty been there in Cordy's place he would have been a dead man by this time. But Dave Glenny had just one qualm of conscience to overcome. It was this little madman who had helped him in his moment of helplessness—that was not going to save him now—but it made the murderer hesitate for a brief space before those hands reached out.

And in that space Cordy saw the rabbit, just as Abraham saw the ram in the thicket. It sat upright, less than twenty yards away, and it was cleaning its whiskers.

The sight of it brought to the country-bred Cordy visions of tender white flesh, easily separated from the bone, baked under flaky brown pastry in company with pink-and-white striped slices of salt pork. A rush of saliva filled his mouth and moistened his lips. The six-shooter, cold and heavy, lay in his hand and the thought of missing the rabbit, cold and heavy, lay in his mind. But Glenny could shoot; he had shot Kevin from quite a distance, only too well. It would be best to trust Glenny, give him the six-shooter and trust him and his luck. It has been good so far.

Cordy turned to offer the chance and the weapon to Glenny, and looked murder in the face!

There was no mistaking it; the uplifted hands, the furtive pose, the purposeful glare in the eye, they announced it as clearly as though Glenny had spoken.

And yet, in that moment, when it was all so clear and plain, while it rushed through Cordy's mind what it was that Glenny meant to do, and why, and how, when almost any word would have been apt, any term of abuse fitting, the pressure of hunger was so fierce and the force of circumstance so potent that the rabbit remained the important thing, and Cordy, staring at murder and cannibalism, said simply: "Rabbit."

The glare faded from Glenny's eyes as he, too, looked at the unheeding animal. His hands dropped. Purpose died. There was left only pain and pitiful hunger, staring at possible food. With a change of motive almost ludicrous in the circumstances Glenny stretched out his hand.

"Give me that," he whispered breathlessly. Cordy even then hesitated for the fraction of a second before shaking his head.

He dropped to his knees and began to crawl forward. The Craddock father had shot the seducer across a kitchen table; there was no hope of attaining that nearness, but he restrained himself and waited, dribbling like a baby, until he was so near that he wondered whether rabbits could smell their enemies. His heart was beating with a curious fluttering motion, as though a butterfly had been trapped in his chest. To his normal anxiety not to miss was added the certain knowledge that if he did so the mad purpose which had shone in the eyes of his companion would be put, unhesitatingly, into action. He halted at last and narrowed his eyes.

He had always been short-sighted, and in the last few days his eyes had been troublesome; not painful like Kevin's throbbing ones, or like Glenny's snow-blindness, but they had left curious gaps in things that he looked at. Now, taking careful aim, he prayed without knowing it to a peculiarly personal and interested Deity whom he had renounced long ago in a Milchester mill. "God, let me see it properly; God let me hit it."

The shot rang out, shattering the quiet. To the left of the rabbit a spurt of snow flew up. He had missed. And simultaneously with that realisation, Cordy took in the fact that the rabbit, beyond stiffening to attention, had not moved. It sat there, as though bewitched. Perhaps it was satisfied that none of its traditional enemies were within sight or hearing; perhaps it was used to the crack of a snapping pine. In any case it sat still and the sight of its immobility roused a wild hope in Cordy's fluttering heart.

In his ear Glenny said, almost sobbing: "You fool, you bloody fool!" Then he, too, saw that the rabbit was still

260

there, and for the second time he reached out to take the six-shooter from Cordy's inept hand. Cordy glanced at him sideways and his eyes took in every line, every furrow, every pore and bristle of that magnified face, so close at hand. Then, very quickly, he raised an elbow and jabbed it into Glenny's mouth with a peevish, childlike nudge which afterwards made him laugh to remember. Glenny, taken by surprise, fell over into the snow and Cordy narrowed his eyes for the second shot. As he did so he knew, with a sense of sinking despair, that his affliction was upon him. Where the rabbit had been there were two black bars, like condensed darkness, and between them nothing but a faint grey blur. Nevertheless he pressed the trigger, felt Glenny get up and run forward, heard him shout as two seconds later he held up the headless animal.

"Well done," he said, grinning at Cordy with good fellowship. "I'm sorry, I nearly spoilt your aim."

"I'm sorry I jabbed you," said Cordy, his heart beginning to beat more steadily.

Glenny's face darkened.

"It'd feed two," he said, weighing the little body contemplatively. "It's no good amongst five."

Kevin, Klara and Scanty were yards away, yet in that wilderness Glenny lowered his voice to the note which has been made fitting by custom to secret proposals. "Come on, now, Warren," he said. "Let's you and me eat it. They needn't know. Come to that, we needn't go back to them. We know the way now. We could make rattling good pace without 'em you know. I'm sorry for them," he threw the sop to Cordy's sentimental nature, "but we're men; we've got a lot to live for. Have we gotta chuck away our chance for a man that's crazy, a loose woman and· a nigger? I say 'No'. What do you say?"

Even against the bleached pallor of his face the white line that Ruth knew so well showed around Cordy's lips, but his voice was as mild as ever as he asked: "D'you want to share this rabbit? Well, it was Furmage's gun, and I did the shooting. Suppose we took it into *our* heads to eat it between us."

Logic was wasted on Glenny, but he recognised Cordy's stubborn opposition. Moreover that wild shot had left him with a mistaken notion of Cordy's skill. Why, oh, why, had he thrown away his own six-shooter in favour of the extra weight of meat he carried? Almost meekly he followed his companion back to the fallen log, where, without waiting to make a fire, the starving company ate the rabbit raw in its entirety, feet, fur and entrails, as a pack of dogs might do. It was a thousand times more satisfying than anything they had eaten since they left the cabin. It put new life into them. They saved the very bones to gnaw as they went along.

After that they starved. They lost count of time. Gaunt, wild-eyed, with broken feet that left bloody tracks in the snow, they staggered along. The country changed as they walked. Leafless deciduous trees lost their novelty; the sun shone; the snow thinned until in places tufts of grass showed above it. (They tried eating it once, but it made them very sick.) But there was still no sign of a human habitation, which alone could offer them hope.

Glenny, still the strongest of them all, continued to measure his pace by theirs, and this fact was suddenly very significant to Cordy, who in addition to his weariness, his self-shouldered responsibility and his hunger, was obliged to bear the strain of constant watchfulness. Life, when threatened, was curiously precious, he found; he walked with the six-shooter handy.

Kevin's period of lucidity decreased. He became obsessed by the thought of losing his arm.

"I was always being pitied," he confided as he stumbled along. "You know, the gloating kind of pity, 'It's a pity about Furmage, no children, you see.' Now it'll be: 'Furmage, fellow with one arm.' One arm! My name has always meant a lot to me. A Furmage fought at Crecy, with twenty of his yeomen; another died at Worcester, on the King's side, of course. There was a Furmage on the *Mayflower,* and my grandfather died at Bunker's Hill. You can't escape a name like that. And I've dragged it in the dust. The end of the line. A one-armed, childless fellow who tried to find a new road and killed a lot of innocent people. You amongst them, Warren. Don't forget that. I've killed you, too."

Cordy heard, but he did not listen. He had his own preoccupations. He wondered whether, after you were dead, there was any consciousness; whether he would ever overtake Susie who had died such months ago; whether there would be recognition. He had moments when he was astonished that he was still alive, capable not only of moving himself, but of keeping the others on the move. Klara and Scanty were failing visibly, and Glenny no longer helped. But for the moment of naked revelation on the day of the rabbit shooting, Cordy would have wondered why the man, still the most vigorous of the party, stayed with them; as it was, he understood the wolfish doggedness. Once indeed, he turned to the big man and said: "Not long to wait now, Glenny, my boy. Make a bid for my brain; it's my softest spot." And Glenny had replied, with a grim gravity which was not lost upon Cordy: "It's your own fault. I offered to stand by you."

And the time was rapidly approaching, Cordy knew, when every bond, every rule would be broken, and the weak would fall by the way, and there would be blood on the snow, and the strong would go on. But even as he realised the inevitability of final drama, he fought it off with every conscious thought and action.

But they were beaten at last. Daylight still held the sky when their limbs failed and even Glenny came willingly to a halt. The meal of rabbit had been eaten three . . . or four . . . maybe even five days ago and nothing else even remotely resembling a hopeful sign had appeared since then. Kevin had sunk from delirium into apathy and moved and stayed at Cordy's bidding; Scanty groaned and muttered; Klara, dumb in this last extremity, staggered, halted, went on again as the others did; Glenny seemed merely to wait. It seemed to Cordy on that bright, chill afternoon that he was in charge of three children and a dangerous animal. Against the latter he had the six-shooter as a last resource; but for the children he could do nothing. He could herd them together and gather the wraps about them, but it meant little. They might as well die of cold as of hunger. He began to wonder whether it were worth while to fend off Glenny any longer. One person might as well come out of the holocaust.

It was twilight when Klara saw the light and yelped like

263

a dog. The Polish which had been spoken beside her cradle and which had served her for the first ten years of her life, sprang to her lips, and to those who had, for days past, listened to Kevin's babblings, it seemed merely that her mind, too, had collapsed under the strain of exposure, fatigue and starvation. Cordy did not even bother to look in the direction of her pointing finger. He tucked in the end of blanket and said: "There, there, Klara," as one would speak to a child.

But Glenny, peering through the gloom, beat his hand on his knee and then sprang to his feet.

"It's a light," he said in a hushed voice. "A light."

"I tell you," said Klara. "A lamp or a lantern. There is people. There is food."

(Mrs. Swabey, whose husband had gone down the valley to the settlement, on business, had put the lantern in the window to guide him home. Swabey felt the cold, and to welcome him home she had, preparing on the stove, a grand stew; venison, from a deer that he himself had shot, onions, potatoes, turnips, and since she was a Norfolk woman born and bred, a formidable suet dumpling. Swabey was late; and he might have drink aboard, so Mrs. Swabey, albeit a little anxious and angry, thought it wise to set the beacon light in the unglazed window and leave the shutter open. She had no idea what that glimmer was to mean to folk she had never heard of, whose existence was unknown, whose state was unbelievable.)

"It's a light," said Glenny again. He leaped to his feet, his strength miraculously restored, and, kicking aside the blanket which had draped his shoulders, set his feet on the snowy ground.

"Wait, wait," said Cordy, struggling into an upright position. "Glenny, wait. We need you. If that is a light it isn't far off and we can all get there, if you'll help us."

Glenny either did not hear, or did not trouble to answer. Scanty gave a groan as Cordy's movements disturbed the blankets, and Klara, grovelling on her knees, began to weep.

Cordy said, in a voice like a schoolmaster's, "Klara, get up and show me that light." She rose and pointed her

264

right hand while her left mopped her face with her sleeve.

"There. You see it? There."

Cordy could see nothing except black bars on the twilight. But he trusted her.

"Klara, you must take Scanty's hand and lead him towards it. Come on now, Scanty, be a man. We'll follow you."

Once more, for the thousandth time it seemed, he roused Kevin, being careful not to grasp him by his injured arm. He murmured encouraging nonsense about the last lap and bearing up and the comforts that awaited them.

For once the snow served them. As the night thickened the figures of Klara and Scanty, instead of disappearing, showed distinctly against the whiteness. The air took on a freezing chill and the thin snow crackled underfoot. Kevin spoke once. "We've gained ten days on the Fort Hall route," he said. And Cordy, raising his voice to compete with the knocking of his own heart in his ears, replied, "So we have. And we'll end the journey in half an hour if you'll put your best foot forward."

So far he had not seen the light at all. The blackness before his eyes increased until he followed the reeling rocking figures of Klara and the Negro by sound rather than sight. Even so he was twenty yards ahead of them before he missed the sound of their footsteps and their breath coming in short hard pants, and realised that he had passed them. Ahead of him he could see nothing save the faint shifting blur of the snow that soon ended where darkness swallowed the ground.

He stopped and listened. Apart from the heavy thump, thump of his labouring heart and the hiss of Kevin's indrawn breath he could hear nothing. He tried to call, but no sound issued from his parted lips. He was spent, finished. He withdrew his arm from Kevin's and Kevin sank at once to his knees with a great sigh of relief. Cordy sat down beside him and drew one, two, three steady, deliberate breaths. Now! He twisted his head and called into his silence, "Klara! Klara!" The breathy, soft name had no carrying power. He realised that with a flash of the intelligence, which, being a mental quality, is one of the last to be destroyed. Gathering his breath again he shouted "Scanty!" and went on shouting it at intervals until from behind him came the sound of hard breathing and a shuffling approach. The Negro, in whom obedience died hard, crawled up on hands and knees.

"Scanty, can you see the light?"

"Yes, master. But Ah's done, finish."

"Nonsense. Point to it."

A long dark arm, with the hand drooping weakly, pointed for a second and then fell, limp.

Cordy fumbled in his pocket, took out his knife, and, since his thumbs were weak and numb, opened the blade with his teeth. Then he rolled back the sleeve of his left arm and bared his wrist. Twice, hardly feeling the pain, he drew the blade across his flesh, dropping the knife as soon as he felt the warmth and wetness of his blood. He thrust his arm towards the Negro, whose lips closed on it, instinctive and unquestioning as a baby's upon the nipple of a breast. "This is my blood which is shed for you. . . ." Where had he heard that? Why did it recall the thin spring sunshine of a Sunday morning at Sibley Strawless?

After a few moments he withdrew his arm and twisted around it the dirty handkerchief that he had taken from his pocket.

"Scanty."

"Yes, master." The voice was stronger already.

"You go back and fetch the girl now. You understand?"

"Yes, master."

"Drag or carry her to that light. You're not to lie down, or stop, or let her either. Do you hear me? You're to come yourself, and bring the girl."

"Yes, master."

"Go on then. Get on your feet. Walk, no more crawling."

The crunch of snow came to Cordy's ears irregularly as the Negro tottered away; but at least he was on his feet again, he would have strength to follow for a little while longer. Now for one last effort. He stooped towards Kevin and shook him, gently but urgently. And as he did so he caught his first glimpse of Mrs. Swabey's beacon light. The blackness seemed to have cleared from his vision, yet he was afraid to remove his gaze, reluctant even to blink, lest the symbol of life and hope escape him again. Keeping his eyes fixed forward he heaved Kevin upwards and began to half push, half carry him along.

No measure known to man could calculate the distance between him and the light, or the time that was spent on the last span of the journey. In this last extremity there were no miles, no moments. He stumbled on in a trance in which a fanatical determination mingled confusedly with abstract thought. At one moment he was conscious only of the need to get Kevin towards that light; by doing so he felt that he would redeem all his past failures and mistakes; at the next moment he was conscious only that he was hovering upon the brink of some tremendous revelation, an act of thought which would explain everything that had ever puzzled the minds of men.

Beating off death with every harshly drawn breath, with every effort of his failing strength, he knew that, behind the stumbling body and the suffering flesh and the bemused mind there lay something, a state, an understanding ... something for which there was no name. He thought of the light which struck down Saul of Tarsus on the road to Damascus, of the understanding which came upon the disciples on the road to Emmaus—and he, Cordy Warren, beating out with his broken feet the last yards of the Furmage Road, felt that a light, a vision, a revelation awaited him as well. Always a road, he thought wildly. God always showed Himself upon a road.

But you, Cordy Warren, in the brutal hell of the Milchester mill, decided long ago there could be no God. No power with understanding and justice within its scope could have tolerated what happened there, what happened in similar places all over the world. What God could sit in Heaven and watch the oppression, the exploitation, the sheer fiendish cruelty which the strong dealt out to the weak? You renounced Him then, and save for brief atavistic moments, like the one when you shot at the rabbit, you have not thought of Him since. How then do you explain what is within you now? Why are you certain that another will than your own is working in you? What does it matter whether you bring in your burden safely or leave it and, lightened, hasten into safety as Glenny has shown you how to do? Who cares? Who will even know?

As though bothered by midges Cordy shook his head impatiently; the answer was there, it would come, he would have it in a moment, and then he would understand everything.

It came, he knew, he understood. He saw that Man, on his way from the ape to the angel, was driven by some urge, which, though it failed often, never died out completely; and that the things which were called gods and moral codes and creeds were in reality standards which Man, in his effort to throw off his limitations, imposed upon himself and conceived within himself. Man stumbled and blundered, he failed, he wronged himself by wronging his neighbour; selfishness, ignorance, cruelty and superstition dragged him backwards, but he gathered himself after each fall and pressed on, on towards some attainable state of perfection which he would reach, in time. The desire for what was right and just and clean and sincere was planted in him, as inherent as an antelope's swiftness or a hound's keen scent. It was because there was no overlordship, no final source of power, no unfailing court of judgment, that a man must live by the light that was within him. That was what the Christ who called himself Son of Man meant when he said that the great sin was to sin against the Holy Ghost—the Holy Ghost who was that urgent, yearning, searching spirit of Man.

The little stumbling skeleton took the onslaught of the force of his own understanding. He saw now that his mother for whom he had grieved, and Susie over whom he had sorrowed, had not in reality been robbed and wasted by the world. They had lived with courage and gallantry and good faith, they had loved without stint, fought without faltering, and although they themselves were dead there was that much more of strength and sweetness in the common heritage of Man. For the first time Cordy thought of his own children without regret. With them (and he did not, at that moment, doubt the possibility of future meeting) he could share this knowledge. They were material, they were steps, infinitesimally small, but of immense importance, in the upward progress of the race.

He was glad suddenly that he had survived to see this moment; glad that this difficult burden had not been laid down and abandoned. Very humbly he was glad that in him Man had triumphed, not over cold and hunger and weariness, but over Man's more deadly foes, over the world, the flesh and the devil, that watchful evil that seeks to halt Man's progress and throw him back into the slime.

Behind him he could hear the gasping and shuffling of the Negro and the girl. Ahead of him, very clear and near, now beamed the beacon light. Kevin stiffened suddenly and said:

"A light. There's a light."

Cordy tightened his stick-thin arm, set his bleeding feet more firmly, pressed forward.

Haggard, ragged, spent and dying, he presented himself before Mrs. Swabey's door. There was very little about him to suggest the conqueror.

On the day when the travellers arrived at the Swabey cabin there was still meat in that other cabin beside the lake on the far side of the Pass. The last of the flour had been used to make the cakes which the travellers had carried with them; and Mahitabel had eked out, with careful fingers, the oatmeal, the dried peas and beans, the three pounds of sugar and the last sack of potatoes. But, save for a little oatmeal, the stores were ended now, and the lives of the company depended upon the frozen meat which, as Madame Jurer often reminded them, belonged to her.

When the travellers set out Mahitabel had watched them out of sight, wishing them well and consigning them to God's care.

When she turned back into the cabin she found Ben up and huddling into his outer clothes. He limped still, and his foot, unable to bear the pressure of his boot, was wrapped in several layers of sacking. He announced his intention of gathering a further supply of wood.

"Branches snapping off right and left," he said. "And we need every one of 'em. Fire'll have to be going day and night."

"Well, don't stand about in the cold, that's all," said Mahitabel a trifle doubtfully. "As soon as you're tired, come in and rest. You'll find you're weak as a cat."

As soon as Ben and little Hendriks had gone Mahitabel sorted out the stores that remained. It was a piteously short job. Flour, which had been most depleted by the cloudburst, since flour is not recoverable from a flooded path, had come to an end with the making of the flat cakes. There was a little oatmeal, a few dried beans and peas, a bunch or two of onions, a sack, three parts full, of potatoes and about three pounds of sugar, set into solid block from damp. Mahitabel faced the fact that except for the meat the food represented about a week's normal consumption. And help—even if it came—might be six weeks or more in reaching them.

As she measured out that day's dinner, so much meat, a handful of beans, a potato apiece, to take the place of bread, she found herself thinking about food as never in all her long dealing with it she had thought before. How seldom did one realise its importance! Why, it had even given men a word which they used, Mahitabel would swear, when food was very far from their minds. Farewell, they said, farewell, and meant it as just a word of leave-taking, as she had meant it an hour ago; but the word went back, far back to a time when food was uncertain and hard to come by, and the best thing that one could wish a friend at parting was that he should find enough to eat. "Write and tell me how you fare," common enough phrase; how surprised, thought Mahitabel with a twist of the lip, would the speaker be to receive a letter giving the literal reply. "I fare well. To-day I ate roast pork with applesauce, greens and gravy . . ."

Oh, for mercy's sake, thought Mahitabel, catching and quelling her errant fancy, don't start thinking about apple sauce and pork, it'll make you hungry.

The midday meal was served at three o'clock by Frank's watch. Its hour had been pushed later and later because it was not easy to fall asleep on an empty stomach, but it meant waking hungry and feeling faint all morning. Everyone was ravenous when the meal time arrived.

270

Shortly before the hour Ben and Hendriks came in, Ben's hand bearing heavily upon the dwarf's shoulder, his face grey with exhaustion or pain. He allowed Mahitabel to divest him of the scarf that had been wrapped around his head, and of his top-coat, then lay down on his bunk and pulled the blanket around him. He accepted his dinner and refused to admit that he felt any the worse for his activity. He spoke of how easily they had found wood and how they would chop it tomorrow. But the grey look remained on his face and his forehead wore a fixed pucker of pain.

The daily dressing of the foot had ceased when the wound had healed, but on this day, in the last hour of daylight, Mahitabel bent over the bunk and despite Ben's protests, insisted upon an inspection. The ridged scars, usually so bright upon the pale flesh, were now hardly visible, for the whole foot was swollen and dark-coloured. Even Mahitabel's careful fingers sank into the doughy substance of it, and the marks remained after the fingers had been withdrawn.

"It's frosted," she said, her composure a little shaken. "You shouldn't have gone out so soon."

"Aw, it's nothing," said Ben, endeavouring to push it out of sight again.

Hiding the fact that her ignorance of the proper procedure appalled her, Mahitabel bathed and anointed that frighteningly unfamiliar foot.

" 'Tain't even paining me now," Ben said. And as though in proof of that, fell asleep almost as soon as she had finished. Mahitabel settled Frank Cooper for the long night, helped Ruth with the children, talked for a little, and then, as the other women grew sleepy from inaction, stirred the fire to a blaze and took out her diary. Crouched by the fire with the red light glowing and paling across her moving fingers, she wrote her brief, undramatic comments upon the day's doings; and then, closing the book, she folded her hands and stared into the fire with the calm contemplation and quiet faith which was one of her methods of communicating with her God.

In the morning Ben complained of pain, not in the injured and frostbitten foot, but in various parts of his body; his back, his head, his throat and wrists all ached. He was evidently in a state of high fever, and Mahitabel longed for plenty of milk gruel, blackcurrant tea and hot sweet spirit of nitre, all the good homely allies against this old enemy. She did what she could with the pitiable resources at hand, but Ben grew worse with startling rapidity. He refused his share of the daily stew lucidly enough, and Mahitabel said, "Maybe you're best without it. I'll make you some oatmeal as soon as I have the pot cleaned." But while she was hastily gulping her own share, having emptied and set the pot to soak, he called to her in a strange hoarse voice, and when she turned, startled, said:

"The cow, Mahitabel, you ain't milked her to-day."

"But, Ben . . ."

"Don't explain, humour him," murmured Frank. And Mahitabel fervently promised to see at once about milking the cow—good placid Dinah, who had had to be killed because no one in the drought-stricken district about Weston wanted another cow to water.

But Ben's troubled mind had already shifted its focus of anxiety. Back it roamed over years when anxiety had never been far away. Relatives long dead, neighbours now far scattered, troubles long ago survived, worried him in turn. The terrible lack of space and privacy in the fetid little cabin added to the nightmare of his delirium. Mahitabel sat beside him, holding his restless burning hands, tilting the cup to his dry lips and trying to follow, with calm reassuring statements, the wild leaping of his mind. With nightfall his mind came to rest, but not comfortingly. He began to call for Mary Ann, and nothing that Mahitabel could say or do would shift his attention. He had always been deeply attached to his children in his quiet, unostentatious way, and of them all Mary Ann was his favourite. Having once called for her and found her absent, he demanded her again and again with increasing violence.

"You've hired her out, that's what you done," he told Mary Ann's mother, with something amounting to hatred in his voice. "Hired out . . . my little girl, breaking her back and spoiling her hands. 'Twasn't called for, Mahitabel. Poor we may be but we hadn't sunk to that. Where'd you send her? You fetch her back at once. 'Tisn't often I hev my way, but I'm gonna hev it about this."

272

Mahitabel, whose prejudices against service were as violent as Ben's own, protested almost unthinkably.

"She isn't hired out, Ben. What put that into your head? She's gone to stay with Aunt Lavinia Raikes over to Edwardstone."

"Ah ..." Ben's voice betrayed his relief. But immediately he added, "Time she was back, then. I like my folks at home. When'll she be home?"

"To-morrow," said Mahitabel rashly. "You must go to sleep now. Try to sleep, Ben. You're worn out and it's very late."

"And Mary Ann is coming home to-morrow? You're sure?"

"Sure."

He murmured and mumbled on, more weakly as the night advanced, but reverting constantly to the subject of his favourite child. Towards morning he fell into an uneasy sleep, and Mahitabel, able at last to ease her position and press her hands to her aching head, wondered whether she had done harm or good by her hopeless promise; wondered about Mary Ann herself; worried about Ben.

As soon as the grey light of morning showed in a line around the blanket that hung over the doorway of the cabin, Mahitabel rose quietly, pushed it aside and stood breathing deeply of the icy air, trying to gain refreshment.

The world lay dead in the iron grip of the frost. It was painful to fill the lungs too deeply; the mere touch of the air stiffened the flesh of the face. Even Mahitabel's spirit could not remain unaffected by the relentless cold, the dead white world where nothing stirred, the depression of being the one living thing awake in the alien, heartless dawn. How, she asked herself, could another day like yesterday be borne? With Ben raving, the children frightened, Madame Jurer and Ruth growing impatient of the disturbance and she herself tiring. And suppose Ben woke with the thought of Mary Ann in his mind?

She sighed, and the sigh was visible on the air, grey-coloured as a sigh should be. Well, no use in sighing and fretting, she thought. There were things to be done. The fire must be mended. There were logs stacked near the heat, but Mahitabel, ever methodical, stooped to the pile by the cabin door and lifted an armful to set to dry in the place of those she would in a moment throw on the fire. As she straightened herself her gaze struck the point where the travelling party had disappeared two days ago round the clump of pines. And there, at the very spot, forms were moving again, moving very slowly and in a curious way, but moving towards the cabin.

Wondering for a moment whether she were not sharing Ben's delusions, Mahitabel stood with her arms full of wood and stared at the figures. There were four of them and they were so muffled and shapeless that it was some moments before she could recognise individuals. Then, with a shock that made her heart bang against her collarbone, Mahitabel saw that the centre one of the three taller figures was Floribel Toit. On either side of her clung another, Mary Ann on the left, Lou Glenny on the right, and upon Lou's other side staggered Evan.

Four had returned, defeated; but at the moment Mahitabel considered neither their defeat nor the fact that there would be four more mouths to feed in the cabin. It was enough to know that when Ben woke Mary Ann would be there, just as Mahitabel had promised. Dropping the wood and heedless of the biting air the mother began to run forward over the hard slippery snow.

They had been absent for less than forty-eight hours; yet their return caused as much excitement and talk in the cabin as would the coming back of travellers from overseas. Lou and Mary Ann, in the last stages of exhaustion, were bundled into the blankets from which Madame and Ruth had just emerged. Heedless of the future Mahitabel heated food and insisted upon their eating their fill. Their delight and relief at having safely reached the cabin they had feared never to see again, lent a jubilant air to the reunion, bridging the essential seriousness of their failure.

"I wish your father would seem sensible that you're here," said Mahitabel, glancing uneasily at Ben. "He kept on about you all day yesterday, wandering-like."

But to-day Ben lay supine. His face was duskily flushed, his eyes glassy between slitted lids. Sometimes he mumbled, and when Mahitabel tried to raise his head and hold a cup of gruel to his lips he screamed, sudden and shrill as a snared rabbit. She laid him flat again and contented herself with spooning the unpalatable mixture between his lips with the cooking spoon.

The excitement of the return died down: monotony, anxiety, and the brief sharp altercation that flourishes amongst strained nerves at close quarters, took its place.

Apart from the children, whose sufferings were physical, not mental, the happiest and most resigned person in the cabin was the one who was most often referred to as "poor Mr. Cooper." He had set out, a sick man indeed, hoping to regain his health in a favourable climate. But the hope, never very strong, had died easily and now he lay, immobile, waiting for death and undeterred by the prospect. Sometimes, waking in the long nights, he wondered whether the paralysing nature of his affliction had affected his mind. Surely to die at the age of thirty-five was a thing to be regretted, rejected, fought against. But the thought could pass through his mind without evoking any feeling save mild curiosity.

He considered his past life. Until he was thirty and the immobilisation of his body had made its first onset, he had lived happily in a worldly and unthinking fashion. He had enjoyed his wealth, his position, his opportunities. He had loved several women, none of them very deeply: he had read considerably, made the grand tour of Europe and twice visited the Orient in one of his father's ships. An aimless, useless, pleasant life it had been, and calculated by serious persons to be of the kind that is bitterly regretted upon a death-bed. But so far as he could see (and he admitted that he might be mentally blind) there was nothing much to regret; he could not remember harming anyone and he died in no one's debt, save Mahitabel's, and he had done his best to repay her as far as care and attention could be repaid.

Of what came after he thought very little. There were so many theories, most of them valid up to a point, all of them flawed. He embraced none of them. He was content to think that he had been alive, had enjoyed himself, been overtaken by disease and was now about to die a little early. If anything of life and personal consciousness remained after the wrench of death, it would doubtless be interesting, and no worse for him than for any other of the millions of dead. So he lay, quiet and uncomplaining, while the muscles of his heart emulated those of his limbs, and he watched Mary Ann when she was within his range of vision and with surreptitious regularity gave away a good portion of his food to one or another of the children.

He died while there was still hope in the cabin and meat in the pot. All the women, save Mahitabel and Nancy, wept for him, scarcely knowing why they did so. Mary Ann, it is true, regretted the foolishness which had made her serve him so unwillingly and behave so ungraciously. Life in the cabin, with its constant emphasis upon the essential and the practical, had swept away those feelings, as it had swept away Mahitabel's false modesty, Ruth's ideas of hygiene and Floribel's interest in her appearance.

Nancy saw nothing to regret in the young man's demise. For weeks now she had grudged him his allowance of food. To keep alive a useless body at the expense of useful ones was plain silliness, in her unsentimental sight.

Mahitabel did not weep. She was sorry, partly that one so young must die, partly because she had undertaken to bring him safely to California and had failed in the task. If she had been firmer and insisted upon traveling the known road he might have been there by now, basking in the sun and improving in health. But his death, like the life and death of everyone on earth, was God's affair. And the fields of Heaven, to Mahitabel's mind, were warmer and more flowery than any earthly ones. In them he would be lithe and lissom again.

The ground, even below the lake, was too hard for digging, so, aided by little Hendriks, Mahitabel hacked out for her passenger a resting place in the snow and patted and moulded it into shape above him.

He had, two days before his death, entrusted the valise to her care. She did not open it, except to lay his watch chain inside. The watch, upon which they depended to keep track of the slow-dragging hours, she set up on a ledge in the cabin wall. But for it, and her own meticulous entries in her diary, time would have silted down into a nameless alternation of light and dark.

276

As it was, merely by writing each day's name and date, even if no entry followed except a laconic, "All is well," Mahitabel kept each week, each month in shape. When the entries recorded an event it was generally a lamentable one: "To-day the oatmeal gave out." "I cooked the last potato to-day." "Ben rambling again. His mind seems to have stored up everything that had been forgotten."

As though death, having gained a foothold in the cabin, was anxious to perform a double errand there, Ben died just eight days after Frank Cooper. The women wept again, but to everyone save his wife and daughter Ben's death was a relief. To gain sleep after a hard struggle, when your stomach is unsatisfied and your bed the draughty floor and your mind a battlefield of warring anxieties and then to be waked within an hour by a sick man's senseless ravings are not inducive to humane feeling. Nights would be quiet now; there was the extra bunk and blankets, and one less to feed.

Mary Ann, who could remember Ben's simple kindness to her as a child—setting her up on the cart-horse for a ride, carrying her into the field and making her snug in the hedge under his coat while he ploughed, scraping a turnip into sweet toothsome pulp for her with his knife, telling her stories at bed-time—only Mary Ann who remembered these things and many others, wept genuinely and visibly. Mahitabel cried over this second grave, but she sent Hendriks away first and no one saw her tears.

Of Frank Cooper she had known little save that he was good-tempered, very sick and anxious to get to California. She had known Ben so well that she was bound to weep for his frustrated hopes. She knew how he had regretted the move from Weston, what he had suffered during those bad years, how urgently he had looked forward to owning "a little place." She wept for those things. And she added a few tears when she remembered how often her efficiency and quick judgment had made her impatient with him, who was never impatient with her. She recalled his kindness, his meekness, his integrity, and how, albeit unknowing, he had rebuilt her self-esteem for her. Heaven, to be sure, awaited Ben, no one could doubt that, and she told herself that she would not have recalled him if she could. But he would have enjoyed settling down again, he was a man who would have liked to have seen his grandchildren ...

Mahitabel wept over that second heap of snow. Shy, awkward, drawling Ben, so kind and unassuming ... who could have forseen your ending here?

Slow days dragging on, new storms piling the snow higher, new frost setting it hard. Christmas Day in this last outpost of civilised people, gathered over the last basin of beans, the last onion-flavoured stew, with two bits of sugar apiece for the children, to mark the day.

There was nothing but meat in store now, and that was perilously low. Once heaped as high as the cabin roof the pile had shrunk, as steadily and relentlessly as a man's span of days. And now there began again that old bickering about the ownership of the oxen from whose carcasses the meat had been cut.

Madame Jurer had borne the position for as long as possible. Now she was frightened; not mildly, or sharply terrified by a bout of fear in the night when all prospects are gloomy: she was coldly, starkly stricken with terror. The meat would be consumed, gently, shred by shred until there was nothing. Then they would starve and die. And Nancy Jurer, who had not known fear for so long that she had forgotten the last occasion, was dreadfully afraid of dying. Besides, why should she die? The meat was there, and it was hers, hers, hers! By far the greater proportion of the beasts that had reached the lake had belonged to her, she had bought them and her usual good fortune had seen that they were preserved when the arrows flew, and the cloud burst. It was not fair that her meat should be used to support a pack of people who had no resources of their own.

Thoughts of that kind occupied her mind for some days before she voiced them. Then, one morning, just as Mahitabel shredded from the frozen block of meat the day's meagre allowance, the old woman's frenzy gained the upper hand and she suddenly waddled forward and cried, "Stop."

Mahitabel poised the knife.

"This won't do! This can't go on."

For a moment Mahitabel thought that Nancy was raving. She looked mad enough; and Heaven knew—thought Mahitabel—that the circumstances were enough to craze a person. She spoke gently.

"Now, now, Madame Jurer. Calm yourself. Sit down and try to be hopeful. Remember help is coming." That last sentence was often in Mahitabel's mind, and on her lips, these days.

"The meat will be gone, at this rate, long before help gets here. And that meat belongs to me. I've shared it with you all for as long as I dare, and I've no wish to see you starve. But right is right. I can't feed you any longer. Do you hear? I can't feed you any longer."

Mahitabel said, "Have you gone mad?"

"No, I've come to my senses. I've kept you all too long. Twelve of you, neither kith nor kin. It's got to stop, I tell you. Put down that knife, Mrs. Smith. I'll carve my meat in future."

"And what . . . ? If . . . ? I never heard such nonsense!" snapped Mahitabel, recovering herself. "What if the meat did come from your beasts, they weren't all yours. And there was the oatmeal and the beans and potatoes, you shared them as long as they lasted. You'll share the meat too."

"Not any longer."

"Then what do you suggest we do? Sit here and starve before your face?"

"Those that can walk must GO," said Nancy flatly. "The others went . . . at least they haven't come back, have they? You and your daughter, the dwarf and the boy and the rest of you, all except the children and Janna. Janna can keep me company and look after the children. I'll give them the broth every day."

"It wasn't snowing when the others left, and they were strong, they hadn't starved for weeks as we have, and they knew the way. What you are suggesting is that we should face certain death so that you may avoid even the threat of it."

"I'm not suggesting anything of the sort. I'm telling you that you can't eat my meat any more."

Mahitabel glanced at the pale, thin, smoke-smeared

faces that ringed the cabin. Consternation, alarm and pure terror showed upon them; Ruth Warren was alreay weeping above her baby's head.

"We're going to share this meat as we've shared everything else, down to the last crumb," said Mahitabel firmly, and laid her hand on the knife. Nancy Jurer flung herself forward and clutched the lump of frozen meat to her chest. It might have been a supremely comic moment, but sense of humour is one of the first deserters in the face of hunger. Mahitabel, about to throw herself upon the joint, suddenly thought better of it. Two grown women must not wrangle like two dogs over a hunk of flesh. Besides, a victory so gained would be very transient. She stood back.

"Very well, have it your way."

A shrill chatter of expostulation broke out amongst the onlookers. Were they to starve? Madame Jurer would see! Let her wait till it was cooked and she'd see whether they'd sit by and watch her eat while they went hungry.

"Wait till it's cooked," said Mahitabel dryly and sat down on the bunk that had been Ben's.

Madame Jurer put the meat in the pot and waddled to the stove. The fire was low, she kicked the ends of the logs together with her foot and set the pot over the little flame. Under the burden the fire wilted and died lower. Nancy waddled to the door. It had been snowing hard for two days and no wood had been cut. The hollow where the logs usually lay was empty. Ordinarily Hendriks would have been returning by this time with a fresh supply, but he had stayed to watch the wrangle over the beef and was waiting now to see what Mahitabel wished.

Baulked, but undaunted, Nancy swept towards Janna.

"Fetch some wood, girl, and be quick."

Janna shrank back against the wall, wringing her hands and mumbling. Nancy slipped off her shoe and advanced with it in her hand. Janna ducked her head. Then Ruth Warren spoke on a high, hysterical note.

"You swear the babies shall have the broth?"

"You hear me say so."

"Then I'll go with Janna."

"You're risking everything, Mrs. Warren," said Mahitabel softly.

"I'm thinking of my babies," cried Ruth. "I wonder you don't, too."

Janna, trying to hold Ruth's hand, went crying with her out into the snow. Silence fell on the cabin. The fire died lower and the temperature dropped like a stone.

In less than an hour Ruth and Janna returned, both in tears. Loose wood had already been collected by Hendriks, and though the women had taken a hatchet with them neither of them was skilled enough to use it nor to keep themselves warm with the work. Their fingers were rigid and lifeless.

Mahitabel moved Ellen from her lap and laid her back on the bunk, but she herself stayed still, except that she ground one thumb into her opposite palm with a fidgeting, mechanical movement.

"You idle, good-for-nothing, misbegotten bitch," screamed Nancy, falling upon Janna and shaking her until her teeth rattled and her head lolled. "How dare you come back empty-handed? What have I kept . . . ?

"Stop it!" Mahitabel rose and stood over the stout furious figure. "We're waiting for you to decide whether you'll eat your meat raw or whether you'll share our fire and your meat."

Without speaking Nancy returned sulkily to her seat. Mahitabel nodded to Hendriks who leaped at the axe.

That evening, Mahitabel, entering the sordid little incident in the day's record, added, "It shows how things will go if matters worsen. Oh God, spare us from seeing what hunger can make of Thine Image."

But God had decreed that nothing should be spared them. Ignorant of the foul weather, the delays and disasters, the false starts and the accidents which were breaking Abe's heart on the other side of the mountains, Mahitabel looked out a dozen times a day, hoping and praying to see the snowy expanse broken by the arrival of the relief party. Day followed day until January was gone and February, with its lengthening hours of daylight, arrived. And always and always the question, what shall we eat? what can we eat? The disputed meat had gone at last. Now the bones must be boiled and boiled until the outer casing was as soft as the inward marrow. They were boiled and scraped and chewed until not a shred of nourishment remained in them. Mahitabel's prayers took on that desperate quality of her earliest ones; and on the day when there was no shred of food in the cabin, she received an answer of a kind. Clearly and distinctly as though a voice had spoken in her she was reminded of those forgotten hides, used for the cabin roof.

She and Hendriks took them down, beat off the snow and cut them to pieces. Then she boiled them until the cabin stank anew, scraped off their hair and shared out the loathsome, gummy strips; and when the glue that had boiled from them had set a little, that too was eaten by the ravenous, though revolted, company. Sickness became the frequent sequel to meals.

Yet there is worse to suffer, said the voice in Mahitabel's mind. Having done all this you must starve yourself, and watch the others starve. You must see those children, already so thin and pale and unchildlike, grow discoloured and misshapen; you must prepare for Death's next blow. And all the time you must know that there is one thing left to do, one weapon untried. You must recognise the unspoken thought that has taken its nightmarish possession of all these minds. And you must, because you are the last of a line of civilised people, fight off this dire suggestion.

"There might," said Mahitabel, at noon of a hungry day, "be some scraps left in the wagon. I'll go down."

"Noding there," said Hendriks with dread assurance; yet when he saw her take her cloak from the bunk he prepared to go with her.

"I'll go alone, Hendriks," she said.

It was only a short way to the wagon and the afternoon was clear. It held in its light a promise of spring, though the grip of the frost was still hard on the land.

Mahitabel walked slowly. She was very weak and her legs quivered. In the face of Hendriks' assurance it seemed scarcely worth while to make the journey, but some unformed hope drew her on. If she could stave off the thing that was threatening for just one more day, help might arrive and it might never have to be done.

The wagon offered no help until she had, with much

difficulty, forced back the sliding doors of several lockers swollen with dampness. Inside the second she found two bottles of red wine and wished she had searched the wagon sooner, poor Mr. Cooper might have benefitted. In the fourth compartment her questing fingers found the only food left in the wagon, half a dozen wizened potatoes and three little onions which had escaped at some time from a broken bag. She took them out and arranged them along the top of the locker. The light fell upon the globular curve of one of the onions, calling out its subtle mixture of colours, pale gold, silver, mother-of-pearl. Mahitabel gazed at it fascinated. She had handled and peeled hundreds of onions without ever noticing how beautiful they were.

And within, still moist with earthy juices, lay the close-packed rings, white, veined with green.

Two seconds later the strong pungent flavour was on her tongue and she was gazing in horrified bewilderment at the smallest onion, now clenched in her hand, marked with the clear strong circle of her teeth. Almost she had eaten it— a wildly disproportionate share, here, in secret, alone. She swallowed harshly. Seldom had she been so deeply shamed.

She bundled the poor booty into the pocket of her cloak, tucked the bottles under her arm and left the wagon. Near the cabin she turned aside where the snow mounds had been obscured by a fresh fall. There was no doubt left in her mind as to what she must do.

Stew again, with an onion flavour and a few crumbs of potato and meat. But there had been no meat in the wagon!

Guilty. That was it, thought Mahitabel, looking round. And why? Why should the air be thick with unasked questions and heavy with a sense of guilt, even as the jaws worked and the eyes gleamed at the sight of food? Only the children, the ugly, skeleton children with their innocent eyes, ate wholly happily. She finished serving the meal and then went and sat between Ellen and Digby Warren, helping them to feed in a manner calculated to mask the fact that she herself was unable to eat. But Mary Ann noticed, halted her spoon, put her head in her hands and began to cry. One by one Floribel, Lou and

Ruth followed her example. Tears came easily to them, these days. It was the worst meal of all, so far.

Yet, barely two hours later, writing the day's entry, Mahitabel dealt with the affair with calm detachment.

"Lately I have thought a lot about the ravens who fed Elijah by the brook Cherith. It doesn't say what meat they brought, but there was a bad famine in the land and I shouldn't think butcher's meat would lay about for birds to pick up. Maybe that was God's way of saving him, and us. So I went to Ben first because he belonged to me. I don't think he would have grudged it.

"It is a little difficult when you think about the resurrection of the body. But you hear of people being eaten by wolves in the north, or by fish in the sea. Mysteries like that are too deep for me." Then, with apparent irrelevance, though the train of thought is clear, she added: "Wolves wouldn't have been sorry, or cried."

The days crawled on; and still the cabin dwellers starved; and still the whiteness between cabin and Pass remained unbroken. It had been Herculean labour lately to gather enough wood for cooking. In the other hours the stove was cold and their sick, thin, suffering bodies gave off little heat. The life-beat, that holy thing, which had been preserved at such cost for so long was very low and feeble before the last dread and nameless source of supply was exhausted.

The day came when the stove stayed cold and the pot was empty.

So now you must die, Mary Ann, Floribel, Lou, all of you ripe for loving, fit for some man's delight: and you, Evan, who would soon have been a man yourself: and you, Digby, James, Zillah and Ellen, whose journey had scarcely begun: and Janna, who in the sun would still have been a happy singing girl, borne up through ordinary trials by your patient African heritage: Hendriks, too, with your capacity for loyalty and your skill with dumb things. And you must die, Nancy and Mahitabel who have at least had a share of life and bent it to your pattern; you, Nancy, will miss some pleasures, and there were useful years ahead of you, Mahitabel.

There was no guard upon the cabin door now. The first man to live upon this planet had learned how to defeat hunger; and hard upon his heels had come the genius who chained fire to man's service; and ever since, with flame and cooking-pot the human race has waged unceasing war upon the ancient enemies, cold and hunger. But the defences are down now; here is a long-held garrison which can resist no more. The stove is cold and the pot is empty. The way is clear, anything may enter.

Death and mania entered the cabin together. Death chose Zillah Warren, mania seized on Nancy Jurer. The breath had scarcely left the wasted little body, before the old woman made her suggestion, logical enough in the circumstances, infamous in the face of Ruth's despairing sorrow.

With little to prop it, Nancy Jurer's mind was collapsing under the strain of her terror. She had never dreamed that such panic existed. Once or twice in the past she had had occasion to turn out her house girls who were overtaken by illness or some other misfortune. Often they had made foolish appeals, saying that they did not know what to do, saying that they would starve. Always she had been inexorable. "That is your affair," she would say. And she meant it; years of unimaginative living had given her a mental immunity. She was incapable of feeling what it meant to be cast adrift, homeless and in danger of starvation.

Now she knew; and as the knowledge seeped into her mind it took with it unsupportable fear. To die; to be blotted out; never to know again the pleasures of good living, the excitement of a hard bargain shrewdly driven, the triumph of a point scored. The thought had the poignance of revelation. Lapped about by material things and dull of soul she had never even thought about her own mortality. She had treated her body as though it would be there to be fed and dressed, painted and pampered for ever. The idea that it might die—and of hunger—was fantastic, so fantastic that for days on end she was stunned by the force of its magnitude.

In a material sense the old woman was no coward. She had often been called upon to deal with furious women and angry men; none had ever seen her at a loss. But in the face of death her brand of courage was of no avail. Quick wits, tough fibre, hard heart, they could not serve her now.

Faint and only half-remembered, the bare tenets of her abandoned faith came back, not to comfort, but to torment her. If there were Purgatory for whom was it meant but for such as herself? She had lived carnally; but had professed no faith, given no alms; she had lived upon the incontinence of other people. She tried to reckon her virtues, but beyond a certain honesty in business she could think of nothing that would commend her very warmly to the judgment of Heaven.

But this phase of self-study, which might have led to some belated resurrection of the soul, could not survive those final days of hunger. She no longer thought of Death, or Hell, or her sins. She became, in everything but shape, a ravening animal, determined to have food. She knew that Mahitabel, though weakening every day, still ruled in the cabin, and she knew Mahitabel well enough by this time to know what she would permit to happen there. But she had no idea that Ruth Warren's baby was not bound, sooner or later, for the fate of Ben and Frank Cooper. She watched it with the unflinching, unfeeling interest of a hovering vulture watching a dying animal on the plain below. There was no horror in her soul as she watched the tiny golden-haired body breathe more and more feebly; no pity for its youth, or for its mother's pain. To her it was not something that Ruth had carried for nine months in heavy discomfort, borne with joy and tended with devotion ever since. It was merely the next thing to be eaten. There was nothing in her regard but an immense hunger.

The child died late in the afternoon. Sunk in their own apathy, so weak that the least movement sent the cabin walls spinning before their eyes, the people—save Nancy only—would hardly have noticed the child's passing if Ruth had not wailed out the immemorial cry of bereavement. Lou reached out her unsteady hands to take the body, Mahitabel staggered over to put her arms around Ruth's shoulders. But Ruth, pushing them both aside, bent over the little corpse, rocking it to and fro, wetting its face with her tears.

Then Nancy Jurer spoke the unforgettable words.

They dropped into the darkest consciousness of every soul in that forsaken company, searching and illuminating, like pine flares dropped into a well. They picked out the acquiescent, bestial thoughts that had their roots in hunger and fear and weakness; but they brought to light also the horror, the pity, the repudiation which alone could distinguish these two-legged carnivora from the beasts of prey to whose level they had been reduced.

At the words Ruth Warren screamed, thrust the small body behind her against the rough wall of the cabin and defied Nancy with eyes almost as mad as her own. The old woman moved forward, and the company saw with horror that she had the knife in her right hand.

Mahitabel, who had moved away when Ruth repulsed her, came forward now and stood between the two of them. Her step, her eyes and her voice were suddenly steady and strong again.

She said, "Have some respect for a mother's feelings, Madame Jurer! We've been brought very low; but we haven't hurt anyone yet."

The words were mildly spoken; and even fierce words would not have deterred Nancy Jurer at that moment.

"When I had meat it was 'Share, share, share,'" she said wildly. "You said it yourself. *You* took my meat."

"And I have given all that I had to give," said Mahitabel steadily. "It is different now. Let the woman mourn her dead in peace."

"So we've got back to owning things, have we?" Without warning Madame whirled round to where Janna, stupefied and drowsy, lolled against the wall. Yelping something incoherent and yet purposeful about owning her, having bought her for a hundred and twenty dollars, she set about the terrified girl with the knife.

What happened then happened too quickly for understanding or intervention. Mahitabel flung herself forward, stumbled on the rough floor and came upright again within reach of the struggling couple. Janna was screaming. With her left hand Mahitabel caught Nancy by the left elbow, with her right she reached over the knife. Nancy twisted and brought her right hand free, probably with no more intent than to push aside this intolerable interference. But the knife was in the hand which was free to push.

Mahitabel gave a gasp and sank on to her knees. As Mary Ann ran forward, crying, "Mother! Mother!" and lifted her, the knife fell out and hit the boughs of the floor. The fringe of Mahitabel's little indoor shawl was darkening with blood. It reddened her daughter's hands as she dragged her to the bunk.

Janna, still screaming, "Save muh, save muh!" tried to take refuge behind Lou as she and the rest of them (save only Ruth, who still wept over her baby), surged forward towards Mahitabel. But Nancy with knife and purpose gone, said in a childish way, "Accident, accident!" and began beating her head against the wall.

Throughout that night Mahitabel's body lay unmolested upon the bunk that had been Ben's. When Ruth's first paroxysm of grief had exhausted her and her arms wearied of the dead child's negligible weight, they tucked it in beside Mahitabel and drew the blanket over them both. Nancy Jurer, like a marionette whose string has broken, sat motionless and silent in her place by the further wall, her hands hanging heavily, her dull unwinking gaze fixed on the floor.

Hopelessness and terror were no new thing within those walls, and yet to the watchful people it seemed that they had never known hopelessness or terror until now. They realised how deep had been their dependence upon Mahitabel, upon one woman who was only a woman when all was said and done, a thing of vulnerable flesh and blood, a frail mortal being who had none the less so contrived that she had imposed order upon Hunger's self and died in an attempt to vindicate her belief that even death should be a decent thing.

There was not, within the cabin, a single mind capable of thought which could bear to think upon the morrow.

Morning broke, very clear and bright. And like ants on a white cloth the small dark forms of the relief party, headed by Abe, showed against the expanse of snow between the cabin and the Pass.